Chirp

ANN EVERETT

ISBN-10:0–9965560–3-6
ISBN-13:978–9965560–3-3

Cover design: Ann Everett, formatted by lisaarts
Images purchased from Adobe Stock Photos and iStock Photos by
Ann Everett
Interior: Integrity Formatting

A *big* thank-you to my wonderful critique partners at TheNextBigWriter and members of my local group, Red River Writer's Workshop: Caryl, Ron, Emily, Andy, and Noelle.

Also to my beta readers, Colby Ray, Jaclyn Parks, Gemma Blair, Bella D'Amour, and Nancy Bowen; you'll never know how much your honest feedback meant to me. Y'all rock!!

A big shout-out to Winestone Goat Products, Lone Star Harley-Davidson, and Debbie Lovelady, cosmetology instructor at Northeast Texas Community College, for answering all of my questions.

Table of Contents

[5]

Chapter 1

Blaze

As Blaze Bledsoe waited for the curling iron to heat, she read her escape list one more time. Watching every episode of *Perfect Crime,* had helped with the plan. Silly. It had been three years, and no one had come, but she couldn't help herself. If she'd overlooked even the smallest detail, they'd find her.

Destroy credit and debit cards.

Buy fake ID.

Transfer files to flash drive, throw computer and cell in lake.

Take the bus to Oklahoma. Pick up the black metallic Chevy Cruze stored there, then double back to Texas.

Stashing the notebook, she stared at the body of Winifred Allen, lying on the mortuary's stainless steel dressing table. "Did you know Dessie Bishop?" Blaze lifted the hot iron and wrapped a thin, silver strand of Winifred's hair around the barrel. "I'm still living in her house." She fluffed

[7]

the wisp and moved to the next one. "I kept her cats, but I have to close them up in the laundry room when I'm not there because they aren't healthy and make a mess."

The lifeless woman barely had enough hair to style, so Blaze dusted it with talcum, then worked the powder into her scalp, and tousled. "I gave you soft curls, added a bit of gray eye shadow, pink lipstick, and a hint of blush. That's what your daughter wanted. Gave me strict orders. I don't like her much. I think she was nervous because of my appearance. But no chopped hair, piercings, or black fingernails for you."

The click of a woman's heels down the hall announced Blaze was about to have company. Within moments, Mrs. Walters leaned around the doorjamb. "Excuse me. Are you done with Mrs. Allen?" Blaze marveled at the secretary's perfection. Honest to goodness, she was so powdered and polished, she could drop dead, and Blaze wouldn't have to do a thing.

"Almost."

"Great. Ms. Elliott is waiting in room three. Be sure and do her next. They've moved the visitation up by an hour." Mrs. Walters retreated down the hallway.

Blaze peered back at her client. "Did you notice the euphonious quality of her voice? That's another word for melodious. Or song-like." Not even noon, and she'd already used her word of the day. Didn't always work out that way, but lately she'd been on a roll. She marked it off the list and pulled a bottle of nail polish from her kit.

She'd barely finished two nails when Cameron Foster, heir to Over the Rainbow Funeral Chapel shuffled into the room. "Hey, there. Church is having a hamburger supper tomorrow night. Wanna go?"

Cam was nice, but Blaze wasn't interested. Not in him, hamburgers, or the Methodists. The boy was a high school senior, and Blaze had celebrated her twentieth birthday two months ago. She lifted her head, looked him in the eye, and smiled. "No, thank you."

His weak chin dropped, and she guessed what would come next. Mind racing, she searched for a response. Dad's numerous instructions flashed in her brain. *Keep your head up. Make eye contact. Think before you speak. Remember not to be rude. Smile. Say thank you.* How could the truth be bad manners? But he'd claimed most people didn't want honesty for personal questions.

The lanky boy propped a bony shoulder against the wall. "Why not? Got something else to do?"

"I don't like crowds or church." That sounded reasonable. She shouldn't have to tell him why.

"What you got against God?"

This was the trouble with Dad's advice. It didn't work. She should have said she didn't find Cam attractive. But she had to play this ridiculous game. "Nothing against God. Just organized religion. Besides, I remember. I do have plans." That should do it, and wasn't a total lie.

"Like what?"

Blaze wanted to order the gangly, feeble-chinned, soon-to-be-graduate out of the room because of his persistence. "I don't date."

He blinked as if she'd spoken a foreign language. "Not at all? Or just guys?"

That did it. If he only knew the hours she'd spent conditioning herself. The constant tutoring on how to handle social interaction. How hard it was for her not to blurt out her true thoughts. *I don't like skinny guys.* She sucked in air, then spit the words out like they tasted bad. "I do not. Want. To go."

Cam stepped back. "Okay, okay. I get it." He didn't give her time to say anything else, which was fine. He spun on his heels and disappeared into the corridor.

With a flourish, Blaze removed Mrs. Allen's protective cape. "Sorry about that. At your age, if you were still alive, I'm sure you'd have lots of relationship advice." Palming her notebook once more, she scribbled on a sheet of paper, tore it out, and folded it. "When you get to heaven, find Grant Montgomery and give him this." She tucked the note inside the woman's bra. "You can't miss him. Big man. Handsome.

Once word spreads you're from Bluebird, he'll probably look you up."

Rollers squeaked as she shoved her chair away. Yep. Ten years younger. No doubt about it. Mrs. A didn't look a day over eighty. Her daughter would be happy.

Blaze reached room three and referred to the next list: Blue eye shadow. Black mascara. Mauve lip gloss. Enhance beauty mark at corner of mouth.

Only thirty-nine years old, Ginny Elliott had met her demise when her biker boyfriend failed to negotiate a turn. Thank goodness she'd worn a helmet. Camouflaging a mangled face presented a challenge. Being tossed ten feet into the air before landing on hard pavement had proved too much for the rest of her bones.

Ginny was dressed in a leather jacket and low-cut tank, her voluptuous breasts swelling over the top. Nothing like formaldehyde to pump up a woman's upper thorax. Blaze tugged at her own T-shirt, conscious of the small boobs she'd been blessed with. Removing the pencil from behind her ear, she scratched out part of the note, and made changes.

Proper shading and contouring made women appear pounds lighter and years younger. Once Blaze had finished, Ginny looked like a Harley Harlot. Blaze always regretted the client couldn't witness the magic. She jotted another message, tucked it into Motorcycle Momma's pocket, and zipped it. "Give this to Larkin Montgomery. You'll recognize her because we look alike." With only a few pictures for comparison, she wasn't sure about that. The older she got, the less she remembered about her mother.

With her supplies back in place, Blaze peeked into the hallway. The coast appeared clear. No Cam waiting to walk her out. Maybe she'd finally been rude enough for him to get the message.

Outside, a sharp February breeze cut at her face, but spring hid right around the corner. Almost time to break up the garden spot. Even though she liked living alone, she missed Dessie. The sweet woman had left the place to her only grandson, but Blaze would never meet him.

Since he was serving a fifteen year prison sentence. She'd be long gone by the time he showed up.

Rance

Rance Keller's biggest regret would always be that Jack Fletcher died before he had a chance to kill him. Son of a bitch had to go and get cancer, and right along with it, he'd gotten religion and admitted to framing Rance. Small consolation. At least in prison, with no distractions, Rance had graduated college *summa cum laude*.

Still, what major corporation wanted to hire an almost thirty-year-old with no work experience except summer construction jobs and bussing tables at Backstreet Willie's Bar and Grill? Especially after being convicted for burning the place down. Didn't matter he'd been exonerated. Statistics proved 20 percent of people would always think he did it.

That was the bad thing about lies; once folks made up their minds, nothing could change them. Not even the truth.

He hoped God hadn't forgiven Jack because the thought of him burning in hell made Rance happy. Maybe the Lord had been busy working a terrorist attack or a ten car pile-up when the scumbag had begged for mercy. Even the Almighty couldn't give back six years. The state had done its part with the annuity and cash settlement, but money didn't replace Rance's lost youth.

Downing his second shot of whiskey, he eyed a duo of leggy blondes at the end of the bar. The one in the tight black skirt dangled a red stiletto from her toes and bounced it in time with the country tune blaring from the jukebox. The other wore leather pants and twirled a pink umbrella in her drink.

Funny how he paid attention to details. When his sentence started, he realized there'd be plenty of things he'd miss. Women—how they looked and smelled and felt.

Driving—freedom to go anywhere he wanted. That's why he'd spent the last year on the open road riding his Harley, letting the wind, rain, and sun restore life to his body.

Never imagined missing something as insignificant as color though. But when everything was taken, he realized the many things he'd taken for granted.

Both babes sported hot pink fingernails—probably fake, and their skin sparkled. Noticed them the minute they came in. Skirt definitely had the better ass. Leather Pants, *mm mm*, killer tits. If he didn't make a move, he'd have to add a missed opportunity to his misery.

Laying one chick a week had turned out to be harder than he'd thought. He could have pulled it off, but some nights—well—he'd been too drunk to care. In two more days, his year of sin would end, and he'd be at the farm his grandmother had left him.

His long-term goal was to get the place in shape with enough square footage to appeal to buyers. Didn't want to keep it. Wouldn't be the same without Gran. Missing her funeral, and not saying a proper goodbye, still galled him. Of course, the damn state had lost the paperwork.

The last time he'd visited, the house had needed repairs. After sitting vacant two years, it would be more run-down than ever. No problem. He had plenty of experience and time.

Right now, though, he needed to focus on the prospect at hand. He motioned to the bartender, swallowed another shot, and went back to the math problem. Two days. Six lays. He laughed out loud. Rhyme sounded like the beginning of a rap song.

Tight Skirt sent him a smile. If he doubled up, he'd make his quota. Hell, might as well get started. He rose from the bar stool and ambled over to the ladies. During the past year, he'd learned females had evolved while he'd been out of circulation, and he didn't even need a pickup line. The best approach? Get to the point.

"Got a room across the street. You girls want to take the party there?"

Tight Skirt fiddled with a gold arrow pendant pointing to her breasts and other southern regions. "You're a big guy. Are you big all over?"

"Nothing like a game of *Show and Tell* to find out."

She licked her lips. "In that case, I'm Mia, and this is Mya."

He doubted that, but hell. *Me-oh, my-oh, I'll fuck you both-o.* "Rance." He stuck out his hand, and when Mia took it, she stroked his palm with her finger. His cock twitched.

Once inside his room, the duo didn't hesitate. No small talk. No games. Just got down to business. Mia started with his shirt, and Mya with his pants.

[15]

The next morning, Rance opened his eyes but didn't move. Either last night's activities—or sleeping three in a bed had made every bone in his body ache. He'd gotten a workout as strenuous as football two-a-days. Correction. Two-a-night. One player. Two cheerleaders. *Harder. Faster.* And damn if he hadn't nearly thrown his back out trying to keep up.

As insatiable as Mia and Mya were, he half-expected them to join him in the shower. But that didn't happen. Shutting the water off, he wrapped himself in a towel. If the babes still slept, he wouldn't wake them. They had until two o'clock to check out.

When he returned to the bedroom though, the girls were gone. Humph. Thought they'd at least say goodbye. His eyes drifted to the dresser and his wallet. Picking it up, he laughed. Fifty-six bucks was all they got. No reason to get angry. The Dynamic Duo was worth a hell of a lot more.

He finished dressing, then ran his hand beneath the mattress and recovered his stash. Silly girls. Ex-cons trust no one.

He stepped outside and followed the aroma of bacon to Bubba's Diner. Just what he needed after going heels to Jesus all night. He removed his last cigarette and tossed the package into the blue trash barrel at the corner of the building. Really should give up the bad habit, and he would. Later.

It occurred to him, the tag-team event with the BFFs, had fulfilled his goal. No more pressure. With an early start and few stops, he could make it to Bluebird in one day. Grab a quick breakfast. Crank up the Harley. Hit the road. Couldn't wait to see the place again. Enjoy the seclusion and relax in his grandmother's old claw-foot tub. That's what he loved about the little country town.

Everything remained the same. Never any surprises.

Chapter 2

Hanna

From her workshop window, Hanna saw dust billowing before the car came into view. Usually, Blaze walked through the woods, but today, she had to pick up groceries. As always, she tried to look the part of a rebel, but couldn't pull it off. More like a pubescent teenager playing dress-up. Even the stud in the cherub's bow of her upper lip, and the ring dangling from her small straight nose, didn't offset the big, innocent, green eyes that dominated her face.

Blaze had revealed nothing, but when she'd arrived three years ago with no prior connection to Bluebird or Dessie, Hanna figured she was on the run from something or someone. She'd decided once their friendship grew, Blaze would be more forthcoming. But that didn't happen.

Once Hanna had discovered the gifted girl's artistic ability, she'd asked for help with packaging her soaps and lotions. All she needed was a break to get attention from a major chain, and the right presentation could be the key.

[18]

Out of the corner of her eye Hanna caught sight of her son as he burst through the trees, stick sword in hand, towel cape pinned around his neck, fighting an imaginary foe. Noah was the center of her life and she was thankful he was happy playing with common things, but he wouldn't always be six. As he got older, he'd want what other kids had, and no way could she afford them, unless she got her business off the ground—or accepted the marriage proposal from a man she didn't love.

There was nothing wrong with Dylan. He'd been interested in her since high school, but they'd never dated until six months ago, and he'd proposed on the first date. Wasn't fair to keep putting him off, but she couldn't bring herself to accept.

Blaze pushed open the door and strolled inside. Black was the only color she wore, a harsh contrast to her delicate features. Despite being puny, Blaze was pretty, but she didn't seem to care about her appearance, which was an incongruity since she worked at making others look good.

"What's up?" Hanna asked.

Head bowed, Blaze slid a folder forward. "Here are the drawings."

Hanna thumbed through them and wanted to cry.

Blaze's shoulders drooped. "If you don't like them, I can do more."

Hanna rushed from behind the table and gave the artist a quick hug. "You're a genius. This is exactly what I had in mind."

Blaze stiffened. "Oh. Okay."

"I love the goat in the bubble bath—and how you've put the bluebird inside the outline of Texas is perfect."

The door swung wide, and Hanna's lifelong friend, Tiffany, flew in like she was on her way to a shoe sale at Dillard's.

"I'm glad you're both here. I have something to show y'all," Tiffany announced. She stuck out her hand to display a bracelet. Hanna reached for it, but Tiffany launched into an animated conversation. "Your soap line got me to thinking I should get my creative juices flowing. I thought about a calendar. They never go out of style and everybody needs one. You know, get hunks to pose in the buff, but that's been done a hundred times ten. Besides, I made a list and only came up with two hot guys in all of Bluebird."

Early evening light streaming through the window glinted off the fake gems in Tiffany's creation. She shook her head. Butterscotch curls bounced around her face. "And Daddy would have a heart attack. Probably do a whole series of sermons about my sinful ways."

Hanna opened her mouth to speak, but Tiffany waved her off. She was on a roll and there was no stopping her. "I know what you're going to say. There's a calendar app." She flapped the air as if swatting mosquitoes. "Sure there is, but I could get my own made and still make a ton of money. But I decided, heck, I should connect to my roots. Texas and Bluebird. So this is my original design."

She thrust her arm out again and dangled her wrist. Hanna and Blaze inspected it.

"How do y'all like it? It's a beer bling bracelet, and it's just the beginning." Tiffany counted off as she recited. "I'll do rings, necklaces, belts, cuff links, key chains, bottle openers, the list is endless." She lowered her voice as if sharing a secret. "I can get the caps for free. I've already talked to Jessie at The Roost. He said he'd be glad for me to have them."

Tiffany's excitement was contagious, but Hanna wasn't sure how big a market was out there for bottle caps and rhinestones.

The perky blonde widened her eyes and raised her voice an octave. "Oh! This is the best part. I have the perfect name for my jewelry line. Are you ready for it?" Tiffany allotted a dramatic pause for their response. Hanna and Blaze both nodded.

Palms out, fingers spread, she announced it as if on a marquee. "'Texas Tiffany's!' Can you believe it? Oh. My. Lord. It's like my momma envisioned my destiny when she named me."

Blaze pulled her brows together. "I thought your fate was to teach second graders."

"Well, that's what I went to school for, because they didn't offer a degree in entrepreneurship. Hanna can tell you, I don't make much more than she does substituting. This jewelry idea could be big. Really big. I might end up on the *TODAY Show*. Just imagine. I, Tiffany Ambrosia Scott, could single-handedly put Bluebird, Texas, population 1,202, on the map."

The way she punctuated the air with her finger as she talked, proved she'd picked up some of her father's pulpit skills. The only thing missing was a Bible to drive her point home.

Tiffany smiled at Hanna. "Well, me and your Nanny Goat Soap line, of course."

Her exuberance always made Hanna feel better. "Thanks for including me. It's a great idea. Maybe you can convince Blaze to design your packaging. Look what she did for me."

Tiffany studied the sketches. "Holy crapoly, these are fantastic." She gave Blaze her puppy dog eyes. "Would you?"

"Sure."

"I'll dance at your wedding."

"What does that mean?" Blaze asked.

"I don't have a clue, it's just something my granny says when you do something nice for her. I gotta get going. While I was checking for hunks, Jacob Mason asked me out. We're driving over to Danvers to eat at that Mexican place."

The jewelry tycoon left with as much gusto as when she'd arrived.

Reaching into her apron pocket, Hanna removed papers, and handed them to Blaze. "I got your shopping and banking done. Here are the receipts."

"Thanks. I need to go, too," Blaze said. "I want to clean out a few birdhouses before it gets dark. The bluebirds will start scouting soon."

"Let me help get your bags."

Blaze

A sensation Blaze hadn't experienced in a while bubbled in her chest. *Pride.* Hanna loved the artwork. Not since Dessie died had anyone praised Blaze's talent. A compliment and recommendation from her friend meant a lot. Along with her goat milk business, the brown-eyed beauty worked hard as a substitute teacher and convenience store clerk. All that and raising Noah.

Blaze wondered about his dad, but Hanna never mentioned him. It was as if the kid had been an immaculate conception. Any man who couldn't fall in love with someone as beautiful as Hanna must have a problem. Her long dark hair, olive skin, and high cheekbones belonged on magazine covers.

By the time Blaze got home, put away the groceries, and fed the cats, it was six o'clock. Still enough daylight left to get some boxes ready. Over the years, Miss Dessie had chaired the committee to promote building and mounting bluebird houses along every county road. Because of her efforts, this hick town was the Eastern Bluebird Capital of Texas. This year, the little berg would celebrate its fiftieth festival.

She raised the lid of the first box and found the hinge screws loose. If Dad could see her working with hand tools, he'd laugh. Before she came here, she'd never held a screwdriver or pliers.

She'd always thought you could hang a birdhouse where you wanted. Turned out, bluebirds were picky. The homes needed to be mounted in sunny, open spaces, twenty-five feet apart. She dug out the old nesting straw and dumped it in her bucket, then lowered the lid.

By sunset, she had all but ten boxes clean, but decided to save them for another day. Still had plenty of chores before she could lounge in a nice hot bath.

Just before midnight she connected her iPod to the Pill speaker and cranked up the music before filling the tub. That was a benefit of living in a secluded area. No neighbors to complain.

Sinking low in the old claw-foot, she inhaled a mixture of almond, coconut and honey, and listened to Meghan Trainor's, "Like I'm Gonna Lose You."

Rance

The closer Rance got to Gran's the faster he drove. On the road for fourteen hours, he was ready for a relaxing soak and feather bed. As he turned onto the home stretch, his heart accelerated. He barreled over the narrow bridge where he and his brothers used to catch tadpoles, then past Mr. Henderson's hayfield.

The last few miles flew by. He'd not seen the house in over seven years. His grandmother always said she'd leave it to him, but he'd never wanted to think about her dying.

Silhouetted by the moon, the homestead looked eerie, and the hair prickled on the back of Rance's neck. The bathroom light was on, and as he brought the motorcycle to a stop, he wondered whose car was parked in the drive. Maybe Gran had hired a caretaker. It was after midnight though. Strange hour for maintenance duties. He removed his helmet, dismounted, unstrapped his duffel, and stepped onto the porch. Finding the hidden house key, he slipped inside.

Nothing seemed disturbed. Actually, the place appeared neater than he'd ever seen it. Housekeeping hadn't been one of his grandmother's strong suits. As his eyes adjusted to the darkness, he noticed more changes. When did she get a big screen TV? And computer?

A sappy love song played from the other end of the house. He grabbed the baseball bat Gran had kept in an antique milk can by the hutch, then edged down the short hallway to the bathroom.

A girl of no more than fifteen lay in the tub with her eyes closed. Mostly nipples and areolas, her small breasts flattened against her chest. Bubble clouds floated over her spindle-thin body.

Shame thickened in his throat. He shouldn't be staring at her, but he couldn't turn away. He didn't know if it was the shock of seeing a stranger here, or that the intruder was a teenager. Whatever it was, he found his voice.

"Who the hell are you?"

Chapter 3

Blaze

Blaze recognized Rance Keller from the stack of pictures Miss Dessie kept in a leather box on the mantle. But he looked different in the flesh. An unkempt beard and mustache surrounded full lips. Long brown hair fringed beneath the edge of a knit beanie. Menacing blue eyes stared back at her.

Blaze rose from the water, reached for the towel hanging on the rack, and wrapped herself, tucking in the corner to secure it.

"Did you escape?"

He blinked like it was a stupid question, but it wasn't. Letters she'd read said he'd been denied parole twice because he wouldn't admit guilt.

"I'm asking the questions. Who are you?"

"Blaze Bledsoe."

He half-grinned as if her answer was a punch line, then snarled. "Blaze? I don't think so."

"Well, I don't care what you think. That's my name and I live here because Miss Dessie said I could."

"New owner. New rules. Get your shit and get out."

His lips barely moved, and she thought of all the villains she'd seen on *Perfect Crime,* but despite his demeanor, he didn't scare her because Dessie had shared plenty of stories about him.

She dried off, folded the towel and laid it on the commode, then pushed past him into the bedroom where she took panties from the dresser and stepped into them. Next, she pulled a faded Madonna T-shirt over her head. "No."

"This is my house and you're trespassing," Rance said.

His voice was low-pitched, and when she faced him, his mouth clamped into a thin line. A muscle in his jaw worked. She reminded herself this was a man just out of prison, yet she still didn't feel threatened. Not after Dessie's tales of how he'd cared for injured animals, and his eagerness to help with any chore. Blaze folded her arms under her breasts. "I have work tomorrow. We can talk in the morning."

At first, he said nothing, just scanned the full length of her body, and she felt more naked than she'd been minutes ago. He locked his eyes on hers, and his gaze darkened. "I'm twice your size. I can throw your scrawny ass out the front door and you can't do anything about it."

"I know. But you won't." Turning down the covers, she switched off the lamp, and crawled into bed.

Rance

Too road weary to deal with conflict, Rance cursed under his breath and slammed the bathroom door. Where did she get off telling him what to do? She was as stubborn as Gran, and his grandmother didn't take crap from anyone. Couldn't help but admire that quality. Yet, this little wisp surprised him. He could chew her up and spit her out, but she hadn't flinched. Hell, she wasn't even embarrassed to be naked in front of him. She'd taken her own sweet time drying off, and when she'd pulled on those black bikinis, his cock had jumped. Dammit, he was turning into a pervert.

Stripping off his clothes, he refilled the tub and spied the bottle sitting on the sink. He brought it to his nose and inhaled. Not sure about the amount to use, he gave it two squirts and bubbles formed. He sank into the foam leaving nothing but head and knees above water. He was too big for the claw-foot, but it felt good to lie back and let the heat loosen his bones.

His eyelids weighed heavy and a vision of the stranger's thin, naked body popped into his brain. He dunked his head, hoping the hot water would melt the image away. Not one damn thing sexy about the girl. Barely had tits and a non-existent ass, and a rocker name like Blaze didn't fit. He didn't trust her, and he didn't need complications. She had to go. But this first encounter told him bullying wouldn't work, so he'd have to come up with a new tactic.

Blaze

When Blaze left for work the next morning, Rance was snoring to high heaven. His arrival created a problem she'd have to face, but not yet. This was her home and she wouldn't leave without a fight.

He should still be locked up. If he escaped, he was crazy to come here. *Perfect Crime* episodes 42, 63, and 86 proved cops checked with relatives first.

As she backed out of the drive, she eyed the motorcycle. Painted in gold across the saddlebag was the word *Outlaw*. It also had a faded bumper sticker on the side of the gas tank. She squinted to make out the words.

It only seems kinky the first time.

Something in her chest fluttered, and she recalled how Dessie had described Rance. *A good man.* He hadn't thrown her out last night, only threatened to, so maybe that was still true. Once he saw what a helpful housemate she was, he'd *want* her to stay.

When she wheeled into the funeral home parking lot, Cameron's truck wasn't there, so that was a relief. She pulled her sweater tight to ward off the chill and rushed inside.

"Good morning, Mrs. Walters."

"Good morning, Blaze. Here are the details for Hadley, Morrison, and Caldwell. All of their services are tomorrow with visitations this evening."

Blaze tucked the list in her jeans pocket. Since the IRS had shut down the only funeral home in the neighboring town of Danvers, business at Over the Rainbow had picked up. Wouldn't complain. She liked the extra hours.

Miss Caldwell was up first. Age thirty-six. Died during surgery. Blaze blinked, then blinked again. Natalie used to be Nathan. She went back to the office and poked her head inside. "Uh, Mrs. Walters. In room one. Female makeup?"

The secretary cupped her mouth and leaned forward. "Well, unfortunately he—she—didn't live long enough for the change to happen. They prepped him, but before they removed the appendage, he suffered a massive heart attack. Physically, he's still male and must be listed that way on the paperwork, but he wished to go out as a woman. Oh, and there shouldn't be a problem with facial hair. He'd been taking hormones for months."

"Okay."

Blaze remembered a TV interview with Billy Graham where he'd described heaven as being whatever made us happy. For him, beautiful golf courses. Blaze didn't know if that was true, but he knew more about the subject than she did, so she'd take his word. Since the funeral would be Natalie's debut for a lot of folks, Blaze planned to make her as gorgeous as possible. Figured her heavenly happiness was to arrive at the Pearly Gates as the woman she wanted to be.

"Miss Caldwell, I want to do something special for you." Blaze chose two bottles of nail polish and shook them. "I'm going to tessellate your nails. That's my word of the day. It means to form or arrange in a checkered pattern." Once she completed the manicure, Blaze lined Natalie's full lips with Peach Petal, then filled them in with Iced Tangerine. She rolled her chair away and eyed the final results. Platinum-tipped blond hair. Warm Umber blended with Golden Mink eye shadow. Coral Tango blush. As Tiffany would say, holy crapoly. The new female looked hot.

Blaze tore a page from her notebook and slipped it inside the woman's camisole. "If you meet Miss Dessie, give her this. She'll be happy to hear her grandson showed up last night. I think he broke out of prison, but don't tell her that part. Anyway, you have a nice trip and I hope you like what I've done with your makeup."

Rance

Rance woke to rain pounding on the tin roof. He stretched, then burrowed deep into the down mattress. Best night's sleep he'd had in years. Even without liquor or sex, there'd been no nightmares. Then he remembered the kid and his temper flared. Swinging his feet to the floor, he grabbed his watch. First on his agenda: settle the squatter situation. He focused on the dial. Almost noon. *Dammit.* She'd mentioned a job, but that couldn't be right. Must have meant school.

He hated passing through her bedroom to use to the john. *Her bedroom.* Hell no. Couldn't think of it that way. When he got to the door, he stopped and peeked in. No sign of her, and the bed was made.

After he relieved himself, he searched for his clothes from last night. Nowhere to be found. She must have taken them. But why? Easy answer. From the looks of things, she was a neat-freak. Good. His messiness alone should be enough incentive for her to leave. He grabbed a clean pair of jeans and a knit shirt, pulled them on, and strolled to the kitchen to make coffee, hoping he remembered how. On the counter was a note.

Do not let the cats out of the laundry room.

Do not feed them.

Pancakes on stove. Microwave for 56 seconds. Syrup and honey on table.

Coffee ready. Push start.

Please rinse your dirty dishes and load in dishwasher.

Wipe table off, careful not to get crumbs on floor.

Drape the dishcloth over the faucet to dry.

I'll run the dishwasher and clean the coffee pot when I get home.

You're welcome.

Blaze

He stared at the paper. *You're welcome?* He needed a cigarette. And something stronger than coffee. But first, he'd eat breakfast. No need to waste it.

The microwave dinged. He removed the steaming hotcakes, smothered them in butter, doused them in syrup, then took a second to inhale the aroma before closing his lips around the fork. *Sweet Jesus.* Whoever she was, she could cook. But that still wasn't enough reason to let her stay. By the time he'd finished the stack, he wavered on that point.

He pushed back from the table, leaving everything as it was, then wandered down the hall. As owner, it was his right to check her room. He turned first to her closet.

Depressing. Six pairs of jeans. A dozen T-shirts. Three sets of shoes. All black. Hell, she barely had more clothes than he did. He moved to the bureau. Panties and bras. At least they were different colors. He picked up a pair of red bikinis and rubbed the lace between his fingers. Forced a sordid image from his head, then turned his attention to the side table. Next to a lamp, sat a framed monogrammed note with a message that read: *You're awesome, loveable, spectacular, and huggable. Goodnight, Birdie. Love, Dad.*

Rance studied the card. At the top, a big letter M, encircled with leaves wasn't much of a clue. Could stand for a first or last name. Birdie must be a nickname, and just as ridiculous as Blaze.

After digging through every drawer, he continued his search in the bathroom. In the medicine cabinet, he found bandages, over-the-counter pain relievers, rubbing alcohol, birth control pills. *Damn.*

Finding no incriminating evidence, he turned back to the bedroom, folded his arms and regarded the mural that covered the whole wall. Trees. Shed. Garden spot. His grandmother standing between a row of pole beans and tomatoes. His throat tightened. She had on the pink bonnet and flowered apron he'd seen her wear a thousand times. Two cats circled her ankles while another pair sat beside her.

He dropped to his knees to look under furniture and found paint cans behind the chair. One didn't have a speck of drips and wasn't heavy. He took his army knife from his pocket and pried off the lid. *Fuck*. It was stuffed with cash and a few pictures. He dumped the bundles onto the spread. All hundred-dollar bills. Had to be thousands here.

His mind raced. Thief? Drug dealer? He picked up the photos. A couple with a baby. Something was written on the back, but it was marked out. He held it up to the light, but couldn't make out any words. Next in the pile was an image of a man in a business suit. Then a woman with an out-of-style hairdo. She resembled the kid. Must be the mother. He compared the two with the family group. Definitely the girl's parents. He replaced everything. No reason to speculate. Didn't matter. As soon as she got home, she was leaving. Right now, he had errands. Leisure time was over and he was ready to get his plans in motion. Bluebird offered little in the way of building supplies, but Danvers had plenty.

Before heading there, he'd visit the cemetery, then stop in town for some smokes and a bottle of whiskey. He already needed a drink.

[36]

Chapter 4

✦

Rance

Rance stared at the headstones of the two most important people he'd had in his life. Mom and Gran. His eyes burned and his chest tightened. After believing in his innocence, his grandmother had died before seeing him exonerated, and that hurt. "I'm home, Gran. Like you said I'd be. Thank you for never giving up on me. It's all that kept me going." He wiped his eyes.

Weeds surrounded most of the stones except for Gran's and Mom's. Someone had tended them. He wondered if it was the girl. He forced the thought to the back of his mind, pulled himself together, and returned to his bike, then headed into town.

One pass down Main Street showed everything Bluebird had to offer. On the north side: Bird's Nest Children's shop, Bird Cage Beauty Salon, A Bird in the Hand

Gift Boutique, Bluebird of Happiness Café, and on the far end of the strip, Birds of a Feather Nursing Home.

Rance thought they'd gone overboard on the theme, but Gran had claimed it made them unique. *Yeah, uniquely nuts.* Other than a few new businesses, the place hadn't changed much since his last visit. Flags boasting the Bluebird Festival hung from awnings. Flower pots full of pansies flanked doors. Twinkling lights outlined store windows.

He wheeled a U-turn and scoped out the other side, Flock Farm and Ranch, The Roost Bar and Grill, Little Peeps Day Care, and Fly-By Quickie Mart, where he slid his bike into a spot near the entrance.

A buzzer announced his arrival. There wasn't a clerk in sight, but a female voice yelled a greeting from the rear. Rance strolled to the counter and waited. A woman came down the aisle, then stopped in her tracks.

"Rance? When . . . what . . . how . . . ?"

It took a second for him to recognize the dark-haired beauty. "Hanna? Is that you? Damn, girl. You've grown up." How awkward. Should he hug her? Pat her on the shoulder? It'd been so long since he'd seen someone he knew, especially a woman, he didn't know what to do. He waited for her to make a move.

She smiled. "You, too. Did you get paroled?"

"No. Free and clear. Guilty party came forward."

[38]

Hanna moved past him and stepped behind the counter. "Just getting into town?"

"Got here last night." His eyes drifted to the magazine rack. *Cosmopolitan.* A quick scan of the articles distracted him. "Gold Medal Sex: How to Cross the Finish Line Together." "Hot Women and What they Crave." Damn. He refocused.

"Give me a carton of Marlboro short reds in a box." Rance tried to remember the last time he'd seen Hanna. She'd been a teenager and he a college student. Beautiful even then, she'd only improved. He glanced at her hand. No ring.

She slid the box and change across the countertop. "Oh. You've been to the house?"

Clearly she was acquainted with the trespasser. Maybe she'd fill him in about the girl. "Yeah. Had a surprise."

"You met Blaze."

Before he could answer, another customer interrupted, so Rance stepped aside.

Hanna looked over the new shopper's shoulder and spoke to Rance again. "I'm due for a break. Meet me out back at the picnic table."

After a trip next door to BB's Liquor, he shoved his purchase into his saddlebag, then moved his ride to the rear of the Quickie Mart. He lit a cigarette, pulled in a long drag and blew the smoke into the air. The breeze floated it into the bare limbs of a tall poplar tree. The mornings and evenings were chilly, but by noon each day, temps hovered into the seventies.

A pair of bluebirds flew to a nearby box. The male poked his head in the hole while the female fluttered to the fence. He danced in and out of the opening, as if coaxing her to come, but she wasn't interested. Damn bird couldn't get the female to stay and Rance couldn't get one to leave.

Hanna came around the end of the building, pulling her jacket tighter. "So, you don't look too bad."

He sucked on his cigarette, then flicked ashes. "Oh yeah. Prison was a real party. Non-stop."

She scooted her butt onto the table top and rested her feet on the bench. "Sorry. I didn't mean to make light of it."

He smirked. "I know what you meant. Been out a year. I've had time to gain weight and get over the beat-down persona. But enough about my exciting life. What about you? Don't see a wedding band. Thought you'd be married with babies by now."

"Not yet, but close."

"Don't see an engagement ring either."

Hanna laughed. "Okay, here's the thing. I'm involved, and he's asked, but I haven't answered yet. Still considering it."

Rance sat next to her. "That tells me a lot."

"What does that mean?"

He should tell her it meant she didn't love the guy or she wouldn't be hesitating. He remembered her being the same age as his younger brother, Seth. That'd make her twenty-five. Old enough to settle down, and there couldn't be that many available dudes in town. But her body language told him the subject wasn't up for discussion. "Forget it. None of my business."

"No, that's okay," she said. "Here are the Cliffs Notes of my life since I last saw you. Almost have my teaching degree by way of online courses. Work part-time here and substitute at the elementary school, while trying to get a bath and body business off the ground. I'm dating Dylan Carver. Did you ever meet him?"

Rance wanted to ask more, but her tone said to drop it. Bottom line: she wasn't available. "Don't think so."

"Was Blaze surprised to see you?"

"Didn't seem to be. Who is she and why is she living in Gran's house?"

Hanna shrugged. "All I know is three years ago, Dessie told me a girl was coming to live with her. Asked me to make friends. So I did."

Rance cocked his head. "No idea where she came from or her connection to Gran?"

"Nope. But it was the best thing that could have happened. Six months after she moved in, Dessie got diagnosed with cancer. Had it not been for Blaze, your grandmother would have spent her last days in a nursing home. She would have hated that."

Rance pulled more nicotine into his lungs. Hanna was right. One of his grandmother's greatest fears had been ending up in a nursing facility. "I don't get it. Gran never said anything in her letters. Seth or Nick didn't mention meeting a caretaker at the funeral."

"Pretty sure Blaze didn't go to the service. She works at the funeral home. Probably said her goodbye there because she's practically a recluse."

"Why isn't she in school?"

"She's older than she looks. Twenty."

"No way."

"She has her cosmetology license and you can't take those courses until you're in high school, so since she had her certification when she got here, that's proof. Are you going to let her stay?" Hanna asked.

"Not a chance. Something isn't right with her. She might be in trouble with the law, and the last thing I want is *any* involvement with cops."

Hanna hung her head. "I'm sure that's not the case. She may be odd, but she's a good person. And Dessie loved her."

Wasn't like she didn't have the means to go somewhere else. It confirmed his theory. Anybody with that much cash would never live in Bluebird unless they were trying to disappear. Like him. "Well, I appreciate that, but she's freeloaded long enough. Time for her to find a new home."

Hanna checked her watch and slid off the table. "Not freeloading. I take care of her business and deposit a rent payment into Dessie's bank account every month. A clear sign of integrity."

Rance dropped his cigarette and ground it into the dirt with the toe of his boot. "You don't want me to kick her out, do you?"

The breeze caught threads of Hanna's hair and blew them across her face. She raked the strands aside and looked up at him. "I understand your concern and I agree she's hiding. But if she had anyone else to depend on, she'd already be gone. Just consider it. She's so shy, you probably won't know she's there."

Rance stared after Hanna until she disappeared. Damn. He hated she was taken. As small as the town was, there wouldn't be much to choose from. Most women his age were already married, or divorced, usually with brats in tow. He didn't need the responsibility of raising another dude's kids. Hell, he wasn't sure if he wanted to produce any of his own.

At least the spot-in-the-road had a bar, and if he remembered right, the neighboring town had several. When he got to Danvers, he'd find out. Just because he wasn't traveling anymore didn't mean he had to give up women. Another reason he needed to get rid of the problem houseguest.

As he drove out of town, he passed Over the Rainbow Funeral Chapel. Must be where the kid worked. Farther down were Bird Bath Spa, Bird Watcher's Optometry, and Bluebirds Fly-Inn. Yep, definitely gone overboard, but he couldn't help but laugh at some prime possibilities they'd overlooked. Bird Brain Psychiatric Hospital, Bird Legs Dance Studio, Bird Shit Sanitation.

Marla

Marla Montgomery pressed one phone to her ear and the other against her breast. "You listen, Felix. I've been patient, but you have no more information about my stepdaughter than you did six months ago. You're fired." She slammed the receiver down, ran her hand over her linen skirt, and took a moment to compose herself before starting the next conversation. She lifted the cell to her lips. "Sorry, Mr. Fraser, but my nerves are stretched thin. If hired, you'll be my fourth PI."

"Well, I've looked over all the files you sent, and honestly, I'm not sure she's still alive. I know that's hard to hear, but when she disappeared, you reported it as a kidnapping, but no ransom demand came. With no sign of forced entry or a struggle, the cops labeled her a runaway. Since she was almost eighteen that pretty much tied their hands," Mr. Fraser said.

Marla clicked a perfectly manicured nail against the cell. "Either way, I need closure. Even though she's not my child, I love her and need to know what happened. I owe that to her father, and I can't bear the thought of my sweet girl's remains abandoned somewhere, with no proper burial." Marla drew a staggering breath. "If she is—gone, I want to lay her to rest beside her dad. Only that will give me peace. Do you grasp what I'm saying?"

"Yes, ma'am. But, I want you to understand the results might not be what you expect."

"Mr. Fraser, I've lived with this for a long time and not given up hope of finding her alive, but I realize the odds aren't in my favor. You'll see from the previous reports, she's not a stable girl. If she ran away, and I'm not convinced she did, it's because she suffered some type of psychological break. She worshiped her father and his death devastated her. Can you promise me you'll find her no matter what?"

"Like I told you earlier, in all my years with the FBI, I never failed to close a case, and I don't intend to start now."

Chapter 5

Blaze

When Blaze got home, Rance's motorcycle was nowhere in sight. She wasn't sure which emotion was more intense: Relief or disappointment. Happy not to face him or depressed about postponing the inevitable. He didn't want her living there, but she couldn't leave. Not yet.

Once inside, she spotted the dirty breakfast dishes. He was baiting her. If he thought he could run her off with messiness, he was nuts. She had experience with people not wanting her around. At least he hadn't let the cats out. She took care of them, then cleaned the laundry room.

Next, she removed his clothes from the dryer, hung up his shirt and jeans and folded his underwear and socks. They didn't look new, so maybe he'd been out for a while. Most likely on the run. No, that couldn't be right. Nobody had shown up looking for him, so perhaps he'd admitted his crime and gotten paroled.

She took out the package of meat she'd moved to the fridge that morning to thaw, laid it on the counter, and washed two potatoes and got them ready to bake.

While the steak fried, she made a salad and set the table. Her phone buzzed as she finished. "Hello?"

"Why didn't you call me about Rance?" Hanna asked.

Blaze lowered the flame on the burner. "I'm sorry. Was his escape on the news?"

"No. He was in the store today. He always claimed to be innocent, and the real criminal finally confessed. So his record is clear. But are you okay?"

Thankful she wasn't living with a fugitive, Blaze smiled and transferred the steak from the pan to a platter. "Yes."

"If you say so, but if not, call me. And one more thing. Don't mention Noah."

"Okay." Blaze clicked off and wondered why Hanna didn't want Rance to know about her son. Was he Noah's father? Shaking the notion away, she put a counter attack in place.

She clipped small twigs from a redbud tree in the backyard and stuck them in a vase Dessie kept on the hutch. On the bottom, carved into the pottery, was *Rance, 1995*. A Bible school project when he was eight. It was one of his grandmother's most treasured possessions.

Blaze brought a pitcher of tea and set it next to the glasses. Outside, a motorcycle rumbled and died. Her heart kicked up a notch.

Rance

Rance finished his business at the building center, arranged for delivery of supplies and got the names of a plumber, electrician, and concrete company. Before heading home, he'd stopped by the Ford dealership to make a purchase. Bright, shiny, and red. The salesman would deliver the truck tomorrow.

He brought the Harley to a stop. Unfortunately, the kid's car was in the drive. He grabbed the carton of smokes and bottle of Jack from his saddlebag.

As he stepped onto the porch, a familiar aroma enveloped him like a warm blanket on a cold night. Damn. Could it be? Gran's chicken fried steak? He salivated at the memory.

The girl stood at the stove, stirring what looked like gravy. She glanced over her shoulder. "Wash up. Supper is almost done."

Said it as if she belonged there, but she looked out of place. A waif playing grownup. It dawned on Rance how careful he needed to be. She could frame him like Jack had. Come up with an abuse story or worse. Who'd believe a big, burly ex-con over a fragile girl who'd cared for an old woman during her last days? His innocence didn't matter, there would always be the stigma. His stomach churned. "We need to talk," he said.

"I know. We will. Over supper. Wash your hands and take a seat."

He went to the bathroom, splashed water on his face, and reminded himself to stick to the plan. He had enough bad habits to drive her away. All he had to do was play those up a bit. Soon, she'd be so disgusted, she'd burn rubber getting out of there.

Seated at the dining table, he barely glanced at her as she slid onto the chair across from him. He spooned gravy, then cut into the familiar recipe with a vengeance. The first bite sent his taste buds to heaven. While he chewed, he loaded his potato with butter, cheese, and sour cream. The only thing missing? Garden fresh onions.

Even the food he'd eaten in cafés across the country didn't compare. If she had apple pie for dessert, he'd forget about running her off and marry her instead. He fought a smile. Wouldn't want her to know she'd done something he liked. It'd only encourage her.

[49]

Her voice brought him to the problem at hand.

"I can't leave. I have nowhere to go."

Blaze picked at her food and his throat tightened. Dammit. Couldn't let her sob story affect him. Sharing his new home with a runaway hadn't been in his plans. "You can go back to where you came from," he said.

"If that was possible, I wouldn't be here."

Rance swallowed another bite and let the silence help with his dirty work. Then, he stabbed another piece, held it in midair, and set his jaw in a firm line. "Listen, kid. If you're in trouble with the law, I want no part of it. I don't know why Dessie took you in. I'm sure she had her reasons, but that was an arrangement between the two of you. It doesn't concern me."

That wasn't exactly true. Gran had a reputation for taking in strays. Sometimes she was too good for her own good.

The girl choked. "I haven't done anything illegal. I swear. I'll cook. Clean. Do your laundry."

He swiped his final bite through gravy and shoved it in his mouth. The kid's cooking skills had to come from Gran's instructions because everything had his grandmother's touch. "I can do all that for myself," he said. Yeah, he could, but after this meal, she had a good selling point. No, he had to scare her skinny ass away. "I'm horny as hell. Guess you could help me with that."

She swallowed hard and for a minute he thought she might faint, but she pulled herself together. "I guess if that's my only option, I could try."

Holy hell. Not the response he'd expected. He looked at her. Really looked at her. This sly little fox was on to him. She was odd, but not dumb. "That's good news. I mean, I've already seen the merchandise and talk about convenient. Doesn't get better than having available pussy on the premises."

She gasped.

He'd called her bet, raised the wager, and backed her into a corner. Put out or get out. His eyes wandered to her breasts, then her face, which had lost all color. He belched and scratched his chest for effect. "So, you ready to get it on or do you want to clean the kitchen first?"

She glared at him. "You're not serious."

Leaning forward, he rested his arms on the table and gave his best evil grin. "I am."

She stood, reached for the hem of her shirt and in one quick motion, jerked it over her head. "If I have to have sex with you to stay, I will. But first, you need to take a bath and brush your teeth. You smell like an ashtray." She turned and disappeared down the hallway.

Rance froze in his chair. She'd called his bluff. Hell. Now what?

Blaze

Blaze didn't know how she'd said those words without falling to pieces, or how she'd removed her shirt and not passed out. But the important part was she'd accepted his offer, and either had to follow through or run.

She walked to the window and gazed out at the shed. No water, heating or cooling, but the roof didn't leak, so she could make do. But even a counter offer to move into it wouldn't satisfy him. He wanted her off the property.

Most likely the sex would only be one-time. With a single previous encounter, she didn't have enough experience to be good at it.

Any minute, he'd cut through her room on his way to shower, unless he decided not to bathe. That made her nauseous. The idea of his sweaty body and bad breath was too much. He wasn't ugly, but when he widened his eyes, he looked downright scary. His nose was okay, and she liked his mouth. She could always pretend he was her fantasy man from *Perfect Crime*, Zack Moy. Who was she kidding? She couldn't do this. Rising, she rushed to the door and locked it, then grabbed her suitcase from the closet. Once Dessie died, Blaze knew her luck could run out but never imagined it'd be over sleeping with a horny jailbird.

As she put the first pair of jeans in the bag, the motorcycle came to life. She sprinted to the window in time to see Rance speed down the road.

She needed to work fast, so she dashed to the kitchen and cleaned everything.

It'd be dark soon. So she grabbed her flashlight and ran out of the house and into the woods. Within a few minutes, she arrived at Hanna's where she found her friend pouring soap into molds. Blaze bent over, gasping.

Hanna jumped up and rushed to her. "Oh my gosh, is he after you?" She craned her neck toward the forest.

Blaze gulped for air. "No."

"Then what's wrong?"

"I agreed to sex if he'd let me stay, but he rode off. What should I do?"

"Tell me what happened."

Blaze told the story, finishing with the last detail. "It's probably true. He's been locked up a long time."

"That S.O.B. is trying to scare you," Hanna said. "He's been out of prison for a year. I doubt he's lacking in the sex department."

Blaze stood and crossed her arms under her breasts. "He's a jerk."

"Yeah, well, maybe so, but he also owns the place. You have to decide if you're willing to put up with him or not. After what you said I'd say he plans to make you miserable. Do you need to stay with me?"

"No. He's rude and doesn't follow directions. I left a list, and he didn't do hardly any of it. I cooked for him and he inhaled it like it was his last meal and never even thanked me."

Hanna laughed. "That may be the key. Do everything you offered—well, all but the sex. Cleaning. Laundry. Cooking. But don't take any crap off him either. Oh, and tomorrow, bake him an apple pie. I remember it being all the Keller boys' favorite."

Rance

The Roost Bar and Grill was across the street from Bird in Hand gift shop where colored umbrellas filled the window displays and a sign advertised "It's Raining Bargains All Week."

If I have to have sex with you, I will. Rance sucked down his first beer and thought of the kid. She had balls. He'd give her that. Should have pushed the limits to see how far she'd go. But as much as he wanted her gone, he couldn't mistreat her. Might be guilty of taking advantage of easy women, but he'd never abused a woman, and hated men who did.

He glanced around the room. Neon signs decorated the walls along with posters of past Bluebird festivals. Scarred wooden tables were crowded close together and there was an open space at the rear for dancing. The aroma of cigarettes and Buffalo wings hung in the air.

The place was almost vacant, but most joints didn't come alive until the sun went down. He belched and couldn't help but smile. When he'd used the word *pussy*, she'd flinched, and her grimace proved she didn't like the bad language or burping. Yeah, grossing her out, plus the threat of sex, made it the perfect plan.

As it got later, Rance watched the chicks gather: a Rhode Island Red, a couple of Leghorns, and a Bantam. All eyeing him. He should join the group, but decided to let nature take its course. Eventually one would leave the brood and head his way.

[55]

By ten o'clock, The Roost was in full swing, and Rance had met Bantam chick, Kayla. A curvy brunette with ample breasts and a mouth that looked as if she could suck a peach through a straw.

As soon as she'd approached him and leaned those Texas-size ta-tas against his arm, he'd limited his alcohol consumption. Didn't want it to affect the performance he planned for later. Plus he had to stay sober to drive.

As they danced Kayla stuck her hands in his back pockets and squeezed. A clear sign to take this party home. It was almost midnight when she parked her Chevy behind his bike. By the time they got to his bedroom, she'd stripped and started on him.

Blaze

The screeching, high-pitched sound woke Blaze with a start. At first, she thought one of the cats was having a seizure, so she sprang from the bed and looked beneath it. All four felines huddled together. Janet growled as if warning a predator. Dianne joined in. Cathy and Peggy cowered.

Blaze rose, and the sound pierced the air again. She eased to the doorway. Maybe Rance was hurt. Stepping into the hall, she tiptoed halfway and stopped to listen. A low moan followed by short, shrill gasps signaled a woman and advertised her activity.

"Yes!" the female screamed. "Oh God, yes!"

Blaze's cheeks burned. She wanted to run, but her feet rooted to the carpet. She pictured a blonde sexpot tangled around Rance's muscular frame, long nails biting into his flesh while he pounded into her. Moments later he grunted, and the room fell silent. Blaze's heart raced. Her body tingled. She'd never been this close to people having sex. Well, except for the time she'd done it with Kevin, and that had been an awful experience. What she'd heard didn't sound unpleasant. She wasn't sure how to describe it. *Wild? Erotic? Pornographic?* A word of the day she'd never used came to mind. Amatory. Yeah. That was it. Expressive of, or inciting sexual love or romance. At last she'd mark it off the list because there was definitely amatory going on in there.

Suddenly Rance came out wearing nothing but jeans, zipped but not buttoned. An unlit cigarette dangled from his lips. She held her breath and froze. Pressed against the wall, she squeezed her eyes tight and prayed he wouldn't look her way. But when she opened them, he glared at her with a menacing grin that would rival the Grinch. He didn't speak, just strolled into the kitchen.

His scowl uprooted her feet, and she ran back to her bedroom. She pulled the covers up to her chin and tried to sleep, but couldn't. Three hours later she socked the pillow over her ears to drown out more amatory.

Chapter 6

✦

Hanna

Hanna stood in the doorway and stared at her son snuggled deep in the comforter, clutching his favorite stuffed animal, a horse with a missing ear. Most boys his age were into superheroes. He liked them, but with a name like Noah, it wouldn't be right not to like animals better. Sunlight streaked through the window and bathed his angelic face in amber. He was such a good boy, and she wanted to do so much for him. Like get him a real pony. He'd asked for one last Christmas, and when Santa didn't deliver, Noah didn't cry. Said he figured St. Nick thought he needed to be a year older.

Her lip quivered and her eyes filled with tears. She should accept Dylan's proposal and make everyone's life easier. Move out of her parents' house and into his country-club, two-story home. No more shopping at thrift stores. Give up her part-time jobs. Purchase a newer car. Get a pedicure. Damn, it'd been years since she'd had one.

Noah shifted and made a little humming noise, then laughed. Hanna laughed, too. His unruly hair poked in every direction. The child needed a haircut. Blaze would take care of that.

The thought of her friend brought Rance to mind. Seeing him yesterday unnerved Hanna and caused long-buried emotions to resurface.

Hanna's mom cleared her throat from the doorway. "He's so precious."

Hanna wiped at her eyes. "I'm going to marry Dylan."

Mom crossed the room and slipped her arm around her daughter's shoulders. "Oh, Hanna. I know you don't love the man."

Hanna caught the disappointment in her mom's voice, but she'd grown weary of struggling. "I'm worn out, Momma. Tired of working two jobs and still not having enough to raise Noah without sponging off you and Daddy. Dylan can provide a good life for us. I care for him, and that will have to be enough."

Mom pulled a tissue from her pocket, wiped her nose, then twisted it in her hands. Even before she spoke, her body language said she wasn't on board with the idea. "Maybe for you, but will it be enough for him? He's got to know how you feel, and I can't believe he'll settle for a loveless marriage. And you aren't sponging. Dad and I love having you and Noah here."

"I know, but I feel guilty that I contribute so little."

"No. No. I won't allow you to do this. In a few months, you'll have your degree, and they've promised you a job in the school district. Once you're teaching, your income will double."

That sounded good, but unless a teacher broke the code of conduct or died, a position rarely became available. "Only if they have an opening, which they don't. That means I'll have to find work out of town. Which means more gas, and I'll need a dependable vehicle. Higher insurance, and I'll see less of Noah. Marrying Dylan will change all that. I won't even have to work because he wants a baby right away."

Mom ripped the tissue and winced as she straightened. "Oh my God! Listen to yourself. Are you even sexually attracted to him?"

"Momma! That's none of your business."

"Sorry. But my daughter's happiness *is* my business, and I'm making a point." She looked at Hanna as if she'd lost her mind, then released a long sigh. "You're willing to swear before God to love this man forever and you don't even love him now. The marriage will be doomed from the beginning. You can't do this. I'm begging you."

Hanna burst into tears and so did Mom.

"What the hell? Did somebody die?" a male voice said.

Hanna faced her dad, but her mother spoke. "Come talk sense into your daughter. She plans to marry Dylan even though she doesn't love him."

Dad folded his arms over his broad chest and glared at his only child. "Hell no, you're not. End of discussion." He turned and ambled to the kitchen.

Hanna swallowed hard. Gerald Oliver Donnelly's initials spelled God, and when in his presence, Hanna believed he was. She'd disappointed him once in her life and swore to never do it again, so if he said no wedding, there wouldn't be one. If only her mother had supported her decision, G.O.D. would have followed suit.

Hanna stood but didn't move. She half-expected Mom to say more, but instead, she shook her head and followed Dad into the kitchen. Hanna guessed it was back to business as usual. On that note, she went to milk the goats. She stomped into the barn and led Sadie, the oldest Nubian, into the stall, grabbed a chippy stool from the counter and a stainless bucket from the sterile closet. After washing her hands, she got busy, still shaking from her dad's commandment.

Mom was right about the lack of attraction. Dylan was kind and patient, but as hard as Hanna tried, she couldn't bring herself to sleep with him. It was wrong to take advantage of his affection, but to have sex would be even worse. It would give him hope for a future together, and just as she'd decided to sacrifice happiness for security, Dad had put the brakes on that plan.

Now she was right back to her financial woes and bleak horizon. After insurance, books, tuition, phone, gas, and Internet service, plus business supplies, there was hardly anything left of her meager earnings. If it wasn't for the money Blaze paid her to run errands, Hanna wouldn't even have pocket change.

Bluebird was a great place to raise Noah, but there weren't many job opportunities. She sniffed and stopped to swipe at her eyes, then returned to the sink to wash again, but couldn't hold back the tears. With a deep breath, she tried to shake the blues away. Damn PMS made her a crybaby every month. Rance had brought this on. Now that he was at Dessie's, it wouldn't be long until his brothers showed up.

"Momma, are you crying?"

Hanna rubbed her cheeks and spun around. "No, baby. Allergies. Come give me some sugar."

Rushing to her, Noah wrapped his arms around her thighs. She stooped to press him closer and kissed the top of his head. "Did you eat breakfast?"

He released his hold and stepped back "Yep, ma'am. It's Saturday. Me-mom fixed pancakes. We saved you some. Can I go play in my treehouse?"

"*May* I go?"

Adjusting the wooden pistol stuck in jeans pocket, he glanced up at her with that aw-shucks expression she loved. "May I go?"

He looked so cute with the kerchief tied around his neck, Hanna wanted to squeeze him. "Sure. Just be careful."

He mounted his imaginary steed, took off his hat and slapped his leg, yelled *yee-haw* and raced away. She should be ashamed of herself. No amount of money could buy a healthy, happy, loving child.

Blaze

Blaze heard him coming before he galloped into view.

"Whoa, boy." Noah untied his bandanna and wiped his brow like he'd been on the trail for days, then dismounted his pretend horse. "You graze right here, Gus. I'm gonna climb up that tree and take a look around."

As Noah's boot hit the top rung, Blaze folded her feet under her hips and sat up straight.

He pulled himself to the opening and leveled his gaze on her. "Whatchoo doing here?"

"The new owner of Dessie's house moved in yesterday and had a sleepover." Last night Blaze had suffered through the noisy sex twice, but that third time, she couldn't take it anymore. So at 4 a.m., she'd gotten dressed, grabbed her flashlight and pillow, and jogged to the treehouse.

"Oh. Does they have kids?"

"No. It's just a man."

The young cowpoke crawled in and sat. "Do you gotta move? 'Cause if you do, you can live here."

"I don't have to move." Blaze hesitated, then smiled. "Thank you for offering. I better go." Rolling onto her knees, she crawled to the door. "See you later."

Blaze took her time getting back to the house and before stepping into the clearing, she stopped to check the drive. The bimbo-to-go's car was gone, but now there was a pickup truck in its place.

Before she could speculate, Rance came from the backyard with a stranger holding a clipboard. The man made notes as Blaze's new landlord gestured as if telling a story. She waited until they walked into the backyard, then rushed inside.

The laundry room door stood open, and no cats were in sight. Didn't he remember the note? Her instructions? She zipped down the hallway and located Janet and Cathy on her bed. After securing them, she returned to look under the chair where the remaining two huddled together.

She scanned the area for damage or accidents, saw none, and relaxed. After a thorough hand- washing, she removed ingredients from the pantry, then pulled Dessie's favorite rolling pin from the drawer and her special pie plate from the hutch. By the time she got the crust ready, Rance came into the room and spoke without looking at her.

"There's too much pussy in this house. You and the fur balls have to go."

Blaze glared at him. If he believed that, why was he bringing in more? "Why are you an enemy of cats?"

"I'm not. But you have a whole damn herd."

"They're not mine. They belonged to your grandmother. She loved them. Named them after her favorite singing group on *The Lawrence Welk Show*. I bought the big screen and paid for cable so she could watch them on Hulu." Blaze pulled out all the stops. She needed to let him know his grandmother wanted her and the cats here.

"Well, Dessie always had a soft spot for taking in strays, but there's too many of you. You're cramping my style."

Blaze's throat burned. He was playing her. Calling her a stray without coming right out and saying it. Gunning for an argument. But he wasn't getting one. He was getting pie.

"No, I'm not. I haven't said anything about that woman you brought here."

Now Rance glared at her. Mouth tight. Eyes narrowed. "Then why were you trying to spy on me? If you want to watch that can be arranged. I'll even let you join in."

"I wasn't spying," she said. "And I don't want to watch or join in."

"Yeah, well, this arrangement isn't going to work for either of us. Best you hit the road."

"You don't even want me to finish the pie?" That got his full attention.

He zeroed in on the perfect circle in front of her, and his angry expression softened. "You're making a pie?"

"Apple."

He froze. Stared. A vein below his ear jumped. Her heart picked up more speed. If this didn't work, she'd be out the door right along with the Lennon sisters. Then he stepped closer.

"What else you got?"

"Fried chicken. Mashed potatoes. Cream gravy. Green beans from the freezer."

Rance

"Dammit to hell." Rance turned on his heel, headed back outside, and wanted to kick himself. He kept letting this intruder get the best of him. But it'd been too long since he'd had Gran's fried chicken and apple pie, and if yesterday's meal indicated his grandmother's training, his expectations were high.

Almost every dream he'd had in prison was about this place. Helping in the garden. Picking blackberries off the fence-row. Swimming in the pond. Sleeping outside. As soon as the weather warmed, he'd do that again. Another thing he'd missed about freedom—a star-filled sky.

For now, he'd let the girl stay, but the mousers were going first thing Monday morning. She claimed to have no attachment, but he bet otherwise. Getting rid of them, combined with last night's activities, should convince her to move on. He didn't understand why he couldn't throw her stuff on the lawn and make her leave, but he couldn't. Something about the way she'd said she had nowhere to go stabbed his gut. He believed her. But she had all that money, so she could book a five-star hotel if she wanted. Wasn't like she'd have to camp in alleys and Dumpster-dive for food.

He'd been about her age when he'd started his time. Maybe that's why he related to her situation. There was so much that could hurt her. The threat of constant danger. He'd dealt with plenty of that. Prisoners who were bigger. Stronger. Older. No conscience. No regard for anything. That's what prison did. It took a person's humanity. It'd taken his for a while. His stomach clenched. If it hadn't been for Hector, Rance would be a lifer for a crime he *did* commit. A chill ran up his spine.

He couldn't bring himself to force her out. That's why it had to be her decision. And from her expression in the hallway last night, his lifestyle would make short work of her wanting to stay. He'd left the room to keep from cuddling with Kayla. Why women wanted to continue hugging and kissing once the action was over confused him.

He lit a cigarette, inhaled a deep drag, and glanced at the oak tree near the end of the porch. Once the lumber arrived, he'd construct a makeshift shower. All he had to do was build a frame, enclose it with tarps, and mount a water hose at the top. That would solve the problem of sharing a tub and bathing around her schedule. Probably wouldn't be for long. He had to be patient. The kid thought she could tolerate his bad habits. He knew better.

The pie was in the oven, but the kitchen was empty. As he rounded the corner to his bedroom, Blaze came out, and he gasped. She looked like a hazmat investigator gone crazy. She was covered from top to bottom in one of his grandmother's old housecoats, the pink gingham with bright blue flowers, along with yellow rubber gloves, a dust mask, protective goggles, orange-and-green striped knee-high socks pulled over her shoes, and a Christmas scarf printed with reindeer tied around her head. Extended away from her body like a bomb was a clothes basket holding his crumpled bedsheets.

"What the hell?"

Her voice muffled through the germ barrier and fogged her eyewear. "I've got to wash these. You need to empty your trash can."

He whipped out his cell and snapped a photo. He'd never seen such a sight and couldn't help but laugh, and once he got started, he couldn't stop.

She pushed past him. "I should burn these."

He wanted to say something, but lost his voice. Staggering back outside, he leaned against the railing, getting control. He hadn't laughed this hard in years.

"Trash. Emptied," Blaze said.

He turned to face her. The instructions weren't delivered as a demand. He'd noticed that about her. Everything she said was in the same calm monotone. Her expression was a different story. Last night, in the hallway, she'd looked like a kid who'd experienced her first roller coaster ride. Come to think of it, he'd had the same sensation inside the room. He chuckled. Full-figured girls like Kayla always tried harder.

He should come back with a smart-ass retort about not dumping the can until it was full of condoms, but thought better of it. No sarcastic remark could top her getup.

"Do you have any idea how ridiculous you look?"

"Yes," she said, then spun around and disappeared into the laundry room.

Damn. She was the strangest person he'd ever met. Later, when Rance went out to meet the plumber, he noticed the kid down the road cleaning bird houses. At least she was back in her regular clothes, something between Goth and punk. He couldn't tell the styles apart.

After the worker left, Rance went to the kitchen and helped himself to a slice of pie. He strolled back to the porch again, sat, and listened to the sounds of nature. As he closed his lips around the first bite, memories of summers, holidays, and playing dominoes with Gran swam in his brain.

The crust, as flaky as he remembered, and the fruit drenched in brown sugar and cinnamon melted on his tongue. When he finished it, he went back for another piece. He'd skipped breakfast, and it was still hours before supper so dessert would be lunch.

From the kitchen window, he saw the delivery he'd been expecting. The young car salesman, dangling keys from his finger, met Rance halfway.

"Not sure the wash job did much good after coming down the dirt road, but the interior is still clean," the guy said.

Rance took the keys. "That's okay. I appreciate you bringing it."

"All the paperwork and manuals are in the glove box. You have my number if you need anything."

The man got in the car with the coworker who'd followed, and drove away. Rance walked around the pickup truck and climbed inside. He loved the smell of a new vehicle. He fired it up and tore out for The Roost. It was the middle of the day, but chicks waited. As he passed the kid, she didn't even glance up.

Tom Fraser

Tom Fraser finished reading over the papers concerning the teenager's disappearance and shoved them into his briefcase. He'd hit a stroke of luck with the original officer handling the investigation. He and Benny Hudson had known each other for years.

Fighting Houston traffic, it was almost two when Tom arrived at the police department. He'd called ahead to make sure Benny was still working. Although his friend was old enough to retire, he hadn't opted out yet.

The elevator doors opened, and Tom got on and rode up to the third floor. He should use the stairs. God knew he needed the exercise, but his knees had given out years ago. And the extra fifteen pounds he'd gained didn't help.

The place hadn't changed much. Same standard-issue metal desks and cubicles, and it reeked of stale coffee and day-old donuts. He stopped for a moment and considered the last time he'd been here. Right after he'd left the FBI and started his PI firm. He'd made sure local guys understood he wouldn't step on any toes when he got an open case. Law enforcement was a country club of sorts. You didn't get to play on their turf without a membership.

Benny glanced up from his desk, unfolded his massive frame from the chair, and embraced Tom. "Damn, Tommy Fraser, how you been?"

"Okay. You?"

"Counting the days."

"When?" Tom asked.

"January first, I'm out of here. Heading to Florida. Deb's mom and dad left her a condo there. We're gonna move in, prop our feet up, and grow old."

Tom laughed. "Don't you mean *older?* We're already old."

Benny gestured toward a chair. "You got that right, and I'm feeling it."

Tom plopped into the seat, the leather squeaking with his weight. "Me, too."

Benny sat again. "So, after you called, I pulled up the file. Put it on a flash drive for you." He slid the small black stick across the desk. "The girl is twenty now. I'm surprised the stepmother is still pursuing this."

"Says she needs closure. Most people do."

"I guess. So, what do you want to know?" Benny asked.

"You didn't keep the case open long. I'm wondering why. No judgment. Just curious."

The cop shouldered back in his chair. "The stepmom insisted it was kidnapping, but there was no proof. I thought she'd left of her own accord, but because she was seventeen, I still worked the case hard with no luck. The courts are so overrun with cases like this, even if I'd found her, she would have been almost eighteen. No longer a juvenile. So the case moved to the back burner." Benny picked up his glasses and chewed on the ear-piece. "You know how it is. We have a stack of missing kids a lot younger."

He shifted in his seat again, opened a file folder, and put his glasses on. "I based my decision on conversations I had with former household employees." He scanned the page. "The nanny they'd had for fifteen years, one Helga Scudder, and the homeschool teacher, Jeanette Lester."

Tom made notes, then looked at his friend. "What'd they have to say?"

Benny removed his specs and pitched them down on the desktop. "The stepmom made this kid out to be disturbed, but that's not the same description I got from others. Odd. Strange. Obsessive. Lacking social skills, yeah, but not crazy. Tutor claimed she had an IQ of 125. When I arrived at the house, I photographed every inch of the girl's room. By that time, the nanny had been fired, so when I showed her the photos, she noticed the girl's cherished concert T-shirts were missing. Now, what kidnapper allows his prey to pack their favorite things?"

"I see your point. The girl ever labeled with a disorder?" Tom asked.

"Dad never allowed her to be tested. That's not all. Her computer and cell phone—gone. Debit and credit cards— never got a hit. She had a college fund she'd cleaned out weeks before she disappeared, and here's the kicker. Daddy Dear had to sign for the withdrawal. Now, you tell me what conclusion you'd get from that."

Tom rubbed his hand over his jaw. "Sounds like the father helped the kid leave."

Benny flicked his finger. "Bingo."

Chapter 7

Blaze

Blaze stood in the middle of the kitchen and took it all in. The simplicity of it. Vinyl flooring. Well-worn Formica countertops. White bead-board cabinets. A drastic contrast to the marble and granite custom work she'd grown up with. She'd been happy here—with Dessie, and then alone. But now *he'd* shown up and spoiled everything.

The men she'd seen and construction plans on Rance's bedside table told her there was about to be more activity than she wanted. But complaining would be another reason in his arsenal to get rid of her. Dealing with the mess and strangers would be a challenge, but she had no choice.

Earlier, when he'd driven away in the new truck, she didn't know if he'd return for supper or not. But to be safe, she'd cooked. After years of prison food, her meals had to make an impression. But more cooking meant more groceries.

After locking her bedroom door and retrieving the paint can from behind the chair, she removed the lid, peered inside, and found the contents out of order. Her family photo should be on top, then Dad's. Had Rance been in her room? Found her hiding place? Gone through her things? He had no right. This was *her* stuff. She counted the bundles. All there. She was being paranoid.

To be cautious, she should find a new location. Under the mattress? No. He'd look there for sure. She stepped into the bathroom. In episode 26 of *Perfect Crime,* drug dealers hid their goods in a plastic bag immersed in the toilet tank. The thought made her queasy. She opened the cabinet below the sink and spied the sanitary napkins. He'd never check there. She transferred the loot, placed the remaining pads on top, and slid the box back in its spot.

If he had snooped, why hadn't he said something? What if he thought the money was stolen, and he'd gone to the police? No. If so, they would have already been here. Maybe he was waiting. But for what?

The sound of a car got her attention. She peeked out the window. He was back earlier than expected. She returned to the kitchen and slid the pan from the oven as he came inside. "Supper will be done in about an hour," she said, picking up a list and shoving it toward him. "Here are the meals I have planned. If there's anything special you want, tell me so I can get the ingredients."

Rance barely looked at the sheet. "I need a drink."

He took whiskey from the cabinet and poured it into a glass already sitting on the counter. Drink in one hand and bottle in the other, he strolled to the back porch. He stayed there until she announced the food was ready.

Rance wandered in, his expression sober. Probably the only thing about him that was, considering the half-empty bottle he held. She joined him at the table and passed the roast his way. He speared a piece, then helped himself to the mashed potatoes. She wanted to tell him she knew he'd been poking around in her room, but his surly mood warned against it. Sitting in silence with someone who clearly hated her made her nervous.

Following the meal, to Blaze's relief, he left again. With her working days, if he stayed gone at night, their cohabitation should work perfectly.

She cleaned the kitchen, secured the cats, then hiked through the woods to Hanna's house. Twilight winked through the trees, and as she drew closer to the workshop, a pleasant aroma grew stronger.

Hanna and Tiffany were busy removing and stacking bars. When the door opened, Hanna glanced up.

"How do you like this scent?"

Blaze inhaled and smiled. "I like it. It's new, isn't it?"

"Yeah. I'm adding a men's line. Sandalwood and vanilla. Cedar and honey. And here's the biggie—cinnamon.

Turns out, it's said to have been used by the Queen of Sheba in her seduction of King Solomon. I'm calling the selection, Stud Suds."

"Holy crapoly! I love it." Tiffany said. "The name conjures all sorts of results without any advertising. I mean, if a guy's already a stud, will it make him more of one? If he's a nerd, will the soap turn him into a stud hammer?" She waved her hands in the air, directing the scent to her nose. "Even if it doesn't, he'll smell good enough to eat, or at least lick."

She stopped the motion with a jerk and widened her eyes. "Oh, which reminds me. My date with Jacob Mason—total disaster. Worst kisser in the universe. *Ack.*" She gagged and shivered. "I love a good French kiss as much as the next girl, but he did this jerking, flicking thing, and I almost puked. Chasing tamales with tongue—not a good combination."

Blaze wondered how it felt to have a man's tongue in your mouth.

Hanna picked up a sheet of paper. "I plan to categorize the soaps. I'll have Baby Bubbles, with light airy fragrances and Sensual Scents for females."

Tiffany stacked the last of the molds and carried them to a nearby shelf. "If you come up with a bar that mimics the aroma of cash and a Corvette, you'll have women going wild!"

"Rance got a new truck," Blaze said.

[79]

Tiffany blinked. "Maybe I should change that suggestion to cash and a pickup truck. And don't leave the older kids out. You can do a line called Teenage Temptations. I bet that'd be a big seller."

"That or Raging Cravings," Blaze said.

Hanna and Tiffany stared at her, then laughed.

"Holy crapoly! Did you make a joke?"

Blaze shrugged. "I don't know. Did I?"

Hanna grinned. "You did, and it was a good one. Speaking of Rance, how's it going with him?"

"He brought a woman home."

"Really? I didn't think he'd been in town long enough to meet anybody, but after what you told me, I guess he found one," Hanna said.

Tiffany cocked her head. "Told you what?"

"Rance tried to scare Blaze into leaving by telling her he was horny," Hanna explained, giggling. "I told her to bake him a pie."

"And I did," Blaze said. "He ate all of it. He's been snooping in my room. Should I say something?"

"Is anything missing?" Hanna asked.

"No."

"Then you shouldn't bring it up. You're hanging by a thread getting to stay there. He may have done it to start an argument hoping you'd leave." Hanna wiped the countertop, raking soap shavings into the trashcan. "Remember, after being in prison, he probably doesn't trust anyone, and since you were a big surprise, you're at the top of that list."

"I saw construction plans in his room. He's planning to build onto the house. Yesterday, a plumber and an electrician came. I don't want all those strange people coming and going, and I hope he doesn't keep finding women."

Tiffany laughed. "You make it sound like he's hunting Easter eggs."

"Like I said, he may be doing this to make you want to leave," Hanna said as she removed her apron, folded it, and put it away. "Y'all stay as long as you like, but Dylan is picking me up in an hour, so I need to get ready."

"I've got to scoot, too." Tiffany pulled photos from her purse and handed them to Blaze. "I took some shots of my latest creations to help you get an idea of the products I have planned. No hurry. I'm in the beginning stages. See you later."

After Tiffany left, Blaze gave Hanna the grocery list and money. "I hate to ask you to shop again this soon, but if I cook every day, I need more things."

"I don't mind a bit. I'll get them for you tomorrow."

[81]

"Thank you."

"You're more than welcome."

Once Blaze was alone, she worked on new drawings for her friend's latest brainstorm. Hanna wanted to play up the bluebird aspect of the business, so she decided it would be the logo shown on the back of each wrapper.

For Stud Suds, Blaze came up empty. No clue how to make a goat studly, so she moved on to Sensual Scents, designing an alluring female with long lashes and pink lips.

She spread Tiffany's pictures on the table. Besides the beer cap jewelry, she'd added shell casings, with colored crystals in the center of each one. Bracelets, necklaces, rings made from different calibers. Blaze couldn't believe it. They were pretty.

It was ten o'clock by the time she got home. Rance's truck sat in the drive with the same car from the night before parked behind it. Blaze's stomach somersaulted. Why didn't that *egg* take him to her roost instead of coming here?

Blaze spun around and went back to Hanna's barn. She raked fresh hay into a pile then curled into it. Good thing she wasn't allergic. As she got settled, she thought about Rance and what she should do. As much as she hated her situation, there wasn't an alternative—unless they traded bedrooms. That way he and his chicks would have access to the bathroom. With that final thought, she drifted to sleep.

She woke early the next morning and hoped the visitor had left. If not, Blaze would come back here, shower, and borrow something to wear.

Strolling through the woods, she found herself wishing the treehouse had a view of Dessie's. That way she wouldn't have to go all the way home to find out if the coast was clear. Just as she feared, the woman's car was still in the drive. As Blaze turned to leave, the stranger came out. The overnight guest was nothing like Blaze had thought she'd be. Short. Not fat, but plump. Dark hair. Big boobs. Rance must like her because this was two nights in a row.

The Booby Babe drove away, and Blaze thanked her stars she hadn't had to listen to the wails and moans of the couple. She eased the door open and tiptoed inside. No need to wake the sleeping giant.

After a quick bath, she dressed for the day, took care of the pets, and wrote a note. She got the peanut butter from the pantry and jelly from the fridge. Lost in thought, she didn't hear her roommate until he spoke.

"What the hell are you doing?"

She jerked upright. "Making a sandwich."

"Are you sure? Because you're bobbing like a pigeon."

"I'm checking to make sure the layers are even and all the way to the crust." This was her opportunity to use her word of the day. "Peanut butter is so *unctuous*. That means oily."

He walked to stand next to her. "No shit. Well, it looks okay to me."

She slid the knife over the bread. "No. See this white strip?" She glided the blade across the filling and pushed it to the outer border. "Now I'm ready for the jelly." She spooned out a glob and swirled it. After a full minute of smearing grape from one side to the other, she backed away, leaned forward until she had it at eye level, and focused like surveying a piece of land. Satisfied with the results, she pressed the pieces together, cut them in half, and put them in a sandwich bag.

He stepped away. "Where were you last night?"

"Hanna's. Is that woman your girlfriend?"

He chuckled. "Not hardly."

"Well, if you keep bringing women here, we should trade rooms."

"An even better idea is you getting your own place."

She ignored his remark. "Furniture, too. Maybe some of the construction workers will help with the switch."

"I bet they'd be happy to pack your stuff."

"Why would they do that? I'm not going anywhere."

"Yeah, about that," he said. "I was at the bank yesterday and see you've continued to pay rent each month, but you know what happens when you get a new landlord."

Blaze turned to face him. "What?"

"Rent goes up. Starting next month. It doubles."

She swallowed hard. He knew about the money.

Chapter 8

Blaze

After work on Sunday, Blaze parked but didn't go inside. Rance's truck wasn't there, so he'd probably gone into town to hunt another *Easter egg*. Instead, she gathered her drawing supplies and hurried to the treehouse.

Doubling her rent was his way of telling her he'd found the cash. Or it might be the other way. He didn't know about the stash and by increasing her expense, hoped she'd look for something cheaper. If Dad were here, he'd say not to read so much into things. He'd flash the smile he reserved just for her and use all those clichés he loved to spout. *It is what it is. Don't make a mountain out of a molehill.* She'd always hated when he did that but now longed to hear the comfort of those corny platitudes. A tear trickled down her cheek. She wiped at it, inhaled deeply, then released a slow, steady breath. *Crying won't change anything.*

Shades of blue and purple draped the forest like a veil. Blaze loved this time of day, when everything hushed and settled. Trees whispered their secrets, and the wind gathered the world's wishes and carried them to heaven.

She'd stalled long enough. She closed her sketch pad, stuck the pencil behind her ear and climbed down the ladder. Even from this distance the fragrant aroma of essential oils permeated the air. The same as every night, Hanna was making soap. Blaze wished there was something she could do to help her friend get her products into the right market. She'd convinced her to get a website, and that was a start. Once she got the packaging designs finished and Hanna got them photographed, she'd establish an online presence.

Sunday nights must not be prime time for picking up women because when Blaze got back home, Rance's truck and Harley were parked in the drive.

The place was quiet, so she eased open the door and crept inside. It was only eight o'clock, but perhaps the previous nights of wild sex had caught up with Rance and he'd turned in early. She tended the Lennon sisters and went to the kitchen. A box of crackers sat on the counter and a dirty bowl and spoon cluttered the sink. On the stove were a pan and empty can. He'd made his own meal but left the cleanup for her.

A shadow on the back porch drew her attention. *Rance.* Even with his back to her, his action was clear. Peeing. She should turn away but didn't. She'd never seen a man pee outside. To see him do that without restraint fascinated her.

[87]

He finished, zipped, and started toward his chair, but caught her staring. Her face burned. She twirled, grabbed the cracker box, and rushed to the pantry as he came inside. Cheeks flaming hotter, she grasped a can in each hand and spun to face him. "This is not right! This is not right!" She moved things around, clanking containers as she rearranged them.

He came closer. "What the hell?"

"Chili goes after chicken noodle!" she said, gritting her teeth and shoving her shoulder into his chest as she put the can in place. Any idiot could see the order. Fruit. Soup. Vegetable. "You're messing up everything!"

"Well, fuck me. Didn't know I had to *alphabetize*. You've got too many goddamn rules. Don't feed the cats. Don't get fucking crumbs on the floor. Dry the dishrag." He set the whiskey bottle down with a thud. "I'm done following instructions. Live with it or leave."

She wanted to say more, but he'd been drinking. Not a good time to argue. He could be a *mean drunk*. She'd seen one on *Perfect Crime*, episode 34. Alcohol sometimes brought out the worst in a person, and she didn't want to risk it. She stormed past him to her room.

For the next two hours, Blaze put the final touches on the mural, then stepped back and admired the results. Clouds as fluffy as cotton candy floated across an aqua sky while a pair of bluebirds circled overhead. Twisting vines climbed the

[88]

wall of the weathered shed, where stalks of pink hollyhocks rose above a mass of zinnias. Miss Dessie stood in the garden, hands on hips, cats at her feet. Everything the old lady loved. Blaze suspected that was the reason she and Dessie got along so well. Simple things made her happy.

By the time she'd cleaned her brushes and gotten ready for bed, it was almost midnight. Rance had gone into his room an hour ago. She slid the laptop onto her thighs, brought up the *Danvers Daily* classifieds, and scrolled to rental properties. Only seven houses listed. One by one she ruled them out. Too big. Bad location. Too expensive.

She snapped the lid closed and flopped back onto the bed. No. She had to stay here. This was where Dad wanted her to live. He and Dessie had an agreement. No matter what, Blaze wasn't leaving.

The next morning Rance waited until he heard his unwelcome houseguest drive away before coming from his bedroom. She was nuts. He'd never seen anyone get so bent out of shape about chili in the wrong place. The fact she had the damn pantry alphabetized was crazy enough, but to go ballistic was another matter.

Later today the construction men would arrive, and if a can being out of order drove her into a fit, having strangers around should make her run away screaming. He turned on the coffeemaker. Next to it sat a saucer with two biscuits covered with plastic wrap, and a note.

Microwave 15 seconds.

Sorry I yelled at you.

Damn kid. If the pantry incident riled her, his next action was liable to give her a stroke. After breakfast, he retrieved the animal carriers he'd bought in Danvers. Once he had the felines in the boxes, he loaded them along with the remaining food and litter, then drove to the shelter.

He'd only been back home a few minutes when the first delivery arrived, followed by workers. As soon as Rance alerted the concrete company the forms were ready, they'd come.

By noon evidence of the renovation was everywhere. Pipes protruded from the framework. While Rance waited for Triple C Concrete, he constructed the outdoor shower he'd planned. Early morning and evening temperatures in March were still chilly but not unbearable. This way he wouldn't have to swap rooms with the girl. One worker commented about the mural and how real it looked. A little too real for Rance. No way would he screw random women in a room with Gran staring at him all night.

At five o'clock the crew called it a day, and so did Rance. His back ached like a son of a bitch, but he didn't care. It felt good to have his mind focused on the future instead of the past. He pulled out the Jack Daniel's along with a glass from the cupboard and headed outside. He held the whiskey up to the light, then filled the tumbler. The bottle was almost empty, so he'd need to make another trip to town. Dealing with the kid meant he couldn't afford to run out.

Blaze

Blaze sighed relief. Lumber sat stacked in piles, but no men were in sight. She surveyed the changes. According to the new foundation, square footage would double in size. Protruding pipes located the bathroom, and it was a big one. Surely they'd finish the project in a month. After that Rance would have his space and she'd have hers, so maybe he wouldn't be so adamant about her leaving.

She went to release the Lennon sisters, but when she opened the door, the room was empty. Had he already let them out? She searched under her bed. With the construction ruckus, the pets would have hidden or run away. Then she remembered what Rance had said about getting rid of them.

She flew to the back porch. "Where are the cats?"

He didn't look at her, just spoke over his shoulder. "Gone."

"What do you mean—gone?"

"They're not coming back."

"Did you kill them?"

That got his attention. He turned to face her. "Hell no! I took them to the Danvers Shelter. They'll go to good homes."

"Okay. Supper will be ready in an hour."

Rance

Okay? That was it? She had nothing more to say? Damn girl went crazy over a can out of place, but no emotion about the cats? Weird.

He turned his chair to watch her as she moved around the kitchen. She didn't look out of place like he'd thought before. She knew where to find everything. Frying pan from the oven drawer. Dishes from the right-hand cupboard. Glasses on the second shelf.

A knot formed in his throat. *Did you kill them?* What kind of monster did she think he was? Well, he was a monster. At least he had been. Still the words cut deep like a metal trap. He shook the notion away and drained his glass, then the bottle. Not near enough to numb him, but it would have to do.

After supper he gave the new shower a try. Not bad. The water was like ice, but the pressure was strong, and a few cold showers would help keep his libido in check. He could always call Kayla again, but he'd already tired of her. Plus, sleeping with the same chick too long gave them the wrong impression. And with his aching back, better to have the whole bed to himself tonight.

He tossed the covers, fluffed his pillow, then sank into the down mattress. Within a few minutes, he was asleep.

Blaze

An odd sound echoed down the hallway. Blaze straightened. Rance didn't have a woman with him, so the noise had to have come from him. She listened and laid the laptop aside. Then another screech. Louder.

She sprang and rushed into the hall. Hearing nothing, she tiptoed farther down, and pressed her ear to his door. Muffled sounds came from inside, then three snorts, as if he was fighting with someone.

"Hector! Hector!"

Was he saying, "Help me"? She burst into the room as Rance sat up, covered his face with his hands, and sobbed. She froze. She should back away, he hadn't seen her, but he was crying so hard. The only man she'd seen weep like this was her dad at Mom's funeral.

Maybe Rance was grieving over his grandmother. Sometimes people didn't mourn until much later. Dad died years ago, and Blaze still experienced sorrow every time she thought of him. She wondered if that sadness would ever go away.

She moved closer and knelt in front of him. "Rance? Are you okay?"

He jerked his hands away and glared at her. Even in the dim light, she saw fire in his eyes. She fell sideways and caught herself on one arm, then kicked her legs out straight.

"Get out! Get the fuck out!"

She pushed with her heels, propelled with her elbows, and scooted on her rear. Once in the hall, she rolled to all fours, scuttled to her bedroom, slammed the door, and locked it. Hugging her knees to her chest, she struggled to breathe. She couldn't stay here. Not with him like this. Legs like rubber, somehow she came to her feet. She grabbed her flashlight, crawled out the window, then ran down the path that led to the treehouse.

Chapter 9

Rance

It took Rance a few minutes to clear his head. Had he struck the girl? She'd fallen backward but he didn't think he'd caused it. At least not by touching her. But what if he had? She'd never believe it was an accident.

He'd come to Bluebird for solitude. Was that too much to ask? That way, when the dreams came, there'd be no one to witness the tough ex-con scream like a frightened child and cry like a baby. He could avoid the nightmares with plenty of whiskey or sex, and sometimes he got by without either. But not tonight.

Rubbing his fingers across the scar on his belly, he sat, shoulders hunched, and tried to erase the memory of blood swirling down the shower drain. Unable to ignore what had happened, he gathered his wits and marched down the hall to Blaze's door.

"Listen, kid. I'm sorry if I scared you. I'd never hurt you—intentionally."

He waited. No response. Okay, she was angry. He got that. "Let's talk about it. I promise to make it up to you. I'll even quit harping about you leaving. Whattaya say?"

Still no answer. He turned the knob—locked. She probably needed time to get over the shock, and he needed a drink.

Blaze

Keeping the beam of light aimed at the ground, Blaze followed the worn trail that curled into the woods. An owl hooted from a nearby tree. Frogs croaked in rhythm. Crickets chirped. She loved the sounds of the night. She'd never known how alive the forest was until she came to live in Bluebird. Even as the world slumbered, Mother Nature worked.

When she reached her destination, she collapsed onto a rock and rubbed her arms before she attempted her climb. Her elbows stung from carpet burn, and the first signs of a headache throbbed in her temples. Closing her eyes, she filled her lungs with fresh air. Strange how a house in a tree with no doors or locks felt safer than the farm.

It took longer than usual to scale the ladder because Blaze's legs were still like noodles. Once she reached the floor, she wrapped herself in the blanket and sat cross-legged. Clutching her stomach, she rocked back and forth. She'd never had a man scream or glare at her that way. She wasn't sure he had seen *her*, but rather some demon from his nightmare. The pain in his eyes made her think of *Perfect Crime*, episode 51, the most heartbreaking of the series, where after years of suffering, parents found out their missing child was dead.

She didn't know how long she sat there with one thought after another swirling in her head. She'd lost track of time. Rance hated her for no reason other than she existed. That wasn't anything new. Sometimes Blaze wondered if God hated her too. He must, since He'd taken away everyone who'd loved her. Mom, Dad, Dessie.

Despite her father's wishes, Blaze didn't belong here anymore. She dreaded having to face Rance again, but she had no choice. No need to wait. She'd return for the things she needed while he slept. It wouldn't take long to pack. Crawl in the window grab her clothes, money, computer, and phone, and leave within the hour. Even if she was contract labor, it would be irresponsible not to give the funeral home notice, but she couldn't help that, unless she stayed at the local motel or Hanna's.

She'd decide that tomorrow. Right now she'd get her things, and in the morning, with a clear head, consider her job situation. Decision made, she climbed down and headed back to Dessie's.

Blaze released a long steady breath. Rance's truck was gone. As she hoisted up a leg and straddled the windowsill, headlights swept over her. She scurried to get inside, but her pajama pants caught on a loose nail. As she struggled to free herself, the fabric ripped right along with the skin below it.

The truck came to a halt, and Rance jumped out.

"What are you doing?"

He didn't sound angry, but she'd seen how quickly his mood could change.

He closed the distance between them, and she froze, expecting him to jerk her back onto the porch.

"Let me help you," he said, offering his hand.

"I can manage."

"Are you going or coming?"

"Both," Blaze answered.

"What do you mean?"

She slid into the room and wiped at her leg. The scratch wasn't deep. A Band-Aid would suffice. She came to her feet and dragged her duffel from the closet.

He leaned inside the window. "About before. I didn't mean to scare you. Had a bad dream. I do that sometimes. Prison stuff."

She turned to face him. "Dessie said you were a good boy."

Rance ran his palm over his weary face, and she saw regret in his eyes.

"I'd never harm you, Blaze. I swear it. No matter what you think of me, you have to believe that."

She considered it. He'd used her name and there was a sadness in his voice she'd never heard before. "I thought you were saying, 'Help me.'"

"In a way—I was. Can I come in?"

He didn't sound dangerous. He sounded—wounded. "I guess."

Within a few seconds, his massive frame filled the doorway. He shoved his hands into his pockets. "I don't remember if I knocked you over or not, but if I did, I'm sorry. I didn't mean to."

Blaze believed him, but it didn't change the fact he wanted her to leave. And she should, because no matter how hard she tried, she wasn't welcome here.

He sighed and rocked back on his heels as if to get his balance. "Where are you going?"

She moved to the bathroom to gather her toiletries, then came back to the duffel. She didn't answer, just shrugged.

He pulled his hands from his pockets and dropped them to his sides. "Stay. I won't badger you anymore about leaving. And the nightmare thing—well, now you know to stay clear when it happens."

He sounded sincere, and she wanted to stay. *Needed* to stay. He zeroed in on her leg and took a step toward her.

"You're hurt. Let me see."

She backed away and looked down at the stream of blood making its way to her ankle. "No. It's just a scratch."

"All right. So, about you staying . . ."

Her elbows burned, her leg hurt, and her heart pounded in her ears. But even with all the tension in her chest, the thought of striking out on her own scared her more than giving him a second chance. "Okay."

"Okay." He turned and walked away.

She wasn't sure why he'd changed his mind, but whatever the reason, she wouldn't question it.

Rance

Rance didn't know why he'd asked her to stay. Perhaps it was because she'd witnessed the dark side of his soul and offered no judgment. The fear he'd seen in her eyes affected him in a way he couldn't explain. He'd terrified an innocent girl, and that scared the shit out of him. And according to Hanna, his grandmother had not only accepted the kid, she'd loved her. Couldn't dispute that recommendation because Gran read people better than anyone he'd ever known. However, the money he'd found made him nervous. But if she was willing to stay after the monster she'd seen in him that led him to think she wasn't hiding from trouble, but from danger.

He could help with that kind of problem, and maybe she could help him find the man he used to be, before his world had fallen apart.

Chapter 10

Blaze

Blaze arranged soap bars into stacks while Hanna admired the final artwork for the wrappers.

"These are so perfect, Blaze. I hate that I can't pay you for them. But if my business catches on, I promise I will."

Blaze considered drawing and painting a hobby and never expected to make money from it even though Dad had claimed she could. When she was twelve, he'd entered some of her paintings in Houston's art competition, and the ribbons she'd won got her a showing in Zimmer Gallery. Having people like her work, thrilled her, but she hated the promotion. Interviews with TV and radio stations made her uncomfortable.

"I don't want you to pay."

"Are you kidding? Do you know how much package design costs? A fortune." She giggled. "But I can barter with a lifetime of free soap."

"I need a favor," Blaze said.

"Now we're talking. What?"

"Over the Rainbow is having a banquet to celebrate its golden anniversary. I need a dress."

"Formal or church fancy?"

"Church."

"I have just the thing. Still has the tag on it. Bought it right before I got pregnant and never wore it. After Noah was born, I increased a dress size. Anyway, I've kept it all these years thinking I'd get back into it, but that's not going to happen." Hanna put the stacks into baskets and carried them to a nearby shelf. "It's pale blue. It'll look beautiful with your skin tone. When we're done you can try it on."

"Okay. Is Rance Noah's dad?"

Hanna gasped. "Why do you think that?"

"You didn't want me to mention him, so I thought— Never mind. I shouldn't have asked."

Hanna sat again. "It was a stupid request. I mean, if Rance plans to make Bluebird his home, sooner or later he'll meet Noah. I just wanted to put it off as long as possible. But, no, he isn't Noah's dad. How are things going with him? It's been, what? Three weeks since the truce?"

"Yeah. He doesn't talk about me leaving anymore, but he doesn't say much of anything."

"Well, that house must be like a tomb."

"What does that mean?"

"You don't converse much either."

"I don't know how to talk to him."

"Ask about his day. The construction. If he needs help with painting. Tell him about your day. Maybe something that happened at work. Oh, here's an idea. If you can invite someone to the banquet, ask him."

"Why?" Blaze asked.

"You mentioned Cameron keeps asking you out, so if you go alone, he'll probably arrange for you to sit together. Plus, doing something social with Rance will help you feel more comfortable."

Blaze frowned. Even though they didn't talk much, things were better, and she didn't want to do anything to upset him. "He doesn't really like me. I mean, he doesn't fuss anymore or use that gruff tone like he did. Mostly ignores me," she said. "Besides, why would he go on a date with me? I'm not anything like the women he brings home."

"It won't be a date. It'll be a plus one. The two of you live together, so you should try to become friends. Tomorrow night at supper, promise you'll say at least one thing to start a conversation."

"If you say so."

"I do. Now let's go try on that dress."

The next day Blaze couldn't concentrate on work for thinking about the promise she'd made. Idle conversation had never come easy, and the idea of making small talk with Rance caused her stomach to cramp. She'd practiced talking to her clients, and it was a good thing they were deceased or all of them would have complained. She'd smeared Mrs. Elmore's nail polish, gotten Mrs. Crane's hair too puffy, and nicked Mr. Rockwell's chin.

The more she thought about it, asking Rance to the banquet was a bad idea. Why would he even consider it? But a promise was a promise. Dad always said if you couldn't keep your word, it wasn't worth anything. He was talking about business, but she got the message. Subtle parenting 101.

She checked the clock once more. Already three. Why was it when she looked forward to something, time crawled, but when she dreaded something, it sprouted wings?

Dusting the excess rouge from her brush, Blaze stroked it over Mr. Robertson's cheeks. What would the town do, now that their local Santa had passed? She'd made sure his cheeks were like roses, but couldn't pull off a cherry nose and droll mouth.

Blaze remembered a photo she'd seen of Rance sitting on old Saint Nick's lap. Couldn't have been more than eight.

After Dessie had gotten sick, she'd looked at that picture and all the others again and again.

A lump grew in Blaze's throat. Nervous or not, she'd invite Rance. All she had to do was picture him as the skinny, freckle faced kid from Christmas long ago. There was nothing scary about that boy.

When she got home, there were no workers in sight and the house was quiet. She didn't see Rance, but both his Harley and truck were parked outside. Since tonight's menu was spaghetti, salad, and garlic bread, it didn't take long to prepare. He came in as she finished setting the table, "Hey, smells good. I'll wash up and be right back."

Within a couple of minutes, he took a seat, and she joined him. The pasta dish was one of her favorites, and by the way Rance lit into it, one of his, too.

She pushed noodles around with her fork, and her chest tightened as her promise to Hanna pounded in her head. Blaze took a deep breath and swallowed hard. "I couldn't use my word today."

"What?"

"My word of the day. I didn't use it." Her heart sped up. "Never mind. How was your day? How is the building going? Can I help with anything? Are you interested in going to a banquet?" The last question squeaked out because her mouth had gone dry. She reached for her glass of water and gulped.

He laid down his fork and half-smiled. "What's the word?"

She looked away. "Uxorial."

"Hmm. What's it mean?"

"Befitting of a wife."

"Can't help you there, but even if I could, it wouldn't count, would it? I mean you have to come up with the sentence on your own, right?"

"Yeah."

"They got the john working in the new bathroom, so I won't have to use yours anymore. As for you helping, maybe when the rooms are ready to paint, I'll let you pitch in. And this spaghetti is delicious."

He took another bite, and she thought he was finished talking. Better he ignored the banquet question. She shouldn't have listened to Hanna.

He leaned back and rested his hands on the chair arms. "Hey, look at me."

She raised her eyes to his and braced.

"Is talking to me making you uncomfortable?" he asked.

She wanted to answer but couldn't get the words out, so she nodded.

"You're not afraid of me, are you?"

That was a good question. She had been when he had the nightmare. But not since then. She lowered her head. "No, but talking is hard."

He reached over and placed his finger under her chin and tilted it up. "I want to understand, so explain it."

His gentle touch and the tenderness in his tone surprised her. A little jolt of electricity caused her cheeks to warm. "I don't always say the right thing."

"Well, you can say anything around me. If I don't get it, I'll tell you. Okay?"

"Okay."

"Now, about this banquet."

"It's a work thing. Golden anniversary."

"And the dress code? Date? Time?"

"Oh, it's not a date. It's a plus one."

He laughed out loud. "I meant the date of the event."

Blaze's face flamed, and she turned away again. "See what I mean?"

"I wasn't laughing *at* you. Your answer was cute."

"Oh," she said. "Two weeks from Friday. Dressy casual. Seven in the evening."

"I'll have to check my social calendar."

"All right." She scooted her chair away, but before she stood, he caught her wrist.

"That was a joke. You know I don't have a social calendar."

She pulled her hand free. She appreciated his attempt to let her down easy, but she'd been right. This was a bad idea. "I know you don't like me, so you don't have to go."

"Whoa. I've never said that."

He frowned, and an odd sensation churned in her stomach. Longing. Desire for his approval. What was that about? She searched for something to say but came up short. An awkward silence hung between them until finally she found her voice. "I'm not dumb. I know I'm odd, and people don't like different."

"Look. When I got here, you were a surprise. I didn't handle it well. But I'm past that now," Rance said. "It isn't that I don't like you, it's I don't know you. We should fix that. I'll go first."

Panic rose in her chest. She didn't want to play this game because she wasn't sure what he'd ask.

"What's your connection to Dessie?"

After a few moments to consider her answer, she decided it safe enough. "My dad knew her."

"How?"

"He and your mom were friends in college."

"Interesting. Your turn to ask me something," he said.

"What are your nightmares about?"

In the blink of an eye, his expression turned grim. "That's the one thing I can't talk about."

"Why?"

"I just can't. Ask something else."

"Why do you call your grandmother Dessie?"

"Good question. When it was the two of us, I called her Gran. But Seth and Nick called her Dessie, and I thought it was easier to do the same. Back to my mom. Did she and your dad date?"

"No. Why do you have to bring women here? Why don't you go to their houses?"

"Here, I'm in control. Somewhere else, I don't know who has a key or who might show up unannounced, and sometimes the chick has kids. Besides, it's been at least two weeks since the last one."

"Nine days."

"What?"

"The last one was here nine days ago. Not two weeks."

He ran his hand over his jaw. "Damn. Sure seems longer."

[111]

She straightened in her chair. "Well, I don't like hearing the uxorial duties they exhibit."

Head cocked, his lips spread into the biggest smile she'd seen since he arrived. Until this moment, she hadn't thought he had that expression in his emotional bag.

"You're welcome," he said.

"What?"

"Because of my bad behavior, you used your word, so you're welcome."

"Is that another joke?"

"Yeah. A sarcastic one. You're on a roll so what else don't you like about me?" Rance asked.

"You smoke too much and drink too much."

"Noted. That's three negatives. Any positives?"

There were a lot of things Blaze liked about him. He was big like her dad, and now that the cats were gone, she liked having another person in the house. And the biggest surprise? She liked talking to him.

"I like that you started washing your own sheets."

He chuckled. "Yeah, well, I wasn't sure my heart could take many more times of seeing you in that crazy getup when you changed them."

"You say please and thank you."

"You go to a lot of trouble. The least I can do is be appreciative," he said.

"I like the way you look without your shirt."

Rance choked on his drink. "What?"

"I like the way you look. . . ."

He held up his hand. "I heard you. I'm just shocked."

"Why? Your chest is very muscular and defined."

"Uh—okay—thanks," he sputtered.

"You're welcome."

Tom Fraser

Tom Fraser parked on the street in front of Helga Scudder's house, a modest white frame with green shutters and a small front yard. Marigolds and pink flowers he didn't recognize filled beds on either side of the cracked sidewalk.

Even though he had all the notes from the previous investigators and the police report, he liked to treat each case as if starting from zero. Ask his own questions. Draw his own conclusions.

When she answered the door, Helga was nothing like he'd envisioned. She wore a bright green yoga outfit accenting her emerald eyes. A tangle of long auburn hair, secured in a ponytail on top of her head, made her look like a genie who'd escaped her bottle.

"Come in, Mr. Fraser."

She flashed him a warm smile and his heart kicked up a notch. "Mrs. Scudder?" he asked.

"Please, call me Helga. Can I get you something to drink? Coffee? Water? Tea?"

"A cup of coffee would be great."

"I just brewed a fresh pot. We can talk while I get it."

He followed her into the kitchen, pulled out a stool at the end of a small bar, and sat. Uncluttered countertops and gleaming white cabinets said a lot about the owner— particular and well organized.

She took cups from a shelf. "So, you're what? Detective number four?"

"Guilty as charged."

Helga laughed as she delivered the drinks and took the seat across from him. "That Marla. She just won't give up."

"You say that as if she should."

"Tom—may I call you Tom?"

The tone of her voice stirred something in him. It had been six years since Janet died. He'd been alone too long. He shook away the memory of his wife and refocused. "Please do."

Helga sipped, then set her cup on the saucer without a sound. "I suspect you'll be the last. Time's running out."

He removed a pen and small spiral from his pocket, then logged her name and the date. "What does that mean?"

"Mr. Montgomery made sure once control of the company passes to his daughter, there won't be much the gold digger can do. Marla will lose her place on the board and the salary that goes with it, so she's desperate."

Tom swirled cream into his cup. "Maybe you should start at the beginning."

"I suppose you know the basic background," she began. "Lark, Grant's first wife, died in a car accident when their little girl was five. Terrible thing. Happened during a strong storm. Poor child was with her dead mother for almost an hour before help came. Anyway, back to Marla. She came into the picture four years later. Mr. Montgomery was lonely, and she was beautiful—and young. No offense, but most men are idiots when a young woman gives them attention."

He grinned. Couldn't deny that. According to background information, Helga was only five years younger than him, and he was already enjoying her company. "None taken."

[115]

"You married, Tom?"

Damn, there was that gut feeling again. "Widowed. You?"

"Nope. Not since I caught him face deep in my next-door neighbor's crotch."

Tom couldn't help but snicker. This woman had spunk. "Sorry."

"Yeah, well, she was younger, too. Sorry, I keep getting sidetracked. At first, Marla was okay, as long as Mr. Montgomery kept pace with her. But then he got sick. The first round of chemo got him into remission, but eventually the cancer came back. The last eighteen months of his life were awful."

Tom propped an elbow on the counter. "Marla seems to think her stepdaughter had a mental break when her dad died."

Helga flapped her hand in the air. "She wishes. Let me clue you in on the widow. The day of the funeral, she fired every last one of us. Brought in her own people."

Tom jotted *Marla the bitch* in his spiral notebook and regarded his hostess. "I understand that's the day the girl went missing."

"It's the day she *left*. If you solve the case, Marla will have a doctor drug the child to get power of attorney. Once

[116]

she has that, she'll stick her in an institution, sell the company, and become a very rich woman."

"I thought she was already rich."

"If you or I had a few million dollars, we'd consider ourselves rich, but not her. The way she goes through cash, that won't last her long. Then all she'll have is a house and a company salary that's about to expire. Besides, greedy people never have enough."

"If the woman is as evil as you say, why hire me?" Tom asked. "Why not a hit man to off the kid?"

Helga laughed. "Mr. Montgomery left Marla the big bucks, hoping it would be enough until she found another husband. But he put things in place in case it wasn't. If anything happens to his daughter, the company will be sold and the proceeds divided between different charities. Marla's only hope is to have things go the way I mentioned."

Tom glanced at his watch, then scooted away from the counter. "Well, I appreciate the information and coffee. I know from our earlier phone conversation you have an appointment, so I'll get out of your hair."

Helga rose too, stepped closer, and laid her hand on his forearm. "I can tell you're a man with a big heart, so do the right thing and forget about finding her. Wherever she is, she's better off."

Chapter 11

Rance

Rance couldn't decide if it was the chick snoring next to him, the approaching storm, or Blaze's compliment that kept him awake. He chuckled. Wasn't sure she considered it flattery. She'd praised his physique with the same emotion as thanking him for doing laundry. If any other woman had mentioned his bare chest, he would have taken it as flirtation, but not with her.

For the first time since arriving in Bluebird, he'd learned something about her. His mom's old college yearbooks were bound to be packed away somewhere. If he found them, maybe he'd figure out Blaze's identity and the reason she'd come here.

Lightning ripped the sky, and an angry burst of thunder shook the house. The weather report claimed a chance of hail, so he'd taken time to move the kid's car into the shed with his Harley. It'd been a while since he'd weathered a violent storm, but he remembered it like it was yesterday. He, Seth, and Nick had spent the last month of summer with Dessie. The heavens had opened and dumped the largest hailstones he'd seen. Once the surge had ended, he'd run outside to gather specimens, and Gran had kept them in the freezer until Christmas.

Was his bed partner Melba, or Melanie? He couldn't be sure. The music had blasted so loudly in the bar he hadn't caught her name. Easy way around that. He'd called her lovey-dovey names. Baby. Honey. Sweetie. Chicks liked that shit. Whoever she was, she snored like a lumberjack. Probably farted like one too.

He wanted a smoke and a drink. The kid's voice rang in his ears. Smoke too much. Drink too much. Why do you bring women home? He'd pass on the whiskey and cigarettes. She was right. He should cut down on his bad habits.

He shifted in bed as the first stone clobbered the tin roof, then another, and another, until the place sounded like it was being pelted by gunfire. All the while, *baby-honey-sweetie* kept right on sawing logs. Just as he turned to look outside, a shadow blocked the light show coming through the window.

He blinked, then blinked again, unsure of what he saw. Wrapped in a blanket, Blaze lay down on top of the cover next to him. He scooted over to make room, then propped his head in his hand and tried to keep his voice down, not that it'd wake the sleeping logger. "What the hell are you doing?"

[119]

She snuggled into him. "I don't want to be in there by myself."

A whispered yell proved to be a challenge. "Well, you can't sleep with me. I have a woman in here."

"You're finished with her."

"How do you know?"

Blaze turned to face him, and her breath floated over his neck. "Weeknights, you do it once. Weekends, multiple times. It's Thursday."

A shiver ran up his spine. "Get out of this bed right now before you wake her up."

Blaze rolled off and settled on the floor. "I'll sleep down here."

He hung his head off the side. "No. You will not. Leave before I carry you out. And if I have to do that, you'll see a lot more than my bare chest. Understand?"

Even in the dark, he saw her eyes widen. "Oh. You mean, you don't have on any clothes?"

"That's exactly what I mean. Now scram. Go to the living room. I'll be there in a minute."

"Okay."

Rance eased off the mattress and pulled on his jeans and T-shirt. What the hell was she thinking? All he needed was for his guest to wake and find another female in his bed.

Especially one who looked as young as Blaze. The bar-babe would label him a pervert and spread the word. He couldn't let that happen. He'd never get laid again.

In the living room, he found the kid huddled on the sofa, chin resting on her knees, arms wrapped tight around her legs. Another crack of thunder caused her to flinch. He sat next to her. "Before I showed up, and it stormed, what did you do?"

"I had the cats," she said.

"Well, you can't come into my room when I have a guest. That's not appropriate."

"Okay."

She shivered, then rose and yanked the blanket tighter. Her chin quivered, and his throat thickened with guilt. She wasn't pretending. The fear in her eyes was as real as what he'd seen in inmates, their first day in the joint. He came to his feet. "Come on, let's get you back to your room."

She followed him down the hallway, slipped into bed, and he slid the corner chair closer. "I'll sit with you until you fall asleep. How will that be?"

"Good."

"Why do storms frighten you so much?"

She wiped at her cheeks and faced him. "Bad things happen then."

He'd begun to develop a soft spot for her and wasn't sure it was a good idea. "What kind of things?"

Another loud clap of thunder exploded, and she grabbed his hand and squeezed it. "My mom died in a car crash on a night like this."

"I'm sorry. How old were you?"

"Five."

Dang. At that age, no way she'd have a lot of memories of her mother. That had to be rough. "How about I hold your hand until you go to sleep?"

"My dad used to do that."

God, he wanted to crawl in next to her. Wrap her in his arms and say it'd get better, but it didn't. He'd suffered the loss of his mother, and even now when he thought of her, he went right back to being that devastated twelve-year-old kid.

Little by little she'd wasted away before his eyes, and he hadn't noticed until it was too late. Barely able to get out of bed, she'd forced herself to go to his football games. She'd stopped jumping up and down though. Just sat quietly, and when he found her in the stands, she always waved and gave a thumbs-up.

Rance's lungs burned, and the pain of losing her lodged in his chest liked it had happened yesterday. If there was any consolation, it was she hadn't seen him go to prison. Blaze's voice shook him from his thoughts.

"I'll try to be quick so you can get back to your lady friend."

He stroked the top of her hand with his thumb. "No hurry. Turns out it's Thursday, and I'm done with her."

"Is that a joke?"

"Yeah."

She yawned and drifted to sleep.

Rance dozed sporadically and didn't know how long he sat there. With all the memories running through his mind, he lost track of time. After Mom's death, he'd gone to live with his dad but never bonded with him or his stepmother. At least Seth and Nick had welcomed him. Even looked up to him, which made things worse once Rance got arrested. Then he became the example of evil. Yeah, he was the bad seed. The terrible influence. The biggest mistake.

Mom was gone. Gran was gone. Dad didn't give a shit. Rance stared at Blaze sleeping peacefully. She depended on him. And it'd been a long time since anyone had. The remark about liking him without his shirt was the last thing he'd expected her to say. He'd never met anybody like her, and she was beginning to trust him. Eventually, she'd tell him what or who she was hiding from.

He picked up her phone and checked the time. In two more hours, it'd be dawn. The storm had passed. Time to return to bed, but getting back to the snoring barfly didn't interest him.

He glanced at the cell. If she didn't have it locked, he might learn more about her. No. Bad choice. They were becoming friends, and he didn't want to jeopardize that. He forced himself to his feet and eased down the hall, but instead of going into his room, he went to the kitchen to make coffee.

Even though he was wide awake, he splashed water on his face, dried it with a dish towel, then neatly folded it. The kid would give him too much grief if he didn't. He poured his coffee, added a splash of milk and whiskey, then wandered toward the back porch. Steam rose from his cup and sent a thin swirl into the damp air. An owl swooped low and landed in a tall pine. Propping a hip onto the railing, Rance closed his eyes and listened to the night.

When he'd first gone to prison, he dreamed of this. The peaceful song of nature. Crickets. Birds. Frogs. This is where he belonged, and he never intended to leave again. He chuckled. Except later this morning, he'd have to drive to Danvers to get the shower hardware he'd forgotten to purchase. While in town he'd buy clothes suitable for the banquet.

He hadn't agreed to go yet, but he would. Hated to leave her without a plus one. He just hoped her contempt for fashion didn't carry over to social events.

The door behind him opened, and *lovey-dovey* stepped onto the deck. "I wondered where you got off to. You're an early riser."

"The storm woke me, and I couldn't go back to sleep."

She rubbed her eyes. "There was a storm?"

Yeah. Almost as loud as your snoring. "Yeah. You slept right through it."

She giggled. "I get that way when I drink. Alcohol puts me out like a light."

"Want coffee?"

"No, thanks. I need to be home to see my kids before they leave for school."

She turned, and he followed her inside. She hiked her purse strap over her shoulder, faced him, and tiptoed to plant a sweet kiss on his cheek. "I had a nice time."

"Yeah. Me too." Total lie. Other than using her for sex, Rance had no interest.

He watched until her tail-lights disappeared, then picked up his cigarettes and shook one out. The kid was right. Too many bad habits, and smoking would be the first to go. He stuck it back inside the package.

"Is your friend gone?"

He turned to face Blaze. She looked a mess. Spiky hair standing in every direction. Dark half-moons under her eyes.

"Yeah. Hey, I'm going into Danvers today to pick up supplies. You need anything?"

"No, thanks."

"Thought I'd buy a pair of khakis and new sport shirt for the banquet. You got something to wear?"

"You're going with me?"

"Why not? Probably get a fancy meal out of it, right? Not that it will be better than your cooking, but I don't want you to be the only one there without an escort. You have a dress?"

"I borrowed one from Hanna."

The answer stopped him. Blaze was all angles and sharp edges while Hanna was rounded corners and curves. "Does it fit?"

"Yeah. She bought it before she got—I mean, it doesn't fit her anymore. It's blue."

Rance went back to the pot and refilled his cup. "Is that your favorite color?"

"I don't know. I guess I don't have one."

"Since you mostly wear black, I thought it was your favorite."

"Not really."

He thought he'd get more of a response as to why she chose the villainess shade, but that didn't happen. "What did you wear to your prom?" he asked.

"I was homeschooled."

That might explain her lack of social skills. Parents thought they were doing the right thing by isolating their kids from the evil of the world, but sooner or later they had to deal with it. "So, no high school dances for you?"

Rance took a minute to recall his senior prom. He'd gotten lucky with Jessica Wilson, head cheerleader and homecoming queen. He'd served as her date and halftime escort. Man. That had been a night to remember. No backseat sex for her. She'd taken him to her parents' lake house. Turned out she had things she wanted to try, and he'd been more than happy to help. "What'd you say?"

Blaze shoved a hand through her crazy hair. "No prom. No dances."

There wasn't sadness in her voice. *No poor pitiful me, I didn't have a prom.* Just stated the facts as if her life was the same as everyone else's. Clearly it wasn't. He could fix that, and this new bit of information gave him an idea.

Chapter 12

Rance

Before Rance shopped for clothes, he made a quick stop by the building supply. While waiting for his order to be pulled, his mind drifted to his brothers. As soon as the renovations were finished, he'd invite them for a visit. Nick's coaching duties would be over, and Seth had a break before starting the new job with his future father-in-law.

At least Dad had two sons to be proud of, but what else was new? Even Rance's full athletic scholarship to Rice University hadn't won Dad's approval. No matter how hard Rance tried, nothing had ever been enough. He'd once dreamed of being CEO of a major company, if for no other reason than to prove he could amount to something regardless of the old man's opinion. But he had no control over how his father or anyone judged him. He'd taken that route. Bent over backward to make the best grades, worked to excel in football and set the right example. That's why the part-time job offer from Dad's buddy Jack had been such a surprise.

Rance had taken the gesture as a sign things were getting better with his father. And they had for a while, but when the place burned down, Dad had been first in line to believe the worst. He'd known Jack for thirty years. No way would he lie. Yeah. Right. Like a quarter million in insurance money wasn't enough motivation.

Why was he even thinking about this? He'd filed all that hurt and disappointment away long ago. Or thought he had. During all those endless days and nights in prison, he'd developed a keen twenty-twenty hindsight, and now realized he'd never gain his father's favor. He'd swallowed that bitter reality and tried to find the good in it. No more pressure. He didn't have to try anymore.

Sharp raps on the back of the truck shook him back to the present. "You're good to go, Mr. Keller. Thank you for your business."

Rance waved to the loader, then drove away. Next stop: Dapper Dan's Duds. Stupid name, but the clothes in the window looked good. He didn't remember the last time he'd bought anything but jeans and casual shirts, so he figured a professional's help couldn't hurt.

Turned out Dan was quite the salesman, and Rance bought more than he needed. As he loaded the shopping bags into the backseat, a young boy approached, carrying a box. A mop of brown hair fell in waves over his small head. An oversize super hero shirt topped his wrinkled plaid shorts. Green sneakers had holes in both toes. He appeared to be about five and should have been in school. Kid probably wanted a handout.

"Hey, mister. You want a puppy? I got one left." He set the box down and removed the scraggly dog. "He's house broke and everything."

Mixed breed for sure, but resembled a wire-haired terrier, mostly brown, with a tuft of gray between its ears and circling its muzzle. Talk about puppy-dog eyes. Those big chocolate peepers stared up at Rance as if begging for a new home. "What's the everything?"

"Huh?"

Rance scanned the street for an adult, but saw none. Who'd let a kid this age camp out downtown with no supervision? "You said house broke and everything, so what's the everything you're talking about?"

"Oh. Well, he ain't got fleas."

Rance felt guilty about busting the kid's balls but couldn't help himself. "Good to know, but I don't need a pet."

The boy shoved the dog toward Rance, and Rance took it without thinking.

"See, Mutt likes you."

[130]

He tried not to look at the scruffy mongrel, but it licked his hand. Rance came to his senses and thrust it back to the boy. "Sorry, no deal."

The child cradled the pup, and sat down on the sidewalk. His lip quivered and tears ran down his dirty cheeks.

Rance reached for his wallet. *Holy hell.* Kids and animals.

When he arrived home, the workers were in full swing. He took care of everything he'd bought, then strapped on his tool belt. In the new bedroom, men taped and bedded sheetrock, while in the bathroom another guy laid tile.

Rance headed back outside to work on the porch addition. Over the last year, he'd given a lot of thought to how he wanted his master suite. Spacious enough for a king-size bed. French doors opening out to a deck. Wood-burning fireplace. Surround sound. Didn't know when it'd happened, but somewhere in the middle of all the planning, he'd decided to keep the place.

By the time the carpenters left for the day, he noticed real progress. Paint and carpeting would come next. Bricklayers still had the chimney to finish, but the stone fireplace and hearth were ready for winter. And soon he'd have an inside shower.

An upbeat country song blared from the radio, and Rance hammered to the beat, nailing the last board. He didn't know why he was in such a good mood. Maybe it was because the construction was going well. Or because he took pride in his accomplishment. Or that he'd bought the puppy from the kid in town. Whatever it was, he shuffled a couple of dance moves, twirled around, and found Blaze standing in the doorway, holding the dog. He holstered the hammer and plastered on his poker face. "Where'd that come from?"

She clutched the animal close to her chest. "I found him in the shed. He's not wearing a collar, so I don't think he belongs to anyone. Can we keep him, or are you an enemy of dogs, too?"

"I'm not an enemy of anything, but you have to admit, the Lennon sisters needed to go. Even the vet said one of them was too sick to save. She was in pain."

"Well, this dog looks healthy. I bet someone dumped him and he needs a home."

Rance moved closer, then leaned down and studied the pooch. "Looks a little wormy." He knew that wasn't true. He'd stopped by the vet's office to get the mutt checked out and caught up on shots. It also provided an opportunity to find out if the three remaining cats had found homes, which they had.

"He's just small," Blaze said. "I'll keep him in my room. You won't even know he's here."

He waited to answer. Wouldn't want the kid to think he'd gone soft. "Tell you what. If you let me name him, I'll let you keep him."

She pulled her brows together. "I've already thought of some. I like Finley, Chesley, or Bentley."

He shook his head. "Sissy names. I'm thinking—Mutt."

"No. That's terrible."

"Let him decide. Put him down."

She eased the scrawny pet to the floor.

Rance crouched. "Here, Mutt. Come on boy."

The dog scampered to Rance and licked his outstretched hand. Smart dog. Wouldn't bite the hand that had already given him treats. "See, he likes it."

Blaze's frown drew tighter. "Well, I don't."

Rance rose to full height and smiled. "Since we need dog food, let's drive to Danvers and get a burger. You won't have to cook."

She lowered her head. "I don't really . . ."

"I know. You don't like crowds. We'll use the drive through, then go to the park and eat in the truck. How about it?"

Wheels obviously turned in her head. Since Hanna did all of Blaze's errands, he didn't think the kid ever left the house other than going to work

"Okay."

"Good. Give me time to shower and change. Oh, and while I was shopping today, I bought you a couple of T-shirts. Something besides black."

"Why?"

"Just because you work at a funeral home doesn't mean you have to dress like the grim reaper. A little color won't kill you."

She frowned. "I have dough in the fridge. I should knead it before we go. Do I have time?"

"For homemade bread?"

"Cinnamon rolls."

"Damn right you have time." He left to get a towel and washcloth.

Behind him, she called the dog. "Come on, Muttly."

Blaze

Blaze put the puppy in the laundry room, washed her hands, and removed the dough from the fridge. She'd learned the cold-rise recipe from one of the cooking shows. She sank her fingers into the soft mound. *Squish.*

Outside, Rance threw the blue tarp open and stepped from the shower. He had one towel wrapped around his waist and another in his hand.

Her mouth went dry. *Squish.*

He draped the extra bath towel over his shoulder and zigzagged it across his upper back.

Squish, squish.

She went stone still. He turned sideways, dried his chest, then ran a hand through his hair. She should look away, or at least close her eyes. Didn't though. She understood why he had no trouble picking up women. Not Hollywood handsome, his broad shoulders, muscled biceps, and taut belly gave him definite sex appeal, not to mention the wicked scar slashed from his breast bone to his belly button.

Squish, squish, squish. She glanced down at her fingers knotted in the bread. "Uh?" Caught up in the moment, she hadn't heard him come in.

"I asked if you were done," Rance said.

She tried to pull her hands free, but couldn't get them to move. "Oh. Yeah. Almost."

"Good, I'll get dressed, then we'll head out."

She hoped she hadn't killed the yeast from all the heat spreading through her body.

Rance

He maneuvered into a spot under the biggest oak in the park, and the late afternoon sunlight speckled the hood of his truck like a disco ball. What little conversation he and Blaze had during the drive concerned the new member of their household. She'd presented her best case to change the dog's name, but Rance stuck to his guns. He wasn't sure if her argument was sincere or gave her the opportunity to use her word of the day: pejorative, which meant expressing disapproval or suggesting something is not good or is of no importance.

Rance swirled a french fry into ketchup. "Turns out, you and I have a lot in common."

"We do?"

"Sure. We've both lost our mothers. We loved Dessie. We like living in the farmhouse."

She pinched off a bite of burger. The kid didn't eat much. Just chased food around her plate most nights. Having her contained inside the truck was the perfect time for another game of Twenty Questions—minus fifteen, because getting her to answer more than five at a time took some doing.

Rance shoved another fry into his mouth. "Tell me about your dad."

"He died three years ago."

"Oh, I'm sorry."

"Why? It wasn't your fault."

Her abruptness always surprised him. "What happened?"

"Pancreatic cancer."

Hoots and hollers from a nearby basketball court where teenagers played three against three got Rance's attention. The tallest of the red team hogged the ball, taking shots and getting his own rebounds, while his two teammates begged for a pass.

Blaze turned, too, then slid low in her seat.

"What's wrong?" Rance asked.

"I work with one of those boys. I don't want him to see me."

"Why?"

"I just don't."

[137]

Rance craned his neck for a better view. Each boy wore a numbered jersey, knee-length gym shorts, and fancy high-tops. "Which one?"

"Number twelve."

The ball hogger. "Has he been mean to you?"

"No. He keeps asking me out."

Rance took another look. The boy put a three-pointer in the basket, then pranced like a show horse. A guy being a guy. He remembered those carefree days. For him it'd been football, but competition was the same in every sport.

"Any particular reason?"

"He's seventeen. I'm twenty."

Rance chuckled. "Don't want to be labeled a cougar?"

"Is that a joke?"

He laughed harder. "Yeah. Kinda."

She gathered her leftovers and crammed them back in the to-go bag. "Are you done?"

He handed her his trash, and she stuffed it in. He wanted to get her talking again. "So, where'd you grow up?"

"Are we playing the question-and-answer game?"

"Sure."

"Okay. In a city."

He faced her and raised a brow. "You're being clever."

"I am? I thought I was avoiding the question. My turn. Where were you raised?"

Damn. This was a side he'd not seen before, and he liked it. "Okay, Miss Smarty Pants." That got a slight smile from her. Another first. "Houston." Ah, something flickered in her eyes. Maybe that was her hometown. He recapped. Raised in Houston. Homeschooled. Both parents dead. He stopped to do the math. If the kid was twenty, and she'd been five when her mother died, that gave him the year of the accident.

Little by little, he was finding out the identity of his housemate. Once he did, he'd figure out why she was in Bluebird and who she was hiding from.

Chapter 13

Tom Fraser

Tom Fraser glanced at his watch and fidgeted in the chair. This was his first face-to-face meeting with Marla Montgomery. He'd worked the case for months and didn't have much to report, but he was making progress. Trouble was, the more he found out about the woman, the less he wanted to find the girl.

He'd entered through a wrought iron gate outside and traveled a pebbled drive to a sprawling two-story Georgian. The interior was just as impressive. Marble floors, and a mahogany stairway curved twenty feet up to the second level. The fancy molding probably cost more than Tom made in a year. Crystal chandeliers hung above him and in the adjoining room. If everything the former housekeeper had said about the widow was true, he understood her desperation. A woman used to this lifestyle would do anything to keep it.

He'd gone back to see Helga Scudder with the lame excuse of following up on a couple of points, but the truth was he liked her and was trying to figure out how to ask her for a date. He'd been out of circulation too long, and she was the first female to get his attention since his wife died.

"Mr. Fraser?"

He looked up at the maid standing in the doorway. "Yes, ma'am."

"Mrs. Montgomery will see you now. This way, please."

She led him into a room with arched bookcases and oval windows with a panoramic view of a small lake. His current employer sat behind an ornate desk. *Holy crap*. Helga had mentioned the widow's beauty, but Tom wasn't prepared for how beautiful she was.

Long dark curls cascaded to her shoulders. Thick lashes hooded emerald eyes. And even from this distance, he could smell her exotic scent. Something floral with a hint of cinnamon. Everything men dreamed of—sex and money. All wrapped in a tight blue silk dress. Grant Montgomery had been one lucky bastard. At least for a while.

She sat ruler straight, as if on a throne. The only thing missing? A crown, and he felt like the court jester.

She smiled and rose to her full height. "Come in, Mr. Fraser. It's so nice to meet you in person." Didn't offer her hand, just motioned for him to sit. Perhaps he should have kissed her ring. Couldn't miss the damn thing. Three carats, at least.

He sat on the black velvet chair facing her.

[141]

Marla reclaimed her seat and shuffled through papers. "I appreciate the weekly reports. However, it seems you've made no new discoveries. Simply verified the prior investigators' findings. That's disappointing."

"True, but I like to check all the facts for myself, and I've barely gotten started. The men before me didn't follow up on sightings posted on the reward website. I'm in the process of doing that. It's a tedious procedure, but that may be our best shot at finding her."

Marla tapped her nails on the desk. "Impressive. But you did say tedious. How long will it take?"

"Hard to say. But I have two computer techs working on it, so hopefully sooner than later."

He wanted to ask about the kid's inheritance and why Marla believed a girl would run away from such massive wealth, but decided against it. No need to rile her. She was paying him damn good money.

She fixed her eyes on him. "Hire more men. Whatever it takes. Thelma will see you out."

He didn't know how Marla summoned the maid, but within a few seconds she appeared. Probably black magic, because the widow possessed the power to cast a spell for sure.

Tom sat in his car and gathered his thoughts, then headed downtown. Next stop: Montgomery Steel's CEO,

William Sherman, who was, according to Helga, the girl's godfather.

As he drove he replayed his first impression of Marla. She wasn't only beautiful, she was smart. Street smart. No doubt she'd educated herself on how to get a man's attention by stroking his ego. Beauty and manipulation were a dangerous combination.

Since the company provided valet parking, Tom pulled right up to the front door. Anytime he could save his knees stress, he took it. The tallest high-rise in Houston loomed over most of the surrounding landscape. Fifty stories of curved blue glass and metal reflected light in all directions. He hated heights, and a glass elevator made the phobia worse. Especially when he had to go all the way to the twenty-ninth floor.

The doors opened into a general reception flanked by two hallways. The young woman sitting at the desk looked up. "May I help you?"

"Tom Fraser to see Mr. Sherman."

She typed something on her computer and nodded. "Sharon will escort you."

Before Tom could thank her, a perky brunette spoke. "Right this way, sir." She led him to the end of the hall. "Go right in."

A gray-haired man rose from behind his desk and stuck out his hand. "Bill Sherman. Have a seat, Mr. Fraser."

Tom shook the man's hand, dropped into one of the leather high-backs, and got right to the point. "What happens to your job once the Montgomery girl takes over?"

"I retire."

Oh, so this was how it would be. Answer questions as if on the witness stand. Say no more than necessary. "Forced or your choice?"

Sherman shouldered back in his executive chair. "My choice."

Tom leaned forward. "I'm not your enemy. Just trying to do my job."

Sherman narrowed his eyes. "I'm not so sure about that. You work for Marla, and that puts you on the opposing team."

"So you won't help me?"

"Grant was like a brother," Sherman said. "He made one mistake in his life—marrying *that woman*. She fooled us all. Even I thought it was a good match. The age difference bothered me, but she seemed to love him. Turned out Marla was a money-grabbing narcissist."

Tom blinked at the strong language. He had yet to find anyone who liked her. "Enlighten me."

[144]

"She wasn't faithful. One of Grant's long-term employees kept quiet for a while because she didn't want to hurt him, but she finally came to me. Once she did, I hired an investigator and gathered proof. By then Grant was sick again. He wasn't up to a bitter divorce battle, so he endured it."

The CEO rested his arms on his desk. "I'm sixty-eight. I was ready to retire three years ago, but I promised Grant I'd stay until the company was safe."

Tom flipped through his notes. "According to her stepmother, the girl isn't capable of running the business."

Sherman's face reddened. "That's bullshit. She's intelligent, detailed oriented, and smart enough to listen and take advice from those with more experience. Grant would have never entrusted the company to a twenty-one-year-old unless he knew she was competent. I'll remain on the board and be her closest advisor. Just like I was to her father."

"Sounds like you might know her whereabouts. Do you?"

Sherman laughed. "Marla thinks the same thing, and believe me, she's offered plenty to find out, but I can honestly say I have no idea."

When Mr. Sherman rose, Tom got the message. Dismissed again for the second time today. *Rich people. Damn.*

As he drove to Helga Scudder's house, he considered what he'd do when he found the girl. It was hard to fight the consensus nobody wanted Marla to succeed. He'd spent twenty-five years fighting bad guys now it seemed he'd joined forces with the wrong side.

He wheeled into Helga's drive and found her stooped over, weeding flower beds. As he strode across the lawn, she looked up, shaded her eyes, and grinned. "Well, hello, you. More questions to clear up?"

"Just three. Do you know the whereabouts of the Montgomery girl?"

Helga removed her gloves and slapped them against her leg to dust the dirt away. "No."

"Would you tell me if you did?"

She thought a moment before she answered, then smiled once more. "Yes. But I wouldn't tell you where."

Damn. Perfect answer. "Would you have dinner with me?"

Blaze

For two days nobody died in Bluebird, and Blaze didn't work. But all the building activity was too much to deal with, so each morning after breakfast, she packed food and art supplies, put Muttly on a leash, and set out for the treehouse.

After blocking the doorway with her cooler to keep the puppy safe, she'd folded a towel and placed it in the corner, where he'd slept for the last hour. She'd spent the morning sketching the dog and Rance. Mostly Rance. She couldn't get the image of his water-splashed body out of her head. Later at the park, the way sunbeams had sifted through the trees cast his strong features in a perfect combination of shadow and light. As an artist she'd wanted to capture the memory before it faded. She'd never used male models or drawn nudes, but something about him excited her. Well, maybe *excited* wasn't the right word.

When she was younger and Helga had helped get her ready for bath time, Helga used to say, "Wash up as far as possible, wash down as far as possible, then wash possible." When Rance came from the shower, Blaze's stomach had tightened when she'd thought about his possible.

Before she finished the thought, his voice echoed through the pines. He was headed her way. She closed the sketch pad and placed it on the floor.

"Hey! Are you up there?"

She leaned out the opening. "What are you doing here?"

"I'm coming up," Rance said.

[147]

She scooted back to let him inside.

Muttly came to him. "Hey, boy." The pup rolled over, and Rance scratched his belly, then looked at Blaze. "I can't believe this place is still in such good shape. When you mentioned it yesterday, I wanted to see it."

He inched deeper inside. "My brothers and I built it. Some of my best memories come from my time here."

If she didn't know him, the scruffy beard and ponytail would be a real turn-off. Scary even. But the look matched his personality. Sexy. Dangerous. Hot. She fought the urge to touch him. To run her hand along his strong jaw. Feel the whiskers beneath her fingertips. She gave herself a mental slap. What was wrong with her? "I like coming here."

He grabbed the towel from the corner, reclined, and propped it under his head. "What do you do up here?"

There was the reason for her desire. She'd spent too much time sketching him. "Draw."

He rolled to his elbow and rested head in hand. "In this?" He picked up the sketch pad, but she grabbed it.

"Those are personal."

"Oh—okay. Sorry." He leaned back again, and the dog crawled onto his chest.

"Hey, I need to talk to you about something. I'm inviting my brothers to the festival. Can you handle that?"

"Where will they sleep?"

"They can bunk in my room, and I'll stay in Dessie's. That way we won't disturb you."

Blaze shoved the cooler back against the opening and reclined next to Rance. She liked being close to him. "Okay."

"Good deal." He yawned. "I may take a little nap."

"You should, because you're a sedulous man."

"Word of the day?"

"Yeah."

He laughed. "Let me guess. It means sexy."

"No. Hard working. But you are sexy."

Chapter 14

Hanna

Scents of coconut and vanilla hung in the air as Hanna sealed the last box of soap, slid it to Tiffany for a shipping label, then puffed a strand of hair from her eyes. "My online presence is paying off." For the past few weeks, she'd invested time on Facebook, following different stores and posting photos of her products. She nodded toward the packages. "Of the six companies that visited my site, those two placed orders."

Tiffany pressed the sticker onto the carton. "I'm familiar with Peabody's in Dallas, but not Ballendorf's in Houston."

"It has everything from bath products to home interiors," Blaze said.

Hanna jerked her head around. Blaze didn't seem like a city girl or the type who shopped in an upscale boutique. But she averted her eyes as if she'd said too much, so Hanna wondered if she'd lived in the city. "You've been there?"

"A long time ago."

Hanna glanced at Tiffany, then said, "I've been thinking I could find someone to represent my line at the home-and-gift show in Dallas next September. That would give me time to build inventory."

"Holy crapoly. I have an idea. Why don't we check into renting a space and do it ourselves? By then, I should have my jewelry line going. That way we wouldn't have to pay a middle man." She pressed a hand to her chest and shrugged. "I've been told I have natural sales skills, so who better to promote our stuff than *moi?*"

Hanna stacked the parcels by the door. "Bad thing about that is we'll have to come up with money and I don't know how much those spots cost." True statement, but she knew how little cash she had, which meant unless they were free, she couldn't afford one.

Tiffany pulled out her phone and tapped. "I've put it on my to-do list. I'll check on that and get back to you." She eyed Blaze. "You all set for your big date?"

"It's a plus one," Blaze corrected.

"Call it whatever you like, but you said he bought new clothes, so I'd say it's a date. You gonna let him kiss you good night?"

[151]

Hanna shot Miss Enthusiastic a glare. "Tiffany!"

"Hey. Just saying she needs to be prepared."

"I'd like to kiss him," Blaze said.

If Blaze kept making unexpected statements, Hanna was sure to get whiplash. This last revelation about caused her to crack a neck bone. "Are you kidding?"

"No."

Tiffany put her cell away. "Has Rance-in-the-pants changed? A few weeks ago you called him a jerk."

"He's not drinking and smoking as much. He hasn't gone out since the bad storm. I think he's been too tired. And he let me keep Muttly."

At the sound of his name, the puppy rose from his sleeping spot in the corner and trotted to Blaze. She lifted him into her arms.

To give her advice more emphasis, Hanna leaned forward and narrowed her eyes. "If you fall for him, you'll get hurt. Those Keller boys aren't really interested in lasting relationships." That wasn't exactly a fact. She didn't know about Rance and Nick, but Seth was another story.

Blaze shook her head. "That's not true. Seth is engaged."

That stopped Hanna, and her stomach spiraled. "Well, I stand corrected."

"Why did you say that?" Blaze asked.

Hanna should have kept her mouth closed, but Blaze was an impressionable girl with no experience with a player like Rance. As a friend, she was duty-bound to warn her. "While Malcom Keller was married to Rance's mom, he had Seth and Nick by another woman, and she was stupid enough to think he'd never cheat on her, but he did." Hanna removed her apron, hung it on a hook by the door, and spoke over her shoulder. "Sad thing about it—the boys knew about his infidelity. He always had a girlfriend on the side. I meant kids learn by example."

"They're coming for a visit," Blaze said.

Hanna's heart pounded. "When?"

"For the festival if he can get the master suite finished in time."

"His dad, too?"

"No. Just his brothers."

"Yeah, that's what I figured. Rance doesn't speak to his father." With the soap molds back in place, Hanna grabbed a rag and wiped the counter. "Let me know for sure, okay?"

Tiffany applied a coat of lipstick, then stuck the tube and compact back in her purse. "Me too. Man, the last time I saw those boys was at Dessie's service. Seth is attractive, but Nick is hot. I wanted to flirt with him, but thought the situation was inappropriate. You know, it being her funeral

[153]

and all." She pulled her hair to the top of her head and wrapped a rubber band around it. "If I was alone with him, I'd need a whole lot of Jesus to keep my panties on." She raked fingers through the strands of her ponytail. "Hey, I don't blame you for wanting to lock lips with Rancelot. But Hanna's probably right. Heartbreak starts with a kiss."

After Blaze and Tiffany left, Hanna grabbed a broom and swept the floor with a vengeance. Rance coming to Bluebird had messed up everything. It was wrong for her to wish he'd stayed in prison, but her life would be easier if he had. Now she'd have to deal with Seth, and that created a problem. She'd never been good at lying, and if he suspected Noah was his, she wouldn't be able to keep it from him. The thought of seeing him again unnerved her, and news of his engagement sent her over the edge.

A sharp pain shot up her arm and ricocheted straight to her heart. If Seth discovered her secret, he'd fight for custody. What if his wife-to-be was a total bitch?

Hanna dragged out a stool and sat. Alternating holidays and weekends was out of the question. She slowly rose, leaned the broom against the wall, and stepped outside into the early evening air to clear her brain. Whiffs of pine, wild privet, and her mother's fried chicken assaulted her senses and caused another flash of torture. From the time Noah could sit in his high chair, he'd joined them at the family table. Would Seth's new wife have family dinners? Could she even cook?

[154]

Hanna shoved her hands into the pockets of her thrift-store cotton dress and took off to the woods. No doubt Seth could provide more for Noah than she could. And once he got used to that, would he think life with his dad was better?

Sunlight filtered through the trees like laser beams, and a pair of bluebirds skittered among the limbs of an elm. This is where Noah belonged, conquering pretend monsters, fighting evil, and saving the planet. Galloping his imaginary steed on a make-believe trail ride. Soaring through clouds into fantasy lands where finding earthworms and frogs made him laugh as much as watching cartoons.

She'd never share her son with a sorority girl more interested in getting her nails done than paying attention to him. She stopped in her tracks to gaze up at the treehouse. Guilt weighed on her chest like a stone. She'd lost her virginity here. Conceived Noah here. If Seth had only loved her, things would have been different.

Regret strangled her. She hated that she'd loved him, and even more that she still did. She cleared her throat.

Noah's sweet face appeared in the window. "Hey, Momma. Whatchoo doing?"

"It's time for supper."

"Come up here. I gots sumpin' to show you."

She couldn't count the hours she'd spent inside those walls. For weeks after Seth left, she'd returned here and dreamed of the day he'd call, or text, or write. When three months passed, she realized she'd meant nothing more than a summer fling. A score. As she'd lain awake at night, she'd thought about how he was probably boasting to all his friends how he'd taken a simple country girl's innocence and how eager she'd been to let him.

One time. The first time. The only time they'd had sex without protection. After that she'd made him use a condom *every* time, but it was already too late. "No, baby. I don't want to come up."

"Please, Momma."

She took in some air and started her climb. When she reached the top rung, she leaned in and focused on the chalkboard mounted on the wall. "That's great, Noah. You're a good artist."

He pointed to each item as he spoke. "This is a pine tree. This is honeysuckle. I had to use my 'magination cause it's not blooming yet. Blaze says to draw good you have to 'member how stuff looks cause sometimes you can't see it."

Hanna smiled. For a first grader, he had real talent. Didn't know where he got it. Her specialty was stick figures. "It's beautiful. Let me take a picture to show Me-mom and Pe-paw. She aimed her phone and clicked.

In that moment it all became clear. She couldn't risk Seth finding out about his son. Not now. Not until she figured out what kind of stepmother he'd have. She punched in a number on her phone, and her grandmother answered on the second ring. "Hi, Gramma. I know. It's been a while. That's why I'm calling. I thought Noah and I might come for a visit. When? I'm not sure yet, but soon."

Blaze

As Blaze made her way home, she stopped to let Muttly sniff a bush. Each time she brought him to the woods, it was like an adventure. He scampered into the underbrush, licked and smelled any leafy thing he could find, and hiked his leg on every trunk.

She wondered if Rance considered the dog hers. She already loved the pet and hated to think of leaving him behind. She gave the leash a gentle tug to get the pooch back on track. He sat and scratched his ear, then took off in a trot. Probably should check him for fleas. Filing that idea away, she went back to her thoughts.

Because of Hanna's disapproving expression, Blaze wished she hadn't mentioned wanting to kiss Rance. But she'd thought about him all the time since the night he'd held her hand during the storm. His lips. His chest. His hands. It was silly, but she couldn't help herself.

Not that he'd ever be interested in kissing her because he wouldn't. The women he liked were older, prettier, curvier, and wilder. The most she could hope for was friendship.

But the tone of Hanna's warning said a lot. She had history with the Keller men. One of them had to be Noah's dad, but which one?

Mr. Keller sounded like a man who wasn't satisfied with one woman. Surely he wasn't the one. No, couldn't be. Hanna wouldn't be attracted to a man his age. Unless he'd forced her. That couldn't be right either. She would have reported that. It had to be Seth or Nick. Seth. When she'd mentioned his engagement, Hanna's face had flushed.

As Blaze reached the house, she caught sight of Rance, shirt off, hammer in hand, nailing a board into place. Sunlight bathed his slick skin as muscles flexed and glistened. Her heart thundered. She didn't just want to kiss him, she wanted to touch him and have him return the favor.

Chapter 15

✦

Rance

The treehouse had been a surprise. Figured it would have been in shambles by now, but someone had kept it up all this time. A few floorboards had been replaced, and the ladder looked new. Rance guessed kids who lived nearby played there. Fine by him as long as they didn't damage his property. *His property.* The words sounded strange. Most of the time he still considered it as belonging to Gran. Probably always would.

The last worker drove away, and Rance took a quick shower. Tomorrow he'd be the kid's plus one. It made him sad she'd missed so much. High school held some of his best memories. Hanging out with friends on a Saturday night. Sitting in the last row at the theater. Making out in the back seat of a car.

The thought stopped his nostalgia. He wondered if she'd ever necked with anyone. Even been kissed? Must have.

Because during his search of her room, he'd seen birth control pills. Hell, just because she hadn't attended public school didn't mean she hadn't had contact with boys.

He stepped from the shower, leaned on the porch banister, and watched a pair of black-bellied whistlers swim in the pond. It was the first time he'd seen them since he'd been back, but they'd been nesting here since he was a kid. He and Seth spent one summer trying to locate their eggs but never found them.

He loved this place more every day. It was his sanctuary. His saving grace. The one place he felt safe. Houston had once been his home, but now it might as well be a foreign country.

After dressing, he strolled into his new bedroom and peered outside. He had a clear view of the garden spot. Like always, the kid was busy planting something. Muttly scampered about, and Rance could tell from Blaze's head movements she was talking to the dog.

Funny how she had no trouble yakking with an animal, but conversation with Rance made her uneasy. However, she was changing on that front. During their dinner question-and-answer game, he'd learned she had no siblings. When it came her turn, she'd been a bit too interested in Seth. Maybe she was simply curious about his brother's bride-to-be, but it seemed like more. She wanted information about his job, his engagement, his wedding date, and if the festival visit had been nailed down.

[160]

The thought occurred to him that she was nervous about having extra people to deal with and planned to stay with someone else. That was probably the reason for the interrogation. She needed to make arrangements in advance.

Blaze

As hard as Blaze tried, she couldn't get Hanna and Noah off her mind. The last few days she'd attempted to get information from Rance without much luck.

She'd learned Seth's new job with the fancy law firm was because his betrothed was the boss's daughter. That called his ethics into question. If he was Noah's father, why didn't Hanna think him worthy enough to tell? And now, his future hinged on nepotism. Maybe he thought only of himself and did whatever it took to advance his career.

She flipped a page in her notebook and studied the instructions for her next client, seventy-four-year old, Clyde Bonner. Men were easier than women. With a little foundation and a dusting of powder, they were good to go. Well, it took longer if they needed a haircut, which Clyde didn't, because he'd been a member of a local country-and-western band and had worn his in a ponytail.

She removed the protective cape, tightened the knot on his tie, then smoothed his shirt and jacket. After checking him off the list, she studied her word of the day. Alacrity, meaning eagerness, willingness, or readiness. She'd been judging Seth unfairly. She hadn't even met him.

At two o'clock she sat in the break room eating a peanut-butter sandwich and enjoying the solitude. The area was small with only one table, four chairs, a fridge, and a couple of vending machines. Since she was about the only person who used it, she wished she could redecorate. A rug would improve the tan commercial tile, and if the white walls had a splash of color, it would cheer the place. Original artwork wouldn't hurt either.

Cam's voice echoed down the hallway and shattered her musing. Hoped he wouldn't make a last- ditch effort to escort her to the banquet. But if he did, now she had a legitimate excuse to refuse.

The door flew open. He stepped inside and gave her the eye. "Hey, how's it going?"

"Fine."

"You coming tonight?"

Her stomach clenched. "Yeah."

"Good. I'll save you a seat."

Before she could answer, Mrs. Walters peeked inside and shoved a white box tied with a ribbon toward Blaze.

"Handy I found you in here because this needs refrigeration."
She retreated, leaving Blaze alone with Cam again.

She stared at the imprint. *Bluebird Blossoms.* The local shop delivered funeral arrangements all the time, but to see a tag with her name on it surprised her. She unpinned the envelope from the bow and read the card. *Looking forward to tonight. +1.*

A rush of adrenaline pushed a knot into her throat. She tugged the satin. Inside was a wrist corsage of white orchids surrounded by baby's breath tied with ribbon the same color as bluebirds. Dad had given her a bouquet at her art show. She'd picked flowers with Helga and then Dessie, but she'd never gotten a corsage. Much less, one from a man—like Rance.

"Looks like I won't need to save you a seat."

She'd forgotten Cam was in the room. "Uh? Oh yeah. I'm bringing someone."

"I didn't think you dated."

She didn't like his tone or the sneer. "He isn't a date. A plus one."

"I'm bringing a basketball buddy. Figured I needed another guy to help me turn a boring banquet into a party."

Blaze wasn't sure what he meant. Were they going to shoot hoops? Didn't have to wait long for an explanation.

[163]

"Yeah, I've already bought the vodka," Cam said. "You can drink it and no one knows because it don't smell."

"You shouldn't do that. If your dad finds out, you'll get in trouble."

"Yeah, well, I already stay in trouble with my old man. He keeps harping about me taking over the business one day. Like dealing with dead people for the rest of my life is what I want to do." He scooted a chair from the table and dropped into it.

She didn't remember inviting him to join her. All she wanted was to be left alone with her fantasies about Rance, because the moment she'd seen the corsage, her imagination had shifted into overdrive. He must like her, or he wouldn't have done something this nice.

Then her euphoria crashed like a jumbo jet. Rance felt sorry for her! She was an idiot to think she meant more to him than just a silly kid. Still, whatever the reason, she should thank him and stop jumping to conclusions with so much alacrity.

Rance didn't know if the corsage pleased Blaze or not. Her solemn demeanor gave nothing away. She'd thanked him, but he'd expected more of a reaction. She'd been acting weird since she got home, quickly disappearing into the woods and taking Muttly with her. He figured she'd gone to the treehouse to sketch. Just as well. Without interruptions he finished the back deck, except for staining. The bathroom was complete and laying carpet was the only thing left to do in the master suite. No more outside baths.

By the time he came from the shower, he heard the water come on in her bathroom. He found his new clothes, pressed and on hangers. Didn't know when she'd ironed, but the proof was before him. He stepped into his khakis, then removed the red-and-white-pin-striped sport shirt along with a navy tie.

Why the hell was he nervous? Easy answer. This would be his first social event since getting out of prison. He'd logged plenty of interaction in bars, but those didn't count.

Tie in one hand and the item he'd taken from Gran's jewelry box in the other, he strolled outside for some air.

He'd spent nights in his cell dreaming of what he'd do here, and now those dreams had come to fruition. He needed bedding. Maybe he'd take Blaze into Danvers to shop. Who was he kidding? She avoided mingling with people, and if tonight's function wasn't required, she'd skip it.

Damn, he wanted a cigarette, but it'd been over a week without nicotine and it was getting easier. At least he wasn't waking in the middle of the night craving one.

"Are you ready?"

Her voice shook the Marlboro urge away. When he faced her, his pulse skipped. Who was this person? Big eyes and long legs. "Damn, kid. You look great."

"Thanks. You, too."

He came inside, reached for the pendant, and dangled it in the air. "I remembered Dessie had this, and it matches your dress. Turn around and I'll put it on you."

Blaze stared at it, then at him. "You don't have to feel sorry for me."

He lowered his hands. "What are you talking about?"

"Agreeing to be my plus one. The corsage. The jewelry. You're trying to make up for the prom I never had, and I don't need you to."

She'd misunderstood everything. Hell, how could he feel sympathy for her when she had a shit load of cash hidden in her room? "That has nothing to do with this. You work hard. Cleaning, cooking, laundry. I wanted to do something nice for you. But excuse me for trying to show some appreciation." He dropped the necklace into his shirt pocket, grabbed his tie, and looped it under his collar. After two

[166]

attempts at tying it, he yanked it off and tossed it onto the back of the chair.

She picked it up and stepped closer. "I used to tie my dad's all the time." She explained as she worked. "This is a four-in-hand-knot. You cross both strips, wrap it twice, bring it up, and back through the bottom loop."

She was so close, her warm breath floated over his skin, and his pulse pounded. When she was done, she slid the knot tight, then rested both palms flat against his chest. "The corsage is pretty, and I'd like to wear the necklace. It was Dessie's favorite."

Rance slipped it around her neck, and she turned for him to fasten it. "Pops gave this to her on their twentieth wedding anniversary. Had it made special."

She pressed her hand over the bluebird. "I know. It has twenty tiny sapphires for the body and twenty rubies for the breast. Dessie said he must have confused a bluebird with a robin."

Rance leaned close to her ear and whispered, "Sorry I snapped at you." God, she smelled good. Like honey and vanilla. "Turn around." Those big green eyes. High cheekbones. Flawless skin. Kissable lips. At that moment he stopped thinking of her as a kid, and just like that, blood rushed to his groin. "Looks great. You ready?"

"Yes."

Two hours later he fidgeted in his chair waiting for Blaze to return from the ladies' room. The banquet food had not disappointed. Delicious steak and a decadent dessert called molten chocolate cake with cherry sauce. As usual, Blaze picked at hers, but Rance devoured everything put before him.

He glanced at his watch. She'd been gone too long. He rose and rushed to the exit. As he came to the end of the hallway, voices echoed.

"Damn, Blaze. How old is your boyfriend? Forty?"

"He isn't my boyfriend."

"Well, then, he won't mind if you give me one little kiss."

"Stop, Cam. You're drunk."

"No, I'm not. I've wanted to kiss you for a long time. That and a few more things."

"Don't touch me, or I'll tell your dad."

"You think he'll believe you over me? Come on, just one little smooch. One little feel."

"Stop it!"

"Get your fucking hands off her." Rance grabbed the boy, slung him into the wall, pinned his wrists, and nudged his knee against the kid's crotch. "Don't you ever touch her again. If I find out you've so much as looked at her wrong,

I'll rip your heart out and shove it down your throat. You *feel* me?"

The boy squeaked out his answer. "Yeah."

Rance went still. Rage coursed through his veins. He hated men who took advantage of women because they were physically weaker. If this kid was already doing it, his path was set.

"Rance!"

Blaze's voice snapped him from his daze. He had the boy by the throat. He let go and stepped back, then looked at Blaze. "Get your purse and say your goodbyes."

Cam slumped to the floor, gasping.

Rance didn't wait for her return. He rushed outside to his truck, pounded the fender, paced, and tried to calm his emotions. He could have killed the boy. The thought terrified him. Damn, he wished he had a shot of whiskey.

She rode home in silence. He wanted to say something, but didn't know what. This was twice she'd seen his dark side. He wondered how many more it'd take before she ran like hell.

He figured she was upset or scared or disgusted. But which one? Well, he'd warned her. Should have made her leave the minute he arrived.

She turned to face him.

He braced.

Then she drew a deep breath.

"My name is Wren."

Chapter 16

✦

Rance

Rance tried not to think about what had happened at the banquet. He'd almost gone too far with the boy, but that skinny bastard had no right to touch her.

Then, on the drive home, when she'd told him her name, his temper had cooled. "Wren," he whispered, and loved the way it felt on his lips. Holy hell, he was lusting for her, and that had to stop. But things had changed in that moment. He finally knew something about her. Real. Honest. True.

Last night he'd dragged the mattress off his old bed into his master suite and slept on the floor. His bones ached, but it was still a hell of a lot more comfortable than a prison bunk. He'd told himself it was to enjoy the new room, but honestly it put him closer to her.

She was a contradiction. Stubborn and strong to a fault, but vulnerable at the same time. He wanted to protect her, not only from the groping coworker, but everything.

Sunlight beat against the sheets he had tacked over his windows, and dust motes floated in the air like glitter. Today he'd go to Danvers to order blinds. Hoped she'd come, too.

He sat up, lifted his laptop from the floor. Her name, along with the monogrammed note he'd found when he searched her room, gave enough information to learn more. Especially if he took into account what she'd shared about her mother's death.

He typed "fatal car accidents Houston, Texas" into the search bar. He'd start there. The look in her eyes when he'd mentioned the city made him think she had a connection to it. Clicking the state archives, he scrolled to Harris County and entered the year he'd come up with. One hundred thirty-six fatalities. Now all he needed was a victim with a last name beginning with M. Within minutes, he'd hit pay dirt. Lark Elise Holland Montgomery. Survived by husband, Grant, and daughter, *Wren*.

He opened another tab and typed her name. The first entry got his attention. "Heir to Montgomery Steel Goes Missing." *Holy shit.* After reading the article twice, he looked at a connecting website where sightings were posted. Hundreds were listed. The most recent was three weeks ago from New York City.

[172]

He wondered how many were bogus. Probably most, since there was a $25,000 reward offered for information leading to her whereabouts. At least the cash he'd found was legit. She was worth millions. So why was she hiding?

He put the computer away, dressed, then strolled into the kitchen. Fresh blueberry muffins sat on a platter, and in front of the coffeemaker was a note instructing him to turn it on. While it brewed he focused on the garden where she walked the length of a row poking holes in the soil with the hoe handle. He smiled. She'd learned the technique from Gran the same as he had when he was a boy.

Muttly played nearby, leaping into the air to catch a butterfly.

Damn, heiress to the biggest steel company in the United States digging in the dirt. Craziest thing he'd ever seen. She should be at a spa getting a head-to-toe treatment. Shopping at Neiman's. Jet setting all over the world. But not her.

He splashed coffee into his cup, took a muffin, and sauntered outside. He was next to her before she noticed. "Morning, Chirp."

She looked up and shaded her eyes. "What did you call me?"

"Chirp."

"Why?"

"Because you're a Wren living in Bluebird. Besides, I can't call you by your real name, and I'm sure as hell not calling you Blaze."

She pulled her brows together as if giving it some thought, then pursed her lips. "I like it."

"You want to go into Danvers with me today? I thought I'd buy furniture for my bedroom. I plan to call my brothers later to tell them their festival visit is a go."

Blaze

Blaze didn't like going into town, but if Rance went alone, he might bring a woman home, and she didn't want that to happen.

Even though Rance's assault on Cam had upset her, she appreciated his gallant defense. But the rage she'd seen in his eyes frightened her. Not that he'd ever hurt her. There was a kindness about him she saw every day.

In the short time she'd known him, he'd changed for the better. It was as if the farm had worked magic and brought him back to life. She was pretty sure she loved him. Couldn't be certain, because she'd never been in love before. But she wanted to be with him more than anybody else. She thought about him all day. Counted the minutes until she saw him. Spent hours sketching his face, hands, body, tattoos. Fantasized about sleeping with him.

Her face heated. She should stop torturing herself. She picked up the pink T-shirt Rance had bought and pulled it over her head. Below the city's logo, it read, Come Fly with Me to Bluebird, Texas.

Startled by the sound of her phone, Blaze stared at the caller ID. Not Hanna or Tiffany. Not the funeral home. Must be a wrong number, but she answered anyway. "Hello."

"Wren, it's Uncle Bill."

Her heart hammered. William Sherman was her godfather, but she'd always called him uncle. And he was the person her dad had trusted most. During the past three years, she checked in with him occasionally so he'd know she was all right, but she never revealed her location.

"Wren? Are you there? I'm using a burner phone so no one can trace the call."

"I'm here. What's wrong?"

"No emergency. Just wanted you to know Marla has hired a new detective. A guy named Tom Fraser, and he seems determined to solve the case instead of taking her money like the others. I know you're being careful, but I needed to warn you because he's working the leads hard."

"Okay."

"Are you doing all right?"

"Yes."

"Come home. Move in with Virginia and me."

"No. I have friends. A job. I have a dog. A boyfriend." She gasped. Why had she said that?

"You do? Oh my God. He doesn't know who you are, does he? Sweetie, there's still a reward in place and if he's not a good person . . ."

"He is, but I haven't told him anything." Not a complete lie. Besides, what did it hurt for him to know her first name?

"You know how folks pretend to be one thing when they're another. We learned that with Marla. Remember, people take advantage of rich people the same as poor."

"No one knows I'm rich, but it wouldn't matter to him."

"Give me his name," Bill said. "Let me at least run a background check."

"No."

If her so-called uncle knew about Rance's prison record, he'd insist she come home. And she wasn't ready. Besides, Rance didn't have a clue she thought of him as a boyfriend. And neither had she until the words spilled out.

Rance called out from down the hall, then stuck his head into the room. "You ready? Oh, sorry, I didn't know you were on the phone." He turned and walked away.

Rance's curious expression didn't escape her, but she'd deal with that later. She turned her attention back to the conversation. "I have to go."

"Are you living with him?"

"Don't worry. I'm okay. I promise."

"I am worried . . ."

"Bye." She clicked off. What was wrong with her? She wasn't involved with Rance and never would be. The stupid idea must have come from the incident with Cam. She'd made that into more than it was.

By noon Rance had all the furniture he needed. A king-size, four-poster bed, two side tables, a chest of drawers, and an oversize chair with matching ottoman. Shopping for home furnishing only fueled Blaze's fantasy. She kept telling herself how ridiculous she was for thinking about something that would never happen, but still couldn't stop gawking at him like a star-struck groupie every chance she got.

She reminded herself of Dad's lecture about how infatuation dismisses flaws and exaggerates virtues. He'd say this was only a crush. Not true. She knew Rance's faults. Even been on the receiving end, and she still wanted him.

[177]

Could be good-girl-bad-boy syndrome. Nice girl attracted to the wrong guy. But he wasn't a bad man. A little rough around the edges, but those had smoothed out since she'd met him.

"Earth to Chirp."

"What?"

"We're here," Rance said. "At Walmart. You've been distracted all morning. Anything wrong?"

Other than picturing you naked? "No, I'm okay."

"I thought maybe the phone call you got upset you."

"No." She could tell he was waiting for her to say more, but he'd made it clear from the beginning he didn't want trouble. If he found out about the private investigator, he'd kick her out for sure. The less he knew, the better.

He reached for her hand and held it. "You can tell me anything. If you have a problem, I'll help."

She took a shallow breath. His touch made things happen. Tingle. Clench. How was she supposed to get over the attraction while picking out beds and sheets? She should have stayed home—and done what? Sketched him?

She faced the window and concentrated on the people in the parking lot. To her left an overweight woman wearing a denim skirt, tube top, and knee boots loaded bags into an old Volkswagen bug with more rust than paint. Across from her, a hairy man worthy of an entry in *Guinness World Records*

[178]

straightened from beneath the hood of a Ford truck, pitched three bright-yellow plastic bottles into the back, then wiped his hands down the bib of his overalls.

She glanced over at Rance and followed his gaze to the entrance, where a woman emerged. The jet-black hair that puffed around her head like a storm cloud was bad enough, but the swimsuit and cowboy boots were too much.

Yep, nothing could kill lust like Walmart customers.

Chapter 17

Blaze

Where were the tube tops and hairy men when Blaze needed them? After the shopping trip in Danvers, Rance had driven through Fred's Fried Chicken and taken her to a different park from where they'd seen Cam.

This time Rance coaxed her out of the truck to sit at a nearby table. Across the lawn, young couples sat on quilts, mothers swung their children, and dads tossed Frisbees with their kids. She wondered what category she and Rance fit into. Friends? Acquaintances? Roommates? Everything she did with him was new, so she didn't know how to define their relationship. She considered this outing as a picnic, but figured to him it was a place to eat.

She'd put too much emphasis on his kindness. Just because he'd been nice didn't mean he had any romantic feelings toward her. But when she'd helped with his tie, there'd been something in his eyes. Longing. Could it be? Finding out was worth the risk.

"Chirp?"

"Huh? What did you say?" Blaze sputtered.

"What's going on?"

"Nothing."

"I texted my brothers, and they're coming to the festival. But no need for you to leave. You won't have to cook for us. We'll either eat in town or I'll throw something on the grill."

"Okay."

He threaded her fingers in his. "Tell me what's wrong. And don't say nothing, because I can see the wheels spinning in that head of yours."

She pulled her hand free, swallowed the lump in her throat, then pointed to a sunny section of the park. "Those people over there are practicing heliolatry because of the lack of trees."

"Preoccupied with your word of the day?"

"Yes. It means sun worship." Not exactly a lie, but she couldn't tell him what was really on her mind—*him.*

[181]

Rance

Rance tossed and turned, loving the softness of the new sheets against his skin. Chirp had been right about the selection and insisted on washing and drying them before use. She was a stickler for following manufacturer's instructions. Hell, she was a stickler for a lot of things. After years of having to follow rules, that should bother him, but it didn't.

She was the most genuine person he'd ever met. Well, her life was full of secrets, but he figured out of necessity for survival. That had to be it. But if he could get her to confide in him, he could help. She'd seen how intimidating he could be, and if she was running from someone, he'd take care of them.

He'd prepared Seth and Nick about meeting his strange housemate. The last thing he wanted was for her to freak out, so he'd warned them about keeping the pantry in alphabetical order. Not to ask her to make a sandwich unless they could wait an hour while she got everything lined up and leveled. And if they planned on getting laid, they needed to rent a hotel room or she'd don her homemade hazmat getup. They'd gotten a big laugh out of the picture he'd sent.

He'd also cautioned them about her lack of understanding sarcasm and absence of filters. Her obsession with making lists, using her word of the day, and keeping the counter cleared of clutter. Dirty clothes needed to go in the hamper. Shoes in the closet. Wet towels in the laundry room. By the time he'd finished explaining all of her quirks, they each had the same question. Why did Rance let her stay?

He'd asked himself that plenty of times. Truth was, she intrigued him. And after seeing her in that dress, he'd been thinking about her in ways he shouldn't.

He flopped onto his back and stared into the darkness. A line of moonlight escaped from between the blinds and marked the ceiling like a carpenter's level. It'd been a week since the banquet and he was still losing sleep over her. He needed a cigarette. Whiskey. Sex. *Damn.*

6 Blaze

Blaze ended the call with Uncle Bill, put her phone aside, and went into the bathroom. No avoiding her godfather. He'd left fifteen messages, so she had to take the time to explain her remark. That Rance was just a friend who happened to be a boy, and she'd simply used the wrong reference. Someone she trusted, who knew nothing about her "real" life. Once she'd reassured her uncle, he calmed down. Good thing. Didn't want him to hire his own investigator.

She rinsed toothpaste from her mouth, gazed into the mirror for a moment, then turned in for the night. Across the hall, Rance thrashed around on his new bedding. It couldn't be uncomfortable because she'd insisted on leaving Walmart and going to the nicest store in Danvers to buy 1,800-thread-count Egyptian cotton. He'd winced at the price, but she'd promised he wouldn't regret it.

She should ask if he did. Or better yet, slide in with him and decide for herself. Stupid. She already knew how great they were. She'd been sleeping on them all of her life. But she couldn't help but wonder how it would feel to be next to *him* on the silky, luxurious fabric. Naked. Skin to skin. His strong arms around her. His lips on hers. She tried to imagine being kissed until breathless. Having him on top of her. *Inside* her.

Her senses kicked into overdrive. She really shouldn't have these thoughts. It wasn't healthy. But, he'd hadn't had a woman in a long time and probably needed one. She scooted to the edge of the bed, and put her feet flat on the floor. Then desire and logic engaged in a serious tug-of-war.

Don't be an idiot, Logic said. *You're not his type.*

Okay, that made sense. She swung her feet back onto the mattress.

[184]

Hold on a minute, Desire chimed in. *Maybe you don't look exactly like the women he prefers, but you aren't hideous. And, you're available—and willing. Two of his favorite things.*

That made sense, too. She sat up again, but Logic wasn't done.

He doesn't want you here and having sex would only encourage you to stay. For once in your life, listen to me. Forget about him. Go to sleep.

With a heavy sigh, she pulled the covers up to her chin.

You love him, right? Desire asked. *So march across that hall and jump his bones. Oh, but whatever you do, don't mention love—romance—feelings—or commitment.*

This time she shot straight up and ran into the hallway, but stopped at his door. She reached for the knob, then pulled back.

Go on. You'll be fine.

No, you won't. This is one more opportunity for him to see how weird you are.

She clamped her hands to her ears. "Stop talking."

When she stepped into his room, he pushed up on his elbows.

"What's wrong?"

She braced against the jamb to steady herself. "I want to have sex."

[185]

At first he didn't speak, and then he raked a hand through his hair. "Not a good idea."

"Okay." She turned, stalked back to her room, and crawled into bed. She should have listened to Logic. A pang of regret twisted in her stomach. At least now she could stop fantasizing.

Rance

Rance came to his feet. Then sat on his bed. What the hell? Sex? He'd considered it for a second, but decided against it. Why? Wasn't as if he hadn't been toying with the same idea. Even in the last hour he'd wrestled with the notion, so why didn't he invite her in and get to it?

Okay, she was horny. Him too. So much his balls ached. He had to give her credit. It was the most straightforward seduction he'd had. He ran his hand over his face. What was wrong with him? When had he ever refused to getting laid? She was an adult. He was a grown-ass man. Hell, his man card could be revoked.

He stood—sat again. No. It'd be wrong. God, her parents would spin in their graves if their little princess

[186]

screwed him. She was upper crust he, a convicted felon. Innocence meant nothing. Ex-con would always be part of his title because he'd done the time.

He rose and took two steps forward, only to turn back again. It wouldn't be right—but *she'd* come to his room. Wasn't like he was trying to take advantage of the situation. But if she'd developed feelings, it would be wrong to encourage her. To hell with it. He owed it to himself to find out.

He grabbed a pair of boxers and put them on. Not a good idea to go to her room buck-naked because she might have changed her mind. Within seconds he was at her bedside.

She looked up at him. "What?"

"Why do you want to have sex with me?"

"Because those women you brought home make it sound like you're good at it."

An excellent answer. He leaned in close to kiss her, but she pulled away.

"I thought you said it was a bad idea," she said.

"I changed my mind."

He leaned low again, but she placed her hand on his chest. "Would you brush your teeth first?"

"Sure. Be right back."

If any other woman had asked him to do that, it would have pissed him off, but not her. Typical Chirp. When he got back to the room, she flipped the cover for him to crawl in next to her.

"I used mouthwash, too," he said.

"Thank you."

Clearly she had no experience in the kissing department, because he had to force her lips apart with his tongue.

For the last hour he'd been thinking about breaking in those new sheets and now had the opportunity. He scooped her into his arms and carried her while she planted quick kisses on his face like playing a game of connect the dots. Damn, she was eager. Once he reached his bed, he eased her feet to the carpet and lifted the nightshirt over her head.

He let the garment drop to the floor, happy she didn't ask to stop and fold it. Then he sat on the mattress and pulled her to stand between his legs. A strong rush of desire surprised him. He slid his hands to her breasts, and they nestled in his palms like two perfect plums.

Blaze

[188]

With moonlight falling across Rance's body, he looked like a god. A chiseled, tatted divinity—with an erection. She'd aroused him. Imagine that. Weird, awkward Wren Montgomery had excited a guy like him.

When he landed that first kiss, her lips stuck to her teeth but he'd taken care of the problem. God, she loved having his tongue in her mouth. And it was so *minty* her taste buds tingled. Then he'd picked her up as if she weighed no more than a rag doll and her heart almost exploded.

Heat raced through her veins as he sucked one nipple into his mouth. Everything left her brain except him—there. He moved from one stiff tip to the other. Licked. Teased. Taunted. Until she thought she'd come apart.

Before she knew it, he slid back on the bed and brought her with him. He was so beautiful. Bronzed and inked. Lean planes and hard muscle. No doubt she loved him, but chances were he'd never feel the same about her. She had too many secrets, and true love couldn't survive without trust.

"I want to touch you."

He whispered a laugh. "God, I hope so." He took her hand, guided it inside his boxers.

Holy crap. She'd never touched a man's penis before. Not even Kevin's. Rance was hard. And big. Now that she was holding it, what was she supposed to do? The answer came quickly as he moved against her slow and steady.

"Damn, Chirp. That feels so fucking good I don't want you to stop, but we have to or I'll get my rocks off before I'm inside you."

That's what she wanted. Him. All of him. She couldn't wait. It would be good because Rance had experience. Unlike Kevin, who'd been as clueless as she. And it'd been over so quickly, there'd been no satisfaction for her.

She let go, and Rance shucked his underwear, took time to roll on a condom, then slid her back onto the bed and climbed on top. He leaned down and kissed her again. Once wasn't enough. She didn't want him to stop. Ever. "I like when you put your tongue in my mouth."

He chuckled. A low, deep tone that got her hotter. He raked his fingers higher, brushing between her thighs. Then his touch became more intimate as he slipped a finger inside her. God help her.

"You're so fucking wet. I can't wait any longer."

He rose above her, and she felt pressure and pain as he entered her. "Wait."

He went still. "What's wrong?"

"It burns. Give me a second."

He pulled back, but she clenched his hips with both hands and coiled her legs around him. "Okay. Start again."

He went deeper, and the stretch hurt even more. She couldn't hold back the tears.

He cursed and tried to pull out.

"No. Keep going."

"I don't think I should."

He tried to stop again, but she dug her nails deeper into his flesh. "Your penis is already in my vagina. I want you to finish!" She bucked hard. Once, twice, and the third time he thrust back and plunged past her virginity. She yelped like a kicked dog.

He uttered more obscenities, angled her up, and drove into her hard. Within seconds he released and slumped forward, pressing his full weight on her.

The pain had been intense. Not his fault. She'd wanted him to get it over with.

He rolled off her. "Goddammit. Why didn't you tell me you were a virgin?"

"I didn't think I was."

He glared at her. "What do you mean? You've either fucked or you haven't."

The anger in his eyes caused her stomach to turn. "I was fourteen. I wasn't sure he'd gotten it in right, until now. And you're bigger than Kevin. A lot bigger."

"Fourteen? How old was this Kevin?"

"The same age."

Rance sighed as if relieved, and she couldn't think of anything to say, so she got up and crossed the hall to her bathroom, where she turned the spigot to fill the tub. Once she soaked in hot water, she'd be okay.

It wasn't long until Rance knocked on the door.

"Come in."

"Are you okay?" he asked.

"Yes."

"Dammit, Chirp. I'm sorry. I should have asked. But I saw the birth control pills and assumed . . ."

He was still mad. She could see it in his eyes. Hear it in his voice. But there was something else there, too. Regret. "They're to regulate my periods. It isn't your fault. There had to be a first time sometime. Right? It'll be better next time."

The muscles in his jaw flexed. "There won't be a next time."

Chapter 18

✦

Rance

Rance disgusted himself. He'd hurt her physically and emotionally, and that was the last thing he'd wanted to do. Her expression when he'd said there wouldn't be a next time filled him with regret. It'd been the same as telling her she was a lousy lay. And she was. Worst sex of his life, and she was the most awkward partner he'd ever had. She didn't know how to kiss, or where to put her hands, or what to do with his cock once she had her fingers around it.

But, dammit, if he'd known she was a virgin, he could have prepared her better. Taken more time. More foreplay. But discovering it in the middle of things pissed him off, and he'd lost his cool. Rammed into her like it was what she wanted. Well, it was. She'd said so, but he should have stopped.

Hell, he should have picked up on her innocence the minute he'd kissed her. But he hadn't, so now what was he going to do? He hoped to hell she didn't want to talk about it. Who was he kidding? She hated talking.

He lay awake for hours telling himself the best plan was to pretend it never happened. But he wasn't sure he could. Her cries of pain kept ringing in his ears. He'd never hurt a woman before. Not during sex or any other time. But he'd never popped a girl's cherry, either. Still, he should have figured that out when his dick felt like it was in a vise. All the clues were there he'd just been too stupid to recognize them.

He sat up and hung his head. She was probably asleep by now. He should go to her. Apologize again. No. It would contradict what he'd said. No more sex. Ever.

The craving for a smoke and drink hit him hard, but he'd given up the cancer sticks so he'd settle for whiskey. He pulled on his jeans and headed to the kitchen. Once he got the bottle and glass, he ambled outside to the back deck and collapsed onto the chaise.

Moonlight shimmered across the pond. A coyote howled in the distance. Humid air settled on his bare chest. Scents of honeysuckle and pine floated to him. All the makings for a romantic evening, but there'd been no romance. And he wanted to make it up to her. Show her what a good lover he could be.

He'd climaxed, but not her. He hated that. Especially after he'd discovered it was her first time. One more thing to add to his guilt. He'd taken her virginity, and she'd gotten zip.

He drained his glass and poured another. His attraction to her confused the hell out of him. Wasn't even old enough to drink. But as quirky as she was, there was something about her he couldn't get past.

He'd already suffered and lost more than most people his age. Finally he had a second chance, but there was still an emptiness inside him from the years when all he'd thought about was self-preservation. Concentrated on making one day at a time. Getting through each twenty-four hours without getting raped, beaten, or killed. When he was with her, he forgot all that.

A splinter. That's what she was. Worked her way underneath his skin until he couldn't take it anymore. He knocked back another drink and mentally kicked himself. He was an idiot to tell her no more sex, because he wanted more. A lot more. To make her scream for reasons other than pain.

He'd had too much alcohol. Wasn't thinking clearly. He held the bottle up to the light. Almost empty. He turned it up and swallowed the last slug, then staggered down the hall and considered acting on the erection straining against his jeans. Still sober enough to know that was a bad idea, he crashed onto his bed.

Blaze

After a sleepless night, Blaze rose early the next morning. She'd made a terrible mistake asking Rance for sex. They'd become friends, and now she'd put that in jeopardy. She'd expected him to storm inside and tell her get out. But he hadn't.

His door was ajar, so she peeked through the crack. Shirtless, but still wearing jeans, he sprawled across the bed. She eased away and slipped quietly into the kitchen. Out on the deck, an empty whiskey bottle and glass sat next to the lounge chair.

He wasn't sleeping. He was passed out.

God, she'd been so bad at sex he'd gotten drunk to forget the ordeal. A sharp pain stabbed her chest. She couldn't stay in this house all day with him and see the anger in his eyes. She grabbed a bottle of water and took off toward Hanna's.

Even at the early hour, the woods were alive. Birds chattered. Squirrels scampered. Crickets chirped. *Chirp*. His nickname for her. She got a little tickle in her belly every time he said it. Mainly because he delivered it with the same affection as when Dad had called her Birdie.

Tears pricked her eyes. She'd ruined everything and didn't know how to fix it.

[196]

As she neared Hanna's place, Blaze knew her friend would be with the goats, so she headed straight to the stalls. Sure enough, Hanna sat on a stool milking Sadie.

"Hey, Blaze. You're out early."

"Seth and Nick are coming to the festival. They'll be here Thursday."

Hanna went almost as pale as the milk. "I was afraid of that. Would you be willing to take over milking duties? I'm going to visit my grandmother. I've convinced Mom and Dad to go with me, so you can stay here."

"Is Seth Noah's dad?"

Hanna spoke over her shoulder. "Yes. But you can't tell anyone."

"I won't. But why haven't you told him?"

"Because I thought I meant something to him, and I didn't. Besides, he had his life planned. So what would have been the point?"

"Don't you want Noah to know him?"

Hanna resumed milking "Yes. But I need to make sure Seth's bride will be a good mother. Easier for me to share Noah if she accepts him."

Blaze understood that scenario all too well. Her dad had been tricked into thinking Marla was the perfect woman, but the minute she had the ring on her finger, she showed her true colors—a lying, conniving, self-centered gold digger who wanted Blaze out of the picture permanently.

"I promise not to tell." Blaze bit her bottom lip. "I slept with Rance."

Hanna whipped around so fast she almost knocked the bucket over. "What?"

"I had sex with Rance, and he didn't like it."

Hanna set the pail aside. "Did he say that?"

"Not exactly. He said it wouldn't happen again, and as much as he loves sex that's all it could be."

"I warned you. You should have told him no. Those Keller boys take what they want without consideration for anybody else."

"I'm the one who asked."

"What?"

"I asked him, and at first he refused but then changed his mind. I've messed up. I bet he's going to ask me to leave."

"Maybe not. Tell me everything."

When Blaze finished the story, Hanna stood, took the milk to the cooler, then turned back. "Why did you ask him?"

"Because I'm in love with him."

Hanna released a heavy sigh. "Oh, Blaze. That can't be right. You hardly know him. I understand the attraction. He's been nice to you of late, and that's confusing."

Blaze shook her head. "No. I think about him all the time. I lie away at night because of nasty thoughts. I wish I'd been better, then he'd still want to be with me. Now he'll bring women home again." Blaze stretched her lips tight to keep them from quivering and didn't understand the urge to cry. But every time Rance came to mind, a knot lodged in her throat.

"It's settled then. Stay here until after his brothers have come and gone. That will give you time to sort things out. Now that you know he's not interested, maybe you'll stop thinking about him so much."

Since the house belonged to Hanna's parents, Blaze didn't feel right about staying there. But she didn't want to go back home either. A quilt and a pile of fresh hay were all she needed. Well, that and the bathroom facilities in the workshop. "I'll agree only if you let me sleep here in the barn."

"Don't be silly. You can crash on the couch until we leave, then take my bed."

"No. It's the barn or nothing."

"Fine. Have it your way."

Blaze spent the rest of the morning making lists of goat chores and notes on how to store the milk. She barely thought of Rance, which made her think Hanna was right. Keeping her distance was the best idea. She supposed that once the guys left, things could go back to how they were when Rance first arrived. Avoiding each other. Or she'd move on. Find a bigger city to get lost in, like—Austin. Its eclectic, creative community would be a good fit.

She pulled out her phone and searched facts about the city. Wow, it had so many events going on each weekend, she'd be invisible.

Her remaining cash meant she wouldn't have to work. Just concentrate on painting. Do pieces good enough to put in a gallery. Once she returned to Houston, her connections to the art scene would get her foot in the door.

She moved to Hanna's laptop and scrolled through rental properties in the area. Plenty of places she could afford until she had to face Marla.

Blaze heaved a deep breath, and the weight of her mistake lifted. As soon as Hanna returned home, Blaze would hit the road.

She'd always have fond memories of this place. Dessie. Hanna. Tiffany. Rance. No, not Rance. She couldn't allow memories of him. Someday she'd look back on how he'd stayed with her during the storm, rescued her from Cam, and let her keep Muttly. But not for a while. Maybe never.

Leaving was the right choice. Cut all ties. When her goat duty ended, she'd say—goodbye, Bluebird, hello, Austin.

Chapter 19

✦

Rance

Rance figured Blaze was at Hanna's because she hadn't been home in days. Fine. Wasn't this what he wanted all along? To have the whole place to himself? Just one problem. He hated it.

Not having her across the hall drove him nuts. Sitting at the dinner table alone made him downright surly. And missing out on her fucking word of the day pissed him off. He'd tried to ease his pain by going to The Roost and hooking up, but he couldn't get interested. He found something wrong with every woman there. Too friendly—too needy—too clingy.

Most nights he had a couple of drinks, came home and got drunk in private, then fell into a whiskey coma, and didn't come to until the booze wore off. He had to stop acting like a teenager with his first crush. He didn't understand it. The sex had sucked, so why did he think about screwing her all the time?

Scrubbing his hand over his four-day-old beard, he shook his head. Didn't even want to shave anymore. Didn't want to do much of anything except drink himself into a stupor.

Thankfully, Seth and Nick would arrive tomorrow and he'd have plenty to do. Fishing. Target practice. Watch sports. Once the festival started, he'd take them into town to check out the barbecue cook-off and antique car show. Rance remembered how much he and his brothers liked the three-legged race and tractor pull. Too old for that now, but the pancake breakfast was always good. He'd talk them into getting up early for that.

He walked to the window, peered into the early morning light, and his heart stopped. Chirp was in the garden, hoeing weeds and dragging dirt around the tomato plants. She wore a shirt he'd not seen before. A blue button-up. The top two were unfastened allowing the fabric to fall open at her neck. Even from this distance he could tell she wasn't wearing a bra.

The memory of having those small breasts in his mouth caused his cock to twitch. *Dammit.* He opened the door and ambled toward her. "Hey."

She didn't look up or stop working. "Hey."

"You been staying at Hanna's?"

[203]

"Yeah."

Why wouldn't she look at him? Easy answer: still pissed. Okay, he got that, but she needed to get over it. "When are you coming home?"

That stopped her, but she still didn't face him. Just leaned against the hoe handle as if considering his question. Then she took a deep breath and went back to working the dirt. "This isn't my home."

"Yes, it is. You pay rent. That makes it yours. My brothers will be here tomorrow. I want you to meet them."

"Why?"

The question caught him off guard. "Because I told them about you. We live together. You lived with Dessie. They'll want to know you." Damn. None of those reasons sounded good enough. Truth was, he didn't care if they met her or not, he just needed her to come back. He missed her. So why couldn't he say that?

"I'll try to drop by one afternoon."

"For God's sake, Chirp. Look at me."

At first she didn't move, but then she faced him with an expression as blank as his brain. "I'm sorry about the other night," he said.

Something flickered in her eyes, and her bottom lip quivered. "I'm sorry I was a virgin. I wasn't trying to trick you. I really didn't know."

[204]

He advanced on her and she backed up. He stuck his hands in his pockets. "I know."

"Then why are you mad at me?"

"I'm not. I'm mad at myself. I should have figured it out the minute I kissed you, and I should have stopped no matter what you said."

She shrugged. "Just one big solecism, I guess."

There it was. Her fucking word. "You don't have to give up your room."

She started hoeing again. "That's okay. Hanna is leaving town for the weekend, and I'm taking care of the goats. I need to stay there."

Rance kicked the dirt and turned to go. There was no changing her mind. He'd only taken a few steps when she called after him, and for a split second, hope overwhelmed him.

"Hey."

He turned and shaded his eyes. "Yeah?"

"Is it all right if Muttly goes with me?"

His chest tightened. "Sure. Take him."

"Thanks."

The heels of Rance's boots dug into the ground as he stomped away. He wanted to wring her neck. Why did she have to be so stubborn? He whipped out his phone and tried typing in *solecism*. Thank God Google knew how to spell it. He read the definition. Mistake. Blunder. Error. *Damn right*. The sex. Her leaving. And most of all everything he'd said.

Even by his standards, it was too early to drink, but he needed something to calm his nerves. Hell, it was five o'clock somewhere. He revved up the Harley and tore out down the road, letting the wind clear his head. Cruising into town, he parked in front of Fly-By Quickie Mart.

Rance stopped at the end of the counter and eyed Hanna. "Thought you were out of town."

She looked past him as if she expected to see someone else. "Oh no, I'm not leaving until later today. What can I help you with?"

"Pack of Marlboro short reds in a box."

She pulled the pack from the rack behind her and laid them next to the register. "I thought you'd stopped smoking. What happened? Fall off the wagon?"

Rance took money from his wallet and handed it to Hanna. "Something like that. So, Chirp's staying at your place."

"Chirp?"

"That's what I call Blaze. Long story."

Hanna rang up the sale and offered his change. "You're breaking her heart, you know."

His hackles went up. "How you figure that?"

"Forget it. I should mind my own business."

What had Chirp been telling her? Except for the bad decision about sex, he'd been as nice as possible. He clenched his teeth. "But you're not, so what the hell are you talking about?"

"She thinks she's in love with you."

Pain pierced his temples like his brain might explode. "Not possible."

"Oh, it's possible, all right. You think she'd ask for sex without an emotional involvement? She's not like the women you bring home."

"I know that. And—well, I thought she was horny, and since I was available." He clenched his jaw tighter. "Wait. She told you about it?"

"The basics. She asked you. It was terrible. And you said you never wanted to do it again. Great pep talk, by the way. You really know how to make a girl feel special."

"Fuck. I hope she told you I tried to stop."

"Yeah, she mentioned that. I'm not blaming you. I get it. She's with you all the time. You've been nice to her. The banquet. The dog."

He held up his hand. "Wait. She knows I bought Muttly for her?"

Hanna widened her eyes. "I meant you let her keep him. But you *bought* him?"

"Yeah. To make up for getting rid of the cats."

"Well, you need to put some distance between you. That's why I have her staying at my place. Maybe by the time I get back in town, she will have come to her senses."

"What does that mean?"

"That it's a crush. You're the first man she's been around so she doesn't have enough experience to know the difference between infatuation and the real thing. Just stay away from her. That way she won't read more into your kindness than you intend."

Grabbing the box of cigarettes, he shoved it into his shirt pocket. "Yeah. Sure." He spun around and stormed out.

Rance cursed himself all the way home. So Chirp had a crush on him. Big deal. Not his fault. She'd known from the minute he showed up what he thought about sex. A basic need with no attachments. He'd never led her to believe anything else. Sure, he cared about her, and missed her. But he'd miss anybody when they were in his face all the time.

Okay, she wasn't in his face, but she was always there. Washing, cooking, and cleaning. She'd made herself useful, and he'd gotten used to it. After so many years behind bars, he figured he deserved pampering, and she'd seemed to enjoy it. Wasn't like he'd made demands. Hell, he'd told her over and over how much he appreciated what she did.

Had she misinterpreted that? Is that why she'd asked for sex? God, he hated when women couldn't separate lust and love. He wanted to screw her. He liked having her around. But that didn't mean he wanted a commitment.

Did she think they'd fuck, and he'd ask her to go steady? He couldn't help but laugh. With her lack of experience, he guessed that's what she'd thought.

Hanna was right. He needed to leave her alone. Maybe he didn't want to give her his class ring, but he sure as hell didn't want to hurt her either. When her goat duties were over and she came back home, he'd keep his distance. No more picnics in the park, or banquets, or unnecessary conversations. He could go right back to the moody son of a bitch he'd been when he arrived. That should make her fall *out* of love with him pretty damn fast.

Blaze

Blaze almost cried when Rance walked away. When she'd claimed this wasn't her home, and he'd said it was, joy bubbled in her chest. But it only lasted a second after he'd pointed out that the rent she paid entitled her to call it that. He'd given her several reasons to come back, but not the right one. He didn't miss her—want her—need her. Hell, he didn't even like her.

Yeah, she bet he'd told Seth and Nick plenty. No question they were eager to meet the freak who'd seduced their big brother and been so stupid she hadn't even known she was a virgin. She'd wager they'd gotten a good laugh.

Just as Helga had taught her, Blaze gulped three deep breaths. In through the nose, out through the mouth. The exercise had worked in the past, but not today.

Her spirits had lifted when Rance came out again because, like an idiot, she thought he'd returned to say he missed her. But instead he climbed onto his Harley and took off like a thief. Appropriate. He'd stolen everything from her. Heart. Innocence. Love. No, not stolen.

She'd given it freely.

Chapter 20

Rance

The next day, Rance glared at the cigarettes but couldn't bring himself to smoke one. If he did, his one month nicotine-free was all for nothing.

While he'd been in town the day before, Chirp had changed the sheets on her bed and made his. The pile of clothes he'd left in his chair were gone. Even after the awkward sex and difficult conversation, she was still taking care of him. He guessed that as an heiress, she was used to people catering to her every whim, but somehow she remained unspoiled. Didn't put herself before others, and he'd never seen a single indication she felt entitled to special treatment.

She'd placed a vase on the dining table filled with Indian paintbrushes and phlox from the field across the road. Gran used to do the same thing. Said she needed to "pretty things up" when company came.

He turned his attention to the hamburger meat on the counter. He hoped he remembered all the ingredients for his special recipe. Later, when Seth and Nick arrived, he'd fire up the grill. Afterward, if they wanted, he'd take them to The Roost. Since the town was gearing up for the festival, the local bar should be flooded with tourists. Hell, maybe he'd even find a woman to suit him.

It didn't take long to get his menu in order, and then he looked around for something else to do. He had time to kill. Could walk to Hanna's and try to reason with Chirp again and straighten out the misunderstanding. Explain that she couldn't fall in love with the first guy who paid attention to her. She had her whole life ahead of her.

At some point, she'd go back to Houston and take her rightful place. Attend galas, operas and appear in the society pages. He'd never fit into that world. He picked up the cigarettes, shook one out, brought it to his nose, and inhaled. Damn, he craved it. Bad. He replaced it, then crushed the box in his fist and tossed it in the trash.

Stepping to the porch, he gazed across the pond. Not a ripple or a whiff of a breeze. A bullfrog croaked a steady rhythm that sounded like a motor grinding. He went back inside, laced his boots, and trekked out to the shed.

A cloud of dust trailed behind as he thundered down the road on his Harley. When he got to town, he noticed most of the side streets were roped off and people were busy setting up food wagons, carnival games, and arts-and-crafts booths. Local business owners hustled to arrange outside tables and shelves for their yearly sidewalk sale.

He made a slow pass down Main Street and parked in front of the bar. The place was already more packed than usual. Normally he'd have a drink, but wasn't in the mood—for much of anything. He wondered if Chirp had attended the festival before. He'd never asked. Gran would have wanted her to but wouldn't have forced her. If she hadn't, he would hate for her to miss the closing ceremony fireworks. He'd try to see her on Saturday and convince her to come. No. What he needed was to stop thinking about her. And he would. Starting now.

After killing a couple of hours in town, he drove home to shower. Now, standing on the porch, he watched a Chevy truck barrel up the dirt road. When it skidded to a halt, Nick emerged first and threw his arms around Rance. "Seth still can't drive worth shit. We're lucky to be alive."

"That is not true!" Seth said. "I'm an excellent driver." He fell in behind Nick and took his turn hugging Rance. "Damn, look at you. Beefed up a little haven't you?"

"Yeah. That's what decent food will do for you. Y'all come in. I can't wait to show you the place."

After a tour and more complaints from Nick, Rance got beers from the fridge and placed them on the table. Seth grabbed his and downed half of it.

Nick pulled a sack from his duffel and pitched it to Rance. "Got y'all some gifts."

Rance pulled out T-shirts and read the first one. "I Didn't Like Prison. They Got the Wrong Kind of Bars. Funny, real funny."

"The blue is for Seth."

Rance tossed it to him.

Seth eyed Nick. "You think I'll wear this?"

"Let me see," Rance said.

Seth turned the shirt and Rance read, "Good Story, Babe. Now Go Make Me a Sandwich."

Nick laughed. "What's wrong? Your little debutante won't see the humor in it?"

"No. She won't."

Rance took two more from the sack. "You went a little crazy on the shirts, didn't you, Nicky?"

"Oh, the green is mine."

Seth smirked. "Free Breast Exams? Damn, you're just asking to be slapped."

Rance stared at the pink one. Irony. The Opposite of Wrinkly. "Who is this for?"

"Your roommate. Since she's hung up on those words of the day and does housework, I thought it was perfect." Nick craned his neck toward the garden. "Where is she?"

"Staying with a friend."

"What? We're not going to meet her? Did you tell her we don't bite?"

"Yeah, but it's not going to work out this time. Maybe next trip. I've got burgers ready to put on the grill."

"Let's wait. I wanted to take a look around," Seth said. "It's the first time we've been here since Dessie's funeral."

"I want to fish," Nick said.

"Okay, I'll get the bait. You get the poles out of the shed, and I'll meet you at the boat." Rance turned to Seth. "You sure you don't want to go?"

"No I think I'll take a walk in the woods. Clear my head of all the wedding crap I'm having to deal with. I don't know why she wants my opinion, because she makes all the decisions."

Once in the boat, as Rance and Nick pushed off from the shore, Rance focused on his little brother. "What's the deal with Seth?"

"Pretty obvious, right?"

"Yeah. Is it the wedding?"

"Between you and me, it's more than that," Nick said. "He's not in love with her, man. I keep telling him to break it off, but he won't do it."

"Then why propose? Oh hell, he didn't knock her up, did he?"

"No. I'm not sure they're even having sex. He got caught up in her world and lost his good sense. I mean, she's rich. Her dad's law firm is the biggest in Houston, and Seth is guaranteed a job there. But here's the kicker. Heather pals around with this loser friend from high school. Claims he's gay, but I'm telling you, the guy's banging her. Seth is about to screw up big time. I hope you can straighten him out."

Nice to know baby brother considered Rance capable of counseling, but hell, he couldn't fix his own woman trouble. "I don't know, Nicky. I should probably stay out of it."

Nick baited his hook, then dropped it into the water. "No. We have to do something. She's spoiled rotten. Gets her way about everything. Plans Seth's life twenty-four-seven. Did you hear his phone dinging? That's her texting about useless shit. Sending pictures of herself at the country club. Shopping. Flowers. Cakes. I can't stand her. The only reason he's here, is because she wants him to break the news that you can't be in the wedding. Can't have an ex-con in the social event of the year. Bitch."

Rance raised a hand in surrender. "Hey, I'll be happy to sit in the back row and pretend I don't know him."

"Not the point. It's his wedding, too, and if he wants you in it, then you should be. I'm telling you, he's going to be miserable. Once they're hitched, she'll never let him see us again. That's why we've got to stop it."

Blaze

Muttly sat up straight and perked his ears, which caused Blaze to do the same. She didn't hear anything, but the dog must have. Closing her sketch pad, she scooted closer to the window and wished it would be Rance. Such a stupid idea. Why did she keep torturing herself with ridiculous fantasies?

The pup whined, and Blaze squinted into the afternoon light. Finally a figure came into view. Too small for Rance, but who? In all the years she'd been coming here, other than Noah and Hanna's dad, she'd never seen another man at the treehouse.

When the stranger got to the thick pines blocking out the sun, she recognized him from Dessie's pictures. Seth. Smaller and with brown eyes, he didn't look much like Rance.

Her heart hammered. Maybe he wouldn't climb the ladder. She slid on her butt to the rear wall, pulled Muttly onto her lap and closed her hand around his muzzle. "Shh."

With only one door, she had nowhere to go. Holding her breath, she heard him take the first rung. Then the second. Third. When his face appeared in the opening, she spoke. "Hello."

He jerked away. "Damn! You scared me."

Muttly growled, but Blaze hugged him tight. She didn't know if he'd bite or not. "I'm sorry."

"That's okay. I wasn't expecting to see anyone. You must be Chirp."

"Only Rance calls me that. I'm Blaze."

"Oh, sorry. I'm Rance's . . ."

"I know who you are. I've seen pictures."

"May I come in?"

She gave it some thought. This could be her chance to help Hanna. Find out about Seth's bride. "Okay."

He propped his hip on the floor, then maneuvered inside. "What are you doing up here?"

She glanced at her tablet. "Drawing."

"I saw the mural. You're good. Which reminds me. We don't need your room. We'll stay out of your way. We were hoping you'd come with us to the festival."

"Why?"

"Because you're Rance's friend, and we want to include you. There's a street dance tonight. Why don't you come? That way, I'll have a partner."

She and Rance weren't friends. Not anymore. She wasn't sure what they were.

Unlike his older brother, Seth had an easy way about him. No bad attitude. No rough voice. She saw kindness in his eyes. "I don't dance," she said.

"Then it'd be a good time to learn. I've been taking lessons because of my upcoming wedding, so I could teach you a few steps."

"What's your bride like?"

"Oh. She's pretty. From a good family. Does a lot of volunteer work."

"What's her name?"

"Heather Banks." He chuckled. "She thinks Heather Keller is hard to say and sounds funny so she plans to hyphenate."

Blaze couldn't help but smile. Acquainted with the family, she remembered Heather and her younger sister, Haley, were about as snooty as they came. Served her right to be stuck with a hyphen.

"You want kids?" Blaze asked.

[219]

Another look of surprise. "Well, sure. Someday."

"Will Heather be a good mother?"

"Uh, I guess. She'll be good at hiring the right nanny. That's for sure."

Blazed picked up her sketch pad. She'd heard enough. Hanna would never want Noah raised by a nanny, but Blaze could reassure her on that front. Heck, she'd loved every minute with Helga. But, then again, Blaze didn't have a mother. "I've got to go. It's time to milk the goats."

"What goats?"

"My friend, Hanna is out of town. I'm taking care of her business."

He slid toward the ladder and waited for Blaze to join him. "When is she coming back?"

"Sunday night."

"Too bad. I was hoping to see her before I left."

"Why?"

"We're old friends. I wanted to catch up."

Blaze took the leash, hooked it in the dog's collar, and placed him on the ground. Then she stuck her sketch pad under her arm. "She works two jobs. About to get her teaching degree next month. Starting up a goat milk product line. That catches you up."

"She seeing anyone?"

"Why do you care?"

"Just curious." Seth pulled his brows together. "You get right to the point, don't you?"

"Yes."

"I like you. Come to the festival with us. I'll even help with the goats, if you need me."

Blaze cocked her head. She couldn't figure this guy out. "You get right to the point, too."

"Yeah. Another reason we should hang out."

Chapter 21

Blaze

Blaze saw no reason to tell Seth she'd already planned to go to the festival with Tiffany. Once her friend had learned about the botched sex and the current situation with Rance, she'd claimed a night out was what a girl needed to heal a broken heart. Blaze didn't think hers was broken. Just cracked. But it wasn't Rance's fault she'd fallen in love with him.

Tiffany didn't make excuses about her ulterior motive, which was to hook up with Nick. According to Hanna, Blaze and Tiffany were both nuts for wanting to get involved in any way with that family. Considering Hanna's history with Seth, Blaze thought her opinion was biased. As much as Hanna protested, Blaze saw the sadness in her eyes every time Seth's name came up. She still loved him. And Noah looked so much like Seth it was spooky. How had she missed it? The big brown eyes. The way he cocked his head. The curve of his lips. Put those two in the same room, and everyone would know Seth was his dad.

Blaze released the last goat from the stall and rushed to take a shower. Tiffany had texted earlier to say she was bringing something for Blaze to wear. Whether she wanted to admit it or not, she'd liked wearing the dress to the banquet. She hadn't worn anything but pants and T-shirts for so long, she'd forgotten how feminine clothes affected her.

She missed that part of her life. And her long hair. And the trips to the spa. What she'd give for a day beneath Janine's hands. Blaze shook her head. If she hadn't thought of the world's best masseuse until now, surely she could block Rance from her mind. All it took was determination and time. Two things she had plenty of.

At six o'clock Tiffany burst through the door like a fireball. The girl never had a bad day. She shoved a clothes bag forward. "You will look so beautiful in this outfit Ranceroni will drool."

"I don't think so."

Tiffany looped a strand of hair behind her ear. "I've been thinking about your dilemma. That conversation you had with him in the garden says a lot. He wants you to come back, and I don't think it's because you pay rent." She flapped her hand in the air. "I know, I know. That's what you think, but he didn't have to come out there and talk to you. But he

[223]

did. Sure, he regrets what happened, as he should, but it's more than that. He just doesn't know it—yet."

"I don't understand."

"That's because you don't know how to play the game. But I do, and I'll help. Nothing gets a guy more interested than thinking you're not interested in him. So tonight, give all your attention to Seth."

"Why?"

"To make Fancy-Rancy jealous."

"But Seth is engaged. Rance knows he's not attracted to me."

"Doesn't matter. What does is ignoring Rance Man. Don't even look at him, and see what happens. If you're right, you'll be able to tell. But if I'm right, and I know I am, he'll make a move."

A spaghetti strap on Tiffany's pink sundress slipped off her shoulder. She put it back in place and raked her fingers through her long blonde curls. No doubt Nick would be attracted to her. Rance too.

As Blaze slipped the white shirt over her head, she considered Tiffany's plan and wasn't sure she agreed. But her friend had more experience with romance, so Blaze figured she might as well try it. She smoothed the hem of the blouse over the full skirt and added a chain belt. Since she had no cleavage, the off-shoulder eyelet ruffle drew attention from that department. Tiffany hadn't missed a detail, from the chandelier earrings to the beaded sandals. Blaze moved to the mirror and cast one last look at the shocking transformation, from Goth to bohemian Cinderella.

In town, she trailed behind her friend as Tiffany shoved open the door to The Roost. The perky blonde sashayed through the crowd like she owned the place. Impressive for a preacher's daughter. But she could fit in anywhere. Not Blaze. She had never even been inside a bar. Sure, she'd been to the country club with her dad when she was a child, but that was different. Every person in the place knew him and his daughter. Here, she wasn't the steel king's peculiar kid, she was just odd.

Dread pooled in Blaze's stomach as soon as she spotted Rance. She quickly moved her gaze to Seth. He rose and came to meet them.

"Hey, glad you made it."

His warm smile and greeting relaxed Blaze a little, but she could feel Rance's eyes on her. "This is my friend, Tiffany," Blaze said.

Tiffany flashed her trademark full wattage. The expression that rendered men speechless and strained their zippers. Seth shook her hand and motioned for them to follow. Blaze hated the heady rush she got as Rance rose from his seat.

The two empty shot glasses in front of him told her he'd not been there long enough to get drunk. She tore her eyes away and focused on Nick, who wore a T-shirt that read Free Breast Exams.

After introductions, Seth pulled out a chair for Blaze, and Nick did the same for Tiffany. Rance plopped back onto his and glared at Blaze.

"Chirp, surprised to see you," Rance said.

Tiffany bumped Blaze's knee under the table as if to remind her of the scheme. "Seth convinced me to come."

Tiffany patted Blaze's leg in approval.

"What do you girls want to drink?" Seth asked.

"Frozen margarita for me," Tiffany said.

Blaze wasn't up for this. She'd been crazy to think she could pull it off. Tiffany nudged her again. "Oh, I can have a soda."

Tiffany glared at Rance, but spoke to Blaze. "Don't be ridiculous. Have something *virgin.*"

"Oh, okay. A peach Bellini."

"Coming right up." Seth walked away.

Tiffany gawked at Nick's shirt.

Nick leaned closer. "You're not going to slap me, are you?"

"Why would I do that?" Tiffany asked.

"Seth said I was asking for trouble by wearing this."

She traced her finger over the word *free*. "Actually, I'd like to make an appointment."

He laughed. "Anytime."

Sweat beaded on Blaze's forehead. Rance's eyes bore into her with such fire, she wanted to run. Afraid to move, she sat ruler straight. Why couldn't she be like Tiffany and say clever things and flirt instead of being awkward? Thankfully Seth returned with the drinks, and that gave her something to do with her hands.

Rance knocked back another shot, then leaned closer and whispered to Blaze, "You look beautiful."

Her heart jumped into her throat. Why'd he say that? She couldn't look at him. If she did she'd fall into his arms and beg him to love her, if only for a little while. She leaned close enough for him to hear her, but averted her eyes. "Thank you."

Seth must have noticed her discomfort, because he came to his feet and held out his hand. "Come on, Blaze. Let's dance."

As nervous as she was to get on the dance floor, it was safer than sitting next to Rance.

Seth tugged her out of her seat and into his arms. "This is awkward."

"I told you I don't dance."

"Not the dancing. You. And Rance. What's going on?"

"Nothing."

"Oh hell. You've fallen for him, haven't you?"

"No." The lie didn't sound convincing even to her. Considering everything about her was a lie, she should be better at it.

"Yeah, you have," Seth said. "As much as I love my brother, he should come with a warning label. He can be pig headed."

At least Seth didn't seem to know about the bungled sex. That was a relief. "We had an argument," Blaze said. "That's all. I shouldn't have come. I didn't want to, but Tiffany wanted to meet Nick. I need to leave. Can you take me?"

Seth brought her in closer and looked over her shoulder. "From the way big bro is watching us, I'd say it's too late to take my advice. So let's get his blood really boiling." Seth twirled her, then pulled her back to him and kissed her cheek.

She stiffened.

"No, don't do that. Smile and say something."

She plastered on a fake grin and connected with his eyes. "I'm not good at small talk."

[228]

"Tell me what a good dancer I am."

"You're a good dancer," she told him.

"Say I'm handsome."

"You are, but you need a haircut."

Seth chuckled. "Maybe you can help me with that. Rance says you're a hairdresser."

"Sure."

He dipped her, then leaned close to her ear and spoke. "Tell me I'm the world's best lawyer."

"But you haven't practiced law yet."

"Just say it."

"You're the world's best lawyer."

"God, you're easy." He laughed again.

"Doesn't Heather ever tell you those things?" Blaze asked.

He pulled his brows together. "No, she doesn't."

"Then why are you marrying her?"

"Want to know a little secret? Been asking myself that same question the last few weeks."

"Oprah says doubt means no. Maybe there's someone perfect right around the corner and you haven't realized it yet." *Or through the woods.*

[229]

"You think?"

"Yes."

"Well, about that haircut. How about tomorrow?"

"When?"

"I'm an early riser, so come at seven."

"Okay."

Rance

Rance rolled one way and then the other. Fluffed the pillow. Punched it down. Finally gave up and came to his feet. After seeing Seth and Chirp together all night, he couldn't sleep. What the hell was wrong with his brother? He'd get married soon, so why was he being so attentive to her? And on top of all that, she'd eaten it up. Talking. Dancing. Laughing. What had gotten into her?

She couldn't have a decent conversation with Rance, but she'd turned into a real Chatty Cathy with his younger brother. She'd looked so damn beautiful, she'd taken Rance's breath away. And Nick. Well, he'd not come home last night, so he'd probably gotten laid.

Coffee. Rance needed caffeine. He'd feel better once he had some. He glanced at the clock. Six forty-five.

No telling when baby brother would be home, and Seth was probably still sound asleep. All that dancing had to have worn him out.

Rance sauntered to the bathroom, took a quick shower, pulled on his jeans and new T-shirt, and headed to the kitchen. When he got to the end of the hall, he heard voices on the front porch. He strolled to a good vantage point and peered out. Chirp was cutting Seth's hair. What the fuck?

He watched as she ran her fingers through the strands, divided a section, and clipped. As she moved around his chair, Seth spread his legs wide for her to get closer. Dammit. A few more inches and his face would be between her breasts.

They were talking, but he couldn't hear what they were saying. He wished he could. She'd fallen into an easy friendship with Seth, and that bothered Rance. A lot. Maybe because of his strained situation with her, but he intended to change that. As soon as his brothers left he'd get the whole mess straightened out.

 Blaze

Blaze caught a glimpse of Rance out of the corner of her eye. "He's watching us."

"Good. Let him get an eyeful. I'll spread my legs apart and you move in closer."

"What's the use? It didn't work last night."

"Oh yeah, it did. He didn't have three sentences to say all the way home. He was pissed."

"Why are you doing this?"

"Because Rance deserves to be happy, and you make that happen."

"No, I don't."

"Yeah. You do. You're all he talks about when he calls."

"Really?"

"Yeah, really. Our dad was a lousy husband but an okay father. At least to me and Nick. Not so much with Rance. They haven't spoken in years. So, given that wrecked relationship, losing his mother at a young age, his fiancée dumping him for his best friend, and the time he spent behind bars, he has issues."

Blaze stepped back, eyed her work, and ran her hands through his hair one last time. "That's better."

"Want to hear something crazy?" Seth asked.

"What?"

"I don't want to go home."

"Then don't," Blaze said.

He chuckled. "Damn. I wish it was that simple."

"If I hire you as my lawyer, you can't repeat anything I tell you. Right?"

He narrowed his eyes. "Right. But money has to change hands. So give me a dollar before you confess."

She pulled a hundred-dollar bill from her pocket and handed it to him. "You're hired."

"Okay. So what do you want to tell me?"

"Nothing, now. But there may come a time when I do. When that happens you'll be there for me, right?"

"Absolutely."

Chapter 22

✦

Rance

Rance wanted to ask Seth what he and Chirp had been talking about, but decided not to. None of his business. If she'd taken a liking to his younger brother, then that got the pressure off him and things could get back to normal. According to Nick, Seth needed to break his engagement, so if his interest in Chirp made that happen, Rance should be happy. Should be, but he wasn't. Not by a long shot.

He poured his second cup of coffee as Seth came in from the porch all chipper, and it pissed him off more.

Seth took a mug from the cabinet, filled it, and turned to face his brother. "You're up early."

Rance scowled. "Nice haircut."

"Thought I'd take advantage of Blaze's skills. She did a good job."

"Yeah."

"What's wrong with you? Run out of Midol?"

"Fuck you, Seth."

"Whoa. What's this about?"

"You know damn well what it's about. She has no experience with guys. You're giving her the wrong impression."

"What? That I want to be her friend? Because she's clear on that subject."

"You don't know her like I do. She takes things the wrong way sometimes. You could hurt her."

"Well, I promise I won't."

"If you do, you'll answer to me."

"Noted. Now what's up for today?"

"If Nicky ever gets home, I thought we'd go knock down some cans. You brought your pistol, didn't you?" Rance asked.

"Yeah. Nick, too."

"Great. Later, we can drive to Danvers. They have a steak house I hear is pretty good."

"Okay. What if Nick wants to invite his new friend?"

"Fine by me."

"And if she wants Blaze to come?"

"Fine with that, too," Rance said.

[235]

"Are you sure?"

"Just spit it out, Seth."

"Last night you didn't seem happy about Blaze being there. So what's going on?"

Rance drained his cup and set it on the counter with more force than he intended. "We've had a misunderstanding. Nothing that can't be fixed when she comes back home."

"If you say so. I'm going to take a quick shower. By the time I'm done, maybe Nick will be here or at least checked in." Seth rinsed his cup, put it in the sink, then walked down the hallway.

Rance called after him because he was in a crappy mood and not ready to give Seth a free pass. "When did you plan to break the news about your bride not wanting me in the wedding?"

Seth stopped in his tracks and spun around. "I've been waiting for the right time. Guess Nick said something already."

"Let me go on record that I don't give a shit, but I got to say your bride-to-be sounds like a real bitch. So why are you marrying her?"

Seth ran his hand over his jaw and thinned his lips into a tight line. "Not sure anymore. In the process of trying to work that out."

Worry lines formed above his eyes, misery apparent, so Rance nodded and dropped it. Seth didn't move for a minute, clearly waiting for Rance to say more, but he didn't. No need to add to his brother's problem.

Taking a deep breath, Seth disappeared down the hall and into the bedroom, leaving Rance to deal with his own guilt. Truth was, Rance didn't want Chirp to go with them. Last night had been so awkward, he'd wanted to leave. Having her around while she focused on Seth put Rance in a foul mood. Wasn't jealous. Only concerned. She'd read too much into his kindness, and he didn't want the same thing to happen again with his brother. Okay, he *was* jealous. The way she'd laughed and danced was a different side he'd not seen. At least Seth didn't seem to know about the sex, but if Tiffany kept making subtle remarks, it wouldn't be long until both brothers figured it out.

When Seth came from the shower, there'd still been no word from Nick. The weekend wasn't turning out the way Rance had planned or hoped. Women. Fucking up everything.

"Would it bother you if Nick and I stayed longer?" Seth asked.

The question surprised Rance. He didn't think they were having much fun. Well, since Nick had hooked up with Tiffany, he was probably having a great time. She was a looker for sure and had latched on to him the minute she sat

[237]

down. "You're welcome to stay as long as you like. But I thought your bride had you on a tight schedule."

"Yeah, but I need a few more days to sort things out."

"You break it off with her, what happens to your job?"

"Goes down the drain."

"Apply at any other firms?"

"No, and Heather's dad can fix it where I won't be able to work anywhere in Houston. I have a lot to consider. My future depends on my marriage. And before you start in on me, I know it was a stupid mistake."

"Maybe so, but marrying someone you don't love would be worse. And you needing to *work things out*, tells me you're not in love with her."

Seth chuckled. "You may be right. Blaze said doubt means no. She also mentioned finding someone perfect."

Rance fisted his hands. "What'd I tell you? She takes things wrong."

"Settle down. She wasn't talking about herself. She's not interested in me. Hell, she won't even let me call her Chirp. Says only *you* get to do that. You see what's happening? If you're not careful, you're the one who'll hurt her."

Those words stabbed like a hot poker because they were already true. But as hard as Rance had tried to make things right, he couldn't bring her around. And how could he if she wouldn't come home? He wanted to explain how wrong he was for her, but couldn't do that without telling her he knew who she was and what she was worth. His snooping would hurt her even more. No, he wanted her to trust him enough to let him in on her secrets.

"I know," Rance said. "And I'm trying to avoid that, but it isn't working out so well." He considered telling his brother everything about her, but going behind her back would be a mistake.

Seth followed Rance to the back porch, then gazed across the pond at a line of turtles on a log taking in the sunshine. "You remember the song Dessie always sang to us when we were kids?"

Rance laughed. "The one with all the gibberish."

"Yeah. Damn, I love that silly song."

"Me too."

For the next two hours, Rance and Seth reminisced about their childhood. Then, just before noon, Nick came home.

"About time you showed up. We decided she must have you tied to the bed," Rance said.

"Naw. We talked most of the night. Fell asleep on the sofa."

"What? You didn't get any?" Rance asked.

"Nope. We made out, but that's as far as it went. I'll grab a shower and hit the sack for a few hours."

"You got plans with her tonight?"

"Yeah. She's cooking for me. Is that okay? I know I came to visit you, but . . ."

Rance cut him off. "It's fine, Nicky. Seth told me you haven't dated in a while, so go for it."

"Thanks."

"Hey," Seth said. "I guess if I wanted to stay longer, you'd be good with that?"

"Yeah," Nick agreed. "Do you?"

"Maybe until Wednesday."

"Works for me."

Seth grinned. "Yeah, I bet it does."

Once Nick grabbed a couple of hours of shut-eye, he was ready for target practice, so the three of them drove to the far side of the property. Rance hadn't been here since arriving in Bluebird. Dilapidated remnants of the deer stand he'd built years ago clung to an old oak tree. With his grandpa looking over his shoulder, Rance had killed the only buck he'd ever shot. Seeing the beautiful animal lying dead had turned him against the sport.

Still hunted ducks, quail, and squirrels, but couldn't bear the thought of killing another deer. He'd gotten the

Remington 243 for his thirteenth birthday. Damn, it'd been fifteen years. A lifetime ago.

Old hay rounds lined the back fence. Rance parked the truck, and Nick got out first, announcing, "I have the paper targets. Ordered special for us." He passed them to Seth.

Seth laughed as he unrolled the package. "You've got to be kidding. Zombies?"

Nick cocked his head. "The apocalypse can happen anytime. Besides, the two of you did serious damage to my psyche with all those movies."

Rance belly laughed. "I'd forgotten how funny that was."

"Funny, my ass. You tied me to a chair and forced me to watch a trifecta of horror."

"What were they?" Rance asked.

"Oh, I'll never forget. *Shaun of the Dead, Land of the Dead, and Dawn of the Dead.* I didn't sleep for weeks."

Seth pinched his cheek. "Poor baby."

Nick slapped his hand. "Just put up the damn targets and let me show you two how it's done." He unzipped his gun case and pulled out his weapon.

"Let me see that," Rance said. "Looks a little girly up beside my Smith & Wesson."

"I have you know the Sig Sauer Mosquito is the most popular twenty-two on the market right now," Nick told them.

Seth hoisted his pistol in the air. "Maybe so, but you can't go wrong with a Ruger."

Rance grabbed a bag of cans and put them in place, then joined Nick again, who was stretching his arms and popping his fingers.

"What the hell are you doing?" Seth asked.

Nick glared at him. "Loosening up."

"To pull a trigger? We're doing target practice, not rock climbing."

Rance couldn't remember when he'd enjoyed an afternoon more. Hearing his brothers' bust each other's balls made him happy. When Seth said they might stay longer, he wished they'd stay forever. Seth could open a small private practice in Danvers, and Nicky could coach at the local high school. Neither would ever get rich, but they'd never have ulcers either.

God, he'd missed them. Their visits, along with Gran's, were all that had kept him going in prison. In the first year, Gran had ridden the bus to Huntsville each month. After that, he'd asked her to stop because the eight-hour round trip was too much. Plus he hated she had to see him in that place.

By five o'clock Seth and Nicky had conceded to Rance. He'd always been a good shot, but he'd not practiced in years, so winning surprised him. He looked at Seth as they came to the edge of the woods.

"I'll take Nicky home so he can get ready for his hot date. Why don't you swing by to check on Chirp?" She was probably okay, but Rance couldn't help himself. He needed to make sure and figured she'd rather see Seth.

"Will do."

Rance brought the truck to a halt. Seth climbed out and took off toward Hanna's.

Blaze

Blaze had just finished spreading fresh hay for her nightly bed when a shadow passed through the light beaming across the opening. She whirled around. Muttly barked.

Seth stood in the doorway. "Hey."

"Why are you here?"

"Wanted to check on you. You doing all right?"

"Why wouldn't I be?"

He grinned. "No reason. But you're here all by your lonesome, so something could happen. Did you hear all that shooting?"

"Yeah. Rance texted earlier to warn me."

Seth shook his head. "Damn thoughtful of him, don't you think?"

She propped the pitchfork against the wall. "Yes."

"He's the one who sent me. He wants you to come home."

"Did he say that?"

"Not those exact words, but he does. You don't have to wait for Hanna to return. You can still come here to milk the goats."

"No. I don't think so."

"Come on, Blaze. He's pretty miserable without you. What do you say?"

She'd thought about the subject all day. Even if Rance asked her to come home and meant it, he still wouldn't love her. He didn't even want to have sex with her. And living under the same roof feeling about him the way she did wasn't a good idea. No. To get over him, she needed to stay away. Far away. "I'm invoking attorney-client privilege."

"Oh, okay."

"I'm never coming back to Dessie's. On Monday, I'm leaving Bluebird."

Chapter 23

SETH

Seth trailed the oak branch in the dirt, stopping now and again to whack at the weeds growing next to the ruts. Dammit to hell. Why had he accepted Blaze's money? It had seemed safe enough, but now she planned to leave, and he couldn't tell Rance.

No doubt when his brother found out, he'd never speak to him again. He could hold a grudge better than most. But considering all he'd been through, and the people who'd disappointed him, Seth couldn't blame him. He just didn't want to be added to the list.

His reason for staying extra days wasn't a lie. He needed to get his head straight about Heather, but more than that, he wanted to see Hanna. She was the one girl he'd never forgotten, and for months he'd thought more and more about her.

The way her skin looked in the moonlight. How she'd fit perfectly against him. The sound of his name on her lips. Oh God, how he'd loved that. No woman had ever said it the same way. Not even Heather, and she claimed to love him. And he thought he'd felt the same. But the closer the wedding got, the more he doubted it.

Nick was right. She planned every moment of Seth's life. Dictated when he could spend time with friends. Demanded his attention to things that didn't matter. He realized his mistake. It'd been over for months. The only thing left to do? End it.

Career suicide for sure. At least in Houston. But that'd been part of the problem. He'd gotten so caught up in her dad's fancy law firm and social status, he'd lost himself.

If he didn't have over a $100,000 in school loans, he could go into private practice. Hell, he already had a client. That made him laugh out loud. A weird runaway hairdresser. Yeah, she should bring in the big bucks, and he'd have that debt paid in no time.

He pulled his phone from his pocket and turned it on. By now Heather was pissed. But he'd grown tired of hearing the damn thing chime knowing she'd sent him some selfie with her uppity friends. All spoiled little rich girls and one loser guy.

Shouldn't think that way because he was no better. He'd promised his soul to be a part of that world, but he'd finally come to his senses. No need to put it off any longer. Time for a little Face Time with his betrothed.

Heather's response to his announcement of staying extra days in Bluebird surprised him, but it shouldn't. She'd flown to Vegas with her gay guy friend. Not unusual. She dropped everything to fly to New York, Paris, wherever she wanted on short notice. He doubted she'd ever find it necessary to use her degree in English, a language she'd been speaking since she could talk, but hey, a degree was a degree if that's all a person wanted.

She wasn't dumb, just unmotivated. No reason to be. She'd had everything given to her. Her goal in life was to wear the latest fashions and appear in the society pages at least once a week. And she was successful at both.

He looked up and saw Rance standing on the front porch. "Took you long enough."

"Sorry, I stopped to call Heather about staying longer."

"How'd that go?"

Seth tilted his head. "Pretty good."

"So, how was Chirp?"

"Doing fine. Her, the dog, and the goats. You should go over there and talk to her. Fix whatever the problem is between you."

"Why? Did she say something?"

Damn. Seth wanted to tell him she planned to leave. But he couldn't. All he could do was encourage Rance and hope it took. "No. But she doesn't seem the type to make the first move, so you should."

"Oh, take my word, she can make the first move when she wants. Besides, I've already tried to reason with her. She'll be back on Monday and we'll hash it out."

No, she won't. "I see my truck's gone, so I guess Nick's left already."

"Yeah. He hightailed it out of here pretty quick. You still want to go to the steak house?"

"Sure, if you do. There's rain in the forecast, so we should hit the road."

Tom Fraser

Tom Fraser gasped for air. It'd been too long since he'd had sex, but damn if it wasn't as good as he remembered.

Helga ran her palm across his chest. "You okay?"

He laid his hand on top of hers. "Better than okay. You?"

"I'm downright giddy."

"Good to know I haven't lost my touch."

"Well, I don't have a before and after comparison, but based on this one performance, I'd give you a gold star."

She giggled, and Tom loved the sound. He'd always appreciated younger women and even fantasized about them now and then, but in reality he would never make a move on one. He needed a woman with patience in case his execution took longer than normal. Thankfully, that hadn't been the case. Turned out, the thought of making love with Helga caused everything to work like he was forty again.

"I have a confession," Tom said.

"Oh no. That's four words a woman never wants to hear right after sex."

He chuckled. "Nothing bad. I haven't slept with anyone since my wife, so I was nervous. Crazy, huh? You'd think at my age I'd have the bedroom stuff down."

"Believe me, you have it down." Helga laughed again.

Damn, he liked this woman. A lot. And he sure as hell didn't want this to be a one-time thing. "I don't want you to stop seeing me because of the Montgomery case."

She sat up, propped a pillow behind her back, and pulled up the sheet to cover her breasts. And they were beautiful. Full, rounded, still firm for a woman over fifty.

"You've found her, haven't you?"

He sat up, too, and took her hands in his. "I think so." What came next caught him off guard.

Helga burst into tears. "You'll ruin her life."

He pulled her to him and spoke into her hair. Thick and red, it smelled so damn good it made him dizzy. "No. I won't. I promise I'll help the kid all I can, yet still do my job."

She gazed up at him, and that luscious bottom lip quivered. "You swear?"

He couldn't stand it any longer, so he took her mouth. And when she pulled away, he groaned. "I swear on a stack of Bibles and the constitution. You've got to trust me on this."

"How did you find her?"

"Been monitoring the reward website. Somebody from Bluebird, Texas, did a search. The IP address belongs to an old woman. With everything I've learned about the girl, it seems logical."

"What do you mean?"

"Obscure town and an old woman with no connection."

"Have you told Marla?"

"No, and I won't until I'm sure. I'm going down there next week."

"And if she's there? What happens next?"

"I'll send my report to Mrs. Montgomery, but who knows? The kid might be gone again before Marla gets it."

[251]

Chapter 24

Rance

By the time Rance and Seth had finished dinner, swung by Walmart, and left Danvers, it was almost eleven o'clock. Little brother had been quiet during the meal, and Rance figured it had to do with the soon-to-be ex-fiancée. Even though Rance had never met her, he was glad Seth had decided to break it off. Earlier Seth had explained if he ever wanted to work in Houston, he had to come up with a way to make her think ending the engagement was her idea. Wasn't sure how he'd go about that, but he was brainstorming.

The best plan so far was for Seth to put his foot down about including Rance in the wedding. He wasn't sure it'd be enough. No doubt she'd throw a fit, but to save face, she'd probably agree.

There'd been something else, too. Seth had insisted on buying a new computer and small television. Rance pointed out those were things Seth could get at home, but for a guy with no job, he'd never seen his brother so adamant.

When they got back to the farmhouse, Rance helped unload the boxes. Once inside, Seth carried his carton to Chirp's bedroom, where he'd been sleeping.

The door banged closed behind Rance, and he yelled, "Hey, don't take the stuff in there. It'll be easier to load into your truck from here."

"No, there's plenty of room in the closet. It's empty except for my clothes."

The wind picked up outside and whistled down the chimney. A loud clash of thunder jarred the house. Rance set the TV on the kitchen counter and sprinted down the hall. "What you mean empty? Chirp has her stuff in there. I know she doesn't have much . . ." He stopped short and glared at the space.

"Nope. As you can see. Plenty of room." Seth slid his box across the carpet.

This didn't make sense. The lights flickered off then back on, much in the same way Rance's brain was processing the discovery, jumping from one thought to the next. Sure, she was upset, but she'd never move in with Hanna. There was no room for her there. He rushed to the bathroom and opened the cabinets. Empty. He flew to the chair, reached behind it, and lifted the paint can. No need to open it, he could tell from the weight the money was gone.

[253]

He rejoined Seth and stared at the blank space. "I don't get it. She's only supposed to stay at Hanna's until Monday. Why would she take everything?"

"Beats me. Guess you'll have to ask her."

A vein throbbed below Rance's ear as a terrible idea popped into his head. Rance slumped down onto the bed. "She's not coming back."

Seth turned to face him. "That can't be right. Can it?"

Rance didn't answer. Just sat in heavy silence.

"Rance?"

He rose and shoved his hands into his pockets. "Hell, if she wants to leave, fine. I don't give a rat's ass."

"I think you do. Go after her. Fix whatever is going on between the two of you. It can't be that bad."

Rance hung his head. "I slept with her. Okay? I thought it was recreational. She didn't."

Seth sat, too. "Damn. We're a pair aren't we? I'm trying to get rid of my woman and you're trying to get yours to stay. You'd think we could solve each other's problem. Don't know about you, but I don't have a clue."

"Guess we should ask Nicky. He seems to have his shit together."

At three o'clock the next morning, Rance was still wide awake. Outside, another storm brewed. Low rumbles moved closer. But it wasn't the weather keeping him from sleep. It was Chirp and the fact she'd taken all her belongings. Well, he'd had enough.

He took time to brush his teeth, slipped his feet into his boots, and grabbed his truck keys. By God, if she wanted to move out, she could, but not until they settled things.

In ten minutes, he was in Hanna's drive. No lights shone anywhere except for a dim glow in the barn. As the drizzle turned to a downpour, he ran inside.

Blaze

Thunder had Blaze hunkered down in the corner of the stall, clutching Muttly so tight the dog squirmed for air. There'd been a flash of light, and she wasn't sure if it was the weather or someone in the drive. Either way, she wasn't budging. Earlier, she'd turned on the battery-operated lantern so it wouldn't be so scary.

The barn door flew open, and even in darkness, she recognized Rance. Six feet two of solid muscle and testosterone. She tried to speak, but her words came out shaky. "What are you doing here?"

In three long strides, he was in the stall, looming over her. "You've punished me enough, Chirp. It's time to come home."

She ignored the gruffness in his voice and hugged Muttly tighter. "I told you . . ."

He pointed his finger. "Just listen. I'm sorry for everything. I want you to come home because I miss you." The soft glow cast most of his face in shadow, but she still saw the determination of his strong jaw.

He held out his hand, and without thinking, she released Muttly and slid her palm into Rance's. He pulled her up and against his chest. "I want you to stop being mad at me. If you want us to be together, I'm good with that. But I'm not the right man for you. At least not long-term. Understand?"

His eyes were dark and dilated, and she could tell he meant business. She wasn't about to argue. Besides, he'd finally said most of what she wanted to hear, so she settled for that.

"Chirp? You still want me, right?"

She struggled to find her voice, but that was impossible with her heart lodged against her windpipe.

"I can't stop thinking about you. Worrying about you. I've already brushed my teeth." Then he kissed her long and deep. And she melted into him.

He pushed away and locked eyes with her. "I have a few rules."

Still unable to put a sentence together, she nodded.

"We're not rushing this time, and I'm in charge. If I want to stop, we stop. You got that?"

Another nod.

"Good. And when we're having sex, you don't get to use anatomy terms. No *penis*. No *vagina*. Unless you want my dick to go limp. Okay?"

The way he looked at her caused a fire to ignite in the pit of her stomach. "Uh-huh."

He dipped his head and pressed his lips to her throat just below her ear. "You were right. You can't get better at sex unless you keep practicing. I shouldn't have said what I did. It was mean. That's what happens when I don't take time to think about stuff before I speak. Forgive me?"

"Yes, and I'll try harder."

He slid his mouth across her cheek. "It wasn't your fault. It's my job to make it good for you. And I will."

Her lips parted, and he fed her a hot, wet, carnal kiss that brought her to the balls of her feet. He slid one hand around her waist, the other past the elastic of her pajamas and into her panties, where he stroked her. "Sweet Jesus, Chirp."

Thunder rumbled overhead and rain hammered the roof. She ran her hands under his shirt, feeling muscle and bone. "Your clothes are wet. Take them off."

"You do it."

She pressed closer and unbuttoned his jeans. He toed out of his boots and let the Levi's drop to the floor.

He'd gone commando and already had an erection. He was as magnificent as the Greek bronze warriors she'd seen at the Museo Nazionale della Magna Grecia in Italy when she was nine.

Dropping to his knees, he reached for his jeans. "Damn. I didn't get my wallet. I don't have a condom."

"Any chance you have an STD?"

"No."

"Okay." She shimmied out of her pj's and panties, then kissed him again.

He pulled her onto his lap. She clutched his shoulders for support. Her skin caught fire and her nipples tightened. An ache settled between her legs. She leaned away.

"Second thoughts?" He asked.

"No." She grabbed the hem of her shirt and tore it off.

He tortured one peaked nipple with his tongue, and she shivered.

With perfect precision, he slipped a finger inside her. Then two.

"Oh, Chirp, you're ready for me. So fucking wet."

And she was. It'd be different this time. She wasn't a virgin anymore, and she had one encounter under her belt. No man had ever talked to her like this, and the rasp of his voice made her blood heat. And as it raced through her veins, it set every part of her on fire. She rocked against him, adjusting her body to get his fingers in the right spot, and when she did, a whimper escaped before she could stop it. He worked her. In and out. Around and around, driving her to madness. And when the orgasm struck with such force, she panted his name.

He started to withdraw, but she put her hand over his. "Not yet." She moved against him again, and within seconds another climax shook her to her core. Deeper this time. She buried her face in the hollow of his neck and sobbed.

"What's wrong?"

"Nothing. I don't know why I'm crying."

He eased her onto the hay and lay next to her, taking her mouth again. "It's okay. I imagine back-to-back orgasms can do that to a girl." He chuckled, a low, mellow tone that caused her toes to curl and raised goose bumps everywhere.

"Now, where were we?" He rolled to all fours and hovered above her, then ran his tongue between her breasts.

[259]

This had to be a dream, but when he scraped his teeth over her skin, she squealed. *Not a dream.*

He trailed his way down to her stomach, where he flicked the silver heart dangling from her belly button back and forth with his tongue. "Sexy."

"Thank you."

He laughed out loud, his hot breath spreading across her skin as he moved lower, and she rose to her elbows. "What are you doing?" she asked.

He flashed her a wicked smile. "Your word for today is cunnilingus. It means dine at the Y. Eat a peach. Tongue fuck."

"Stop talking. I know what it means."

He laughed harder. "Yeah, well I'm about to give you a new appreciation of vocabulary."

She went perfectly still. The thought of his tongue—there—turned her bones to ash. But she'd agreed to let him be in charge. And then he hit home with his first stroke. She dug both hands into the hay and lost herself in the passion. Everything faded away except the roaring in her head. She writhed against him, feeling every delicious lash. Over and over again until she came undone.

He kissed his way back up her body and placed his lips next to her ear. "Now, let's hear you use that in a sentence."

She gasped for breath.

[260]

"Come on. You're about to get the main event, but not until I hear you use the word. So make it a good one."

Her whole body shook, and she thought she might have a coronary. But if she was going to die, she wanted it to be in his arms. "Okay. Rance is good at cunnilingus."

She loved how his lip quirked up at the corner when he fought a smile. "Not your best work, but I'll give you a pass."

"Thank you."

He nudged her thighs apart with his knee and leaned next to her ear to whisper. "And, no, I'm not brushing my teeth again. It turns me on to know you'll taste your own juice."

"Why do you have to talk so nasty?"

"Because you like it."

She should be repulsed. But she wasn't. Not by a long shot. She loved every filthy word. She kissed him with a fierceness she didn't recognize.

He deepened the kiss, and the dirty dance of his tongue made her think of where it'd been and the pleasure it'd caused. She licked inside his mouth, and when they parted, he laughed. "I thought so. Open your eyes." He slid inside her. A little at first, then more. "Oh yeah. Slick and tight."

Before he moved again, he raised his brows as if to ask if she was okay. She bit her bottom lip. "More, please."

There was that wicked grin. "Oh, baby. So polite."

Then he gave her more, and she responded by arching up to bring him closer. Deeper. She heaved the word out. "More."

"I'm not hurting you, am I?"

"No."

"Good, because you feel so fucking good, Chirp." He thrust harder.

Gaze never wavering, she dug fingers into his hips and bucked against him. "All of it, please."

A low growl came from deep in his throat. "Since the other night, all I've thought about was how good you felt wrapped around my cock."

His words made her dizzy with desire. His touch rendered her senseless. Nothing mattered. Only him. Flesh pressed against flesh. His big hands moving over her.

He cupped her hips, tilted them until he stroked high into her. How did he already know how her body worked? He pressed, and she arched. He gave, and she took. And when she couldn't stand it anymore, she shattered, locking her legs around him until he emptied into her.

They stayed that way for a long time, their bodies jerking with aftershocks. Lying pressed against him, Blaze closed her eyes. She loved him. More than she'd ever loved anyone. Now her only problem—how to get him to love her back.

Chapter 25

Rance

For the first time in a while, Rance woke with a smile on his face. Last night all his macho bullshit about cuddling had been shot to hell when he'd wanted Chirp pinned right next to him. He loved feeling the rhythm of her breathing against his chest.

Barn. Hay. Storm. Mind-blowing sex with an almost virgin. First time he'd had that combination. Hell, a screen writer couldn't have written a more perfect scene.

A few stalls over, she hummed as she worked. The sounds of a satisfied lover. And she had been, multiple times. It'd been years since he'd gone down on a woman, so he was glad to know he hadn't lost his touch.

Today she'd come home with him and forget all about leaving. And she understood the arrangement. Just sex. No strings. No promises.

In the corner of the stall, his clothes were stacked and folded. *Little Miss OCD strikes again.* He got dressed and went to join her. Busy with the goats, she didn't notice him, so he cleared his throat.

"Need help?"

She turned to face him. All bright-eyed and glowing. Damn, if she hadn't gotten more beautiful overnight. "Do you know how to milk goats?"

"Never done it, but how hard can it be? All I do is wrap my fingers around a teat and squeeze, right?"

She took her bottom lip between her teeth. "You even make that sound nasty."

He chuckled. "Not my intention, but I can see it got you going." He raised his brows as he zeroed in on the front of her T-shirt, where her nipples stood at attention.

Crossing her arms, she covered both breasts. "You're terrible."

In two short strides, he captured her in his embrace. "That's not what you said last night. I remember you telling me how good I was. Several times."

She looked up at him. "You were good." Tiptoeing to reach his mouth, she kissed him like she meant it. Then her hands were everywhere. Under his shirt. At the top of his jeans. Lowering his zipper. And when she slipped her hand inside his boxers and circled his erection, he groaned. God help him. She was killing him.

Abandoning her mouth, he trailed his lips to her breast and tortured the nipple through the thin fabric. He'd never wanted a woman the way he did her, and that was wrong. But with her wrapped around him, it was impossible to wrap his brain around logic.

Within minutes, he had her naked, back in the hay going at him like a wild animal. And once he delivered her first orgasm, he twisted her beneath him, and she welcomed him inside her small body. When he finally broke the connection, she whimpered as if he'd taken part of her with him. He fell back onto the hay gasping. "Damn, Chirp. When we get home, I want you to move into my room."

"Okay."

He rolled to his elbow and traced a finger down her cheek. "Now talk to me."

Her warm breath floated across his chest. "About what?"

"Everything. What you're running from. Who's after you? All of it. Whatever it is, I'll protect you."

At first he didn't think she would say anything. But then she began. When she finished, he lay quiet for a moment, dealing with the part that bothered him most.

Finally, he spoke. "So, in December when you turn twenty-one, you're going back to Houston."

"Yes. I don't have a choice. Uncle Bill wants to retire, so even if I don't want to run the company, I'll have to pick someone to take over."

"Can you do it? I mean, it's a big job and you . . ."

"Why? Because I'm a woman?"

"No, that's not it. You don't have experience is what I meant."

"Dad and I talked about this before he died. You're right. I'll need help, but it was his dying wish, and I promised."

One thing missing from her story was the can of cash he'd found in her room. Wasn't sure why. Maybe she didn't completely trust him or figured he already knew. Either way, he'd heard the fear in her voice. Running a company was the last thing she wanted, but she was right. Her dad had built it from the ground up, and he'd want her involved. Rance shifted the conversation. "Never slept with an heiress before."

Her brows scrunched together. "Heiress. Sounds funny."

"You mean you've never thought of yourself that way?"

"No."

"Guess that comes from always having money."

She had a strange look but said nothing. Rance wondered what was going on in her head. He couldn't always tell with her, so he dropped it. "Why were you taking my picture earlier?"

"I thought you were asleep."

"Dozing."

"I like taking pictures of you."

"Naked?"

"Yes."

"Why? They won't show up on the Internet, will they?"

She rolled her eyes. "Your body is beautiful. I like to sketch you. They're just for me."

He sat up and stretched. "Well, we'd better take care of these goats and get you home." Busy- work. He needed it, because when she'd told him that in eight months she'd leave, something had twisted in his gut. Come this time next year, she'd be back in her world of money and power, and he'd still be here. Alone.

Blaze

Blaze heard it in Rance's voice when he'd said the word *heiress*, and again when he drew the conclusion about her wealth. Somehow he thought less of himself because of it. He had no reason. It was true, she'd never struggled financially, but money didn't mean anything to her. Even with a big bank account, Dad had taught her not to flaunt her affluence. He'd set a good example by giving much of his wealth away, and she planned to continue his legacy.

She hated the company was in Houston. Because of that she saw no future with Rance. He'd made it clear Bluebird would always be his home. She'd make it hers too, if he asked.

God, she sounded like the lovesick women on every cheesy soap opera Helga had watched. Shaking the ridiculous notion away, Blaze returned the chippy stool to the counter and wrote the date on the milk container before sliding it into the cooler.

Outside, Rance threw a stick and tried to get Muttly to fetch. He wasn't having much luck. The dog kept rolling over, wanting his belly rubbed. Blaze couldn't help but laugh. She liked it when Rance rubbed her, too.

He stepped inside. "You ready?"

"Am I a slut?"

He bent with laughter, holding his sides.

"Not funny. There's something wrong with me. Sex is all I think about, and that can't be normal." She slumped onto a stool. "I've always been odd, and now I'm a sex maniac, too."

Rance tried to straighten, but he was laughing too hard.

"Stop it. This is your fault. With your big penis, and your magic tongue, and your nasty talk."

He crossed the room, pulled her into his arms, and got control. "You're fucking adorable. That's what you are." Then he tilted her chin until she met his gaze. "Everybody goes a little nuts when they have great sex. Trust me, you're as normal as it gets in that department."

"Are you sure?"

"Hell yeah. We'll go to town and buy a copy of Cosmo. It's bound to have an article that will set you straight."

Chapter 26

SETH

Even as a boy, walking through these woods calmed Seth. A bee buzzed around his head and brought him back to the route he was following. The cool morning air. Sunlight winking through the trees. The sounds of the forest. Man, how he wished to go back to those carefree days if only for a little while.

He'd played out this scene in his head a thousand times, but now his stomach knotted. Who was he kidding? With Hanna's beauty, she'd probably had a dozen lovers since him. No way would she still be carrying a torch—or a grudge.

He swung the door wide. She looked up, and her breath caught. The same sound she'd always made right before she came apart in his arms. She was even more beautiful than he remembered.

"Hey, Hanna."

"What are you doing here?"

She was stirring something in a bowl. Bottles of different sizes lined the counter. The place smelled of lavender and something else. Coconut. "Nick and I came to visit Rance."

Hanna's eyes darkened, and she swallowed hard. "I know that. I meant what are you doing *here?*"

The tone of her voice warned him he wasn't welcome. But he couldn't let that change his plans. "I wanted to see you."

"After all these years? Why?"

"Lately, I've been thinking about you, and I . . ."

She cut him off. "Why in the world would you do that when you thought so little of me before?"

He advanced on her, and she stood her ground. No longer a fragile, innocent teenager, she glared at him. Maybe he wasn't the only guy who'd hurt her. "That isn't true. I've always thought about you."

She stopped mixing. "What do you want from me, Seth? Forgiveness? Absolution for taking my virginity? Letting me believe I meant something to you?" She put her palm in front of him and made the sign of the cross. "You're absolved. Go on with your life."

He reached out to take her hand, but she backed away.

"You did mean something to me."

That got a humorless laugh from her. "Once a liar, always a liar. You should leave. I have someone in my life now and if he finds you here, I'll have to explain more than I want." She turned her back and shuffled pans on a shelf.

"Well, if you're so in love, why are you still pissed at me? What happened between us shouldn't matter anymore."

She spun on him, tears streaking down her cheeks. "I loved you! You were my first love! My first everything! FYI, a girl never gets over that." She swiped at her nose.

He couldn't stand it anymore. He rushed around the counter and took her in his arms.

She jerked away. "Oh, I understand. Thought you'd get a little *stray* before you tie the knot? And who else better than easy Hanna, right? Well, I'm not so easy anymore."

He shoved his hands into his pockets. "I never thought that. What did you want from me? I was eighteen." God, he'd said it like that fixed everything, but from the way she was shaking, it didn't.

"What'd I want? A phone call. Text. Letter. Anything to make me feel as if I mattered. I waited, Seth. Weeks. Months. You used me and then pretended it never happened."

He took another step forward, but she stepped back again. He jammed his hands deeper to fight the urge to hold her. "You mattered. It's just I was in Houston. You were here. Living five hours away, I didn't see how we could . . ."

"How we could what? Keep screwing? Yeah, you're right. That was impossible, which made it clear that's all you wanted. I meant nothing more than a good time."

He couldn't fight it any longer. He wrapped her in his arms again, holding her tighter this time. The memory of her beneath him flooded back with such force he thought his chest would explode. "That isn't true. Every time I came to visit Dessie, I tried to see you, but you were always conveniently out of town. Seems you were avoiding me."

She broke free and glared with so much hate, he staggered backward. Her words dripped with venom. "Go home, Seth. There's nothing for you here." She pushed past him and slammed the shop's door behind her, leaving him alone. Within seconds, he heard another wood-splintering crash as she went into the house.

This didn't go the way he'd expected. God, he'd hurt her more than he thought. She was right. He hadn't spoken to her after he'd left that summer. But not for lack of trying. Hell, she didn't even come to Dessie's service. Why put this all on him? He didn't get it.

He stepped out into the sunshine and headed home, kicking rocks as he walked. When he got back to the farmhouse, he found Rance in the laundry room.

"Where'd you run off to so early?"

"Hanna's."

"Really?"

"Yeah. A long time ago, she and I had a thing."

Rance finished stuffing clothes into the washer, added the detergent, and closed the lid. "Where was I when this *thing* was going on?"

"It was the summer your trouble started."

"She have anything to do with your decision about Heather?"

Seth raked his hands through his hair. He'd not been sure until today, and now it was too late. "Doesn't matter. She made it pretty clear she hates my guts."

"Why?"

"I never called after I left. But in my defense, the next summer when I came for a visit, I tried to see her, but she'd gone to her grandmother's." Okay, maybe that wasn't a good excuse. He had waited a year, but long-distance relationships didn't work.

"So, you're saying to hell with it?"

"I guess. What I don't understand is why she's still mad. Claims to be serious about a guy, so our past shouldn't matter."

"I thought you were leaving today," Blaze interrupted.

"Decided to stay a little longer."

Rance straightened. "Hey, what are you doing home so early?"

"No bodies."

He went to stand next to her and spoke to Seth again. "No way she's serious about the guy. She told me he'd proposed, but she hadn't accepted, and that was weeks ago. Unless you saw an engagement ring, she still hasn't."

Seth glanced at Blaze, who had an odd expression. "Then why say that?" he asked.

Blaze averted her eyes. "I don't know."

Seth had taken part in enough mock trials to read body language. "I think you do. So what's up?"

She fiddled with her hair, twirling a spiked strand in her fingers. "Maybe to get rid of you."

Rance nodded and draped an arm around her shoulders. "Makes sense. If she's involved, no need for you to see her again."

"Probably shouldn't anyway." Seth said.

Blaze shook her head. "No!"

Her outburst caused Seth to flinch. "Why not?"

"You shouldn't give up."

"Appreciate the encouragement, but she practically threw me out. Can't go back. She was leaving for work."

"You should go there. To the Quickie Mart. She can't make a customer leave. She works until midnight. Did you tell her you weren't getting married?"

"Didn't really get the chance."

"You should tell her. And if you still like her, tell her that, too."

Before Seth could say anything else, Blaze turned and walked away.

He looked at Rance. "What do you think?"

"If you still have feelings for her, then Chirp is right. Go for it." Rance's phone chimed. He read the text, then smiled. "I'm needed in the bedroom."

"You remember the lecture you gave me about hurting her? You're on dangerous ground."

Rance laid a hand on his brother's shoulder. "Anytime you're between a woman's legs, it's dangerous. She understands our relationship. I made sure of that before I brought her back home." He strolled away.

Seth sauntered out to the back porch. Hanna confused him. She'd cried. Women didn't cry over men they hated. They screamed. Cursed. Threw shit. She'd overreacted, and that didn't make sense. He came to his feet. He fished keys out of his pocket and quietly closed the door behind him. Blaze was right. Hanna couldn't kick out a paying customer, so that's what he'd be.

Hanna

Two hours into her shift, Hanna still felt sick. Why hadn't Seth left? And why had he come to see her? Stupid. He wanted one last fling before giving up his freedom. Even though she still loved him, she'd never let that happen.

Regardless of how Seth had treated her, he deserved to know his son. But after what Blaze had said about Heather, Hanna couldn't bring herself tell him. Not yet. She'd fantasized about Seth spending time with Noah, but according to Blaze, his new wife would be against it. She'd hire a nanny so she and Seth could socialize. So what would be the point? Child support? Sure, she could get money out of him, but that wasn't what she wanted. No need to worry. After how she'd treated him, he had probably left by now and her secret was safe for a while longer.

She turned her attention back to the candy rack she was refilling and thought of more logical things. Like contacting more businesses about her soap line. Another order had arrived from a boutique in Houston, so that was encouraging. The Facebook page was paying off. But she had to give credit to Blaze. The wrappers she'd designed were real eye-catchers.

Hanna discarded the empty box and moved to the next one. Since the festival was over, the town was dead. If business continued to be slow, she'd get all the stocking done before her shift ended. She loved when that happened. The door chimed, putting an end to her musings. She slid the carton aside and called over her shoulder, "Come in."

The customer went down the next aisle, so Hanna tossed the empty box into the storeroom behind the register. When she turned around, Seth stood before her. He handed her a family-size bag of chips and a jar of salsa.

Her heart jumped into her throat, and she struggled to get the words out. "Will this be all for you, sir?"

"I believe so." He pulled his wallet from his back pocket.

She rang the sale and bagged it. "That'll be seven dollars and thirty-three cents."

He slid a ten-dollar bill to her.

Instead of handing him the change, she placed it on the counter. "Thank you."

He turned to go, then hesitated. "You know what? I should get something to drink with this."

He left the purchases, walked to the refrigerated case, and returned with a soda.

"Will this be all, sir?" And there was that damn smile again. Her knees weakened.

"I think so."

She put the money in the register. "Thanks."

"On second thought, I might want something sweet after I eat this." He disappeared around the corner and came back with two candy bars.

"Will *this* be all, sir?"

"Not sure. Let me think a minute." He folded his arms across his chest, looked up, and tapped his foot.

She didn't need this aggravation. "Milk, bread, eggs?"

He shook his head.

"Cereal, butter, cheese?"

"No."

"Athlete's foot powder, hemorrhoid suppositories?"

That got a laugh from him, and God, how she'd always loved his laugh.

"Now we're talking."

She fought a smile. "What does that mean?"

"It means we're talking, and that's what I want. For us to talk. Without anger. Without hate. Can we do that?"

"I never said I hated you." Her stomach rumbled, and she didn't know if it was from hunger or misery.

"Good to know, because from our earlier conversation, I would have sworn you did."

"Well, I don't. So you can go home now."

"Okay." He gathered his bags and left.

Hanna braced against the wall and hung her head. *No, Seth. I don't hate you. I hate myself because I'm still in love with you.* She rushed to the window and found the parking lot empty. *Thank God.*

For the next few hours, her mind ping-ponged between her soap business and Seth, with him winning most of the time. She wanted to hate him but couldn't. It had taken every ounce of willpower not to throw him to the floor and rip off his clothes. She'd reached a new low. Lusting for another woman's man. He belonged to someone else, and she needed to accept that.

Someday she'd confess, but not now. Not when he was about to start his life with *Heather.* Note to self: *throw out all heather essential oils. Don't want to be reminded of Seth's wife every time you make soap.*

At eleven-thirty, the owner, Mr. Ross, showed up to help close. She checked the sales, and he took out the trash. When he came back inside, he joined her at the register.

"Slow tonight, huh?"

She studied the detail tape, then wrapped it around the bundle of bills. "Real slow. Only thirty-one customers all night."

"People are still recovering from the festival. It'll pick up again in a day or two. Why don't you go on home? I'll lock up."

"Okay. See you tomorrow." Hanna grabbed her purse from the back room and headed to her car, parked behind the building. When she rounded the corner, she saw Seth leaning against her fender.

"I noticed you have a flat, so thought I'd offer you a ride home."

She jerked her head toward the Chevy. Dad had been after her for months to get new tires. She should have listened. "That's okay. I'll call Tiffany."

"She and Nick are on a date. No need to interrupt them. Besides, I'm already here. Just get in the truck. I'll have you home safe and sound in no time."

He had a point, but the last thing she wanted was to be alone with him. "Not a good idea."

"Why?"

"Just isn't."

"Have it your way, then." He walked to his vehicle.

He was right. She shouldn't depend on Tiffany, and she hated to wake her parents. "Okay. It's only a ride. Right?" *Oh, God. Don't grin. Don't grin. Don't grin. Damn.* His lips curled into the most delicious smile, and her knees weakened again. She ran her hand along the hood to steady herself, then opened the door and crawled inside.

He backed out of the parking lot, pulled forward, then stopped. "You hungry?"

"No." Her stomach betrayed her and growled.

He chuckled. "I think you are. Burgers and Fries is still open. Let's swing by."

"That isn't necessary. I can get something at home. We'll be there in fifteen minutes."

He turned onto the highway. "Come on, Hanna. I'm leaving tomorrow. Spend a little time with me."

"Why?"

"Because we have unfinished business."

If you only knew.

Chapter 27

Hanna

Hanna placed her hand against her chest. *Unfinished business?* A light bulb came on in her head. "You let the air out of my tire, didn't you?"

Seth looked at her, and his lip quirked up. "Yes."

"So you're kidnapping me."

"Not hardly. You got in of your own free will."

God, she wanted to slap that grin off his face. Or kiss it off. Yeah, that sounded better. "Only because you tricked me."

"Guilty. But still—didn't force you."

"Why? And what unfinished business could we possibly have?"

He ignored the question and whipped the truck into the drive-through lane. "You want the Bluebird burger with mayo, no onions, no pickles, and a vanilla coke. Right?"

[284]

She blinked. "You remember?"

He licked his lips. "I remember—*everything*."

So did she, and that was the problem. He was about to marry someone else and all Hanna wanted to do was screw his brains out. But she couldn't let that happen for a multitude of reasons. He didn't belong to her. And, more importantly, she wasn't wearing sexy underwear.

In all of her Seth sex fantasies, she'd worn a hot-pink cheeky panty and matching French-cup bra. He'd been so eager to get her out of them, he'd ripped them off. She was a terrible person. Lusting for an unavailable man. She didn't know which was worse—shame or desire, because those two emotions were battling it out.

"So, Blaze says you're about to start a new job with a big law firm. Congratulations."

He placed the order and moved to the next window to pay. "That's not going to work out."

"Oh, I'm sorry. I thought you'd already been hired."

"I believe everything happens for a reason. Like the timing of my visit here."

"What does that mean?"

He drove forward again, got their food, turned back onto the highway and headed south. "I've been trying to sort some things out and coming here helped me do that. Quiet time in the country cleared my head."

[285]

"That's good, I guess."

"Blaze told me you have a project going with bath products. I figure that's what you were doing earlier. Right?"

"Yeah. I'm trying to get it off the ground but not having much luck."

Hanna noticed her surroundings and panicked. "Where are we going?"

"Back forty. Did some target practice there the other day. Thought it'd be a quiet spot where we could talk."

Sitting with him under a full moon and starlit sky would only add fuel to her burning desire and misery. "I should get home."

Too late. He'd already made the turn and within minutes, he parked, then handed her the sack. She'd lost her appetite. Why wasn't he going to work for his soon-to-be father-in-law? What had he been trying to sort out? Her brain flooded with questions, but she didn't dare ask. The best thing to do was eat her hamburger and get away from him as fast as she could. Because being this close to her only lover, her son's dad, the man who still owned her heart, was taking its toll.

"Are you all right?" Seth asked. "You've hardly touched your food."

"I was more tired than hungry. It's been a long day."

He reached into the back seat, found a blanket, and handed it to her. "Come on. Let's look at the stars."

"No. Take me home, please."

He reached over and unsnapped her seat belt. "Oh, come on. Let's go back in time. Remember how we gazed at the stars that summer?"

Of course she remembered. That's why she needed to get away from him. She drew a staggering breath and closed her eyes. "Why are you doing this?"

"What?"

"You know what. Please, just take me home."

"Not until I find out."

SETH

He cupped her face and crushed his lips down on hers. She clutched his shirt to bring him closer. God help him. Nothing had changed. He remembered how her sweet, warm mouth had welcomed his kisses so many times. Every time. *This time.*

Suddenly she jerked away, and her words came in a whisper full of pain. "Don't do that. You're getting married."

"No, I'm not." And in that moment, everything became clear. This is why he couldn't marry Heather. He'd never gotten over Hanna.

She looked up at him. "What?"

"I'm not getting married. The wedding is off. I don't love her. Hell, I don't even like her. I love you. I always have."

She covered her face and sobbed.

He gathered her in his arms and spoke into her hair. "And you love me. I wasn't sure until that kiss, but I am now."

Hanna drew one ragged breath after another, then stared up at him. "You can't say that unless you mean it. I won't survive losing you again."

"You'll never lose me. I swear." Seth's fingers speared into her hair, holding her face just right for him to devour her mouth again. God, he loved her mouth and everything else.

She planted her hands on his chest and worked the buttons of his shirt. Fast and frenzied, she undid them all, then grasped the zipper of his jeans. "I want you, Seth. I want you so much."

He pulled away. "Come on. I want to make love in the moonlight."

This time she didn't hesitate. She slid across the seat, out the door, and into his waiting arms. While she spread the blanket, he shucked all his clothes. Then jumped into the bed of his truck next to her.

He placed his hand low on her belly and slipped his fingertips back and forth around the band of her pants. "Take these off."

She did and knelt before him. He fisted the hem of her shirt, then tore it off in one motion, slid his hand between her legs, and stroked her through her panties. "I remember the first time we did this. My cock got so hard I thought it might rip. Damn, I want you."

She removed her bikinis and straddled him.

"Christ, Hanna." He slid into her so easily his head spun. She moved against him—then stopped.

"What's wrong?"

"Condom. You have to wear a condom."

"I don't have one. But I'm safe. I haven't had unprotected sex since you."

"Not even with Heather?"

"No. She can't take the pill."

"I'm not on the pill either, so we can't do it."

"Shit. No. I don't want to stop. I'll pull out. I promise."

"No. It's too big of a risk."

He pulled down the cups of her bra, forcing her breasts to spill over the top, then rubbed his thumb back and forth across one stiff nipple. "I swear I won't come inside you. Please don't make me stop." He sucked the sweet peak into his hot mouth, and Hanna shivered, then rocked against him.

"You're not playing fair," she said. "You know my secrets."

She was right. He knew how to make her climax. He'd spent that long-ago summer perfecting the formula. He moved his mouth back and forth between her breasts sucking each nipple into his mouth. She was already close. He could tell by the way her nails dug into his shoulders. How she angled to get in the right position. Then she stiffened, threw her head back, and repeated his name as if it were a prayer. God, he loved watching her come. That dark hair flying in the moonlight. Her body quaking with satisfaction.

She collapsed onto this chest. "Oh my God."

He rolled over, trapping her beneath him, then thrust into her again. "I want to come inside you, Hanna. I'm willing to risk it. Please let me. You feel so fucking good. Please."

She gripped his hips to stop his motion. "No. You can't. You promised."

"Okay. Okay. Just a little more. Yeah. Like that. Damn. Damn." He jerked out of her and spewed onto her stomach. "Sweet Jesus." Then he rolled to lie next to her and stared toward heaven. He'd just gone there. "Come with me tomorrow."

She took the corner of the blanket and wiped away his pleasure. "Where?"

"Houston. I've got to break the news to Heather that the wedding is off."

Hanna bolted up straight and screamed at him. "What? You haven't told her? Oh my God! I've had sex with you, and you're still engaged!"

"No, I'm not. I decided to end it days ago. I just haven't made it official. That isn't something to text. I need to face her."

She covered her face with her hands and cried. "Oh my God. Oh my God. I'm the other woman."

Seth raised up and forced her into his arms. "You're the only woman. My woman. What just happened has nothing to do with me breaking up with her. I told you. I made that decision days ago. You've done nothing wrong." He offered his best wicked smile. "You've done everything right." He flopped back down onto his back. "Damn. I'm happy. For the first time in months, I'm actually happy."

Hanna pulled air into her lungs. "Well, that's about to change, because I have something to tell you and when I do, you'll hate me."

He propped his arm under his head and faced her. "There is *nothing* that could make me hate you." He stroked his finger down her cheek. "I love you. I've always loved you. I'll love you forever."

"Don't be so sure. I just don't want you to hold it against him or let it affect your relationship. Okay? Promise me that."

Seth swung his body up and sat cross-legged. "Oh hell. Did you sleep with Rance?"

"No! I've not had sex with anyone but you. Ever."

"What? Are you kidding? Not since high school? Why the hell not?"

"I've always been in love with you. I didn't want anyone else."

He gathered her into his arms. "I'm sorry." Then he pulled away and smiled. "Not about you doing without sex. I kind of like that I'm the only one. Damn, I must be *really* good to ruin it for every other man in the world."

"Seth, this isn't funny. It's serious. As serious as it gets."

"Oh God. You're not dying, are you? I mean, we can take you . . ."

"Stop it! Just let me say it and get it over with."

He threw up his hands in surrender. "Okay. Okay. What?"

Her lip quivered for a second, then she bit it. Whatever it was, he could tell this was killing her. She grabbed for her shirt and covered herself as if her nakedness made it worse. She swallowed so hard, a gurgling sound came from deep in her throat, like she might throw up. She drew a shallow breath. "You have a son. *We* have a son."

What did she say?

"I'm sorry. I'm so sorry. Please don't hate me. When I didn't hear from you again, I figured it'd be best not to tell you. Clearly you didn't want anything to do with me, so what would have been the point?"

He rose to his full height and glared down at her. "The point? The point is you had my kid. I had a right to know!"

Now she pulled the blanket over her and sobbed. "I know. I know. But if you had, you would have insisted on marriage. I was seventeen and pregnant. I couldn't help you. I couldn't work. You would have had to drop classes and get a part-time job. Move out of the dorm. Lose your scholarship. How long would it have been before you hated me for ruining your life?" Her voice cracked. "I know now you hate me anyway, but at least you finished law school."

He dropped to his knees and threw his arms around her. "I don't hate you. I'm pissed. Yes. But I could never hate you."

[293]

She cried into his chest. "But you don't love me, either, right?"

This was a dream. Or a nightmare. He wasn't sure which. He had so many questions, he didn't know where to start. How could she do this? Keep a child, his child, from him. Why hadn't Dessie told him? Or Rance? His brain spun. Okay, Rance couldn't know because of prison. But Dessie? No, she must not have known either. He ran his hand over his jaw to ease the tension. "I need a few minutes." He slid off the tailgate, put his feet on the ground, and walked away.

Hanna's sobs pierced the night.

God, he needed to get his thoughts together. Truthfully he'd always dreamed of having a son—and now he did—with Hanna. And he loved her. Really loved her. Had always loved her. Nothing else mattered. He returned to the truck and climbed in. "Don't cry. It's okay. Tell me about him."

She'd gotten dressed while he'd sorted things out. She pulled the hem of her shirt to her eyes and wiped. "He looks like you. Even the way his hair grows on the back of his neck. The little swirl you have here." She pressed her fingers to the spot. "He has it too. And when he half-grins—she touched her fingertip to his mouth—"his lip quirks up the same as yours."

Her breath hitched between each sentence and tears flowed down her cheeks. "His name is Noah David."

Seth cocked his head. "You gave him my middle name?"

"Of course I did. He's your son."

"Were you ever going to tell me?"

"You have no idea how close I came to calling, and I must have written fifty letters, only to throw them in the trash. And just when I decided to tell you, I found out about your engagement. Not the best time to spring fatherhood on you and your bride. I know you may never forgive me, but someday I hope you can."

"What have you told him about me? Does he think I don't care?"

"No. I would never let that happen. He asked once, and I told him you lived so far away you couldn't come here."

"Christ, Hanna. Where the hell would that be? Mars? What kind of man would never want to see his kid?"

Now her breath came in gasps. "I know I've done everything wrong. But regardless of the mistakes I've made, I'm a good mother. I swear I am. I'll let you see him anytime. I'll share custody. You can hate me because I deserve it, but please don't take him from me."

His chest burned as if he'd been sucker punched. But he needed to ask himself some hard questions. What would have happened if he'd known about the pregnancy? Probably wouldn't have a law degree. She was right. A baby on the way would have forced him to change his future. And as angry as he was, she'd made all the sacrifices. And he loved her. That was the most important part. No matter what she'd done, he loved her. And she loved him. And they shared a child. "Only one way you can make it up to me."

She sobbed into her hands. "Anything."

"Marry me."

Chapter 28

Rance

Someone pounded on Rance's bedroom door and he woke with a start. He vaulted to his feet, jerked on his boxers, and grabbed his pistol. Chirp sat up straight and pulled a pillow to her chest.

"Rance! Wake up," Seth yelled.

Rance yanked the knob. "What the hell? You're about to get your ass shot!"

Seth pushed past him and paced back and forth, babbling. "I have a son. Can you believe it? I'm a dad." He turned to Chirp. "You knew about Noah, didn't you? That's why you said not to give up."

Rance looked at her. "Who the hell is Noah?"

"He's my kid! I haven't met him yet, but I will in a few hours. Hanna says he looks like me," Seth said.

Rance held up his hands, the gun still gripped in one. "Whoa, whoa, whoa. You have a kid with Hanna? What the fuck?" He faced Chirp again. "Is that true?"

She stared wide-eyed at the weapon, so he put it back on the dresser. "Chirp? Does Hanna has a kid?"

"Yes."

"Damn. Why didn't you say something?"

"She asked me not to. But I encouraged her to tell Seth. Every man should know his children."

Rance reached out and grabbed his brother. "Stop the damn pacing. You're wearing out my new carpet."

"Sorry. I can't help it." Seth dropped onto the end of the bed. "Me. A dad. I want to buy him something." He twisted to face Chirp again. "What would be a good gift? Wait." He raked his hand over his face. "I don't have a job. How the hell am I going to provide for them, much less spring for a present?"

Rance put a hand on his brother's shoulder. "Don't worry. I'll give you some cash."

"Okay, but what about the gift?"

Chirp leaned forward. "He wants a pony."

"A real pony?"

"Yes."

"Damn. Where will I get a horse on short notice and at this hour? Wait! Is Mr. Henderson still alive? He used to have horses."

This time Rance grabbed both of Seth's shoulders. "Go to bed. We'll call him first thing in the morning. If he doesn't have a horse, he'll know where we can find one." He nudged his brother toward the door. "Now get the hell out of my room."

"Okay, okay. I'm going." Seth made it to the hallway, then turned back. "Oh, one more thing. I asked Hanna to marry me, and she said yes."

"Damn, Seth. Now you're engaged to two women?" Rance said.

"Technically, yes, but in my heart, only one. I love her, man. Always have. I know it sounds crazy, but when I saw her, I knew. And we have a child. God, I can't believe it."

Rance ran his hand over his stubble. "What I don't understand is why you're not pissed. But we'll add that to the discussion for tomorrow."

"You know I won't sleep!" Seth shouted.

"That's your problem. See you in the morning." Rance crawled back into bed, and Chirp scooted next to him.

"It's good they're getting married. I mean, now Noah will have both parents. And if two people love each other, they should be together."

Rance shifted to spoon her. "Don't do this."

"What?"

"Try to start a conversation about love and marriage shit."

"I'm not."

"Yes, you are. I thought we were clear about our situation."

She pulled away and rolled to her back. "Perfectly clear."

Rance hated the sadness in her voice. He'd been too harsh. Gathering her in his arms again, he nuzzled at her ear. "I didn't mean to be so gruff. I'll always protect you, but I'm right, and you know it. We're from different worlds, Chirp. I'm not the guy to attend operas or dine at the country club, or do any of that rich-people shit. And I never will be."

"Neither am I."

"You are and don't even realize it because you've always had money. Besides, a piece of paper doesn't guarantee fidelity."

"So Seth won't be faithful?"

"He will. But not because of a legal document."

She stiffened. "Stop talking."

"Dammit. What do you want from me?"

"Nothing."

"Yes, you do." He propped on his elbow and stared into her eyes. "As long as we're sleeping together, I won't have sex with anyone else. That's the most I can offer. You have to decide if it's enough."

God, she gazed up at him with those big eyes shimmering with tears and he wanted to take it all back. Why had he pressed the subject? He should have dropped it, but he couldn't let her expect something he could never give.

"What if it isn't?"

His lungs burned at the thought of losing her, but he had to stand his ground. "Then I guess we're done."

"Then I guess it's enough." She snaked her hands around his neck and pressed her lips to his.

The next morning Rance let Chirp sleep while he and Seth went to see a man about a horse. Rance had never seen his brother so happy. Which was nuts, because he still had an engagement to break and no future job in sight. But his luck was changing, because Mr. Henderson had several ponies that fit the bill for a young boy.

Seth wanted to saddle one up and walk him home, but the old man talked sense into him.

Rance stuck his checkbook in his back pocket, and as they reached the truck, Seth's phone rang. He looked down at the number and pulled his brows together. "Hello—yes—what?" He leaned against the fender as if needing it for support.

Rance tried to read his face. Confusion? Worry? Hell, was it bad news?

Seth's eyes widened, then he smiled. "Yes, sir. I can be there next week. Yes, sir. Thank you." He clicked off and stared at Rance. "You won't believe this. I got a job offer. And a damn good one."

"From a law firm?"

"No. The legal department of Montgomery Steel."

"Montgomery Steel," Rance repeated.

"Yeah. They're the biggest . . ."

"I know who they are." Rance climbed in the truck.

Seth opened his door and slid onto the seat. "They want to see me next week."

"To interview?"

"No. To make an official offer. He mentioned a signing bonus. I don't understand this. How the hell did a company like that even find out about me?"

"Hey, don't question it. Consider yourself lucky."

"Damn straight I won't question it. I'll sign that contract so fast Mr. Sherman's head will spin. Another thing. Since when does the CEO personally call a new hire?"

"Thought you weren't going to question it."

"Yeah. You're right. Do you know what this will mean for Hanna, Noah, and me? We can buy a house. Maybe a place big enough to keep his horse. Damn, somebody upstairs must be watching out for me."

"Yeah." *Or somebody back at the house.* "Must be Dessie."

"Right."

Rance glanced at him. "Well, you look like shit. Did you sleep at all?"

"No. Couldn't stop thinking about meeting my son. Think he'll like me?"

"You're giving him a fucking pony, of course he'll like you. Give me a horse, even I'll like you."

"Shut up. You like me now."

Rance smirked. "Yeah, I do, and I'm happy for you. You'll be a great dad."

"I hope so."

"Tell me something. What'd you ever see in Heather?"

Seth stretched his lips tight against his teeth and sighed. "I guess I went a little crazy. Take somebody like you and me, we don't fit in that circle."

"Yeah."

"Now you tell me something. What's really going on with Blaze?"

"What do you mean?"

"Are you in love with her?"

"What makes you think that?"

"You were upset when you thought she wasn't coming back, so if she isn't important to you, why go after her?"

Rance tightened his grip on the steering wheel until his fingers tingled. If he was a better man, worthy of her, it could be more—would be more. He'd make sure of it. But he wasn't. "It's just sex."

"You sure? Because I see how you look at her."

"So what? Now that you've found your one true love, you're psychoanalyzing me? Don't waste your time. I'm a lost cause when it comes to forever."

Seth chuckled. "You're living together. I'd say there's already an element of commitment on your part."

That evaluation hit hard. Rance had made plenty of mistakes. He'd brought her home, moved her into his bedroom, and expected her to accept his rules. No wonder she'd mentioned the love and marriage crap. Thank God he'd set her straight. "I know she has a big-time crush on me, but she doesn't plan to stay in Bluebird. It'll run its course, and she'll move on."

"If you say so," Seth said.

"Well, I do, so drop it and worry about your own love life. You've got double trouble."

Even as Rance said, "She'll move on," his heart ached. No. He couldn't allow himself to have feelings for her. He cared. That was all. The pain had to come from giving up the sex. Hands down the best he'd ever had, which was crazy since it started out as the worst. But the way she gave herself to him was as if she wanted to seep into his soul, and that made him feel something he'd never felt before. No. It was just sex. That's all it could ever be.

Seth's truck was in the drive when they got home, so Nicky was back. Chirp stooped by the shed planting seeds. Probably zinnias because that's what Gran always put in that spot, right next to the hollyhocks.

Rance brought the Chevy to a stop. Seth got out and went inside while Rance made his way to her. "Planting zinnias?"

She shaded her eyes. "Yeah."

Damn, she looked so natural there. As if she belonged on a farm, digging in the dirt, but she didn't. No more than he belonged in her world. "So—Seth got a job offer from Montgomery Steel. Imagine that."

"Good. Now he can support Hanna and Noah."

"Thank you."

[305]

She went back to work. "No problem. Just wielding my *heiress* power."

From her tone, last night's talk had not set her straight, only pissed her off. Damn.

Hanna

Hanna spent most of the night rehearsing how she'd break the news to Noah. Sitting on the edge of his bed, she ran her fingers through his hair. His big brown eyes blinked open, and he reached out his arms. She pulled him in close. "Good morning, sweet boy. I have a surprise for you."

He sat back and scanned the room. "A present?"

"Better than that."

"What?"

Unable to hold back, Hanna burst into tears.

"What's wrong, Momma? Why are you crying?"

She pulled him into another hug. "Because I'm happy. You're meeting your daddy today."

"He's here? To see me?"

"Yes."

"Where?" Noah bounced out of bed and stripped off his pajamas. "Hurry, Momma. Help me get my clothes on."

In spite of her tears, Hanna couldn't help but laugh. "Not so fast. He won't be here until ten."

"No. I want to see him now!"

"Okay. Okay." She pulled her cell from her pocket. "Why don't you call him? I'll dial the number." She punched it in and handed the phone over. "When he answers, tell him who you are."

"Hello, this is Noah. I want you to come see me now." He listened for a second, then grinned. "Yes, sir. But you better hurry cause Momma's crying."

By the time Seth parked in the drive, Hanna's emotions still weren't under control. She didn't wait for him to knock; she jerked open the door and threw herself against him.

He stroked her hair and whispered, "Don't cry. It's okay." Then he focused on his son, knelt, and stretched out his arms. But the little boy didn't move.

Hanna walked to where Noah stood, and he clung to her legs. She patted him. "It's okay. He's your daddy, and he loves you." She gently nudged him away. "Don't be bashful."

Seth thrust his arms wide again. "I've been trying to get back to you and your momma for a long time. I promise, I'll never leave you again." Noah ran into his waiting arms. Then it was Seth's turn to cry, and Hanna's heart swelled. She dropped to her knees and hugged both of them.

She stood after a few minutes, but Seth continued to hold his son and whispered in his ear, "Guess what?"

"What?"

"I'm taking you and your mom to Mr. Henderson's house for you to pick out a pony."

Noah widened his eyes. "A real pony?"

"Yes."

Wheeling around to face his mother, Noah shouted, "He's getting me a real pony!"

"Seth!" Before she could say anything else, he raised his hands.

"Come on, Hanna. I have a lot of years to make up for. I need to give him something spectacular. After the horse business is squared away, we'll go to breakfast, because I have another surprise. Let's go."

"Wait!" Noah ran to his bedroom and came back wearing his cowboy hat and carrying his bandanna. "Tie this on me."

Seth looked at Hanna. "Let me do it." He draped the kerchief around the boy's neck and knotted it. Then he pulled him into a hug and kissed his cheek. "You look like a real cowboy."

Noah took off in a gallop around the room. "I'm getting a pony! I'm getting a pony!"

On his third pass, Hanna grabbed him. "Settle down, or you'll be too tired to ride the real one."

He pulled away from her and hugged Seth's legs. "Thank you, Daddy."

Seth lifted him into his arms. "You're welcome."

Noah leaned toward Hanna and patted her shoulder. "Aw, Momma. Don't cry again."

She wiped her face. "Sorry."

Seth set Noah's feet back on the floor, and he ran out the front door. As Hanna and Seth caught up, she looped her arm in his. "What's the surprise? Don't make me wait. I can't take much more excitement."

Seth chuckled and told her about his job offer. When they reached the truck, he leaned her against the fender and took her mouth. "I love you, Hanna, and I promise I'll spend the rest of my life making you happy."

"Stop smooching and come on!" Noah yelled.

Hanna and Seth laughed.

When they arrived at Mr. Henderson's, the old man had two ponies in the corral. Noah ran over to them as soon as Seth opened the door.

Seth waved. "Hey, Mr. Henderson."

"Good morning, Seth—Hanna. Either one of these will work for the boy." He focused on Hanna. "I told Seth yesterday, Noah needs to learn to ride bareback before he uses a saddle. But when he's ready, I have several to choose from. I'll even give him lessons."

"I'll take you up on that offer," Seth said.

One pony stuck his nose through the rails and nickered.

Noah patted him. "Hi, boy. My name's Noah. What's yours?"

"That's Toby," Mr. Henderson said. "He's a nine-year-old pinto. You want to give him a try?"

"Yes, sir!"

Hanna had never seen her son so happy. Heck, *she'd* never been this happy.

Seth leaned in close. "I'm going home tomorrow to handle the Heather problem. Only staying one night, then I'll be back. I wish you and Noah would come with me."

She waved at her son as Mr. H led him around the corral. "No. It'll be hard to tear him away from Toby."

Seth climbed down, helped Noah off the horse, and hugged him close. "I love you, Noah."

"I love you, too, Daddy."

Hanna wiped at her eyes, then turned to Seth. "How'd you know he wanted a pony?"

[310]

"Blaze."

"Is she okay?"

"Yeah. She's sleeping with Rance."

"He's going to hurt her."

"I'm not so sure."

"What do you mean?" Hanna asked.

"I think he's falling for her."

Chapter 29

✦

"

Rance

With one brother on his way to Houston, the other sound asleep, and Chirp gone to work, Rance headed out to mend the fence for the pony's new home.

His brother's excitement about fatherhood proved contagious. "Uncle Rance" sounded pretty good. Could be projecting his own secret desire, because since hearing the news, fleeting thoughts of parenthood had crossed his mind more than once.

There'd been a time when he'd dreamed of having his own family, but prison had killed that hope. He'd pushed the idea to the back of his brain and concentrated on staying alive. But freedom created a whole new list of problems. In the number-one position: Chirp, and what to do about her.

He swung the truck around and opened his door. Muttly bounded out and hiked his leg on the nearest post. Rance pulled on his gloves and got to work, but couldn't concentrate on the job. Seth's questions had stirred up emotions he didn't want to deal with. Why try to make more out of sleeping together than just plain sex?

The dog barked at a grasshopper while Rance grabbed the digger. Once he had the new post in place, he attached the stretcher, connected the two pieces of barbed wire, looped them together, twisted, and nailed.

Okay, so maybe his relationship with Chirp was stronger than physical, but what did everyone expect? She was the one who'd wanted it, and he was giving her what she asked for. Well, he wanted it, too, but she'd started it, and now he was paying the price. Seemed she and everyone else expected more from him, and he had no more to give. Especially not to her. A twenty-year-old rich girl mooning over the first guy who'd given her an orgasm. That was a hell of a long way from from—from what? He didn't know. That's what bothered him most.

"Muttly! Don't wander off, because when I'm ready to go, I'm not coming to find you." The pooch looked at him as if to say he knew better. Rance moved farther down to the next problem area and spliced wire to repair it. Once done, Toby would have plenty of pasture to graze, and when winter came, Rance could buy hay from Mr. Henderson.

The small pond on the property still had plenty of water. Enough for one horse. The pup scampered to the edge and drank, then went back to the grasshopper.

[313]

Rance hoisted himself onto the tailgate, palmed a bottle of water, and took a long pull. Maybe he'd buy a few head of cattle or another horse. Noah was too young to ride alone, so that way he or Seth or even Hanna could go with him.

The idea made him smile, but as quickly as the happy image appeared, it vanished. What was he thinking? Once Seth started his new job, he'd move his family, and they'd rarely come to Bluebird.

A few months ago, Rance had dreamed of being alone in Gran's house with simple, quiet freedom. The thought of his brothers leaving made him sad. Fast forward to December, when Chirp turned twenty-one. She'd leave, too. Suddenly easy, silent, liberty lost its appeal.

Dammit.

Muttly trotted up carrying a stick and dropped it at Rance's feet.

"Oh, so you want to play fetch?" He picked up the small branch and gave it a toss. The dog took off, returned, and dropped it again. "Okay. One more time. That's all."

He threw it as hard as he could, and seconds later, Muttly was back. "This is the last time."

Fifteen minutes later Rance issued the same warning as he hurled the stick. "I mean it, Mutt. Last time." When the dog came back, Rance closed the tailgate and opened the door. "In, boy."

The pooch rolled over, and Rance gave him a quick belly rub. "Play time's over. Get in the truck."

When he arrived home again, Rance found Nicky sitting at the kitchen table eating cereal. "Who the hell are you, and what are you doing in my house?"

"Very funny."

"Come to think of it, you look a little familiar," Rance said.

"I know. I'm supposed to be visiting you but haven't been around much. Sorry about that. And, it seems a lot has happened in my absence."

"Yeah, Seth became a father and got another woman to agree to marry him." Rance broke into laughter. "And I thought I was a player. You two are outplaying me on every level. You proposed to Tiffany yet?"

"Not yet."

Rance pulled his brows together. "You say that like you plan on it."

Nicky turned up his bowl and slurped the remaining milk, then wiped his mouth on his sleeve. "I sure like her. Could turn into love."

Rance shook his head. "What's gotten into you and Seth? Leave the city, come to Podunk, USA, and fall for country girls. Crazy."

"You're one to talk. You have a bed partner. Last I heard, you weren't even speaking."

Rance didn't want to risk another love lecture, so he changed the subject. "What you got going today? Back to your new honey's house?"

"Later. I thought I'd go with you to move the pony. You get the fence fixed?"

"Yeah, and there's enough water in the pond to hold him for a while. Mr. Henderson has a trailer we can use, so if you're ready, we'll go."

"Lead the way. I'm right behind you."

Tom Fraser

Tom Fraser had been in the detective business long enough to know local watering holes were a wealth of information. As he came to a stop in front of The Roost, he figured it wouldn't be any different. Bartenders kept their ears to the ground.

One good thing about private practice was he no longer had to wear standard black suits. In a country town, jeans, knit shirts, and cowboy boots filled the bill.

He sauntered in and slid onto the stool at the end of the bar. Too early for happy hour, the place was empty except for three old guys at a corner table.

The bartender approached. "What can I get you?"

"You got Atrial Rubicite?"

"Sure 'nuf."

"Give me a bottle of that." Tom placed a twenty on the counter.

The barkeep delivered the tall boy and a pilsner. He stepped to the register, then returned with Tom's change. "You passing through?"

"Yeah. Looking for an old friend. Thought I might stop by her place and catch up. Lost touch. Dessie Bishop. You know her?"

"Yeah, but sorry to tell you, she died a while ago."

Tom tilted the glass, poured in the brew, and gave his best fake expression of concern. "Sorry to hear that. They sell her place?"

"Naw. Left it to her grandson. Rance Keller. Ever meet him?"

"No." Tom gulped, then smacked. "Damn, I don't know if it's the well water or the raspberries, but that's good beer. He living there?"

"Yeah. A few months now. Got an early release from prison."

Tom's stomach clenched at the thought of an ex-con visiting the reward site. "Dessie never mentioned a trouble-maker in the family."

"I don't think he is. Never caused a problem in here."

"So he's a regular?"

"Was for a while. I think he was catching up if you get my drift. Left most nights with a woman on his arm."

Tom chuckled. "Maybe one caught him. Happens when we least expect it." He thought about Helga and how he'd already fallen for her.

"So, what line of work you in?"

"Retired FBI," Tom said.

"Cool."

"Take my word, the job isn't as sexy as they make it on TV. So, how was the festival? I remember Dessie looked forward to it every year." Tom remembered no such thing, but he'd done his homework. Lying was an art form and if you wanted to master it, you had to have your Intel in place. Which meant learning what the area was famous for and reading past issues of the local paper. Didn't take much to find out Dessie helped to get bluebird houses mounted on all the county roads.

Within fifteen minutes, Tom had extracted all the information he needed. And thanks to Google, he located the house and learned all about Rance Keller.

Rance put the last plate in the dishwasher and stared out the kitchen window at the dust kicking up. "I don't recognize this car pulling into the drive, so stay out of sight."

Chirp busied herself wiping the table while Muttly searched underneath for stray crumbs.

Rance dried his hands on the cup towel, then stepped onto the porch as a middle-aged stranger got out of his silver Chevy Equinox. "You lost?"

The guy shaded his eyes against the setting sun. "No. Looking for Rance Keller."

"You found him."

Rance eyed him. Dark hair graying at the temples, he looked to be in his mid-fifties. About six-foot. Still in good shape, but getting a little paunch around his middle.

The stranger narrowed his steely gray eyes and stuck out his business card. "Tom Fraser."

Rance read it, then focused on the investigator "How can I help you?"

"I'm working a missing person case, and my investigation has led me here."

"Me? Missing? Case solved."

"Not you. A young woman. Wren Montgomery."

From the moment of his arrest, Rance discovered law enforcement didn't want the truth they only wanted to be right. Lying with a straight face became second nature—and to be good at it, he never said more than necessary or defended his answers. "Sorry, can't help you."

"So you don't know her?"

"No."

"Never even heard of her?"

"No."

"She's heir to Montgomery Steel. Familiar with them?"

"Sure."

"Aren't you curious why your place landed on my radar?"

"Not really."

Tom shifted his weight from one foot to the other. "Someone at this IP address visited the data site for Miss Montgomery. That tells me you know who she is and *where* she is."

Rance kept his poker face. "Like I said, can't help you."

Tom screwed his mouth around, and Rance decided the PI was arrogant enough to be military police, or worse—FBI.

Tom closed the distance between them. "Look, Mr. Keller. I'll be honest with you. I don't like my client much, but I've committed to the job and won't stop until I find the girl. Pretty sure I have. She may not be here on your property, but I'd be willing to bet my left nut she's in this town. So two days from now, I plan to report what I believe to be the kid's location. When that happens, somebody'll show up to get her."

Rance smirked. "You'll be able to live just fine with one nut."

Tom smiled, turned to go, but stopped and faced Rance again. "Too bad the girl's not married, because then nobody could touch her. Any decisions about her mental health would fall to her husband."

As Rance watched the man drive away, his stomach twisted. Chirp had heard every word. Two days. Two fucking days to decide her next move. He waited until the car disappeared, then opened the door to find her plastered against the wall. Big eyes filled with expectation. An answer he couldn't provide.

She took a shallow breath. "Say something."

He wanted to speak, but his throat closed off. This was his fault. If he hadn't done the fucking search. But he hadn't known who she was, or that anyone was looking for her. Hell, if she'd told him the truth from the beginning—damn.

Her bottom lip quivered. "Please. Say something."

His head pounded. There was plenty he should say, but he needed to think the situation over before he came up with a way to fix it. "I . . . I'm . . . I need a drink." He grabbed his keys and rushed to his truck.

Chapter 30

Blaze

Paralyzed with fear, Blaze pressed against the wall like a cat burglar. So much for Rance doing everything he could to protect her. What a lie. It'd all been lies. He'd known who she was because he'd looked on the Internet, and now they'd found her. Eight more months. That's all she'd needed to be home free, and she'd been stupid enough to think she'd make it. Even a bigger fool to trust him.

Shaking her head to clear it, she pulled her wits together. She'd disappeared once. She could do it again. Had to. She found her feet, rushed down the hall, grabbed her bag from the closet, and stuffed everything into it. After that she took a pen and paper, wrote a note, stuck it in her pocket, and returned to the kitchen for food items. The PI was probably watching the house, so she escaped through the back door. She was in Hanna's workshop within minutes, heaving out the words, "I have to leave. I need your car."

"Oh my God. What's wrong?"

She gulped air. "No time to explain. Give this note to Rance. He'll tell you everything and give you my car. Even trade."

"What are you talking about? Your car is worth twice as much as mine. I don't understand."

"Please, give me the key."

Hanna scrounged in her purse, handed it over, and followed Blaze outside. "Where are you going?"

"I don't know. But I'll be okay."

"Please, Blaze. Don't go. Whatever it is, I'll help you. Seth will, too."

"Nothing you can do unless you'll let Seth marry me."

"What? Marry you? Why do you need to get married?"

"Joking. I should be good at that since the joke has been on me. Thank you, Hanna, for being my friend." Blaze climbed into the Toyota and started the engine. "I'll call to let you know I'm okay. I promise."

Blaze shoved the car into gear and sped away with Hanna calling after her. When she reached the city limits sign, she glanced in her rearview mirror. *Goodbye Bluebird.* Then she pushed Rance from her mind and concentrated on a plan. Drive to Dallas, ditch the car in a bad part of town, and leave the key in it. Take a cab to the bus station and buy a ticket to Waco, where she'd spend the night. That would give her a chance to dye her hair and get new clothes. Time to lose the

Goth image. The next morning, another bus trip to Austin, and if the apartment she'd found online was still available, she'd rent it. Guess the searches she'd done while taking care of the goats had paid off.

She glanced at the speedometer and eased off the pedal. Wouldn't want to get a ticket. Needed to avoid anything traceable. Thank goodness Hanna's car didn't have GPS. Blaze added a new phone to the list because Rance had her number, and if he called, she might answer in a weak moment. She was taking a lot for granted. He wouldn't call. Not after the detective had shown up. That was the sort of attention Rance didn't want or need. Now, with her gone, he'd go right back to the lifestyle he loved. Drinking, smoking, and screwing strangers.

As much as she hated the thought of him being with other women, she needed to get over it. He didn't love her and never would. At least he hadn't lied about that. He'd made it crystal clear there was only one thing he wanted. She couldn't blame him. She'd thrown herself at him. A more than willing victim.

But now it was time for a new beginning. No more Rance Keller. No more Chirp.

Rance

Rance wanted to get shit-faced and forget about what he'd done, but wasn't in the mood. Liquor wouldn't solve anything. When he sobered up, he'd still be the one who'd allowed Chirp's wicked stepmother to find her. The question now—what to do about it? Marry her?

Maybe it wouldn't be such a big deal. A quick trip to Vegas. And once she turned twenty-one, she could divorce him. It'd be perfectly acceptable. The rich girl finally came to her senses and realized she'd had a lapse in judgment concerning a bad boy. Plenty of uppity girls slummed.

Why had the PI even mentioned marriage? Why was he waiting two days to report? He'd said he didn't like his client, but he was risking a lot. If the woman found out he'd given Chirp time to disappear again, he'd lose his fee. Something wasn't right about that guy. It was almost like he had a conscience.

Rance knocked back his second shot, then called it a night. He'd go home and fix this mess. Besides, he'd promised to take care of her—keep her safe. And he always kept his word.

When he got home, he breathed a sigh of relief. Chirp's car was still there. Not that she'd leave before he got back.

She knew he'd need time to wrap his brain around the situation and come up with a plan. Besides, she had forty-eight hours before anything happened. Unless Fraser had lied which was possible, but Rance believed the guy.

He got out and took the porch in three steps, then yanked open the door. "Chirp!"

No answer. His heart kicked up a notch. Hurrying down the hall, he called again. Still no response. He rushed to the closet inside the master suite. Her things—gone. He checked the bathroom. Toothbrush, makeup, every personal item—cleared out. Dammit. He hurried to his truck and peeled out toward Hanna's.

She was closing up the shop as he pulled into the drive. "Hey! Chirp here?"

Hanna turned to look at him, and he didn't like her expression. She'd been crying. "What's wrong? You and Seth have a fight?"

"No. Blaze is gone. Took my car." She reached inside her pocket and pulled out the paper. "She left this for you."

Rance grabbed the note, unfolded it, and stared down at the single sheet of paper.

Tell Hanna everything. Give her my car. Even trade.

Blaze

She couldn't have said, "Fuck you" better if she'd spelled it out. Not even a, "Goodbye. I'll call. Thanks for everything."

"Where'd she go?"

Hanna shook her head. "I don't know. Not sure she had a plan. What's going on, Rance? She wouldn't explain anything."

He folded the note and stuck it in his pocket along with the PI's card from earlier and began the story, leaving out how it was his fault they'd found her and how he could have saved her. When he finished, Hanna placed her palm to her throat. "Montgomery Steel. Seth's job. She did that for him. For us." She fisted her hand and pounded Rance's chest. "Why did you leave? You should have known she'd panic."

"I didn't expect her to do anything without talking to me. Dammit to hell. How long?"

"Over an hour. You'll never catch up to her. Besides, we don't know which direction she went. Go home, Rance. She promised she'd call to let me know she was okay. When she does, I'll try to find out where she is."

He climbed into the truck, but Hanna wasn't finished because she followed and leaned against the fender. "She made a joke about marriage. What was that about?"

He ran his hand over his face. "The guy said if she was married, her stepmother wouldn't be a threat."

"Damn you, Rance. Why didn't you offer to marry her?"

"If it came to that, I would have. We could have worked this out. I could have protected her. Tell her that when she calls."

"Yeah. Like it'll make a difference now." Hanna turned and stomped into the house.

When Rance returned home, he decided getting drunk *was* a good idea, so he broke out the whiskey. He lumbered to the deck, plopped onto the lounge chair, and turned up the bottle. He had a buzz within fifteen minutes. Hell, he had plenty of reasons to get plastered. He took another long pull and felt the burn.

Letting Chirp stay had been his first mistake. He should have kicked her ass out the morning after he arrived. Going to that fucking banquet. Seeing her in that dress. Hating how that boy touched her. Damn. Another drink and he'd feel better.

The mother lode of all regrets was going to the reward website. But if she'd been honest with him. No. This wasn't all his fault. Running away proved nothing. He slugged another gulp. Jack Daniel's might not fix everything, but it could sure as hell get him through the night.

"Rance! Wake up!"

The voice came from far away, and Rance tried to open his eyes but only squinted. God, it was dark. And wet. Where the hell was he?

"Help me get him up," Seth said.

"Damn, Rance. What's got into you?" Nick asked. "It's coming a storm."

Rance's head weaved. *Hell, hell, the gang's all her. I mean— here. Shit. Chirp's afraid of storms. Damn her.* His lids fluttered, but he couldn't get his eyes to roll down. "Oh, hey, Nicky."

"We've got to drag him inside." Seth's voice came in a fog.

Rance tried to raise his arms, but they were too heavy. *Rain must have soaked me to the bone.* "Give me a minute. I'll get up."

They tugged him forward, and he opened his eyes. "See, I can do it by myself."

"No, you can't. Dammit, Rance," Seth said.

He squinted up at Seth and slurred his words. "What day is it? I thought you were in Houston breaking up with bachelorette number one."

"Yeah, how'd that go?" Nicky asked.

"Once I told her about Noah and how I planned to get custody, she said that was a deal breaker and handed me my ring. Didn't even shed a tear."

[330]

Rance chuckled. "Her or you?"

"Her, you fucking moron. Now, on three, we're pulling your sorry ass up and getting you out of the rain. One. Two. Three."

A minute later they let go of him, and he fell onto the couch.

"I've been on the road all day and half the night so I wouldn't have to stay in Houston," Seth said. "Then I come home to this. She's gone, Rance, and she's not coming back. Understand?"

"Fuck you and the horse you rode in on, Seth. She is coming back because I'm going to find her."

Blaze

Blaze rinsed her hair and raked her fingers through it. Looked strange to see her natural color. She'd liked being blonde. The brunette staring back at her in the mirror would take getting used to.

Just as planned, by now Hanna's car had probably been stolen. Even the taxi driver warned Blaze about being in that part of town. She'd used the excuse her jerk of a boyfriend had dumped her there. Thank goodness the cab had arrived minutes after she'd parked. The dark street had given her the heebie-jeebies.

After opening a package of peanut butter crackers she'd bought at the bus station, she took a bite out of one, washed it down with water, then stacked the remaining squares in a neat column. Those two items could keep her going for days.

Whispering Pines motel wasn't fancy, but it was clean and they accepted cash. She walked to the window and stared out. Not much of a view. A parking lot with the hotel sign flashing No Vacancy. Desk clerk said she'd gotten the last room. Even though the fear of starting over squeezed air from her lungs, things were falling into place, which convinced Blaze she'd done the right thing.

But there was also a sense of relief. No more lying to people she'd grown fond of. By now Hanna knew the truth. Soon, Nick, Tiffany, and Seth, too. Then they'd all hate her, because friendship was based on honesty, and her whole life was a lie.

She ate her last cracker, brushed her teeth, and settled onto the scratchy sheets. If only the PI hadn't found her, she'd be curled next to Rance listening to his steady breathing. She dug her fingernails into her palms, the pain taking her thoughts. No. No more dreaming about a guy who'd never love her. Instead she forced her mind to Muttly. What she'd give to have him here. But traveling by bus made it impossible. With that final thought, she drifted to sleep.

The next morning, she got up early, ate an apple, and finished her remaining bottle of water. She should be in Austin by noon, hopefully have an apartment by the end of the day, and reinvent herself one last time. Blaze Bledsoe. Austin artist.

Chapter 31

✦

Blaze

Blaze sat on a park bench and read the ad again.

Constructed with the same quality and style as the one-hundred-year-old main house, the furnished single bedroom garage apartment provides a private entrance. Hardwood floors. Washer and dryer. An upper patio overlooks an arbor to the courtyard and fountain. Located in the historic district.

The place looked vacant. Nobody going in or out. No lights on. Leaves littered the stairway and porch. Palming her phone, she dialed, and a woman with a French accent answered.

Once she found out the place was still available, she walked across the street, set her duffel bag down, and rang the bell. When Odette Fontaine opened the door, she wasn't anything like Blaze had pictured. She'd imagined someone older and fat from years of eating rich cuisine instead of the beautiful woman with dark eyes. Her black hair was twisted into a messy bun, and wisps dangled around her flawless face.

[334]

A beaded turquoise necklace, weighing at least a pound, rested against her orange-and-red brocade tunic.

Odette eyed Blaze from top to bottom and Blaze felt uneasy. Although she'd removed her nose ring and dressed in basic black slacks and a white cotton shirt, she hadn't completely filed away her punk identity. She picked up her bag, straightened, and pulled her shoulders back.

"Mrs. Fontaine?"

"Yes. Come in, my dear."

Blaze followed her into a dizzying cacophony of color. It'd been a while since she'd thought about French décor, but she hadn't forgotten how gaudy it could be. The woman eased into one of two orange velvet chairs and motioned for Blaze to sit. She chose the opposing crewelwork Victorian. On either side of the fireplace, urns full of leafy plants sat on stone columns, and a wall tapestry depicting a grape harvest hung above the mantle.

Odette removed a sheet of paper from the top of a French antique two-drawer chest and handed it to Blaze. "I'll leave you alone to fill out the application. I had chocolate croissants for breakfast. Would you like one with a glass of champagne?"

Apparently Blaze's new identity made her look old enough to drink, but it was one o'clock in the afternoon. However, those pastries sounded good. "I'd love a croissant, and water is fine."

Her hostess flapped a hand in the air as if swatting flies and rattled in her native tongue.

Blaze had not spoken French since she was fifteen, so the only thing she understood from the rant was absolutely not! She'd have to brush up on the language.

"Oh, I'm sorry. I slip into my language from time to time. You can't drink water with pastry. I'll bring you some fresh-squeezed orange juice. *Oui?*"

Blaze nodded. "Yes, thank you." Once alone, she made short work of the application. As she stared at the blank lines, her hope sank. No chance of being approved. She glanced around the room again. A painting of sunflowers in a blue vase resting on an easel caught her eye. She walked to the canvas and squinted to read the signature. "O. Fontaine." If she played her cards right, she'd close this deal.

When the woman returned, she placed a silver tray on a small ottoman.

Blaze passed the paper and took her first bite. After nothing but peanut butter crackers and an apple, the pastry shocked her taste buds. As she ate, Mrs. Fontaine studied the application.

"So, I see you have no credit cards. No bank account. No job. No references. No former employment. You list a previous landlady—deceased. Your parents, as well."

She looked up at Blaze as if waiting for an explanation.

And she had none. "I don't have any pets. I don't party. I'm not messy. I can pay six months' rent in advance, if you'll accept cash."

Lacing her fingers together, Mrs. Fontaine relaxed back in her chair. "With no job history, I'm forced to wonder where your money comes from."

Blaze could have listed Over the Rainbow, but she'd decided it was better to keep as many secrets as possible. "I inherited it." The woman's pinched expression said she was about to send Blaze packing, but she couldn't let that happen. "All I want is a nice quiet place to concentrate on painting."

That got Odette's attention. She leaned forward with renewed interest. "You're an artist?"

"Struggling."

"Do you have anything I may see?"

"Rough sketches."

"Show me."

Blaze unzipped her bag, removed the pad, and handed it over. At first Odette turned the pages quickly, then more slowly. Suddenly her eyes popped so wide, Blaze thought they might shoot from their sockets. "Well, hello there," Odette said to the drawing, then held out the sketch and pointed. "This man. Your lover? *Oui?*"

In her excitement, Blaze had forgotten to take *that* picture out. Rance. Every inch of him. "Yes."

[337]

She raised a brow. "Ah. More than that. You are *in* love with him. *Oui?*"

Blaze's throat thickened. She bit her bottom lip and nodded.

"But he doesn't love you?"

This wasn't going the way she'd planned. The last thing she wanted was to discuss Rance and remember how it felt to run her hands over his beautiful body. She bit back tears. "No."

Odette shook her head, said something in French, then corrected herself. "Oh, sorry, *chérie*. I said, men give us their cocks, and we give them our hearts. He broke yours and this is why you want solitude. *Oui?*"

Blaze nodded again.

"When can you move in?"

"Now. This bag is all I have."

Mrs. Fontaine returned the drawings and motioned for her to follow. "I'll show you the place, and if you approve, it's yours."

Blaze couldn't help but smile. As soon as she began to paint, she'd forget all about Rance and the rest of her problems.

Her new landlady spoke again. "Where are your painting supplies?"

"I need to buy some."

"Not necessary. I have many. I can no longer hold a brush. Arthritis." She slid her hand into her pocket and pulled out a key. "I thought it an old person's disease. I am only fifty. Still young, but yet I suffer with the affliction. So unfair."

Inside the apartment, Blaze turned in a circle. The online pictures didn't do the place justice. Marble countertops. Dark wooden cabinets. Stainless appliances. Eight months here would be a dream come true. Natural light poured through the windows. She couldn't wait to get started on her first canvas.

"I love it. I promise I will be the best tenant you've ever had."

The proprietor laughed. "No doubt, because you're my first. This was my studio, but once I accepted I'd never paint again, I hated to waste the space. You, my dear, were sent to me as an angel. Watching you create what I no longer can will be my joy. Perhaps you will let me teach you."

"Yes. I would like that very much."

She cocked her head. "This lover. He was good?"

Blaze's cheeks heated. She hadn't expected the question.

"Oh, *chérie*. I'm sorry. I have embarrassed you. It's just from his endowment, I assumed he was."

[339]

"Yes." She couldn't imagine a better lover than Rance. Maybe someday she'd want another man, but not now.

Mrs. Fontaine fingered the beads of her necklace. "I had a lover like him once. I still shiver when I recall our time together."

Blaze's chest tightened. "Did you marry him?"

She chuckled. "No. He was already married. I've had countless lovers, but he was the best. Perhaps it was because he was younger. So virile. So insatiable. I bring this up so you will understand you, too, will have many, if you choose. That is the thing with women. We are the ones who set the rules of lovemaking." She laid the key on the counter. "I'm sure you noticed the market down the street. And I hear the coffee shop is good. However, I have breakfast each morning at eight, and I would be happy for you to join me. I would welcome the company. My housekeeper stays until noon each day, but she is too busy to provide companionship."

"Okay." Blaze reached into her bag and pulled out six stacks of bills banded together. "Here's the rent."

"You were convinced I would accept your application?"

"No. But I wanted to be prepared."

Rance

Rance disconnected, threw his phone onto the bed, and cursed. He didn't care if he called Hanna a thousand times; he needed to find out if Chirp was all right. Why in hell hadn't she contacted her friend like she'd promised?

It had been a week, and during that time he hadn't slept more than two hours a night. Hanna's old Toyota wasn't dependable. Chirp was alone, and according to Hanna, had no plan. Who strikes out with no idea of where they're going? She could have had car trouble and ended up with a serial killer. Okay, he was letting his imagination get the best of him. Sleep deprivation did that.

But still, she had no right to leave without talking to him. Coffee. Caffeine would make him feel better. That or whiskey, and it was too early for the hard stuff. He stomped to the pantry and eyed the cans arranged in perfect order. He didn't need this shit, or her. Grabbing peas in one hand and chili in the other, he moved everything around like playing a game of checkers. *Alphabetical order my ass.*

Busy-work. That's what he wanted. Something to keep his mind off her and drinking. He still had scrap lumber to clean up, so that should do the trick. He was tired of worrying. And his damn nightmares were back. In full force.

He got the wheelbarrow and tossed blocks of two-by-fours into it. After he rolled the first load to the burn pile, he came back for more. Every way he turned, something reminded him of her. The overgrown garden. Wildflowers across the road. Bluebirds darting in and out of their houses.

He pitched more wood into the cart and thought of Tom Fraser. Rance had expected the PI to come back, but he hadn't. And what about the stepmother? Guess the detective figured his warning worked, because only a fool would have hung around, and Chirp was no idiot. She'd been smart enough to cover her tracks for three years she could do it again. That's what bothered him. He'd never find her unless she wanted to be found.

One hint. That's all Rance needed. Something to point him in the right direction.

He stared into space. Desperate times called for desperate measures. He didn't know who said that, but it was true. He palmed his phone and punched in Hanna's number again. She answered on the first ring.

"Look, Rance. I told you I'll let you know when I hear from her."

"That's not why I'm calling. I want you to report your car stolen."

Chapter 32

Blaze

With her phone camera app, Blaze waited for the perfect shot of Ethan as he trimmed shrubs in the courtyard. He came each Thursday, quickly removed his shirt, and tied a bandanna around his head like an Indian warrior. More than once Odette had tried her best to get Blaze interested in the gardener, and he *was* nice to look at. Lean planes, hard muscles, and a light dusting of hair on his tanned chest. From an artist's standpoint, Blaze wanted to capture his image on canvas, but figured she'd come across as creepy if she asked him to pose.

A photo would be enough. She waited until he fired up the hedge trimmer again, then framed his image within the screen and clicked several times. Across the way, Odette watched through binoculars. Blaze understood she wasn't a dirty old woman; the artist in her couldn't resist a beautiful body.

The male form fascinated Blaze. Powerful hips. Bulging biceps. Defined abs—and his manhood. She found it most beautiful. Sculptors and artists had admired the human physique since time began. Not that she couldn't appreciate females, but they didn't captivate her in the same way.

She strolled back inside and finished the bowl of grapes and strawberries she'd brought home from breakfast with Odette. Funny. That sounded like a movie title. She popped a grape into her mouth.

Hard to believe it was almost the end of July. She painted every day, and other than two portraits of Muttly and one of Noah, she'd been obsessed with Rance. Canvas after canvas leaned against the walls of her bedroom, all in different phases, but none completed. Torso. Backside. Frontal view. Half-naked. Nude. She should toss them out. Build a bonfire. See if she could burn out her burning desire. Funny. Not funny. Looking at his image was torture. She didn't understand why she did it. He'd lied to her. She should never want to see him again. Maybe that's why she'd avoided adding his face to any of the paintings.

The motor on the hedge trimmer died, and Blaze stepped back to the porch. Odette came across the courtyard. Dressed in white slacks with a hot-pink silk blouse, a turquoise cuff bracelet adorned each wrist and a matching oversize dragon fly pin rested at her throat. Her shoes were orange with sequin owls on the toes. The woman was a palette of color and design. Blaze wished she could get away with that style, but she'd feel like a clown. Probably look like one, too.

Within a minute, Odette tapped on the door, opened it, and fluttered into the room like a butterfly searching for a flower. "I saw you photographing Ethan. Have you changed your mind? An orgasm would help your creativity. The furrows between your brows, *chérie*, well, they tell me you need a man." She swept her hands through the air. "Look at my face. Do you see any lines? No. Because I am not sexually frustrated." As she talked, she moved to the porch to stare at him. "Oh, if I was only ten years younger. I would take him for myself."

Blaze did the math. Even with the reduction, Odette would still be forty, almost twice Ethan's age. To have that much self-esteem would be wonderful. "No. I don't want a date. I want to paint him."

"Are you sure? Come here." Odette slipped an arm around Blaze's waist and nudged her forward. "Now, focus on his chest. How it glistens in the sun. Concentrate on that pale ring of skin where his jeans ride low. The muscles in his back. How they flex as he works that clipper thing." She turned to face Blaze. "Anything? A tickle? An ache?"

Blaze shook her head. "Nothing."

Odette threw her hands in the air. "You are hopeless! Bring those canvases."

Blaze left, then returned and set them against the wall.

[345]

"Spread them out, so I may see your progress."

As Blaze placed the art, Odette clicked her tongue and paced in front of the lineup. "This will not do. I demand you finish each of these. I am giving you two weeks."

"I've tried. Really, I have. I just can't."

"*Chérie*, you are thinking of things the wrong way. You must not dwell on what you've lost, but what you've gained." Odette grabbed her by the shoulders and guided her to stand at the canvas with Rance's naked torso. "Do not desire him. Instead, channel that into your creativity. Let your talent catch fire the same way your body did when his breath floated across your skin. Or when he was deep inside you. Allow that passion to come out in your work. I know it is difficult to lose a good lover, but find inspiration from the memories you have from the experience."

That was the problem. Blaze couldn't stop thinking about him and the way he'd made her feel. Odette was the one who didn't understand, because she didn't fall in love. She took pleasure when she wanted and left it at that. Two nights a week, Blaze saw a guy leave her home. A younger man in a business suit. "You don't love the gentleman who visits you?"

Odette fluttered her lashes. "No. But I love our time together."

"Is he married?"

[346]

"Yes. And with his wife, he must be proper and polite. With me he can be dirty and take my word. Men want that in the bedroom. They like for a woman to tell them what they desire, and when they deliver, they need praise for a job well done. It is our responsibility to make them better lovers. His wife does not know what she is missing."

"You don't feel guilty?"

"Why should I? She doesn't want to be bothered with him. Besides, I'm not trying to take him from her."

"He could be lying."

Odette smiled. "I know it to be true, because I know her. Enough about me." She pointed her finger. "Two weeks, *chérie*. That is all I'm giving you."

She didn't wait for Blaze to say anything else. She spun around and disappeared out the door. Blaze swallowed hard and glared at the paintings. Odette was right. She should finish them.

Rance stood on the front porch and knocked back another slug of whiskey. Didn't know how many he'd had. He'd lost count.

Even in the dark, the garden mocked him. Tomatoes dried on the vines. Beans had shriveled in the hot sun. Bare okra stalks stood as tall as Rance. The only things he'd watered were the zinnias and hollyhocks, and that was because they'd meant so much to Gran. Didn't have a damn thing to do with Chirp.

He studied the almost-empty bottle, turned it up, and swallowed the last bit. Damn her. Damn the vegetables. He staggered off the porch and stumbled to the shed. After two tries, he pulled himself into the driver's seat of the tractor and fired it up. It still had the disc harrow attached, which was a good thing because he didn't think he was sober enough to connect farm tools.

He backed out and wheeled around to face the patch, revved the engine, put it in gear, and lowered the blades. After one pass, he swung wide, realigned, and repeated. When he got to the end of the row, light beams swept over him. Seth and Nick stood nearby, in their underwear and bare feet, both holding flashlights.

He waved to them and made another round.

Yelling, they ran after him.

He killed the engine.

"What the hell are you doing?" Seth screamed.

Tongue thick, Rance pushed the words out. "Getting rid of the garden."

"At four o'clock in the damn morning? Have you lost your mind?" Seth asked.

Nick chimed in. "Yeah, he's lost it, all right. Get off, Rance."

Rance weaved in the seat and swung his hand in the air. "No, I'm plowing all this under. She's not coming back, and it's her fucking garden. It needs to go. Same as her."

"And what will that prove?" Seth asked. "That you're a jackass? Leave it alone. Come inside and go to bed. You haven't slept in days."

Rance leaned forward and almost fell from the seat, but grabbed the steering wheel. "Where is she, Seth? Hanna knows. She's got to."

Both brothers dragged him off.

"She doesn't know. I swear. If she did, I'd tell you."

Rance tried to take a step, but his feet were too heavy. "Chirp wanted too much from me."

"Well, you don't have to worry about that now, do you? Got him, Nick?"

"Yeah."

[349]

Seth looped Rance's other arm around his shoulder as Nick had done, and they maneuvered him inside. "You've got to stop drinking, Rance. It's getting out of hand."

"It's my fault, you know. I went to that reward site trying to find out who she was, and that brought the PI here. I fucked up. I fucked up, and I can't undo it. She hates me now. Didn't even say goodbye. Kiss my ass. Nothing." Tears streamed down his face.

"She doesn't hate you," Nick said.

"Yeah, she does, and I deserve it."

"Let's get him onto the couch," Seth said.

They eased him into position and let him fall onto the sofa.

"I've got to find her. I don't know how, but I have to."

Seth removed Rance's shoes, while Nick propped a pillow behind him and ran his hand across his forehead.

"We'll help you." Nick said.

Seth knelt next to his big brother and patted his cheek. "Nick's right. We'll help find her, but only if you promise to stop drinking. We can't spend all our time trying to keep you sober. Because it *ain't* working."

Rance patted his brother's cheek and tried to look at him but couldn't. "I love you, Seth. You too, Nicky. I knew I could count on you. I promise I'll do better." He closed his eyes.

Seth slapped him, and Rance's eyes popped open. "Listen, Rance. Doing better won't cut it. You've got to swear you'll quit the whiskey. Crawling into a bottle won't change anything. If you don't stop, then you're on your own. Understand?"

"Yeah," Rance said, and wished for another drink because he was still conscious.

Chapter 33

✦

Blaze

Blaze slid the blouses across the rod and wondered why she'd agreed to this outing. Easy answer. Odette was rewarding her for finishing the paintings.

The woman got her way about everything. Plus, Odette's late night visitor had stopped visiting, and that had put her in a foul mood. Claimed a shopping spree would lift her spirits.

"Ooh, look at this. It would be beautiful on you, *chérie*. Sexy, even."

Blaze eyed the black embroidered-lace peasant top with a sheer midriff. She'd never worn anything so revealing, but had to admit it appealed to her. Maybe Odette's fashion sense was rubbing off on her. "It is pretty."

Odette shoved it toward her. "You must try it on. It will be perfect with either skinny jeans or a skirt." She pointed to a nearby table. "Strap on those wedge heels, and you'll be the hottest thing around." She turned back to the display. "And this one, too."

Now Odette flipped a sleeveless royal-blue peplum from front to back to display the sheer insets. What was with her? Everything she selected exposed skin.

"You're so small, this will look lovely. Perfect to wear to your friend's wedding."

Blaze snapped her head around. "I told you I'm not going."

"Why? Because your former lover will be there?"

"That isn't the reason." She'd been a blabber-mouth during their morning breakfasts. But there was something about Odette that pulled out information before Blaze knew what was happening. She'd shared too much about Rance and everyone else in Bluebird. Well, she hadn't told her what city they were in. She wasn't a total fool, but had a hard time resisting Odette's persuasive powers.

"You should wear revealing things while you're young. Soon you will be old and feel the need to cover most of your body. Liver spots. Crepe skin. No matter how hard you work to maintain your face, the rest will betray you." Odette waved her hand in the air. "You think I am being silly. You are barely twenty, but so was I just a few months ago." She giggled. "Time goes so fast. That's why we must grab all the joy we can."

[353]

"I'll try them on, but I make no promises."

"Your word today is démodé. It means out-of-date. We cannot have you dressing that way. Especially now that I've arranged an exhibit for you at Kennamer Gallery."

Blaze spun on her. "What? No! I don't want my work shown. Why did you do that without discussing it with me?"

"Calm down, *chérie*. It is your responsibility to share your talent. Your nudes are some of the best I've seen. You will show them. I will not allow you to refuse."

Blaze couldn't do this. People would expect the artist to appear. She collapsed onto a sofa and lowered her voice. "No. Odette. You don't understand. I can't make public appearances or sign my work."

The woman narrowed her eyes. "You say that as if it's dangerous. Is it?"

She nodded.

"So, there is more to your story than a broken heart?"

Another nod.

"This lover. Did he mistreat you?"

"No, no. He was good to me. It's someone else I need to avoid. Please, I can't be in the spotlight."

Odette ran her thumb over Blaze's cheek. "I understand. But that will make the show even more popular.

A new artist who insists on remaining a mystery. I love it! I'll arrange everything."

Blaze wished she could get as excited as Odette, but she couldn't. At least not about the art show. The clothes were a different story. Once she'd tried on everything, she'd fallen in love with the way the fabric felt against her skin.

Later that night she tried to sleep, but too many thoughts flooded her brain. She finally gave up and climbed out of bed. Maybe hot chocolate would help. A stupid thought. The drink was not a sedative. She poured water into a pan and set it on the burner, then took a cup from the cabinet.

All the way home, Blaze had begged her landlady to cancel the show, but she didn't get Odette to budge. She admitted Odette seemed to have the problem worked out. She'd handle all the personal contact. Even so, Blaze should leave. Pack her things and get out of Austin. But where would she go? She ripped the cocoa package open and emptied it into the cup, poured in the water, and stirred.

Closing her eyes, she blew a steady breath across the surface and thought about the time she had left—and Rance. God, she hated that he kept popping into her head. She missed him. And Muttly. The treehouse. Working in the garden.

Taking a slow sip, she put the cup on the counter, and returned to the canvas she'd started earlier.

[355]

Rance

Two months sober. Shouldn't he get a chip or something for that milestone? Nope. He wasn't an alcoholic—just a guy drinking to forget a woman. Well, he should give testimony somewhere because it sure as hell didn't work. An ocean full of whiskey wouldn't be enough to forget Chirp. To make matters worse, without her curled against him, every night, bad dreams tormented him.

He leaned his head back, turned up the radio, and recalled the last time he'd seen her. Right before she'd packed her things and left. He could have fixed everything is she'd waited. As always, he'd done the wrong thing and now suffered the consequences.

He clung to the smallest hope she'd show up at Seth and Hanna's wedding, but he knew better. Once Chirp committed to something, she kept with it.

After all this time, his only lead was Hanna's car being found in Dallas. A dead end. From there he had no idea where to look next. Might still be in Big D.

The dog raised his head and perked his ears, then Rance heard the noise. He rose from his chair, walked around the end of the house, and found Tom Fraser halfway out of his car. A woman sat inside.

Rance adjusted his sunglasses. "What the hell do you want?"

"Thought I'd follow up on the girl."

"Get off my property."

Before Tom said anything, the woman got out and pinned Rance with her gaze. "Mr. Keller, I'm Helga Scudder. I practically raised Wren and I need to know if she's okay."

That was true. Chirp had told him about her nanny, and her description matched right down to the red hair. "Sorry, can't help you." He turned to leave, but she called after him.

"Please, Mr. Keller. I'd not thought about your grandmother in a long time, but once Tom told me he was coming to Bluebird, I remembered a photo from Mr. Montgomery's college days. He and your mother were friends."

Rance kept walking, and Helga continued to talk.

"Tom is good at what he does. We know you've been in prison."

Rance spun around, jerked his glasses off, and spoke through clenched teeth. "I'd never hurt her."

Helga gasped and put her hand against her throat. "You care about her."

True. But he'd explained to Chirp he wasn't the man for her, and Helga agreed, because she'd already judged him unworthy. And he deserved it. He was innocent of arson, but guilty of much worse.

"Like I said. Can't help you." This time Rance made it to the porch before she spoke again.

"I'll bet she brought out a kindness you didn't even know you had."

The woman was right on every level. He faced her again. "She was fine when she left. I don't have a clue where she is. I wish to hell I did." Rance grabbed the screen door handle and pulled it open.

"I can trace her to Waco," Tom said.

Rance wheeled around to focus on the PI. "How?"

"I had a guy staked out on the main road. If she was here, I figured she'd run. Also knew she wouldn't use her car. He followed her to Dallas, where she ditched the vehicle. Took a bus to Waco, but then he lost her. As far as we can tell, she's still there. You sure she hasn't contacted you?"

"Why didn't your guy grab her?"

"Hired to find her, not return her. Marla has goons for that."

"Why are you telling me this?" Rance asked.

Tom raised his brows and glanced at Helga.

Women and their power. Rance's stomach knotted, the same as it had every day since Chirp left. "I didn't handle the situation well. I'll be the last person to hear from her."

Helga folded her arms beneath her ample breasts. "Then what are you going to do about that?"

"Nothing I can do."

"Go after her. Find her. Protect her," Helga said.

"Don't you think I would if I could? My brothers and I have brainstormed about every possible way to locate her. No luck. Dallas. Waco. They're big cities. It'd be like trying to find a minnow in the ocean. Thousands of miles. One of me."

"So you're giving up?"

"I have no choice. I appreciate the information, but I don't see how it helps." He glared at Tom. "If you can't find her, what makes you think I can?"

"Thought you might have inside info. Maybe she mentioned someone in Waco."

"If she'd shared her past with me, I would have never gone to that website, and we wouldn't be having this conversation." Rance opened the door and went inside. Helga was right. He had to do something, but what? For the first time in weeks, he wanted a drink. He grabbed the keys to his Harley.

When Rance got to The Roost, the place was almost empty except for a trio of older guys and three forty-somethings dressed too young for their age. All bright colors and bleached hair made him think of Chirp's cleanup garb. He pulled up the photo on his phone and couldn't help but chuckle. But then he thought about never seeing her again, and his mood turned dark.

Today he'd stick with beer and skip the whiskey. He ordered his drink, and when the bartender gave it to him, Rance headed to a back table. He should be glad about the information the PI had shared, and he was, but it was no help. More than anything, it reminded him this whole situation was his fault.

Lost in gloom, he didn't notice the man staggering toward him. The short, skinny dude was almost to the table when Rance saw him. He set down his bottle and rolled his eyes up to look at the guy. "S'up?"

"I seen you eye-fucking my woman."

The last thing Rance needed was trouble. But that was what this idiot wanted. He reminded himself he wasn't in prison anymore, and had nothing to prove. "I apologize." No clue which of the three bar-babes the guy was referring to, and it didn't make much difference. This nut was looking for a fight.

The redneck's ego deflated. He'd expected a confrontation and didn't get one, but he was too sloshed to give up. He raised his voice. "Well, I don't accept your apology. I'm gonna whip your ass."

Rance leaned forward and plastered on a smile, but added steel to his voice. "Listen closely. I'll give you a way out of this as to not embarrass yourself, but if you don't take it, we'll step outside and I. Will. Put. You. Down." Rance stood, raised his hands in surrender, and spoke loud enough for the guy's friends to hear. "Again, I sincerely apologize— to you and your lady. I meant no disrespect."

He towered over the wimp by a good six inches and outweighed him by forty pounds. The fool had no muscle, probably from spending too much time in here. Rance's defined physique came from years of perseverance. He could snap this opponent's neck like a fresh green bean. He just hoped the chump had enough remaining brain power to make the right choice.

And then he saw the sweat glistening on the man's forehead and recognized his expression. Fear. Rance backed away and eyed him. "We good?"

He nodded.

It was time to get the hell out this place. All Rance had wanted was to enjoy a beer in peace. So much for that. As he straddled the Harley, his phone chimed.

"Hey, what's going on?"

"Come to the shop. I need to talk to you."

The tone of Hanna's voice worried him. "What's wrong?"

"Are you coming or not?"

"On my way."

During the fifteen minutes it took to get there, Rance's mind raced. Was there already trouble in paradise? Seth was living in Houston during the week and in Bluebird only on weekends. Rance wasn't sure the arrangement was a good one, but Hanna was busy planning the wedding and they still needed to find a house. Until then, she didn't want Noah having to change schools.

He came to a stop and dismounted. In three long strides he was inside. Hanna stood behind the counter, glued to her laptop. "Are you in love with Blaze?"

Rance shook his head. "What the hell? All the way over here I've been going crazy wondering what you wanted to talk about—and that's it? What damn difference does it make? *She* left me. Remember?"

"I didn't lie when I said I didn't know where she was, but if I did, I'd need a good reason to tell you. I mean, what would be the use of finding her only for you to hurt her again? She wanted you to love her. So, do you?"

"Goddammit, Hanna! If you've heard from her, tell me."

"I haven't, but I still need to know how you feel about her."

Rance ran his hand over his face. "Fuck. First the PI comes calling, and now this shit. Contrary to what you think, love doesn't fix every problem in the world. So if you've got something to say, say it."

"What did the PI want?"

"Said he'd tracked her to Waco, but lost her there."

Hanna smiled. "Then it makes sense."

"What?"

"I was clearing out my history on my laptop, and during the time Blaze was taking care of the goats, she searched for rental property in Austin. I think she's there."

Chapter 34

Blaze

Blaze spent the morning watching Ethan, the yard hunk, move pumpkins from one place to the next as Odette directed. Wasn't sure if the woman had really been undecided or wanted to see Ethan's muscles flex and his jeans dip low as he bent to arrange them.

Whatever the reason, it had paid off because the courtyard looked like an autumn magazine cover.

Blaze refocused on the canvas she'd finished. Ethan was a fine specimen. She'd gotten to know him over the past few months, and it turned out he wasn't the least bit offended to learn she'd been painting his portrait.

Clearly Odette hoped Blaze would develop more than artistic interest in him, but that hadn't happened. He was a nice young man, but when she was near him, nothing tingled or tightened. Guess it was a good thing since she'd learned he had a steady girlfriend. That information had burst her landlady's matchmaking bubble.

She glanced at the mesh blouse, leather skirt, and wedge heels laid out on the chair. Add chandelier earrings, and she'd have the perfect ensemble for tonight's special dinner at Odette's house.

Closing her eyes, Blaze thought about her upcoming birthday, less than two months away. She'd concentrated on hiding for so long, the soon-to-be freedom frightened her. She'd be able to do anything she wanted without looking over her shoulder. As crazy as it sounded, it would be an adjustment. But she'd have Hanna. By then her friend would live in Houston. The downside? Crossing paths with Rance at some point. Wasn't sure how she'd handle that. Being in the same room with the love of her life and not touching him would be agony.

She went back outside and eased onto the lounge chair, pulling a blanket around her. It was only the middle of September, but a crisp breeze cut at her face, and the odor of burning wood tickled her nose. There was something peaceful about a crackling fire. Over the years she'd enjoyed plenty of evenings in front of Dessie's. She shook the memory away. No need to dwell on Bluebird, because every time she did, sadness overwhelmed her.

Rance

Rance had been in Austin for two weeks checking all the ads Chirp had searched on Hanna's computer, but so far no luck. Each rental company had pages of properties, and there was no way to know which ones she had considered.

He'd compared what had been available during that time to what had leased since then. Once he made that list, he drove by each location and staked it out until he saw the new tenant. Knowing Chirp, she'd avoid apartment buildings, so he'd concentrated on individual dwellings and duplexes. That narrowed the possibilities, but there were still hundreds.

He parked his Harley and strolled inside Rise and Shine breakfast bar. Staying at a nearby motel, he'd found plenty of places to eat. This one had been a godsend. Locally owned, they offered a buffet with fifteen different bacon flavors.

He grabbed a complimentary newspaper from the end of the counter and slid into a booth. Within a few seconds, the waitress came to get his drink order. While he waited, he helped himself to the buffet, then returned to his seat and scanned the headlines. Texas Book Festival Expecting Record Turnout. Texas Mom Convicted of Man Slaughter. Austin Police Body Cameras on Hold.

The server brought his coffee and sashayed away. He folded the paper, laid it aside, and texted Seth. His brother was working long hours but loved his job. Chirp had done a good thing because she was a good person. Better than Rance deserved.

He finished his pancakes and fought the urge to smoke a cigarette. Following a meal was when he wanted one the most. Would the craving ever go away? He wondered that about her, too. Would he ever stop wanting her? He didn't think so.

He slid across the plastic seat and knocked the newspaper to the floor. As he gathered the pages, something caught his eye. He sat again and stared at the events section. Kennamer Gallery Hosts Anonymous Artist. There, in the center of the page, in all his glory, Rance's torso. The scar on his belly proved it. *Holy shit.*

Board chairman Odette Fontaine discovered the local talent. The artist, who wishes to remain a mystery, has caused quite a stir among art critics. Located on Congress Avenue.

His pulse raced.

It didn't take long to find the address, and he angled into a spot in front. A park next door provided a good place to wait until the gallery opened. His insides jumped. He'd found her. Really found her. He couldn't believe it. She'd never agree to go public with her paintings. Not while hiding.

[367]

What was the woman's name? Why hadn't he brought the paper?

God, he wasn't thinking straight. He palmed his phone. Fumbled. Dropped it. Damn, hoped he hadn't broken the thing. *Calm down.* He took a deep breath and retrieved the cell. Thankfully it was still in once piece. He pulled up today's edition. Odette Fontaine. With a few more taps, he had her address.

The lights came on in the building. Once inside, he wandered from painting to painting. It was as if he'd fallen into a dream. Canvases of his body hung on every wall.

"It's beautiful work, isn't it?"

Rance turned to face a young perky blonde. "Yeah."

The woman placed her palm against her windpipe and got all dreamy-eyed. "Every stroke is so intimate. Almost erotic. Clearly the artist is in love with the model." The girl traced the line of his scar in the air with her finger, then snapped out of her trance. "Look at his fingers. So detailed. The way the cuticles hug the nails."

Without thinking, Rance held out his hand and inspected it.

The girl gasped. "Oh. My. God. It's you! You're the model."

He shook his head so fast his brain rattled. "No. No. I'm not. I imagine most men have similar hands."

She narrowed her eyes. "It's you, all right. See this freckle?" She pointed to the spot on his thumb. "Only a person in love with you would add such a small detail. I'll bet if I could see your stomach, I'd find the scar. Wait here. Mr. Kennamer will want to meet you."

As soon as the girl disappeared, Rance found the nearest exit. Didn't want to risk her ripping his shirt open to prove her point.

As he drove away, he thought about his next move. He wanted to rush over to the Fontaine address and see if Chirp was there, but that wasn't the best strategy. No, he'd rent a car. That way he'd blend in. He grinned. Modern term for his plan: stalking. But his motivation was different. For all he knew, this Odette person stole Chirp's work. She could have Chirp tied up in a cellar. Okay, his mind was going wild again, but honestly, that was the only thing that made sense. Not the cellar part, but the stolen art part. Anyway, he needed to be sure before he charged in like the cavalry.

By five o'clock, everything was in place. He'd rented a car, returned to the motel, showered, and dressed in the new clothes he'd bought. He was like a teenager going on a first date. But if Chirp was there, showing up road-weary wouldn't help his cause. Not if he wanted to make things right between them. Apologize and confess. That's what he had to do. But once he did, chances were she'd never want to see him again. Couldn't blame her. He'd pushed her away, and up until two weeks ago, had refused to admit his feelings for her.

[369]

He loved her.

Had from the moment she'd helped with his tie. He'd just been too much of jerk to admit it.

He found a spot with a clear view but far enough away not to be noticed. Tinted back windows in the rented Camry provided good cover. A courtyard separated the main house from a garage apartment. This was the kind of place Chirp would choose. She was here. He could feel it.

It was almost six when a brunette came out onto the balcony. His heart sank. The girl was dressed all in black. Typical, but too modern for Chirp. She dropped into a chair and covered herself with a blanket. After a few minutes, she went back inside. He wished he'd bought binoculars.

Time crawled, and he'd about given up when the door opened. She came down the steps and strolled through the courtyard to the main house. Definitely Chirp. Now all he had to do was wait.

Blaze

The suspense was killing Blaze, but she suffered through the meal until Odette was ready to make whatever dramatic announcement she had planned. It must be big, because she'd gone all out. Caterers served each course as if she and Odette were dining in a Paris restaurant. For dessert she'd had her choice of raspberry macrons, apple galette, or crepes Suzette.

The server popped the cork on a bottle of champagne.

Odette smiled. "You will be old enough to drink in two months, and that is close enough to celebrate this special occasion."

The waiter poured, and Odette raised her champagne flute in a toast. "*Chérie*, you have been invited to exhibit two of your paintings at the Aurora Gallery in New York City. Congratulations! This is quite the accomplishment, and I could not be prouder." She clinked her glass with Blaze's.

Blaze's head spun. Not wanting to be rude, she'd intended to sip, but now she gulped, then asked for more, and again, drained it in one long swig. "I don't know what to say."

"Merci will suffice. This is the beginning of a wonderful career for you, and I am so happy to be a small part of it."

Blaze didn't want to be ungrateful, but she'd never wanted this. However, the sparkle in Odette's eyes proved her excitement, and Blaze couldn't bear the thought of disappointing her. "Yes, merci. Which paintings, and when will they show?"

"Not until January. A new career in the new year. So wonderful!" Odette rose and twirled, her chiffon caftan

[371]

fluttering like a butterfly emerging from its chrysalis. "They want the full frontal and back nudes. I think you should send the one from your bedroom."

Blaze choked on her third drink. "No! You weren't supposed to see it." It was the one of Rance lying in the hay after the best night of her life. The only one she'd done that included his face.

"I understand. It was merely a suggestion. Are you okay? You're a little pale."

"It's the champagne. I'm not used to drinking. I should go home."

Odette cupped her elbow. "Yes. It's the result of this wonderful surprise. How I would have loved an opportunity like this at your age. Oh, *chérie*, your talent has brought such bliss into my life! Go. Rest. You'll be better tomorrow."

As Blaze walked across the courtyard, she wanted to scream. Odette had taken over her life. She was making decisions for her. At least the exhibit didn't start until January. By then she'd be in Houston running Montgomery Steel, and it would be fine for her to reveal her identity. Even so, the attention would be too much. People not only judging her work, but her, too.

Dizzy from the alcohol and the news, she passed the last pile of pumpkins and stepped to the bottom of her stairway. A figure, sitting in the shadows, startled her. Breath rushed from her lungs.

"Rance."

Chapter 35

Rance

An hour earlier, when Chirp had disappeared into the house, all Rance could do was wait and rehearse what he'd say.

The wind picked up and scattered leaves from beneath the maple trees lining the street, creating a swirl of red. It wouldn't be long until the weather turned cold for good. He'd thought about lying in front of the fireplace with her curled against him. But what if she didn't want him anymore? Served him right.

He glanced at his watch, got out of his car, and ambled across the street. Shrubs hid the view of the stairway from the main house, and he settled on the second step. A catering van sat in the drive, so they must be having a party. There were no sounds of music, laughter or conversation, but that meant nothing. Chirp might even have a date.

He texted Seth and Nick. Wanted them to know he'd found her and promised an update later. Then he turned off his phone so he wouldn't have any interruptions once he had her alone.

A door closed across the way. Footfalls. A cadence he recognized. He sucked air into his lungs as she rounded the corner. He eyed her from head to toe, trying to make her plain, back at the farmhouse in jeans, digging in the dirt, planting flowers. No luck. Not with her dark hair, trendy clothes, and dangling earrings. She wasn't Blaze Bledsoe anymore. She was Wren Montgomery. Beautiful. Sophisticated. *Rich*. And he wasn't good enough.

"Rance." Her hand flew to her chest and her voice trembled. "What are you doing here?"

"You left without saying goodbye."

"There wasn't time." Unsteady, she grabbed on to the railing.

Even in the faint light, he saw how pale she was. He wanted to touch her, feel her softness. Have her arch against him as he buried deep inside her. Whisper his name. Beg him for more. "Are you okay?"

"Champagne went to my head."

"You've been drinking?"

"A little. But I'm all right. Let's go inside."

He stepped back for her to pass, and she opened the door without a key. "You really shouldn't leave your place

[375]

unlocked. Never know when an ex-con might show up on your doorstep."

She faced him. "Are you being sarcastic?"

"Yeah. You're getting good at recognizing that." He scanned the room, his eyes settling on the painting of a half-naked man. A young, handsome dude. Clean-cut. About her age. Rance leaned down and studied the guy's cuticles. Hell, he couldn't tell if they hugged his fingernails or not. He nodded toward the canvas. "Somebody important to you?"

"He mows the lawn."

"But—you'd like him to be important?" Rance straightened his shoulders and prayed for the right answer. What if she'd moved on and didn't love him anymore? Or realized it'd been a crush all along. She'd never said the words because he hadn't allowed it. His stupid rules. But she'd told Hanna, and women confided in their best friends things they didn't share with anyone else, so it had to have been true. But now?

"No." She turned away, but not before Rance saw a tear roll down her cheek. He wanted to grab on to her and never let go. Tell her what a fool he was. How he'd finally come to his senses. But not before he got everything off his chest.

She walked into the kitchen calling over her shoulder, "Do you want something to drink? All I have is water."

What he wanted was to get her naked and fuck her into next week, but that wasn't a great opening line. He shoved his hands into his pockets. "It's my fault the PI found you, and I'm sorry. Curiosity got the best of me, but I should have waited until you were ready to tell me about yourself."

"It's okay. I don't blame you anymore. I mean, I did at first. But not now."

He rocked back on his heels. "Well, I do, and I'll never forgive myself for it."

She took a glass from the cabinet and filled it with water, gulped, wiped at her eyes, then faced him again. "You look terrible. Not ugly terrible. Because you look really good. I mean, you look worried terrible. So, what's wrong?"

"Everything."

She rushed to him. "I love you. I know you don't want me to, and I've tried not to, but I can't help it. I kept telling myself if I could make a whole day without thinking about you it would mean I was getting over you. But it's been 153 days, and it hasn't happened yet."

Damn. He'd been doing the same thing. He'd argued with himself about how wrong it was on so many levels. She had no business falling for the first man she slept with. An ex-con would never fit in with her rich friends. But the most important reason was the deal breaker. "Once you know me, you won't love me."

"But I do know you."

For a moment, he didn't speak, but confession was supposed to be good for the soul, and his was in trouble. With the secret tightened around his throat, he felt like a man about to be hanged. Other than Hector, no one knew the truth. "No, you don't. I—I—I murdered a man, Chirp. And it wasn't self-defense. I thought about it. Planned it. Watched him die. And even now, after all this time, the only regret I have is that I can't kill him again. I'm glad he's dead."

Her gaze didn't waver, and there wasn't a hint of judgment in her eyes. "Is that what your nightmares are about?"

"Yes."

"Was he the one who gave you the scar?"

The memory flashed through his mind as vivid as if it happened yesterday. Donald Wayne Pittman. Inmate #05192106. Rance had been tormented by Pittman. Almost killed by him. Lived in fear of him, until he couldn't take it anymore. Rance had memorized everything about the guy. Every tattoo, scar, blemish. He'd never hated anyone the way he'd hated him. Not even Jack for putting him in that hellhole to begin with. Rance swallowed hard. "Yeah."

She slid her arms around him and rested her cheek on his chest. "Then I'm glad he's dead, too."

He'd opened up to her, and she hadn't batted an eye. She was the one person who'd seen him at his worst and now knew his darkest secret, yet she loved him in spite of it. How could she overlook everything he'd done and still find good in him? The part that wanted to take care of her. Protect her. *Love* her. He pulled away and took her hands in his. "Marry me."

She stumbled backward. "What?"

"Marry me."

She shook her head. "I heard the investigator. You're trying to save me, but I only have a few more weeks. I'll be fine."

Everything he'd denied for so long crashed down on him with an unbearable force, bringing the truth with it. "I'm not trying to save you. I need you to save me."

"From who?"

"Myself."

There. He'd gotten it all out. Almost. "I'm a selfish prick, and you'd be better off with someone else. But without you that old house has been more of a prison than Huntsville ever was. I'm suffocating, Chirp. I don't want to wake up another day knowing I can't see you. Touch you. But being with me won't be easy. Everyone will use me against you. Claim I only want you for your money. You'll be hurt, and it'll be my fault. But I love you so damn much. I . . ."

She pressed her hand to his lips. "Stop talking." Then she kissed him. Hard. Hot. Wet. Lust ripped through him with as much force as the jagged knife Pittman had used. Rance had been without her too long. She was still Chirp. Soft, warm, giving, and *his*. Desperate to be inside her, *own* her, he grasped the button on her skirt, undid it, and opened the zipper. "Get rid of this."

She stepped back enough to let the garment fall and pool at her ankles. Then she kicked out of it, grabbed the hem of her blouse, and stripped it off. She wasn't wearing a bra, and the sight of those perfect little tits caused his cock to jump. God, it felt like years since he'd touched her, tasted her, held her; he wanted to do everything at once.

He gripped her waist, then nudged her back until she bumped the counter. "Keep the shoes."

She shivered, and he spun her around, pulled her backside tight against him, and whispered in her ear, "Ease your panties down." Damn, watching lace slide off her sweet ass tore him up inside. His balls drew so high and tight, he thought they might pop out the top of his head.

Once she was naked, he turned her, dropped to his knees, and flicked the belly button ring with his tongue. "I'm glad you still have this." His hot breath teased one inner thigh, then the other, until he palmed her hips with both hands, brought her to his mouth, and licked into her.

[380]

Blaze

Blaze struggled to pull air into her lungs, but only managed to half fill them. She tried to pinpoint when things changed between them, but couldn't concentrate on anything but the sound of his moans as he tasted her. And when he brought her leg over his shoulder to go deeper, her mind went blank. God help her. A second later he hit the right spot, and she gripped the edge of the bar for support because her legs turned to rubber.

Low in her stomach, it began to build. She braced for impact and came hard. As the orgasm claimed her, he didn't stop the torture. He gave her only a few seconds to recover, then sucked her into his mouth again, and a second wave of pleasure attacked. Every muscle stiffened while her bones turned to liquid.

He rested his forehead against her belly. "Don't ever leave me again. I'll die if you do."

He rose and took her in his arms. Neither of them spoke, but he was hard, and she needed to take care of that. Pulling away, she slipped her hand in his and led him down the short hallway. No need to turn on a lamp the light streaming through the windows from the courtyard provided enough.

When they reached the bed, she unbuttoned his pants, pulled down the zipper, and let him take over. She removed her shoes while he got rid of his clothes. He lay back on the mattress. Now it was her turn to drop to her knees. She'd never done this before, but she'd thought about it.

He looked down at her and raised his brows. "Chirp?"

"I want to put it in my mouth. Not all of it. Just some. And don't ejaculate. Okay?"

He laughed. "Hell yeah." Then he leaned back to rest on his elbows and grinned. "Have at it."

She closed her fingers around it, licked the tip like an ice cream cone, and he must have liked it because he released a long sigh. Then she swirled her tongue, and he moaned. She glanced up. He had his eyes fixed on her. "Do you have to watch?"

"Yeah."

"Why?"

"Because I want to."

"Don't. It's my first time. I won't be good at it. It makes me uncomfortable."

A low rumble came from his chest. "FYI, no such thing as a bad blow job, unless you bite it off. But I can't keep this boner forever, so we have to do *something*."

"Okay." She went back to work and took more of it this time. He arched into her, and she got her rhythm. Slow at first, then faster. A sound she'd never heard him make before came from deep inside him.

He fisted her hair. "Stop, stop, Chirp, or it'll be too late." He jerked free and lifted her to straddle him, and slid into her with such ease, her head spun.

"Finish me. Go slow. It's been so long. I want to feel you." He placed his hands on her hips, and she loved the roughness of them.

"Oh yeah, just like that."

Her heart raced because she loved when he talked during sex. She rocked into him and he lifted his head to kiss her. Something was different. It wasn't just about satisfaction anymore. There was tenderness. She saw it and felt it. He'd let go of everything he'd kept buried. Pain. Fear. Guilt. And he'd trusted her with all of it.

When a tear dropped onto his chest, he stilled and gazed up at her. "What's wrong?"

"I don't know."

He tangled his hands in her hair and drew her closer, then thrust his tongue into her mouth. A kiss so sensual and hungry with need, it took her breath. She wanted to melt into his skin. That's the only way she could get close enough.

He whispered her name. Shifted. Rolled until he was on top. She coiled her legs around his hips to bring his thick, hard, length deeper.

"I'll never get enough of you," he growled as he pumped into her.

She dug her nails into his flesh and hung on. She knew his next move because he had her body memorized. He lifted her hips and stroked high into her. Within seconds, she climaxed and so did he. Collapsing next to her, he tried to get his breath back. "You okay?"

"Why wouldn't I be?"

"The blow job."

"I liked it."

He chuckled. "Good to know."

She rested her head on his chest. "With practice, I'll get better at fellatio."

He laughed so hard the bed bounced. "Damn, Chirp. I never know what will come out of that sexy mouth of yours."

She raised to look at him. "You think it's sexy?"

"Everything about you is sexy. You're the best thing in my life. All I want. All I think about. You never gave me an answer, but you'll marry me, right?"

[384]

"Yes."

"You got ID with your real name? I've got to marry Wren Montgomery for it to be legal."

"Yes."

"You can keep it, you know," he said.

"I don't understand."

"Montgomery connects you to your company, so if you don't want to take my name, it's okay."

She ran her fingers across his lips. "I want your name. Do you have a dollar?"

"In my wallet. Why?"

She slid out of bed, retrieved the billfold from his pants, and handed it to him. "Give me one."

He pulled his brows together, but took the money out and offered it.

She folded it neatly, then placed it on her side table. "Now it's Montgomery-Keller Steel."

Chapter 36

Rance

Rance sat straight up in bed and couldn't believe what she'd said. Sex affected her in ways he didn't understand. Give her an orgasm, she gives him a company. "Not a good idea, Chirp."

"Why not? You'll be my husband."

She looked so wide-eyed and innocent, he wanted her again. But that would have to wait. "Weren't you paying attention when I said people will judge you?"

She frowned. "I don't care."

"Well, I do. Besides, your dad would never want you to give part of your legacy away. Especially not to me."

"He . . ."

Rance folded his arms across his chest. "We're done talking about this. Now come to bed."

She flopped down next to him. "You're bossy."

He grasped his pants, and she groaned, "Stay naked."

"I am, but I have something for you." He reached inside his pocket, then settled beside her again. "It isn't a big rock, but it belonged to Dessie, so I hope the sentiment means more than a price tag. Let's make this official." Rance slipped the ring on her finger and she held it up in the soft light. Damn thing was so small it didn't sparkle much, but she stared at it like it was the Great Star of Africa.

"Perfect fit. I love it."

"I'll buy you something bigger later. Say, maybe for our first anniversary."

She switched on the bedside lamp, then poised her hand in midair. "I don't remember ever seeing Dessie wear this."

"After Pops died she put it away. The middle stone is from her original engagement ring. He added the circle of diamonds for their twenty-fifth anniversary. It'll have to play double duty for now, but later we'll have a custom band done. Whatever you want."

"Nothing could ameliorate this. That means *make better or improve*."

He gathered her in his arms. "Damn, I've missed your word of the day." From the corner of his eye, he caught a glimpse of the painting leaning against the opposite wall. "Holy shit!"

Chirp jumped at the outburst. "What?"

He pointed. "I thought you said nobody would see the picture you took in the barn. Damn, Chirp. You've painted me in living color on—what is that, a five-foot canvas?"

"Yeah."

He ran his hand over his face. Something about seeing himself naked and supersized made him uneasy. He thought the exhibit paintings were bad, but this was pornographic. "Thank God you didn't include this in the gallery."

"You've been to Kennamer Gallery?"

"It's how I found you. Well, one of the ways."

She clutched her throat. "Since you found me, Marla can, too."

He wrapped her in his arms. "It's okay. By then we'll be married, and no one can touch you." For the next few minutes, he gave her the details of how he'd come to Austin and fate had intervened. That's all it could have been. He'd had little clues, but someone upstairs made sure they'd been enough. Probably Gran.

Chirp shook her head. "Why is Helga helping the investigator?"

"I think she's helping *you*, and that's why he gave you a head start and came back to point me in the right direction."

She turned to face him and narrowed her eyes. "Why would he do that?"

"From the way he looked at your former nanny, I'd say there's something going on between them."

"Oh. I guess that's possible."

"Yeah." He pointed to the portrait again. "Now, about that. You've got to get rid of it."

"Why? It's art. And it helps when I—Never mind." She clamped her mouth tight.

"When you what?"

"Nothing."

Well, well. Little Miss Innocent wasn't so innocent. "Holy hell. You look at it while you Jill off, don't you?"

"There's nothing wrong with masturbating as long as you do it in private."

Not a sign of embarrassment. He thought about the first time he met her. Naked in the tub. She'd been shameless that night. He didn't think she had either emotion. But he did, and no way in hell he'd take a chance on the world seeing him in his birthday suit. The shadowed paintings were bad enough, but this one showed *everything*. He took a second to imagine her using it as an aid to pleasure herself. "I want to watch you."

"Why?"

"Because it'd turn me on."

Her eyes tracked south. "You're already turned on just talking about it."

He brushed his lips over hers. "Promise."

"I won't have to anymore because you're here now."

"Damn. I think you're probably the only woman who's ever fantasized about me while diddling the skittle."

She shoved him. "You're so nasty."

He chuckled. "Yeah. I'm the nastiest nasty boy you'll ever have."

"Stop talking."

"No. Not until we settle this picture dilemma. There isn't a single place you can hang that thing without the risk of someone seeing it. Do you want Hanna or Tiffany to see my junk? I don't." He rose from the bed and moved to the artwork.

Chirp laughed.

"What's so funny?" he asked.

"You, standing next to it. I did a really good job."

Rance looked down at himself, then at the canvas. "Yeah, you did, but like you said, you have the real thing now, so you don't need this." He turned it to face the wall. "That's better." He crawled back into bed and spooned her close. "We need sleep. In the morning, we'll get our license, and since there's a three day waiting period, you can use that time to plan the wedding."

She snuggled into him. "I want to go home."

"To Houston?"

"No. To Bluebird."

He raised her face to his and kissed her. "Do you have any idea how happy you make me?"

"No."

"You saved me, Chirp. For the longest time I didn't care about anybody but myself. Trust, compassion, love— well, those words weren't in my vocabulary anymore, until you."

She trembled in his arms.

He held her tighter. "Okay, I promise not to say any more mushy shit."

"I like the mushy shit."

He didn't say anything else. Just held her until she drifted off to sleep, loving how she felt in his arms. Finally his

[391]

world made sense, and he wasn't about to let anyone take that away.

$\mathcal{B}laze$

The next morning, Blaze opened her eyes and stared at her husband-to-be. Before she met him, the men in her fantasies didn't look like Rance. They'd been smaller, prettier, sophisticated. But here she was, hopelessly in love with a hard-living, nasty-talking hulk of a man who made her quiver at the sight of him. In spite of her quirks, he claimed to feel the same. And she believed him.

Offering half of the company had been a test, and even now, she wondered what she would have done if he'd accepted. Send him away? No. Not in a million years. She loved him too much. But he was right. Everyone would think he was after her money. Why else would he marry her? Well, she didn't care what people thought. She slipped out of bed, made a trip to the bathroom, took care of business, brushed her teeth, and slid in next to him again.

He rolled to face her. "Haven't changed your mind, have you?"

"About what?"

"Marrying me."

"Why would I?"

"Thought once you slept on it, you might have reconsidered," Rance said.

"Never. Now go brush your teeth because I want to have sex."

He chuckled.

"Why is that funny?"

"You're so direct."

"Is that bad? If it is, tell me how you want me to say it, and I will."

"No, baby. I like it, but you can send me the same message without saying anything." He took her hand and moved it south. "French kiss me or touch me right here, and it'll be pretty clear what you want. But the direct approach works. I need a shower. Come with me."

While the water warmed, Chirp sat on the edge of the tub, and Rance brushed his teeth. When he finished, he stepped into the spray and pulled her in with him.

She ran her fingers over his lips. "Mine?"

"Yeah."

Hungry for him, she trailed her hot breath across his chest, scraping her teeth over his nipples, then wrapped her fingers around his erection. "All mine?"

[393]

"Forever." Then he kissed her hard. Licked her throat. Bit her shoulder. His words echoed in her head. And she got lost in the passion. In him. Because he belonged to *her*.

He slid his hand down her belly, then lower, where he pushed his finger inside her and stroked.

"Oh yes. Don't stop," she begged. And he didn't. He knew what to do. Where to go. And after the first orgasm, he didn't waste time. He spread her legs wider and gave her all he had.

Water pelted. Steam swirled. Mist shrouded. Two bodies slick with need and desire moving as one. *Oh God.* There it was again. Like riding a roller coaster. *Climb. Climb. Climb.* Her body jerked, and she went mindless.

He buried his face in the crook of her neck and gasped, "Sweet Jesus. Just when I think it can't get any better, it does."

An hour later Blaze held Rance's hand as they walked across the courtyard. After what they'd done in the shower, the simple gesture shouldn't be so intimate, but it was.

Odette's eyes widened as she opened the door. "Come in, *chérie*." She zeroed in on Rance and took him in from top to bottom, hesitating at his crotch. She smiled and lifted her gaze to his face. *"Encore plus délicieux en personne."*

Rance looked at Blaze and raised a brow.

"Even more delicious in person," she translated.

"You speak French?"

"Yes. Rance, this is Odette Fontaine."

"Nice to meet you."

She latched on to his hand until Blaze gave her the evil eye. "I came to tell you I'm leaving."

"No! You must not leave me."

"I'm sorry, but I have things to take care of. I promise I'll return in a few weeks and go public with my art."

"So you and Rance have reconciled, *oui?*"

Rance slipped his arm around Blaze's waist. "We have, and I'll make sure she comes back."

"Oh, *chérie.* I will miss you so much."

"I'm sorry."

Odette threw her arms around Blaze. "Very well. If you must."

When Blaze and Rance got back to the apartment, he helped gather her things. With so little to pack, it didn't take long. She laughed when he shoved his portrait under the bed.

"You don't think Odette will take this to the gallery while you're gone, do you?"

"No."

[395]

He shook his head. "I hope to hell you're right. Hey, I came to Austin on my bike, but I rented a car, so we'll drive it home. I can return it in Danvers, but I'll need to arrange storage for the Harley."

"Let's ride it."

"You serious?"

"I've never ridden a motorcycle. It'll be fun."

"Are you sure? It's a long trip for a first timer."

Perfect. He wouldn't be able to talk, and that should give her enough time to figure out a way to convince him to live in Houston.

Chapter 37

✦

Wren

Relief washed over Blaze when the county clerk didn't recognize the name Wren Montgomery. Rance had been right. A missing heiress was old news, and no one remembered. She gazed at the signed marriage license. Blaze Bledsoe had served her purpose and no longer existed.

At nine-thirty, Rance drove the Camry into the lot at the rental place and reclaimed his Harley. Stuffing the paperwork into the saddlebag, he secured her duffel with a bungee cord. He handed her the only helmet, then straddled the seat, and her heart pounded at the memory of how those strong thighs had boxed her in hours earlier.

She eyed the bike from front to back. "What kind is this?" She didn't care about the answer. Only wanted time to work up the courage to get on the metal monster.

He grinned. "Street Glide Chopper. Vintage 2008. Badass, right?"

Wren swallowed hard. This might have been a bad decision. The machine had appeared harmless enough parked at the farmhouse, but now, standing next to all the black metal and chrome, it looked dangerous. Like the rider. "Yeah. Badass."

He cut his steely eyes over at her, and his mouth quirked up. "We're ready to roll. You ready to ride?"

He looked downright wicked in the best possible way. Bandanna tied around his head, ponytail hanging below the knot. She put on the helmet, took her place behind him, and snaked her arms around his waist.

"Hold on, baby." He kicked the engine to life, shot out of the parking lot and onto the highway.

She screamed, tightened her grip, and felt his laughter vibrate against her chest. He was testing her, or trying to scare her. She wasn't sure which. Blaze Bledsoe wouldn't be fazed, but Wren Montgomery was anything but a biker chick.

Once on the interstate, he weaved in and out of traffic like a choreographed dance. The wind tore at his hair, whipping strands loose.

As soon as he got out of the city, he took the first exit onto a state highway. Apparently he was taking the scenic route. Fine by her. Snuggled tight with his back muscles flexing against her and the vibration between her legs turned out to be a good combination.

Soon the mowed boundaries of the interstate gave way to butterfly weed, goat foot, and wild morning glories, which reminded her she had a wedding to plan. As soon as she got home, she'd find a dress online and have it shipped overnight. Rance would need a suit. *Wren Keller. Mrs. Wren Keller. Mrs. Rance Logan Keller.* She loved how each of those sounded.

Her thoughts bounced around between style, fabric, flowers, and cake. Even with a simple ceremony, tradition was important. She wanted a dress with lace. She could wear her mothers, but it was in storage. Uncle Bill had a key to the place, but he'd never find it among all the other stuff. No, she'd buy her own. Not enough time to get her mothers and have it cleaned and ready in three days. But she needed to contact Bill and ask him to give her away. Other than Helga, he was the closest person she had to family.

Rance stopped at a red light and leaned into her. "You doing okay?"

"Yes." The word echoed against the helmet like being in a well. The light changed, and this time he eased into the throttle, brought one booted foot off the pavement, placed the other on the foot pad, and gracefully leaned back, putting his neck in reach of her lips, and she couldn't resist. She planted a kiss first on one side and then the other. He reached back and gave her leg a squeeze, and she shivered.

Town after town flew by, some smaller than Bluebird. Wren tried to concentrate on her surroundings because she'd never been in this part of Texas. Banners for festivals and flea markets flashed by. Time slipped away, but as the sun moved behind them, she knew they had to be at least halfway home.

When they reached the city limits of a one-traffic-light town, he angled into a spot in front of a convenience store. Next to it was a taco/snow cone stand. An odd combination, but the aroma of grilled onions and peppers hung in the air, and Wren's stomach growled.

Rance spoke over his shoulder. "You get off first. The bathrooms are inside, and the last time I was here, they were decent. The tacos aren't bad either."

Wren dismounted, removed the helmet, and stretched. She was stiff all over, and her butt was numb. Rance didn't seem any worse for wear. His windblown hair and facial stubble only made him sexier. Inside, two teenaged female clerks gawked and pointed to the word painted on the metal saddlebag. Outlaw.

Rance swung his leg over the chopper and adjusted his junk. The two teens widened their eyes. Wren couldn't blame them. He deserved the title. If they only knew how bad he was, and by bad, she meant good, she might have a fight on her hands. She shivered.

"You cold? I have a sweatshirt in my bag." He walked to stand next to her and pulled her into his arms. "Or we can move around behind the building and I'll warm you up."

The girls inside were getting an eyeful. "Okay."

[400]

He sucked in air and coughed. "You're calling my bluff, aren't you?"

"Yes."

"Maybe later?"

"Maybe."

"That's my girl." He tilted up her chin. "You don't mind kissing a guy with bug juice on his teeth, do you?"

"Hush!" She wiped her mouth with her sleeve.

He laughed out loud. "I'll get us some tacos before we leave. Davy Crockett National Forest is right up the road. We can have a picnic."

When they arrived at the park, Rance found a good spot and angled the bike in between two tables. Wren had never seen a place so beautiful. A thick mixture of elm, oak, cedar and dogwood towered over the area with some of the leaves changing colors.

Crisp, cool air settled over her and she rubbed her arms. Rance pulled out the sweatshirt and draped it around her shoulders. She put it on, sat, then tore open the sack of tacos and spread the paper bag as a place mat.

He unscrewed the lids on two sodas, passed one over, and joined her. She crunched her food and washed it down with a big gulp of Diet Dr. Pepper. "It's so pretty here." A steady cadence echoed through the forest and Wren sat straighter. "Is that a woodpecker?"

[401]

Rance answered around a mouthful of food. "Uh-huh."

"Can I ask you something?"

"Sure."

"The guy you killed. How did you not get caught?"

He didn't answer at first, and she regretted asking. Then he took a deep breath and met her gaze. "My cell mate, Hector, took the fall. Said it wouldn't matter since he's serving life without parole. Some days the guilt gets to me, but I send money each month to his family, and add to his canteen account. That will never repay what he did for me, but at least he knows I'm not forgetting about him."

"I won't either."

For the next few minutes, she didn't speak, and neither did he. Just enjoyed the silence. A nice change from the roar of the engine and highway noise. After they finished their meal, Rance gathered the trash and put it in a can a few yards away. He joined her again and looped his arm around her, leaned in close, and whispered, "Let's make love on this table."

"It's against the law to have sex in a public place. This is a national park. It would probably be a federal crime."

"Then let's rent a cabin and spend the night."

She scooted around on the bench and laid her head in his lap so she had a great view of those dangerous blue eyes.

"We're only three hours from home. Don't you want to sleep in your own bed?"

"Sure, but I want to get you naked in a strange place even more." He stroked her cheek.

"Wasn't the shower strange enough?"

A hawk circled overhead and landed in a tall oak. Wren dragged the scent of damp earth and fermenting leaves into her lungs. The combination, along with the trees, birds, and his fingers trailing down her face, caused her toes to curl, and her resolve weakened for a moment. Her eyes fluttered. God, she could drift off to sleep.

"Yeah, that *was* good, but having your body pulse against me for two hundred miles has me horny as hell."

She felt the same way, but someone had to be level headed and neither of his heads reacted logically when it came to sex. But the lower one was definitely reacting now. She jerked upright and glared at his crotch. "Stop that! We need to go."

He followed her. "I hate you're wasting a perfectly good hard-on."

She remounted the motorcycle. "It isn't like it's the last one you'll ever have."

"It could be."

"Stop talking."

He laughed harder and fired up the Harley.

It was seven o'clock by the time they reached Bluebird. When she saw the old house, joy bubbled in her chest. She'd found safety here. Made friends. Fallen in love. If she left, could she be happy? She wasn't sure. What if Rance refused to move? She needed to find out before the wedding because living apart was out of the question.

The thought of being without him overwhelmed her. She tightened her grip to get closer. He must have sensed her need because he patted her thigh. She slipped her hand to his crotch.

He drove inside the shed, eased to a stop, and turned his head toward her. "What are you doing?"

She removed the helmet. "I thought you said if I did that, you'd know. Leave the motor running." In a flash, she dismounted and stood next to him. "Stand up."

He pulled his brows together. "I like where this is going and damn glad I invested in a center stand." He kicked it into place.

She knelt and removed his boots, then made short work of opening his jeans.

He didn't wait for her next move. He slid pants and underwear off in one steady motion, then kicked out of them.

From her vantage point and with the hum of the engine, she imagined it was like a scene from an X-rated movie. Not that she'd ever seen one. But she bet Rance would love to furnish her with that experience. She bent to remove her shoes, then rose to her full height. He stepped closer, his eyes dark and hot on her, and her mouth went dry, because she'd been thinking about this for the last fifty miles.

Grabbing the hem of her sweatshirt, he ripped it off, bringing the undershirt with it. Wren unfastened her bra and let it fall to the floor. While she did that, he got her pants and panties down to her ankles, then pulled her tight against him. "This makes up for your refusal in the park," he said, his voice husky, full of promise of things to come.

"Get back on the bike." Her instruction, more command than request.

"Okay. This might not be sexy, but I need to put my boots back on or I could get burned."

While he did that, she folded and stacked their clothes. Then, she faced him, threw her leg over the seat, slid forward, and leaned back against the gas tank, which was so warm it caused her to shudder with delight.

He pushed inside her with such force, she lost her breath. Taking a few beats to regain composure, she moved against him with a slow, steady rhythm. Pressing her lips against his, she whispered the important question, "Will you be all right living in Houston?"

His rough hands slid down her back, and she lost her train of thought for a second. Then he pressed his lips to hers. Long, slow kisses that made her hot and wet as she rocked against him "Will you?"

"What?"

"Move. To Houston."

"Do we have to talk about this *now?*"

He leaned her against the handlebars and thrust into her harder and she couldn't think anymore. Only feel. His tongue against hers. His fingers clamped to her butt, pulling her closer. Burying himself deeper. All that and the throb of the bike made her crazy. He nuzzled in her ear. "Say something dirty."

She stilled. "Like what?"

"Use your imagination."

Her mind raced. No anatomy terms. He didn't allow those. She swallowed hard. She'd never talked dirty in her life.

He picked up his rhythm and every nerve in her body caught fire. With him wide eyed and pumping into her, she fisted the grips of the handlebars.

His upper lip curled, and he gritted his teeth as if holding back a scream. "One thing, Chirp. One dirty little sentence."

He licked into her mouth as if to coax the words out, and all that heat flared to full flame. She'd do or say anything he wanted. Panic clutched her, then she regained her wits, lowered her voice, and spoke in French.

Even if he didn't understand she'd said, "I'm so glad we have a dog. I think he'll need a bath, "her delivery affected him, because now he was going at her with a vengeance. He rose from the seat, grasped her thighs with both hands, pulled her forward, and pounded into her like a madman. He grunted and growled her name against her throat. Suddenly he grabbed a handful of her hair, jerked her head back, put his mouth to her breast, and sucked the nipple in hard.

A low guttural rumble came from deep in his chest, and he plunged one last time as he released.

Resting his head against her shoulder, he caught his breath and killed the engine. "I'm *never* getting rid of this bike. Damn, I'm sorry, Chirp. I didn't even let you come, but that French talk did something to me. I don't know what you said, but it sounded nasty. I didn't hurt you, did I?"

"No, and I did kind of have an orgasm from the motor vibration."

"First one today? Or was that happening the whole trip?"

She ignored the question. She was done with dirty subjects. At least for now. "What about Houston? Can you live there?"

[407]

He closed his eyes, then opened them and heaved for oxygen. Even before he answered, her heart cracked.

"No, I . . ."

Chapter 38

Wren

Wren flung her leg over the seat, barely missing Rance's cheek. She grabbed the clothes, stomped across the yard, and let herself into the house with the hidden key. Within seconds, he was right behind her, yelling.

How could he do this? Come all the way to Austin, aware of her obligations, and propose marriage with no intention of living there?

As she reached the bedroom, he caught up and spun her around. She shoved against his chest. "I don't want to hear any more taradiddle from you." She slammed the bathroom door behind her.

"Not sure what that word means, but it has diddle in it, so it can't be all bad."

"Stop talking. Go away."

"Not happening. You know I keep a key right here, so I'm coming in." He turned the lock and stepped inside. "You didn't let me finish. I can't live in Houston all the time. But since you're the boss, I figured you could set your own hours and it wouldn't be a big deal."

She looked at him. Big mistake. Defined muscles and broad shoulders. In spite of her anger, she wanted to touch him. He reached out and pulled her close.

"I love you, Chirp, and if I have to live there to be with you, I will. But you've got to understand. Every bad thing that ever happened to me, happened there. My dad leaving. Mom dying. Losing my scholarship. My friends. My freedom. Any good memories I had of that place have disappeared."

"We'll make new ones. I'm a hairdresser. You have a business degree. I need you to help me."

"We'll work it out. Split our time between here and there. Can we do that?"

She nodded, loving the way his arms felt around her. "I'm sorry."

"Don't apologize. I'm glad you need me." He reached over and started the shower. "Now, once that gets warm, we'll get in and I'll let you taradiddle me all you want."

Even after Wren explained the word meant lying or fibbing, Rance still concentrated on the diddling part, which was fine with her since she reaped serious benefits from it. Later, when he fell into a sex coma, she pulled the laptop onto her thighs and looked at wedding dresses.

After narrowing her search to four, she texted Uncle Bill to tell him of her plans and ask him to give her away, and to use his credit card, since she didn't have one. That many dresses in two sizes, shipped overnight, tallied to a chunk of money. But she wasn't sure about the size. She'd never tried on wedding dresses. After deciding, she'd return the other three, but still, he was a conservative man and spending that much cash might cause him to have a stroke.

Then she contacted Helga. Wren wanted her at the ceremony. Helga was the closest thing she had to a mother. After that, she closed the laptop, snuggled close to Rance, and tried to think about how they'd split their time between Bluebird and Houston.

The next morning, Wren got up early because she'd been too nervous and excited to sleep. In two days, she'd be married and had tons of stuff to do. Rance was still down for the count, so she dressed and headed to Hanna's.

The forest was more alive than ever, or maybe Wren's mood made it seem that way. She shuffled her feet, scattering autumn leaves as she traveled the trail. Two squirrels chattered playing a game of chase along a low-hanging oak limb. Birds sang. A cool breeze whistled through the trees. She inhaled and caught a whiff of vanilla.

When she arrived at the shop, Muttly bounded from the corner and circled her ankles. She leaned down to pet him. "Hey, boy. Look how big you are." He ran his tongue across her cheek, and she shuddered. "Oh no. Don't do that." She rose, went to the sink, and washed the dog's kiss away.

Hanna came from the supply closet and gasped. "Blaze, I mean Wren." She pulled her into a hug. "Which do I call you?"

"Wren. I'm sorry I lied."

Her friend waved her off. "Please, if anyone knows about keeping a secret, it's me. I can't very well pass judgment." She plopped down on a stool and motioned for Wren to sit. "Thank you for giving Seth a job. I just wish it wasn't in Houston."

"Why?"

"Noah. He's so happy here, we hate to move him to the city. He's such a loner. We're not sure how he'll do there."

Wren had not considered that, but she was an expert on not fitting in. "I have the same problem."

Hanna's brows rose. "I don't understand. I thought you grew up in Houston."

"I did. Rance doesn't want to live there. We can fly back and forth. The company has a plane."

Hanna's eyes twinkled like Christmas-tree lights. "That would be so great!" She vaulted from the stool and threw her arms around Wren again. "We could buy a house here and

Seth would be home every night. We wouldn't have to uproot Noah. I can't tell you how much that would mean."

"Okay. I'd better go. Rance and I are going to Danvers to get things ordered for the wedding."

"I don't know how you'll put it all together in such a short time. I've been working on mine for months and still don't have everything finished."

"Ours is simple. Rance, me, and the minister. I ordered dresses. When they get here, I'll need your advice."

"Glad to help, and that reminds me. I want you to be my matron of honor."

"Oh—okay."

Hanna grinned. "You're about to be my sister-in-law and Noah's aunt."

Wren's hand flew to her chest. "I hadn't thought of that."

"Yep. The Keller clan. I sure like how that sounds."

So did Wren. For the first time in years, she'd have a family.

When she got back to the house, Rance was in the kitchen shoulder-deep in the pantry.

"What are you doing?"

"Fuck! I didn't hear you come in."

"You were talking to yourself."

She took two steps, and he stopped her. "Don't come any closer. While you were gone, I got a few cans mixed up. I'm putting them back in order."

"I can do it." She tried to pass, but he blocked her.

"No, Chirp. I'll fix it."

She craned her neck to see around him, then widened her eyes. "What happened?"

"Calm down. I'll have it back the way it was in no time."

"No! Step aside."

She got to work, and when the last can was in place, she glared at him. "Never do that again."

"I won't. I promise. Don't know how it happened." He pulled her into his arms. "One more reason I need you. To keep the beans before the corn."

She frowned. "Are you being sarcastic?"

Then he kissed her and all her anger disappeared.

The dresses arrived at noon the next day. Hanna and Tiffany decided on a white, vintage-inspired, long-sleeve, full-length silhouette sheath, made of lace and tulle with intricate bead work. Wren smoothed her hands over the fabric. She loved their choice.

Rance had found photographer, Travis Hardy, online. Once he'd seen the photo of the bride on the motorcycle, he wouldn't consider anyone else. Travis had driven all the way from Dallas, and had no idea who Wren was, but he'd been suspicious when Seth demanded he sign a nondisclosure agreement and not post any of the photos on his site for thirty days.

"Now hold your bouquet down by your side, and don't look into the camera," Travis said.

Wren snapped out of her trance and asked the photographer to repeat the instructions.

Hanna adjusted her veil while Tiffany stood close by. A gust of wind caught the tulle and whipped it into the air.

"Beautiful! Now, keep your body in that position, but turn your head to face me."

Wren had been as determined about the treehouse as a backdrop as Rance had been about the Harley. He'd also insisted on using a haystack in Hanna's barn. Obvious reason. Hubby-to-be had a dirty mind.

Travis opened his camera case. "Okay, that should be enough in this location. If the groom is gone, we can head back home for the motorcycle shots."

Tiffany nodded, and curls flew in every direction. "Oh, he's gone, all right. His brothers took him to the bar in town.

By the time he gets home, he may be three sheets to the wind."

Hanna spoke up. "No, he won't. I gave Seth strict instructions not to let that happen."

Rance

Down at The Roost, Rance leaned back in his chair and eyed Seth. "You get the paperwork done I asked about?"

His brother opened his briefcase, removed a folder, and slid it to him. "Yep. Sign at the arrow."

"We don't need a witness or anything?"

"If Wren had asked for the prenup, then yes, we'd want witnesses, but you'd be the only one to contest this, and a handwriting analysis would prove it's your signature. Besides, are you ever going to tell her about it?"

Rance put the pen to paper. "Probably not, but hell, I knew I needed one when she tried to sell me half of Montgomery Steel for a dollar. She's a smart girl, but she was letting her heart rule her head. Tongues will wag anyway, but if it's clear I'm not after her money, claiming her place in the company should be an easier transition. Be sure her uncle and all the board members get copies."

"Well, this document overrides divorce or transfer of assets. No matter what happens, for the next ten years, if she dumps your ass, you get zilch."

Quiet until now, Nick leaned forward. "That will never happen. She worships him. We should be so lucky."

Seth stiffened. "Speak for yourself. My woman waited seven years for me." He puffed out his chest. "I ruined it for every other dude on the planet."

"Easy to do when her world stopped at the city limits. Few dudes to tempt her," Nick said.

Rance chuckled. "What's wrong, Nicky? Still can't round all the bases with Tiffany?"

Nick swigged his beer, then set the bottle down hard. "Nope. She's making me work for it. Says we should form an emotional relationship before a physical one. All those stories you hear about preachers' kids being wild—total lie. Tiffany is anything but promiscuous."

Seth finished his brew and signaled the bartender. Then he turned back to Rance. "Sure you don't want at least one drink?"

"No, I'm good. But I'm wondering how much longer it'll be."

"Hanna said she'd text when the coast is clear. Until then, we've got to hang out here. Wouldn't want you to see your bride in her dress and start out with bad luck. This time tomorrow you'll be a married man. Are you nervous?"

"No."

"No last-minute jitters? No cold feet?"

"None. Why? You having doubts about yours?"

"Nope. Not since Wren told me I can commute to work. Living in Houston during the week and only being here on weekends hasn't worked for me. I've missed Hanna and Noah so much I've been miserable."

The waitress brought the drinks, then sashayed away. Rance turned to Seth again. "I have an offer for you. Actually, both of you. If y'all want to build on Dessie's place, I'll deed you some property. Free and clear."

"I'm in," Seth said.

Rance laughed out loud. "Damn. I thought you'd at least discuss it with Hanna."

"Are you kidding? No way in hell she'll turn down the deal. Do you know we have never had sex in a bed? She won't do it in her parents' house because she's afraid they'll hear us."

"Are you serious?" Nick asked.

"Hell, yeah. We do in the barn, her shop, the treehouse, my truck, her car. Everywhere but the one natural place we should do it."

"Bummer," Nick said.

"No shit."

Rance raised his brows. "Well, I'll fix that. I'll get both of you a room for the night. My treat. That way Chirp and I will have the house to ourselves. Now, back to my offer. What about you, Nicky? Interested in building on the property? I bet you can get a coaching job here."

"No. I like living in Houston."

"You'd have more time with Tiffany. These once-a-month visits don't seem to be good enough."

"I appreciate it, but for now, I'm staying put," Nick said.

"I understand. But if you change your mind, the offer is always on the table." Out of the corner of his eye, Rance caught sight of a man moving toward them. "Holy hell. What is he doing here?"

Seth and Nick both turned, then Seth spoke. "Who is he?"

Rance rose from his chair. "The PI who's been looking for Chirp."

Chapter 39

＋

Rance

Rance wasn't sure what category to put Tom Fraser in—friend or foe. The man seemed to work both sides of the street. He was out of character for an ex-lawman, and as much as Rance appreciated the head start the PI had given Chirp, the fact remained, he still worked for Marla Montgomery.

Tom set his briefcase on the table and stuck out his hand. Rance ignored it. "What do you want?"

The PI pushed his palms out in front of his body as if surrendering. "No need for hostility. I'm here to help, not cause trouble."

Rance nodded at the last vacant chair. "In that case, take a seat. Only fair to warn you though: nothing—and I mean *nothing* will mess up my wedding day."

"I understand." He glanced at Seth and Nick. "I take it you're the brothers."

They both cut their eyes to Rance, then back at Tom, but didn't offer their hands. "Correct. I'm Seth, and this is Nick."

"Nice to meet you both." Then Tom swung his attention to Rance again. "Here's the deal. I still work for Mrs. Montgomery, and I plan to collect my fee. I've put in too much time not to get the final installment. So tomorrow morning, I'll notify her that Wren is in Bluebird. Once I do, the widow will head this way."

"So far I don't hear the *helping* part of this plan," Rance said.

Tom leaned forward. "I figure the earliest she can get here is one o'clock. Since your wedding is at two, I suggest you move the ceremony to an earlier time. Say—before noon."

"Why not postpone your call?"

"Can't do that. Notification needs to look like I contacted her as soon as I located the girl. Besides, according to Helga, all the wedding guests are already here, so no need to wait."

"I'll talk it over with Chirp. If she's good with it, then so am I."

[421]

"Okay, now that's settled, let me buy you guys a round of drinks."

Seth drained his bottle. "Rance isn't drinking, but even if you are the enemy, Nick and I will take you up on it."

Tom motioned for the bartender to send three more beers, then shouldered back in his chair and focused on Rance. "Once you're married, Wren might be safe, but you won't be. Anything happens to the girl, the company must be sold and proceeds divided among a list of charities. But, Marla can off you and leave Wren vulnerable again. So here's where my help comes in. While I've been searching for Wren, I've had Marla under surveillance. And I've investigated her all the way back to childhood."

The waitress brought the drinks, and Tom took a long pull. "She ran away from home when she was sixteen. Turns out she spent time in juvie for breaking and entering. Had a real knack for picking locks. After that she used her beauty to her advantage. Made a habit of hooking up with older men who had a little money, but once they couldn't afford her, she moved on."

Tom opened his briefcase, pulled out a folder, and slid it to Rance. "If Marla gets you out of the picture, she'll have Wren in a facility and take over the company before anyone knows about it. Once she has power of attorney, it will be hard to undo."

Thumbing through the file, Rance's gut clenched. Doctors, lawyers, and a judge willing to say or do whatever it took to prove Wren incapable. Fake documents outlining erratic behavior.

What? Attempted suicide? Bull shit.

As successful as Chirp had been in hiding out for three years, she'd be no match for Marla. Not with this many people on her stepmother's payroll.

Rance eyed Tom. "So she fucked her way to the middle until she decided she could rise to the top with Grant Montgomery."

Tom nodded.

Rance closed the file. "Why are you doing this?"

"I've spent the majority of my life putting people like Marla where they belong. It took a while to figure out what kind of person she was, but once I did, I decided not to let her get away with it. And everything I've learned about Wren tells me her stepmother's claims are false."

On the way back to the farmhouse, Mother Nature reminded Rance that the ultimatum he'd spouted about nothing ruining his wedding day didn't pertain to her. Because now dark clouds rolled in and made themselves right at home.

The house was quiet. He rushed down the hallway, stepped into the bedroom, and found Chirp clutching his pillow to her chest, sound asleep. He walked over, sat on the edge, and kissed her cheek.

Her eyes fluttered open. "Are you drunk?"

"No, ma'am. Are you okay?"

"Yes. I'm just tired." She straightened and leaned against the headboard, then tilted her head toward the doorway. "Seth and Nick with you?"

"Nope. Got the place all to ourselves. Hanna came and picked them up because I rented rooms for them at the motel outside of town."

"But I'm supposed to spend the night at Hanna's."

"Yeah, we'll talk about that. Right now I want to shower." He headed to the bathroom, then stopped and leaned against the jamb. "We already act like old married people. Going to bed with the chickens the night before our wedding when we should have parties with strippers."

"Hanna wanted to take me to one. But I'm not old enough to get in."

Rance chuckled. "Maybe I'll strip for you."

"Really?"

"It could happen. You want to shower with me?"

"No. I've already bathed."

[424]

Chirp was still awake when Rance came from the bathroom and crawled in next to her. "Let's change the wedding to eleven o'clock. Okay?"

"Why?"

He pulled her into his arms. "The sooner we're married, the better." That answer probably wouldn't be enough to satisfy her, but he'd be damned before he'd tell her anything about Marla.

Chirp trembled, and the warm breath from her deep sigh floated across his skin. He clutched her tighter. "What's wrong?"

"You always sleep naked, and you're not. You want to move the wedding up. Are you afraid you'll back out?"

He loosened his hold, tilted her face to his, kissed her, and snugged her against his chest. "The day I got out of prison was the best day of my life, until you accepted my marriage proposal. The next day you climbed on my bike, wrapped your arms around me, and held me all the way home—and that was the best day. Now, with you next to me, breathing my air, this is the best. Tomorrow, when you become my wife that will be the best. You're one best day after another, Chirp. Back out? Never."

"Okay."

"Okay. Now, about going to Hanna's. I want you to stay here."

"You'll see me in the morning. That's bad luck."

"You trust me?" Rance asked.

"Yes."

"I promise I won't look at you. It'll be fine. Now close those pretty green eyes. We got a big day tomorrow."

She snuggled closer. "Can't we have sex first?"

"Nope. We're abstaining until we're married."

"You're being mean. An orgasm or two would help me sleep."

He chuckled. "This might be a good time for me to watch you get yourself off. I'll even talk dirty while you do it."

"No."

He laughed harder. "Okay, but I'm going on record right now—that's what I want for my next birthday."

"Stop laughing. Do couples do that? Watch each other?"

"Baby, anything a couple agrees to do together is okay. It isn't perverted."

"So if I wanted you to tie me up and spank me—you would?"

"I said if *both* parties agreed. Want to make love in strange locations? I'm your guy. Try different positions? Hell yeah. But I don't swing, swap, or do fifty shades of anything.

You submit because I get you so hot you can't help yourself, not because I demand it. If I do something you don't like, say so, and I won't ever do it again. My job is to keep you satisfied. And believe it or not that plays a big part in my satisfaction. Understand?"

"Yes."

"Good. Uh—you don't really want to be tied up and spanked, do you?"

"No. But I have a list of places where I want to have sex."

He bolted upright. "You're shitting me."

"No."

"Like where?"

"Airplane. Boat. Car. Deck. Elevator."

"Stop! Let my brain catch up." After the motorcycle sex, he should have seen this coming. Of course she'd have a list, *and* it would be in alphabetical order. "Okay, between the two of us, we have those places. Go on."

"Float."

His hand went back into the air. "A parade float?"

"Yeah."

"Damn, that's a problem."

She smiled. "Garage. On a horse. You think Toby is big enough to hold both of us?"

"I'll buy a bigger one."

"That's the first eight places. Should I get my list?"

God, the woman drove him nuts. "No, and we're done talking about this because I'm getting a bitching boner."

She flashed the innocent look he recognized as fake.

"If you want to get *yourself* off, I'll watch and talk French while you do."

"You wicked woman. Right now, spanking you sounds tempting."

Wren

Wren opened her eyes and let them adjust to the dark. A low rumble of thunder announced the threat of rain. Her stomach knotted at the thought of stormy weather on her wedding day.

She glanced at the clock. In four hours Rance would be her husband. Then she remembered last night and how she'd gotten the best of him. But even if she'd turned him on, he'd stuck to his guns. No sex.

She needed to leave before he woke and saw her. As she scooted away, he touched the small of her back. "Where do you think you're going?"

She pulled the sheet over her head. "Don't look at me!"

"Relax. I can't."

She lowered the cover and stared at him. He'd blindfolded himself with his bandanna.

Moving closer, she ran her fingers over his lips. "Do you have any idea how sexy you look?"

He pointed to his eyes. "Duh. Blindfold."

"Oh—yeah. I want to take your picture."

"Is it going to end up in a gallery?" Rance asked.

She jumped out of bed and grabbed her phone. "Maybe."

"At least I won't be *nekked*. That'll be an improvement."

As she snapped, he continued to talk. "Have you thought about what you'll tell our kids when they see all the naked paintings of Daddy?"

She froze in place.

"Chirp? You still here?"

"Yes."

"What's wrong?"

She eased onto the mattress next to him. "Kids."

He felt his way up her arm to her throat, then cupped her face with both hands and kissed her. "You want kids, right?"

"If I don't, will you still marry me?"

"Yes. But why wouldn't you?"

"They're messy."

He leaned back on the bed and made room for her. "You'll be a great mom. By the time we're ready to start a family, I'm willing to bet you'll want children."

"But what if I don't?"

His answer came without hesitation. "Then we won't have any."

By ten o'clock the rain had passed, and the sun shone from a watercolor sky. Wren had been at the church for hours visiting with Uncle Bill, Aunt Virginia, and Helga. But now her nerves were getting the best of her. She smoothed her veil and fidgeted with her bouquet.

"Stop picking at everything," Hanna said.

"I can't help it. I think the hands on the clock are stuck."

"Good Lord. It's a good thing you changed the time. You would have never made it until two."

[430]

Tiffany rushed into the room. "Okay, Helga and your aunt have joined everyone else in the sanctuary, and your uncle is waiting in the hallway. So let's get this show on the road."

"The church is beautiful," Wren said. She reached for Hanna's hand, then Tiffany's. "Thank you."

"No big deal. As the minister's daughter, I had access to the arch and candelabrum. Mother Nature provided the fall leaves, and I threw in a few pots of mums, tied ribbon on the pews, and voilà! Oh, and since you moved the time, your uncle Bill arranged a catered lunch following the ceremony. It's all set up in the fellowship hall."

"Did I hear my name mentioned?" Uncle Bill stepped through the doorway and wrapped his arms around Wren. "While I waited, I spent time with your groom. Seems like a good man."

She broke his hold and smiled up at him. "He is. Did you bring the ring?"

He reached into his jacket pocket and slid a wedding band into Wren's palm. "Your mother would be happy that you're using the ring she gave your dad."

"I hope it fits."

"Pretty sure it will. Rance and Grant are about the same size."

"I'll tell the piano player we're ready to start," Tiffany said.

Uncle Bill offered his arm. "That's our cue. You ready?"

Wren slipped the gold band on her thumb, swallowed hard, and nodded. With a deep breath, she curled her arm through his and started the long walk down the hallway to her future.

Chapter 40

✝

Marla

Marla couldn't hold back a smile. For the past month, one question had tormented her. Would Tom Fraser be another disappointment? So she'd gotten downright giddy when the text came. *The girl is in Bluebird, Texas.*

The timing couldn't have been better. She was down to under a half million dollars. A lot for some, but if she continued to keep pace with her rich friends, skiing in Aspen, vacationing in the Hamptons, and attending Fashion Week in Paris, she'd need more. A lot more.

Tired of having to please a man to get what she wanted, she'd planned for Grant to be the last one. He'd been attentive until his diagnosis of cancer. And then, when she'd suggested enrolling Wren in a private school that dealt with problem children, he'd held that against her.

God, how she hated the kid and her childhood tantrums over the most ridiculous things. If a book wasn't in alphabetical order or if a blue stuffed animal got put in with the pink group, and later, after Grant got sick, how she had to spend almost every waking moment at her father's bedside. And he'd encouraged it. That's what she despised most. Wren always came first.

Today Marla would start the process of getting what was rightfully hers. She'd spent the last four years of her marriage stuck in that house. She'd had no choice. If she wanted to gain sympathy as the devoted wife and stepmother, she couldn't jet-set all over the world with him fighting for his life.

Thank God she'd found comfort with some of the hired help. If not she would have dried up like an old maid. She eyed Tony and Frank in the front seat. Big. Strong. Young. Just her type. But she didn't have time for any extracurricular activity. Not now. Not with so much riding on getting control of the company.

The car came to a stop, and Marla scoped out the place. The dreary country scene was a long way from what the little princess grew up with. And the report she'd gotten from Mr. Fraser stated the weird heiress was living with an ex-con, to boot! That was the best part. God, how she wished Grant were alive to see his little darling shacked up with a thug.

There didn't seem to be anyone at home. No cars in the drive or the carport. No sound came from inside. Good. It would give her time to pull herself together because her nerves were on edge.

She whispered a laugh. After all this time, the wait had been worth it. Other than money, appearance was paramount. Marla needed to come across as only wanting the best for her stepdaughter. Wren involved with a felon proved she wasn't capable or stable enough to run the company. A damaged girl making bad decisions. Everyone would applaud Marla for taking measures to protect her from ambitious losers.

But as happy as that made her, it created another problem. If this Rance-what's-his-name knew who his lover was and how much she was worth, he might put up a fight. Clearly a man like him only got involved with someone like Wren for one of two reasons. Sex or money. But then again, he was probably a dumb lug with more brawn than brain and he'd jump at the chance for some cash. She could pay him off. If not, she'd have to put him down.

A dog barked and broke her concentration. She removed her sunglasses, hung the stem in the top of her blouse, then strolled to the front door. After knocking with no response, she took a hairpin and made short work of the lock. Funny, she still remembered how to do it.

She turned to face her partners. "Remember, this guy is an ex-con, so things might get physical. But nothing will stop me from rescuing my stepdaughter. Understand?"

"Two of us, one of him. No problem," Frank said.

Marla strolled inside with both men right behind her. A dog yelped from the back porch.

"Where'd you learn to pick a lock?" Tony asked.

She spoke over her shoulder. "When I was a teenager, I'd sneak out at night. Had to learn how to get back in without a key." That wasn't the real story, but it sounded better than admitting she'd been a thief. She moved to the sofa and sat.

Tony ran his hand through his wavy hair. "Now what?"

She cut her eyes over at the hired muscle. "We wait."

Wren

A wave of panic washed over Wren as she changed from her wedding clothes into jeans and a T-shirt. The earlier conversation concerning kids made her realize how little she knew about her new husband. *Husband.* The word caused her chest to tighten.

No doubt she loved him, and he'd said he loved her a million times, and she believed him. But was that enough? Sure, living together had provided some insights to his habits,

[436]

but there was more to compatibility than not squeezing the toothpaste tube in the middle and liking the same foods.

She hung her wedding gown on the hanger and covered it with the clothes bag. It really was the most beautiful dress she'd ever seen, and from the way Rance had gazed at her when she'd appeared at the end of the aisle, he agreed. However, if he saw the price tag, he'd have more to say about her being rich.

When she'd joined him at the altar, he'd taken her hand and kissed it, and she'd almost collapsed from happiness. And then later, during their first dance together, her heart had pounded.

The door opened with the sound of a tap. Rance leaned against the jamb and smiled. "Mrs. Keller, you ready to go?"

Hearing her new name startled her. This was the happiest day of her life. Yet gloom settled over her like something bad was about to happen.

He rushed forward and took her in his arms. "What's wrong?"

She rested her forehead against his chest and inhaled his scent. She loved how he smelled and the comfort of his embrace. "What if I mess up?"

He led her to a small bench and pulled her down next to him. "If anybody should worry about screwing things up, it's me."

"I have more money than you."

"So I hear. But that makes no difference in how I feel about you. Lose it all tomorrow, I'm still your guy."

"Okay."

He placed his hand beneath her chin and tilted it up. "Look at me."

Those beautiful blue eyes she loved stared back with nothing but adoration.

"Sometimes I'm restless and reckless and a real jerk, but I love you more than life. There'll be times when I piss you off. But I'm the one person you can depend on no matter what—and I'll be damned before I let anything or anyone come between us. Even my stubbornness. Understand?"

"Yes."

He stood and brought her back into his arms. "Okay. We good?"

She nodded. "I want to make you happy."

"Baby, you are my happiness. After all those miserable months I spent without you, I know that for a fact. Stop worrying. We'll be fine. I promise." He leaned to whisper in her ear, "Do you have a church on that list of yours?"

"No!"

He laughed. "Just checking, because if you did—I mean, we're already here. Don't want to miss an opportunity."

"You're bad."

"Guilty, but sometimes I'm good, like now, because I have a surprise for you."

"What?"

"I know we didn't discuss a honeymoon, but with the help of your aunt Virginia, tomorrow morning we're flying to Fishers Island, New York, where Montgomery Steel owns a cottage. We'll have the whole place to ourselves for a week. She even arranged for a staff. So we need to get home and pack."

Rance

Rance wouldn't worry about Chirp's insecurity. The wedding had happened so fast, she just had a case of the jitters. He had more pressing matters. Like making sure they got away from Bluebird before her wicked stepmother showed up. When he got to the farm, the hair on the back of his neck prickled. A strange SUV sat in the drive.

[439]

Chirp leaned forward. "Whose car is that?"

"Don't know, but I'll find out." He brought the truck to a stop. "Seth and Hanna aren't far behind us, so you stay put until they get here."

"I want to go with you."

He narrowed his eyes. "No. There might be trouble waiting inside, and I want you out of harm's way. Don't argue with me, Chirp."

"It's Marla, isn't it?"

"Maybe. Probably. So stay here. Please."

She grabbed his arm, and her bottom lip quivered. "Don't go. Let's drive away. We can buy everything we need for the trip."

He patted her hand. "That won't prove anything. Sooner or later we have to face her. I'll be okay."

"Then I'm going with you."

"Dammit, Chirp." Her expression told him there was no use in arguing, so he did the next best thing. "Okay, but you stay on the porch out of sight. I go in alone. Understand?"

She nodded.

He'd already played out the possibilities a hundred times in his head. Face-to-face meeting? Ambush? Gunfight? He'd tried to cover all the options and what action to take.

The disadvantage between a personal and prison confrontation was not knowing your opponent. Inmates were all pretty much the same, with limited weapons, location, and opportunity. But a beautiful, evil, rich woman posed threats Rance could only imagine.

Palming his cell phone, he tapped the screen and dropped it back in his shirt pocket. He glanced over at his bride, then got out of the Ford into the crisp October air and filled his lungs with oxygen and determination.

As he stepped onto the porch, his instincts kicked into high alert. Adrenaline coursed through his veins just as it had in prison when he'd sensed danger. Everything he'd learned from Chirp and Tom Fraser told him Marla was as lethal as any guy he'd encountered in the Big House. Even more, because according to the photos he'd seen online, she didn't look dangerous. Just the opposite. The sort of woman most men wanted to get close to.

He grasped the knob, eased open the door with his foot, and took one step into the room. Marla sat on the sofa, making herself right at home. She was more beautiful than all those society page photos. Creamy skin and voluptuous curves. But there was something else about her more obvious. Cold, dead eyes.

Two men with bodies capable of bench pressing at least three hundred pounds stood behind her. They were dressed in jeans and T-shirts stretched tight over their bulging physiques, and an array of familiar tattoos snaked from beneath their sleeves, indicating they'd spent some time in the slammer.

"If you know what's good for you, you'll get out of my house, off my property, and never look back."

Marla sneered. "Not without Wren."

The transformation from fake socialite to genuine bitch jolted Rance into defense mode. "I was going to ask how you got in, but I guess you've returned to your old skill set of picking locks."

Despite her attempt to remain cool, Rance saw that his statement rattled her.

Marla fisted her hands like a street fighter. "You know nothing about me."

He didn't give her a chance to say more. "That's where you're wrong. I know every doctor, lawyer, Indian chief you have in your pocket. And for everyone who'll do your bidding, I have two who will contest anything they say."

"I don't care about your threats. I came for Wren, and I'm not leaving without her. Where is she?" Marla craned her neck as if expecting her stepdaughter to appear.

Rance moved closer, keeping his eyes on the two goons who seemed rooted to the floor. "Apparently you didn't get your invitation. Wren and I got married a few hours ago, so she's not going anywhere with you—ever."

Marla's face lost all color. "What are you talking about?"

"It's a done deal. She's my wife. My responsibility. And no way in hell I'll let you hurt her."

Marla came to her feet. "I've heard enough!" She glared at the goons. "Kill him."

The guy on the left jerked his head toward his boss. "You're kidding, right?"

"No. There's a bonus for whichever one of you shoots him."

Chirp burst through the door. "No!"

Marla curled her lips into an evil grin. "Hello, Wren."

Rance turned to face his wife. "Go back outside— please."

The witch focused on Chirp. "Did you really marry this loser?"

"He's not a loser."

"Really? He's a twenty-eight-year-old ex-con, and the last job he had was bartending. If you think he married you for anything other than your money, then you're more delusional that I thought. Did you even have him sign a prenup?"

"No, but . . ."

[443]

"Of course you didn't, which proves how easily influenced you are by the wrong people."

Rance took two more steps closer to Marla. "She didn't have to ask. I signed one. You're still on the board for a few more weeks, so you'll get your copy in the mail." He advanced again.

Marla ignored him. "No worries. We'll get the marriage annulled as soon as we get home." She looked at the two steroid studs. "Frank, you take care of him, and, Tony, you get her."

"Not a good idea," Rance said to the brute.

"Nothing personal, man. But I've got a job to do."

Frank rushed forward, and Rance landed a quick jab to the big guy's windpipe. Frank clutched his throat as he wheezed in pain. In the background, Chirp screamed. If there was one thing Rance knew how to do, it was fight dirty. A power kick to the man's groin brought him to his knees with a shriek of agony. He curled into a ball on the floor, one hand grabbing his nuts, the other wrapped around his gullet. Rance hammered a fist to the back of Frank's head and rendered him unconscious.

Then he turned his attention outside. Tony had Chirp around the waist, her hands flailing and feet kicking in midair as he struggled to put her in the SUV. "Let me go!"

"I'm not going to hurt you, so stop kicking and get in the car."

Rance ran forward and tackled them, knocking the pair away from the vehicle. Tony released Chirp and concentrated on Rance, throwing three quick punches, failing to connect with any of them. Rance weaved and bobbed, then answered with a blow to his opponent's jaw. As Tony drew back for another go at Rance, Chirp came from the end of the porch, shovel in hand. She raised the spade and bashed Tony's head, dropping him in his tracks.

"Oh good God, do I have to do everything for myself?" Marla yelled from the porch.

Chirp's eyes went wide, and Rance followed her gaze in time to see the queen bitch point a gun and fire. Rance's hand flew to his shoulder as the bullet made contact. Stunned for a moment, he lost sight of Marla. She was halfway to Chirp when he spotted her. Then he ran full charge. She turned and pointed the weapon. Just as he reached her, she squeezed off another round, shattering a flower pot on the porch before he wrestled the pistol away.

"Oh my God! She shot you!" Shovel still in hand, Chirp rushed to help, but by the time she got to them, Rance had Marla in control.

"I'm okay. Small-caliber mouse shooter couldn't do much damage."

Seth's car came to a screeching stop, and he and Hanna jumped out to join the fray. Hanna removed her scarf, and Rance tied Marla's wrists. She glared at Chirp. "Believe me, you'll regret marrying this man. He'll take you for everything you're worth, and you'll end up with nothing."

Rance wiped blood from his wound. "That's a prediction that won't come true, but here's one that will. You're about to get a free membership in a new kind of country club."

"You idiot. Who do you think the cops will believe? An upstanding widow who donates time and money to a multitude of worthy causes, or a worthless ex-con? I'll say you attacked me. Frank and Tony will back me up. Your only corroboration is from a runaway who has been lying about everything for three years. So good luck with that."

Rance pulled the cell from his pocket and wiggled it in the air. "Don't think so. I recorded our entire conversation. There's enough on here to prove everything I have to say to the cops."

Seth came from inside. "That guy is still out cold, but I tied him up, anyway."

"Yeah, and after I called 911, Wren and I took care of the other one," Hanna said. "She held him down with the shovel, and I used a piece of rope from the shed to bind him. Good Lord, my hands are still shaking."

Seth wrapped his arm around Hanna.

[446]

As sirens blared down the road, Chirp looked up at Rance. "We'll postpone our honeymoon."

"No, we won't." He glanced at the blood spot on his shirt. "I'll get this taken care of, and then we'll leave."

"Are you sure?"

"Damn straight. Oh, and one more thing." He stood, scooped her up and into his arms. "I still need to carry you over the threshold" He pushed the door open with his foot and walked inside.

"Did you really sign a prenup?"

"Yeah."

"You didn't have to do that."

"I know. That's why I did it. I love you, Chirp. Always will. But remind me to never get you mad when you have a shovel handy."

The End

Epilogue

Wren got off the elevator and stepped into the foyer of the penthouse located two floors above Montgomery Steel's executive offices. She and Rance lived here during the week, but returned to Bluebird each weekend. So far the arrangement worked.

She'd hired a decorator to change the interior from contemporary to farmhouse country, so he'd feel more at home. The style suited her as much as it did him. She planned a courtyard garden for next summer. He'd laughed when she told him she intended to grow tomatoes and peppers. He'd suggested throwing in zinnias for good measure, and she'd taken him up on it, even though she knew he was being sarcastic.

Muttly lunged from the sofa and came to her. She leaned down and petted him, then eyed the crate against the wall. The artwork from Odette's had arrived.

Lighted candles on every table bathed the room in a warm glow. She read the note stuck to the mirror. *I'll clean the rose petals up later. For now, follow the path.* So she did. From the entry, down the hallway, into the master suite. A bottle of champagne chilled in a silver bucket. Soft music played on a Pill speaker. A printed Happy Birthday banner hung across the headboard. Rance was nowhere in sight, but the light in the bathroom was on.

"Rance?"

"Hey, babe. Take your shoes off, prop yourself against all those bed pillows, and let me know when you're done."

She didn't know what he had planned, but whatever it was, no doubt she'd like it. "I see my paintings arrived."

"Yeah, and don't get any bright ideas about hanging the diddle-skittle. We're hauling it to the farm for a bonfire."

"We'll talk about it."

"No! We won't. I told you, it's got to go."

"We'll talk about it."

"Not going to argue with you on your birthday. So are you ready yet?" Rance asked.

She got comfortable and settled the dog next to her. "Yes."

"Good. Now, take the iPod, scroll to "The Only One Who Gets Me," and push play."

The music blared through the surround sound. Rance threw the door open and began to dance, pantomime, and unbutton his shirt. Wren's smile turned into giggles as he rolled his shoulders, slipped one sleeve down part way, then pulled it back up and wiggled his brows.

She took her bottom lip between her teeth. Muttly buried his head beneath the pillows.

Then Rance clutched both sides of his shirt, ripped it off, swung it in the air, and tossed it to her.

She caught it and squealed.

He grabbed the jamb, gyrated against it, and undid the top button of his Levi's.

Her mouth formed a perfect O.

Moving to the next button, he turned away from her, hooked his thumbs in the waist of his pants, inched them down, then back up. Twirling to face her, he released another button and winked. "You want more?"

Wren widened her eyes and nodded.

When the song got to the word *strong,* he flexed his biceps like a bodybuilder.

Hands above his head, he hip-swayed toward her, then stopped at the edge of the mattress. "Happy twenty-first birthday, baby." He pulled her into his arms, and they danced.

[450]

She took a deep breath, melted against him, and kissed the scar from the bullet wound. God, she'd been so scared. Even now, the memory caused her stomach to hurt. The best and worst of times all rolled into one. He'd recovered, and Marla was behind bars.

"All the women were jealous today when I got flowers every hour. They think you're the perfect man."

"But you know better."

He twirled her, then dipped her low. "Are you nervous about the press conference tomorrow?"

"A little. Uncle Bill said we have bids from several magazines to do an exclusive interview."

"Well, it's the official passing of the torch. That's plenty newsworthy. It's your call, but it's a good time to let the world know about the changes."

"I have an idea," Wren said.

"About what?"

"Start a foundation to finance education for prisoners or their children. We can use the money from the magazine interview. You got your degree there, and look how great you turned out."

He grinned. "Yeah, but I seduced a rich girl to get ahead."

She punched his shoulder. "Your cell-mate, Hector. You said he has a son. Maybe he could be our first recipient."

Rance let out a long sigh, and his eyes misted. "I'll never figure out how why you fell in love with me, but I'm sure glad you did." He planted a hot, wet kiss. The kind that made her toes curl.

She leaned away and gazed up at him. "You're nice, too. You hired Tom Fraser as head of security."

"Yeah. He has the credentials. And since he's marrying Helga that almost makes him family. Seems our social calendar is getting crowded. Their wedding in two weeks. Seth and Hanna's in three. Then your art show in New York. You okay with all that?"

"Are you?"

"Yeah, if you can tolerate my fans wanting to tear my clothes off for a better look." He broke into laughter.

"And they haven't even seen you strip."

"And never will. This is a private performance. But fair warning—now that you're legal to drink, I plan to get you drunk and talk you into all sorts of *lascivious* things. How's that for a word of the day?"

"I don't have to be drunk to do lewd things with you."

"Yeah, well, right now I want you to take a relaxing soak in the tub because I have dinner coming from Frisco's. All your favorites. Shrimp platter, filet mignon, château mashed potatoes, asparagus, and since you can never make your mind up between the strawberry cheesecake and bread pudding, I ordered both."

She slid off his lap and pushed him back on the bed. "See, you are nice."

He slapped her on the butt. "That's my job, babe. To keep you happy. So get a move on. They'll be here at eight."

"Okay. But before that, let's mark the elevator off my list."

He grinned. "I like how you think."

She hooked a finger in a belt loop on each side of his jeans, tugged them down, and smiled. "Happy birthday to me."

All About Ann

Award winning and Amazon best-selling author Ann Everett embraces her small-town upbringing and thinks Texans are some of the funniest people on earth. When speaking to writing groups, businesses, book clubs, and non-profit organizations, she incorporates her special brand of wit, making her programs on marketing, self-publishing, and the benefits of laughter informative and fun.

She lives on a small lake in northeast Texas where she writes, bakes, and fights her addiction to Diet Dr. Pepper.

Ten more things about Ann

She's married to her high school sweetheart.

She loves shopping at thrift stores.

She doesn't remember her first kiss.

She hates talking on the telephone.

A really sharp pencil makes her happy.

She secretly wants to get a tattoo.

Being a charter member of the National Honor Society in high school remains one of her proudest and most surprising moments.

She's thankful wrinkles aren't painful.

She sucks at math.

An Invitation
TO MY READERS

Hey y'all,

If you liked my book, pretty, pretty *please* go to Amazon or your other favorite online retailer and leave a review. I will appreciate it very much!

Stalk me:

Facebook

Pinterest

Amazon UK Page

Amazon Page

Goodreads

I love hearing from readers. Email me at: ann.everett@rocketmail.com or reach me via my website: www.anneverett.com

My heartfelt thanks,

~Ann

Preview
TELL ME A SECRET

New Adult Romance

Chapter One

According to scientific studies, Maggie knew even good girls got aroused by bad boys. The personification of that research, Jace Sloan, strutted into the campus library with the confidence of a peacock, leaving a trail of pheromones to settle on every coed in the room. A wave of whispers circulated, each female mesmerized by his imaginary plumage.

Maggie surveyed his approach. He appeared to shift into slow motion, his stride lyrical, as if shuffling to a soulful beat, leaving no doubt as to why girls found him irresistible. He looked as if he could take you to hell and you'd enjoy the trip. Leaner than the men in her fantasies, he had the same blue eyes and dark hair, and a small, paper-thin scar on his chin made him just dangerous enough.

Drumming fingers in rhythm with her throbbing headache, she glanced at her watch. Thirty minutes late, as

[458]

expected. This wasn't her first experience with a college jock. Sophomore year, she'd tutored Texas Tech's star quarterback, and what a jerk he'd turned out to be. But this time Dr. Adams assured her it would be different. Apparently the professor had made a mistake.

At least she was sitting in one of her favorite buildings, surrounded by the comforting scent of books. Technology was great, but holding a hardcover, the pages and words transporting her to places she dreamed about, made her happy.

A strand of unruly hair fell into her eyes and she puffed it away, then slid her glasses up on her nose and decided to look on the bright side. Given Jace's reputation, he'd never stick with tutoring and she'd be off the hook. Besides, helping a self-centered pretty boy pass anatomy was the last thing she wanted to do.

"Maggie Fielding?" He looked sure of himself, and she felt uneasy. "I'm sorry I'm late. My truck had a flat."

Motioning for him to take a seat, she checked the time again and frowned. "I understand, but I also have to study, so try to be on time."

His grin disappeared. He grabbed the chair across from her, spun it around, and straddled the seat like he was doing it a favor.

She got right to the point. "There's a technique that may help you. Do you know what a *mnemonic* is?"

"No. Sorry."

"I'm sure you do, just not the word for it. You use the initials of words to help memorize information. For instance, to name the cranial bones, we'd use Old People From Texas Eat Spiders. Old would be occipital, People would be parietal, From would be frontal, and so on. Get it?"

"Yeah." His answer came out warm enough to raise the temperature in the room. It elevated hers, and she scolded herself.

"If you agree with the method, that's what we'll use."

Before he answered, Maggie caught sight of a curvaceous blonde wearing a halter top slightly larger than a baby's bib. When she reached Jace, Booby-babe leaned down, planted palms flat on the table, and provided him a clear, full view. A necklace with the number ten and a half escaped from between bulging breasts and dangled in midair. Maggie thought how horrifying it'd be if every girl wore a numeric rating, realizing hers would be a five, at best.

The girl handed him a note and whispered, "Are we still on for Friday night?"

"You bet."

"Well, here's my number just in case you lost it."

The bottle blonde retreated with long fluid steps, the sway of her hips enough to tempt any man. Maggie wished her own butt looked that good in jeans. Shaking the notion from her head, she gave attention back to her new student.

He stuffed the note in his shirt pocket as if nothing had happened. "Yeah, that'll work."

"Okay, here are some test cards." She shoved them toward him. "I'll quiz you on them next Monday."

He shuffled through the deck, then arranged them in a neat stack with the same enthusiasm as the card with Blondie's phone number.

Across the room, another young woman headed their way, boobs jiggling, bleached curls bouncing with each step. Maggie expected her to throw hands in the air and lead a cheer.

"Hey, Carla," he said.

Miss Perky Perfect tossed her hair and beamed at him. "After the other night, I expected to hear from you."

"Sorry, I've been busy. You know, practice, studying." He gestured toward Maggie, then lowered his voice. "I promise I'll call you later."

She eyed Maggie with a what's-he-doing-with-you glare and walked away.

God, what's with all these blondes and their double-D-dumplings? Maggie rounded her shoulders and tried to disappear into her B-cups. From the looks of both girls, Jace preferred cookie-cutter Barbies.

Maggie sucked in a deep breath and frowned again. She gathered her books, shoved them into her backpack, and attempted to look unconcerned. An old familiar burn started in the pit of her stomach, rose to her chest and squeezed the air from her lungs. A sensation she hadn't experienced since age sixteen while crushing over Daniel Radcliffe in a Harry Potter marathon movie weekend. She swallowed the knot in her throat. "We're done for tonight. As I explained in the e-mail, this was a meet-and-greet. I'm doing this as a favor to your professor, so if you can manage to be on time next Monday, we'll have a regular session."

Jace stood and leveled an incandescent gaze. "I'll try not to let it happen again. You want me to walk you to your car?"

She tried to match his stare but couldn't pull it off, so as a diversion, she rummaged in her purse, produced a business card and snapped it toward him. "Well, in case you have another flat, here's my number. I'd appreciate a call." She slung her bag over her shoulder. "And no, I don't need an escort."

He accepted the card, and stuffed it in his jeans pocket. "No problem."

She walked away.

At nine fifteen, Maggie dropped her backpack onto the floor and strolled into the kitchen. Still upset about her new student, she grabbed a bottle of water from the fridge and downed half of it in one gulp. She'd watched him play football plenty of times but had never taken a close look until she'd googled him. Roommate Sarah Henderson interrupted her thoughts.

"So what's your opinion of Jace?"

"Not much."

"Whattaya mean?"

"I mean, I wasn't surprised. He came in late and made an excuse, but I'd be willing to bet he was with a groupie." Maggie slid the band from her ponytail and shook it loose. "I admit he's gorgeous. As a matter of fact, he's the most beautiful man I've ever seen." She stared into space and spoke in a far- off voice. "He's like a box of candy—and every girl in the room wanted a piece." She snapped from her trance. "It was pathetic."

"Come on, Maggie, just because your mother sucked at the choices she made doesn't mean every man in the world is a jerk. But in this case, Jace is a charmer, so you should be careful."

Maggie walked past her into the living room, plopped onto the sofa, and folded her feet under her hips. She took another swig of water, then held the bottle as if toasting. "He's not my type."

Sarah broke into a full laugh. "My God, you've been on three dates in your entire life. I'm not sure you know what your type is, or if you even have a type."

Maggie grimaced. Sarah was right. She didn't have any experience with men in the dating arena for sure, and not many role models. "From the looks of fans who came over to talk, unless I have gargantuan breasts and big-bar hair, I should have said I'm not his type."

Her friend crossed her legs Indian-style and Maggie expected a lecture, but instead, Sarah said, "Sam tells me Jace has never had a long-term relationship. He sleeps with a girl a few times, and he's done. That pretty much makes him a man-whore. Will the interruptions be a problem?"

"Not for long. While I waited I made a decision." She finished off the water, replaced the lid, and picked at the label. Sarah's warning wasn't necessary. Maggie realized the moment she'd seen Jace, he'd be trouble. "I'll meet with him a couple more times and call it quits. That should satisfy Dr. Adams. I agreed to try tutoring and made it clear if Mr. Football Superstar didn't apply himself, I'd end it." She wadded a piece of the label into a small ball and rolled it between her fingers. "For the record, I can already tell. Jace Sloan will be a total waste of my time."

In three long strides, Jace crossed the room and dropped his bag onto the floor, still thinking of Maggie. She was a strange one. All business.

His roommate, Sam Morgan, glanced up from his book. "Hey man you're cutting it kind of close to curfew. How was the tutor?"

"Plain with a brain." He sat on the edge of the bed and retrieved his notes.

"Definitely not your usual sort."

"What do you mean by that?"

"You don't go for the smart ones, and you seem a little pissed. What's wrong? She wasn't dazzled by your charm?"

The dorm reeked of dirty socks and burly football players. Jace toed out of his boots. "We got off to a bad start. I showed up late. It went downhill from there."

"How come? You left in plenty of time."

"Yeah, well, I stopped by the store where the new cheerleader works."

"How was she?"

"Flexible. Very flexible."

Sam grinned and widened his eyes. Jace knew he wanted details, but he wasn't in the mood.

"I guess it's a good thing teacher isn't hot. At least you'll be able to keep your mind on the subject and out of her pants."

"I said plain, not ugly." Jace wasn't about to admit his new tutor didn't seem to be impressed with him. He tapped the index cards on his leg, then flipped through them.

"She's got wild red hair and beautiful green eyes, but she had on sweats two sizes too big, so I couldn't tell much about her body."

"What's her name?"

"Maggie."

Sam's brows rose. He put his book down and plastered on a smug grin. "Maggie Fielding?"

"You know her?"

"Hell yeah. I can't believe Sarah didn't mention this. She lives with Maggie." Sam reared back in the chair and folded his arms across his broad chest. "Oh man, this is too good."

"If Sarah lives with her, then why haven't I ever met Maggie?"

"She doesn't have a social life. Studies or works all the time. She does come to the games when she can, but that's about it."

"From the way she looked, I can understand that."

Sam grinned. "You'd better take notice, bro. Maggie's a dancer, so under those baggy clothes, she's hot. I'm talking smokin' hot."

"Maybe so, but tonight she didn't dress to impress, if you know what I mean." Jace cocked his head and narrowed his eyes. It was unlike him not to notice the potential in a woman. But with all the attention from the other girls, Maggie had faded into the background. "What kind of dancer?"

"That ballroom crap. She and Sarah take the same class. They've got a recital in a few weeks. You should go." Sam laughed again.

"What's so funny?"

"The two of you together. The stud and the virgin."

"What the hell do you mean?"

"Hey, I got the inside scoop, and the virgin princess has never been laid."

Jace leaned forward. The word *virgin* hadn't been in his vocabulary for years except in a biblical sense. "What is it, a religious thing?"

"Not sure. Sarah said she's not interested in dating."

"Hell, is she a lesbian?"

"Naw. It has something to do with her mother. I don't know the whole story."

"Well, when I first got there, I fantasized about taking the band from her hair and running my fingers through it." He moved to his desk, scooted out the chair, and sat. Sarah had probably told Maggie plenty concerning his reputation, which explained his tutor's cold reception.

"Damn, man. Is there any woman you don't want to have sex with?"

"Yeah. Sarah."

"Well, thanks for that," Sam said.

Jace stood, removed his shirt, and draped it over the back of his chair. The note from the ten-and-a-half blonde fell out of the pocket. He reached for the phone, punched in the number, and, when she answered, he said, "Hey, you want to get together tomorrow night?"

An hour later he lay wide awake, still thinking of the earlier meeting. So they'd gotten off on the wrong foot. He could fix that. No doubt he'd screw her, and although patience wasn't his strong suit, he was up for the challenge.

Sam came back into the room finishing a call. "Yeah, I love you too, baby. Bye."

Jace rolled up on an elbow. This was an opportunity he couldn't pass up. "What did Sarah say?"

"Nothing."

"C'mon, what'd she say?"

"Oh, you mean what did Maggie tell Sarah about you?"

He hated Sam having the upper hand. "Cut it out, man."

"Damn, this is funny. You've finally met a girl who doesn't wet her panties over you, and you can't stand it."

"Hey, I'm stuck with her, and I've got an advantage. The least you can do is tell me what she said."

"Well, she didn't buy your flat-tire story, and she thinks you're a friggin' box of candy."

"What?"

"Yeah, that's right. You're a box of chocolates, and every girl wanted a piece. Sorry bro in spite of your sweetness, your days are numbered."

He stiffened. "Whattaya mean?"

"I'm saying she's going to meet with you a couple more times and then cut you loose. Plans on telling Dr. Adams it isn't working."

Veins pulsed in Jace's neck just below his ears. A mixture of anger and determination burned in the pit of his stomach. He'd never met a female he couldn't charm, and he wouldn't allow Miss Plain Brain to be the first. "No, that's not happening."

"Why are you so upset? Oh. Wait. I get it. She's the virgin princess."

He didn't appreciate Sam's tone, and if they hadn't been friends and roommates for the last four years, he'd take him down a notch or two. "If anybody ends this arrangement, it'll be me. I've never been ditched, and I'm not going to be dumped by the likes of Maggie Fielding."

Amazon

Preview
TWO WRONGS
MAKE A RIGHT

Contemporary Romance

Quinn Dorsey had kissed her share of toads, and now, months before her thirty-fifth birthday, her efforts would finally pay off.

Brad squirmed in his seat and didn't complain about money or work. Yes, tonight, he'd pop the question. Why else bring her to Chez Suzette in the middle of the week?

Not that she was counting, but after dating for three years, two months, and twenty-one days, she expected a ring. It didn't matter that hot desire no longer shot straight to lady-town when he kissed her, or she didn't get googly-eyed when she saw him. She was too old for that. Those emotions ran rampant in her twenties.

A vivid image of Andrew popped into her head. He could kiss and burn her to the ground in a split second. But when Andy moved on, Quinn swore off men for a while.

[471]

Until Kevin. She hadn't thought of him in a long time, and wondered why these former lovers came to mind. Maybe because she was about to be off the market, and a trip down memory lane made it that much sweeter. After devoting three years to Kevin, he'd dumped her for a twenty-year-old yoga instructor. Girls with the flexibility of a Slinky got a man's attention.

Quinn cast a loving look at Brad while he studied the menu. An attorney with a prestigious firm, no doubt he'd make partner someday. Quinn's mother had been quick to point out that Brad's condo near the university campus, was in a more upscale location than Quinn's apartment. Yes, Brad was the complete package in her mother's eyes.

He shot hoops with his buddies on Sunday afternoons and took part in charity events, but he also treated *every* dime as if it were the last one he'd get. No, not perfect, but close.

Smiling, Brad tilted the menu down and peered over it. "What are you having? Oh, never mind. You always get the same thing." He closed the folder, placed it on the table, and leaned in close. "But if you want to try something new, go for it. Tonight the sky's the limit. You should even save room for that dessert you love so much."

Meringue and caramel floating in a pool of crème Anglaise. The image made her mouth water. Could the night be more perfect? Candlelight shimmered and reflected off the crystal chandeliers. Soft music drifted through the room, carrying wonderful aromas on every note. Red roses in silver

[472]

vases sat on tables draped in black satin. Yes, there was romance in the air and a ring in Brad's pocket.

The waiter brought wine and took their orders. Brad rattled off the choices in perfect French. Perhaps if she got him to recite food items during sex, it would be hotter because that was the one department in which he needed help. He'd become more interested in his own satisfaction than hers. But she'd never find a man who looked more handsome in a suit, or one with better grooming. Every hair in place. Coal-black, with a natural wave skimming his forehead, just right. With his square jaw and blue eyes, if he donned a cape, he might leap tall buildings.

When she pictured their children—because she wanted kids—they got his looks and her personality. Her original plan: married by thirty, two little ones by thirty-five. She'd given it her best shot with Andrew and Kevin. But as the saying goes, third time's a charm, and with the family curse of early menopause looming, an engagement couldn't happen at a better time.

Questions jumped in her brain. Location of the ceremony? What china pattern? Where would they live? Well, that was easy. Since her apartment was a rental, his condo was the only choice. It wasn't as convenient to her work, but she submitted her newspaper column electronically, so fighting traffic one day a week when she went to the office wouldn't be a big deal.

[473]

The waiter returned with their food. Quinn took her first bite and wondered if she should mention the brochure she'd seen in Brad's open briefcase. She hadn't snooped. It had been in plain view. New York City. She'd never been but wanted to go, and said as much when the subject of vacations came up at the last Christmas party. She scolded herself for not giving him enough credit in the romance department. Here she was at her favorite restaurant. The one he never chose because of the expense, and he planned a honeymoon in the Big Apple. She forked a spear of steamed asparagus dripping with butter.

He swirled the wine in his glass as if judging it, then focused on her again. "Have I told you how nice you look tonight?" Holding her gaze for a moment, he sipped the Cabernet Sauvignon.

"No. But thank you. You clean up pretty well yourself." How odd he was dishing out compliments, which convinced her he was putting forth extra effort to make this night special.

"Is that a new dress?"

"Yes. I splurged."

As much as she appreciated the pleasantries, conversation wasn't going the way she'd imagined, but he was probably nervous. She waited for him to say something else, but he didn't. He poked another bite into his mouth and chewed it, as if making sure he got his money's worth.

Slumping in the chair, she reassured herself. No need to rush things. Let him take his time. It'd already been 1,176 days since their first date, so what were a few more minutes?

Holding his fork in mid-air, he bobbed it up and down to punctuate his question. "What are you working on?"

Unbelievable. He never asked about her articles. Never even read her column. This was an opportunity to steer him in the right direction. "Since Valentine's is coming up, I'm doing a piece on love, romance, and happily-ever-after." *Perfect. What better segue into a proposal?*

Her mind raced. Since he'd brought up dessert, perhaps he'd made arrangements to have the ring hidden in a pastry? So unlike him, but so creative. Her heart fluttered. The anticipation was killing her, so she concentrated on less talking and more eating.

Brad must have had the same idea because he gave full attention to his food.

Once they finished, the waiter came to take their plates and asked for dessert choices. Quinn opened her mouth to order, but Brad held up his hand. "Can you give us a few minutes?"

"Yes, sir. Signal when you're ready."

Alone again, Brad stared into Quinn's eyes. Her heart hammered against her rib cage. This was it. The moment she'd waited for. The one to erase the years she'd wasted on

Andrew and Kevin and all the other toads. She sat up straight, licked her lips, and gazed back at Brad, waiting for the question.

"I've had something on my mind for days."

She pulled her brows together. An odd way to start a proposal, but this was a big step.

"We've been together a long time." Now it was his turn to take a deep breath. He leaned forward. "I've been offered a position in New York. I'm taking it."

Inside her head, the world went silent. No more chatter. No more music. Just her brain trying to process his words. She searched his face for the slightest hint of love, and there was none. "I'm not sure what you're saying. Are you asking me to move with you? Because I can't leave Dad right now. I mean, he's not finished with chemo, and when he is there's no guarantee he'll go into remission."

"I know."

She hesitated. Waited for him to talk her into it or suggest joining him at a later date, but he didn't. She dropped her hands into her lap, laced her fingers so tightly they tingled. "Well, I must be the dumbest smart girl in the world. I expected a proposal. But you're breaking up with me."

"I don't see a choice. You can't move and long distance relationships never work."

Her throat closed off the same way it had the day her dad had told her he was moving out. "What was this all about?" She waved her hand around the room. "You assume breaking up in my favorite restaurant would make everything okay? I'd say, 'Oh, great, Brad. Good for you. Go to New York, and have a wonderful life—without me.'" There was bound to be a good argument to offer, but for the life of her she couldn't think of anything else to say. She scooted her chair away from the table and stood.

He rose from his seat. "Wait. Please, sit down. This was a hard decision."

"Oh really? Which part? Taking the job or dumping me?"

"Both."

Collapsing back into the chair, she tried to keep calm, but her emotional investment pounded in her head. It was over without a payoff. No proposal. No marriage. No family. Just a penny-pinching, good-looking, ladder-climbing, fool. No, she'd have to claim the fool part, because the one thing she knew in life was that, men leave. Andrew left. Kevin left. Dad left. Why'd she think Brad would be different? But there it was, that tiny glimmer of hope. He could still come through and at least try to convince her to go. But he didn't. He stood there as if waiting for her to make the next move. "I can't believe this. I thought you loved me."

He sat again. "I did—I mean, I do."

[477]

From the look on his face, it'd been over for months. Maybe he had never loved her. Tears burned her eyes, but she wouldn't allow him to see her fall apart in public. Probably why he'd brought her here. Well, if he thought he could rip her heart out with no consequences, he was mistaken. "I guess it's settled. You're starting over and leaving me behind."

His eyes wandered to his drink, the flowers, over her shoulder. "I knew you wouldn't go, and that's why I never brought it up. But as much as I care for you, I can't pass up this deal." His attention landed back on her again, and he smiled. "There is a silver lining. My condo will be available. This is a perfect opportunity for you to get out of that dreadful part of town. I'll give you a great price."

The announcement had her blinking and wondering why she didn't slap him. "Are you kidding me? You want me to buy your condo?" Fire burned in the pit of her stomach like she'd swallowed a hot coal. The nerve of him. Then she got control. "That isn't going to happen, but thanks for the *generous* offer. Now I'm ready to order dessert. You said money was no object, right?"

"Yes. Get your heart's desire. I'm glad you're being reasonable. Didn't much think you'd take me up on the condo offer, but if you change your mind, I'm not putting it on the market for a couple of weeks." He motioned for the waiter.

[478]

Pushing aside her disappointment, she decided payback would taste sweeter than anything she ordered. She beamed up at the server. "I want a slice of Charlotte à la Framboise, two dozen madeleines, twelve profiteroles, three chocolate crepes, and six pistachio éclairs." She closed the menu and stood. "Oh, I almost forgot. Also a Floating Island and three bottles of Dom Perignon Rose 2002. All to go, please."

Brad's mouth fell open. "Are you insane? Those bottles cost over four hundred dollars each!"

She smiled down at him. "Yes. I am insane for wasting three years of my life and believing you loved me. I'll take a taxi home." She didn't give him a chance to respond, just slung her purse over her shoulder and hurried to the ladies' room.

Staring at her reflection in the mirror, she adjusted her skirt, then smoothed her hair. How could she have been so blind? It sounded like a song lyric, but it was a valid question. Sure, sex hadn't been so great lately, but all couples went through dry spells. Work stress and schedules took their toll. Or her first idea was right. He'd never loved her.

Shaking her head to clear it, she decided the reason didn't matter. Only the result. Bottom line: he didn't want her. A tear slid down her cheek, and she wiped it away. She had to pick up her order before Brad refused payment. Squaring her shoulders, she rushed to the counter, got the goods, and made her getaway.

[479]

As the cab pulled from the curb, Quinn opened one of the to-go boxes, removed a madeleine, and shoved it into her mouth. The cake felt like sawdust against her tongue. She stared out the window at passing cars, licked her lips, and tasted salty tears. *Damn him.* She sniffed, wiped them away with the sleeve of her jacket, and reminded herself crying was useless. It was over, and that was that.

An hour later, sitting on her sofa polishing off her third éclair, she took stock of the place. As much as she hated to admit it, Brad had a point. It was depressing and in a bad location. Given his reputation as a tightwad, he should appreciate her thrift store furniture and lack of décor. He'd told her he admired her because she didn't need fancy things. Guess she wasn't fancy enough.

Holding the glass of champagne up to the light, she played back his expression. It was worth $400 and change. The tag hanging around the neck of the bottle caught her attention. She removed it and read it: "The bouquet's lilting and even radiance presents an orange-red gleam. On the palate, experience an aggressive occurrence that has rich completeness along with caressing depth."

Too bad a drink had to furnish her with completeness and caressing, because Brad sure as hell never would. She reached for another pastry, and the phone rang. Maybe he'd come to his senses and realized a life without her wasn't worth living. She grabbed her cell without looking at the caller ID and pressed it to her ear. "Brad?"

"It's Megan. Did he pop the question? I couldn't wait until morning to find out."

Quinn sniffed, then stared at the cream-filled profiterole to concentrate on the sugar high she had going in place of her broken heart. "No. He didn't. We're done."

"Oh God. We're coming over."

"We?"

"Yeah. I'll stop and get Raynie on the way."

"No! Don't come . . ." It was too late. The line was dead.

She sank deeper into the couch. The good Lord knew she loved her two friends, and they were great to want to offer comfort. But she wanted to be alone, in her miserable apartment, with her thrift store furniture, binging on French desserts and taking pure pleasure knowing the money she'd forced Brad to spend had his butt hole clenched so tight, he wouldn't be able to crap for a week.

Amazon

[481]

Preview
SAY YOU'LL NEVER LOVE ME

Contemporary Romance

Thankful today the wind wasn't strong enough to stir dust, Raynie headed south with no idea of where she was going. She needed to leave that house with all its secrets and lies and the pretend life Celeste and Evan shared.

The sound of a jackhammer shook her from her worries, and she noticed her surroundings. Construction workers were busy adding a section to the Episcopal Church. She gave attention to the parking area. A man loaded boxes into the backseat of his crew-cab pickup truck. When he closed the door, she saw the marker: Associate Minister J. Sloane.

"Father?"

He spoke over his shoulder. "Sorry, but I'm not . . ." He turned. Paused. His gaze drifted over her. "How may I help you?"

He wasn't what Raynie expected. Weren't ministers supposed to be older, fatter, and balder? This guy appeared to be about her age, and gorgeous. Dark hair, brilliant blue eyes, and when he smiled, dimples deepened like sugar down a funnel. Not dressed like a preacher should, either. He wore jeans and cowboy boots. Silly her. What did she expect from a west Texas town with nothing but farmers and cowboys? "I was wondering what support groups your church offers."

He fished keys from his pocket, but continued to keep his eyes on her. "What kind do you need?"

"New mother."

Raising his brows, he eyed her from top to bottom. Not in a sexual way, but more as if judging her appearance. She hadn't put on makeup, and her hair, well, he'd probably never seen straight, crimped, and braided combined.

"That's okay. I see you're about to leave. I'm sorry I interrupted." She turned to go, but he stepped forward.

"No bother." He scanned the area. "So you're a new mother?"

Facing him again, she shook her head. "No. Yes. No."

Now he pulled his brows together. "Is it multiple choice?" And there were his dimples again.

Why was she so nervous? Must be his profession. She swallowed hard. Who was she kidding? Preachers needed her type. Sinner deluxe.

[483]

"No children of my own, but I recently became guardian to a six-year-old. I thought my sister had the perfect life, and today learned it was anything but that. I'm a mess right now and don't know what to do." She flapped her hand in the air. "I should work this out on my own."

He moved two steps closer. "Are you unable to discuss this with your husband?"

"No husband. No boyfriend. Nobody. I don't even live here."

He offered a handshake. "I'm Jared."

"Just Jared? No Father Sloane or Father Jared?"

"No. I was about to go down the street to Caprock Café. Why don't you join me and we can talk."

There was kindness in his voice. Surely a tone he'd practiced to offer sympathy and understanding to parishioners. She slid her palm into his. Warm and soft. Clearly he didn't do physical labor, but he must work out. What else could explain the broad shoulders and the way his butt filled out those jeans? *Holy crap.* She shouldn't be looking at his body parts or the shape they were in. "Okay, I'm Raynie."

He held the door for her, and she climbed in his truck. He walked around and slid behind the wheel, then started the engine. "So where are you from?"

"Austin."

[484]

"Hmm. Nice city. How long you been here?"

"Two weeks. I'm staying until the end of the school term. I thought a move this soon might be too traumatic for my niece."

The café came into view, and he parked near the entrance. Raynie got out before he did and met him at the front of the truck. Inside the eatery, every stool, occupied. Conversations hummed. Waitresses in black aprons worked behind a long wooden counter like ants gathering food for the winter. Jared pointed to a corner booth. "How about that one? It'll give us privacy."

She nodded and headed in that direction. Once seated, he opened the menu. "You want something to eat? I haven't had had lunch."

She panicked. No money. No purse. But she hadn't eaten either.

He peered over the folder. "My treat."

"In that case, sure."

"Great. I hate to eat alone."

Raynie wondered what made a guy who looked like this go into the ministry. Harrowing experience? Family tradition? Low testosterone?

The waitress came for their orders, taking Raynie from her daydream.

When the server walked away, the padre rested his arms on the table. "So why are you a mess?"

"I can't understand why she died. Celeste was the good one."

"Compared to who—you?"

She nodded.

"So, you're bad?"

Another nod.

"And why is that?"

"The short version? Two arrests. Two divorces. A penchant for bad boys."

He chuckled. "You didn't kill anybody, did you?"

"Public intoxication back in college."

"Well, none of those things make you a bad person. We all make mistakes, especially in college."

She wondered what trouble the good father had gotten into. Something really bad like staying out past curfew. Or was he wild before he converted? She'd like to have known him then. Lord. What was wrong with her? She had enough on her plate without wicked fantasies.

She leaned forward and threaded her fingers together. She should give him the long version. "I know I'm not a horrible person. But today I discovered Celeste's marriage was on the rocks and now she and Evan are dead. A friend said the craziest thing. That God took them to avoid divorce. Do you think that's true?"

"I think we interpret things to fit our needs."

He looked as if he might say more, but the waitress returned with their drinks. Once alone again, Raynie went back to the conversation. "I've had this child put in my care, and I'm no good at it."

"You're asking for advice, so I'd say you're not giving yourself enough credit."

Raynie took a sip. "You know what I hate most? The constant uncertainty. I'm a strong, independent business owner. Ask any of my friends, and they'll tell you I'm self-assured to the point of being a smart-ass. Oh, sorry. I'll watch my language."

She waited to be scolded, but instead he smiled, those deep cheek dents distracting her. She glanced away. "But in my current circumstance, I doubt everything I say and do. I'm so afraid it will be the wrong thing and Silbie will suffer because of it."

The food came, and Raynie didn't say anything else, just concentrated on eating, and he did the same. He wasn't like any clergy she'd ever met. She expected him to sermonize, but he didn't. Mostly listened.

He swigged his tea, then trained his deep blues on hers. "Well, you haven't complained about your niece being a burden, or having to give up your so-called bad-girl lifestyle. I think you'll be fine."

"You know, padre, I thought you'd be all preachy, but you're different from any minister I've ever met."

He double dimpled her. "People forget ministers struggle like everyone else."

For the next few minutes they fell into another comfortable silence, and Raynie tried to read his expression, but couldn't. He was so handsome, she wondered why he wasn't married. The church didn't prevent it, and first impression, said he was a real catch. Oh God. Maybe he was gay. No. Her gaydar was pretty good, and no alarms had sounded.

He glanced at his watch. "I have an appointment, so I've got to go, but if you'd like to meet here again tomorrow, I'll put it on my calendar."

She shouldn't agree, but he put her at such ease, and she needed adult conversation. But with a hot preacher? "I'd like that."

"Okay."

She drew a silent breath. How dangerous could it be? She'd bet he didn't have a tattoo anywhere.

Amazon

Sneak Peek
TIZZY/RIDGE TRILOGY

Think you might enjoy some small town sass, sizzle, and suspense?

Check out Ann's Tizzy/Ridge Trilogy

Here's a sneak peek at each book.

Book One

Laid Out and Candle Lit

Not only did Tizzy Donovan think her cup was always half-empty, she was pretty sure someone had spit in it.

The last leg of her daily jog took her through Jenkins Cemetery. She stopped and inhaled the scent of freshly mowed grass and the musk of fertile earth. It was spring, and she should have a bounce in her step. But the approaching anniversary of Boone's death pushed any sense of renewal away. To become a widow and single mother before the age of twenty-five had not been in her plans.

Closing her eyes, she willed the notions away. Many thought her ritual morbid. Except to her, it remained a chance to start the day among people she had loved most in her life. She didn't consider the departed as eerie or macabre. She thought of them as peaceful. All the pain, suffering, disappointment, grief, and demands of living were over. Granted, so was the *earthly* joy, but she believed the afterlife held much greater happiness. That is, unless you ended up in hell.

She inhaled, feeling strangely alive among those who were no longer of this world. Her muscles eased as she reverently moved past the headstones. Just as they did each morning during her run, childhood memories flashed through her mind. Hours she'd spent with her grandmother in the kitchen learning how to cook, her grandfather McAlister taking time to teach her to drive. The recollection of steering his old jeep over a vacant field of bumpy cornrows made her laugh out loud. She stopped to catch her breath.

Even though many of the dead had spoken to her for years, not one had ever *appeared* to her. But this morning something caught her eye. Something different. At first she thought the spring haze created an illusion. But, as she blinked and looked again, she spotted someone kneeling at the foot of Boone's grave, *praying.* Apparition or not, she got a full-blown, head-to-toe case of the heebie-jeebies. Every

[490]

hair on her body snapped to attention. She rubbed her arms. Squeezed her eyes tight. *Okay. I'll count to ten and they'll be gone . . . nine . . . ten.* She opened one eye. Damn!

"Hello? Can I help you?" The words trembled across her tongue.

She moved closer, brain scrambling to understand the scene. With each step her heart pumped faster. Knees grew weaker. The figure was not so much kneeling as it was slumped, and not so much praying as staged. Its head rested limp against its chest, and its lifeless arms were spread wide. Tizzy's scream came out as a weak yelp.

She staggered and struggled to keep her balance, but it was no use. Falling against a tree, she retched and slipped downward until her butt hit the ground with a thud. She panted like a dog, then leaned forward, hugged her belly with both arms, and fought to make sense of things. Who could it be? She stood and edged two steps closer. Recognition sent Tizzy's stomach into a death spiral. She gasped, wiped her lips, reached inside her bra, and pulled out her cell phone. She punched in the numbers. "Hello, Dan? Dan, there's a dead body in the cemetery!"

Her brother laughed. "Ha-ha, very funny, Tizzy. I get it. April Fool's!"

"Dan, I'm not kidding. There really is a dead body in the cemetery, and I think it's Marlene."

<u>Amazon</u>

[491]

Book Two

You're Busting my Nuptials

Twenty-four hours ago Tizzy Donovan was naked in Ridge Cooper's bed, screaming to get God's attention. She loved everything about Ridge. How his dark hair curled at the nape of his neck when he needed a haircut. Steel-blue eyes set against the hard lines of his face. Broad shoulders, thick chest, the way he held the steering wheel of his truck. She pictured him, standing straight, thumbs hooked in his front jeans pockets, cowboy hat settled just right. The more vivid the image, the hotter she got.

A knock at the door snapped Tizzy from her daydream. She twirled from the window as matron of honor Rayann Tatum peeked into the room and held out a mug.

"Is he here?" Tizzy accepted the drink.

Rayann flipped her long blonde hair back and widened her green eyes. "Not yet."

"He's not coming." Tizzy put the cup to her lips and gulped. "Holy crap!"

"Sorry, I should have warned you, that's tequila, not punch. I thought you needed something stronger by now, but go easy on it because I don't think you've eaten since yesterday."

"Wonderful. Now I'm going to hell for drinking in the Lord's house. Not to mention all the fornicating I've been doing with Ridge, and today he doesn't show up to make an honest woman of me."

Tizzy knocked back the rest of the drink and thought of every possible scenario for her groom's absence. *Wrong church? There was only one Methodist Church in town. Flat tire? He lived close enough to walk to the ceremony. Cell phone dead? Two land lines were at his disposal. Heart attack? The chance of that couldn't be high, but it would be the best excuse.*

"It's been over an hour. He isn't answering his phone. Daddy went to his house. His truck's gone." She paced. Her bare feet sank into the deep carpet, a small comfort against heartache. "What's wrong with me? Boone joined the Marines to get away and now Ridge doesn't show up for our ceremony. Am I that bad?"

Rayann fell in beside Tizzy and matched her pace. They zigzagged across the room like a band formation during a halftime show. "C'mon, Tiz. It has nothing to do with you. Boone enlisted to avoid Marlene. You know better than anybody what a witch his sister was. He didn't want to spend his life working with her at the bank."

Tizzy stopped at a small table and picked up her engraved invitation. *James Ridge Cooper and Marjorie Louise "Tizzy" Donovan request the honor of your presence.*

Until an hour ago, it had been a perfect day. The sun shone across a heaven of endless blue, and the temperature hovered in the upper sixties. It held promise of being one of the best days of her life, and now might be one of her worst. "Ridge told me he fell in love with me at first sight. *You* knew I was in love with him before I did."

"Oh, honey." Rayann embraced her. "You'd been a widow and without a man for five years. To say you were horny would be an understatement. You named your vibrator."

Amazon

Book Three

Tied With a Bow and No Place to Go

Jay Roy Hobbs held the county record for talking women out of their panties. At least that's what Tizzy Cooper had heard. Rumor said ladies ignored his lack of good looks and fell for his quick wit. Now, staring at him through binoculars, she wasn't so sure humor was his main appeal.

She swallowed the lump that'd been lodged in her throat since arriving on the scene. It wasn't the sight of a dead body that bothered her. She'd seen plenty of those over the years. Her talent for talking to the dearly departed made it a frequent occurrence. But while the rest of Brownsboro's citizens were having their first cup of coffee, she was five miles out of town, at the edge of a field, swatting mosquitoes. Not the way she intended to start her day.

Sunlight filtered through naked limbs of an old tree and cast shadows across colonies of bishop's weed standing tall like lacy parasols. The only thing ruining the spring array?— Jay Roy's lifeless body.

At first Tizzy considered he might be asleep or unconscious, but after calling out to him with no response, and given the color of his skin, along with the buzzards overhead, she decided on a third choice.

Stepping onto an old stump to get a better view, she focused the field glasses. About fifty yards away, the man lay naked, except for boots and a bow, on a patchwork quilt, face toward heaven, arms outstretched. Something twisted in Tizzy's chest. Jay Roy and her mom had graduated high school together, which made him much too young to die.

A few feet to the right, Tizzy's friends Synola Harper and Rayann Tatum shaded their faces and squinted toward the dead man. Tizzy stepped off the stump, adjusted the straps of her sundress, and decided they must be as surprised as she was by the sight because neither of them uttered a word until she passed the field glasses to Synola.

"Lord, can you believe the size of that thing?" Synola let the binoculars dangle around her neck. She tugged her red tank top against warm mocha skin, tucked it into the slender waist of her jeans, and smirked at Rayann. "I don't suppose you've ever seen anything that big."

Rayann tossed her head, blonde curls bouncing with the movement, then narrowed her green eyes and frowned. "Of course I have. I watch HBO."

Amazon

www.ingramcontent.com/pod-product-compliance
Lightning Source LLC
Chambersburg PA
CBHW070827260626
47170CB00007B/2285